Classic Love Stories

Edited by

DAVID PICKERING

ISBN: 1482012839
ISBN-13: 978-1482012835

Cover: David Pickering, after *Seated Woman Combing her Hair*
by Edgar Degas (*c.*1887).

CONTENTS

Introduction

The tales included in this volume of *Classic Love Stories* have been chosen after much careful deliberation, romantic absorption and dreamy contemplation. The final selection of twenty classic tales will take readers to different continents, historical periods, and romantic situations. Some tales constitute happy, optimistic, even jovial, depictions of ideal love realised and reciprocated. Others expose the heart-rending tragedy of love unreturned or seemingly doomed to failure by fate, circumstances or human frailty.

Every reader will have their own favourite. The selection begins with one of the most touching and celebrated depictions of a loving and giving relationship ever committed to paper. It continues with impossible infatuations, the exquisite agonies of first love, the dangerous intensity of forbidden desire, the passion and remorse (or otherwise) of adulterous affairs, and the forging of unlikely but unbreakable matches that transcend all obstacles. Finally, it ends where it all began, in the Garden of Eden, with the very first love affair of them all. These are no idle tales undeserving of attention by the serious reader but enduring masterpieces from the hands of such great writers as Anton Chekhov, O. Henry, Oscar Wilde, Thomas Hardy, F. Scott Fitzgerald, Kate Chopin and D.H. Lawrence.

This book comprises a companion volume to *Classic Short Stories* and two volumes each of *Classic Ghost Stories* and *Classic Horror Stories*; it is hoped that readers will enjoy building a library of classic stories that will introduce them to, or renew their delight in, some of the world's finest literature.

David Pickering, Buckingham, 2013

The Gift of the Magi
O. Henry

One dollar and eighty-seven cents. That was all. And sixty cents of it was in pennies. Pennies saved one and two at a time by bulldozing the grocer and the vegetable man and the butcher until one's cheeks burned with the silent imputation of parsimony that such close dealing implied. Three times Della counted it. One dollar and eighty-seven cents. And the next day would be Christmas.

There was clearly nothing to do but flop down on the shabby little couch and howl. So Della did it. Which instigates the moral reflection that life is made up of sobs, sniffles, and smiles, with sniffles predominating.

While the mistress of the home is gradually subsiding from the first stage to the second, take a look at the home. A furnished flat at $8 per week. It did not exactly beggar description, but it certainly had that word on the lookout for the mendicancy squad.

In the vestibule below was a letter-box into which no letter would go, and an electric button from which no mortal finger could coax a ring. Also appertaining thereunto was a card bearing the name 'Mr James Dillingham Young'.

The 'Dillingham' had been flung to the breeze during a former period of prosperity when its possessor was being paid $30 per week. Now, when the income was shrunk to $20, though, they were thinking seriously of contracting to a modest and unassuming D. But whenever Mr James Dillingham Young came home and reached his flat above he was called 'Jim' and greatly hugged by Mrs James Dillingham Young, already introduced to you as Della. Which is all very good.

Della finished her cry and attended to her cheeks with the powder rag. She stood by the window and looked out dully at a grey cat walking a grey fence in a grey backyard. Tomorrow would be Christmas Day, and she had only $1.87 with which to buy Jim a present. She had been saving every penny she could for months, with this result. Twenty dollars a week doesn't go far. Expenses had been greater than she had calculated. They always are. Only $1.87 to buy a present for Jim. Her Jim. Many a happy hour she had spent planning for something nice for him. Something fine and rare and sterling—something just a little bit near to being worthy of the honour of being owned by Jim.

There was a pier glass between the windows of the room. Perhaps you have seen a pier glass in an $8 flat. A very thin and very agile person may, by observing his reflection in a rapid sequence of longitudinal strips, obtain a fairly accurate conception of his looks. Della, being slender, had mastered the art.

Suddenly she whirled from the window and stood before the glass. Her eyes were shining brilliantly, but her face had lost its colour within twenty seconds. Rapidly she pulled down her hair and let it fall to its full length.

Now, there were two possessions of the James Dillingham Youngs in which they both took a mighty pride. One was Jim's gold watch that had been his father's and his grandfather's. The other was Della's hair. Had the queen of Sheba lived in the flat across the airshaft, Della would have let her hair hang out the window some day to dry just to depreciate Her Majesty's jewels and gifts. Had King Solomon been the janitor, with all his treasures piled up in the basement, Jim would have pulled out his watch every time he passed, just to see him pluck at his beard from envy.

So now Della's beautiful hair fell about her rippling and shining like a cascade of brown waters. It reached below her knee and made itself almost a garment for her. And then she did it up again nervously and quickly. Once she faltered for a minute and stood still while a tear or two splashed on the worn red carpet.

On went her old brown jacket; on went her old brown hat. With a whirl of skirts and with the brilliant sparkle still in her eyes, she fluttered out the door and down the stairs to the street.

Where she stopped the sign read: 'Mme Sofronie. Hair Goods of All Kinds.' One flight up Della ran, and collected herself, panting. Madame, large, too white, chilly, hardly looked the 'Sofronie'.

'Will you buy my hair?' asked Della.

'I buy hair,' said Madame. 'Take yer hat off and let's have a sight at the looks of it.'

Down rippled the brown cascade.

'Twenty dollars,' said Madame, lifting the mass with a practised hand.

'Give it to me quick,' said Della.

Oh, and the next two hours tripped by on rosy wings. Forget the hashed metaphor. She was ransacking the stores for Jim's present.

She found it at last. It surely had been made for Jim and no one else. There was no other like it in any of the stores, and she had turned all of them inside out. It was a platinum fob chain simple and chaste in design, properly proclaiming its value by substance alone and not by meretricious ornamentation—as all good things should do. It was even worthy of The Watch. As soon as she saw it she knew that it must be Jim's. It was like him. Quietness and value—the description applied to both. Twenty-one dollars they took from her for it, and she hurried home with the 87 cents. With that chain on his watch Jim might be properly anxious about the time in any company. Grand as the watch was, he sometimes looked at it on the sly on account of the old leather strap that he used in place of a chain.

When Della reached home her intoxication gave way a little to prudence and reason. She got out her curling irons and lighted the gas and went to work repairing the ravages made by generosity added to love. Which is always a tremendous task, dear friends—a mammoth task.

Within forty minutes her head was covered with tiny, close-lying curls that made her look wonderfully like a truant schoolboy. She looked at her reflection in the mirror long, carefully, and critically.

'If Jim doesn't kill me,' she said to herself, 'before he takes a second look at me, he'll say I look like a Coney Island chorus girl. But what could I do—oh! what could I do with a dollar and eighty-seven cents?'

At seven o'clock the coffee was made and the frying-pan was on the back of the stove hot and ready to cook the chops.

Jim was never late. Della doubled the fob chain in her hand and sat on the corner of the table near the door that he always entered. Then she heard his step on the stair away down on the first flight, and she turned white for just a moment. She had a habit of saying a little silent prayer about the simplest everyday things, and now she whispered: 'Please God, make him think I am still pretty.'

The door opened and Jim stepped in and closed it. He looked

3

thin and very serious. Poor fellow, he was only twenty-two—and to be burdened with a family! He needed a new overcoat and he was without gloves.

Jim stopped inside the door, as immovable as a setter at the scent of quail. His eyes were fixed upon Della, and there was an expression in them that she could not read, and it terrified her. It was not anger, nor surprise, nor disapproval, nor horror, nor any of the sentiments that she had been prepared for. He simply stared at her fixedly with that peculiar expression on his face.

Della wriggled off the table and went for him.

'Jim, darling,' she cried, 'don't look at me that way. I had my hair cut off and sold because I couldn't have lived through Christmas without giving you a present. It'll grow out again—you won't mind, will you? I just had to do it. My hair grows awfully fast. Say "Merry Christmas!" Jim, and let's be happy. You don't know what a nice—what a beautiful, nice gift I've got for you.'

'You've cut off your hair?' asked Jim, laboriously, as if he had not arrived at that patent fact yet even after the hardest mental labour.

'Cut it off and sold it,' said Della. 'Don't you like me just as well, anyhow? I'm me without my hair, ain't I?'

Jim looked about the room curiously.

'You say your hair is gone?' he said, with an air almost of idiocy.

'You needn't look for it,' said Della. 'It's sold, I tell you—sold and gone, too. It's Christmas Eve, boy. Be good to me, for it went for you. Maybe the hairs of my head were numbered,' she went on with sudden serious sweetness, 'but nobody could ever count my love for you. Shall I put the chops on, Jim?'

Out of his trance Jim seemed quickly to wake. He enfolded his Della. For ten seconds let us regard with discreet scrutiny some inconsequential object in the other direction. Eight dollars a week or a million a year—what is the difference? A mathematician or a wit would give you the wrong answer. The magi brought valuable gifts, but that was not among them. This dark assertion will be illuminated later on.

Jim drew a package from his overcoat pocket and threw it upon the table.

'Don't make any mistake, Dell,' he said, 'about me. I don't think there's anything in the way of a haircut or a shave or a shampoo that could make me like my girl any less. But if you'll unwrap that package you may see why you had me going a while at first.'

White fingers and nimble tore at the string and paper. And then an ecstatic scream of joy; and then, alas! a quick feminine change to hysterical tears and wails, necessitating the immediate employment of all the comforting powers of the lord of the flat.

For there lay The Combs—the set of combs, side and back, that Della had worshipped long in a Broadway window. Beautiful combs, pure tortoise shell, with jewelled rims—just the shade to wear in the beautiful vanished hair. They were expensive combs, she knew, and her heart had simply craved and yearned over them without the least hope of possession. And now, they were hers, but the tresses that should have adorned the coveted adornments were gone.

But she hugged them to her bosom, and at length she was able to look up with dim eyes and a smile and say: 'My hair grows so fast, Jim!'

And then Della leaped up like a little singed cat and cried, 'Oh, oh!'

Jim had not yet seen his beautiful present. She held it out to him eagerly upon her open palm. The dull precious metal seemed to flash with a reflection of her bright and ardent spirit.

'Isn't it a dandy, Jim? I hunted all over town to find it. You'll have to look at the time a hundred times a day now. Give me your watch. I want to see how it looks on it.'

Instead of obeying, Jim tumbled down on the couch and put his hands under the back of his head and smiled.

'Dell,' said he, 'let's put our Christmas presents away and keep 'em a while. They're too nice to use just at present. I sold the watch to get the money to buy your combs. And now suppose you put the chops on.'

The magi, as you know, were wise men—wonderfully wise men—who brought gifts to the Babe in the manger. They invented the art of giving Christmas presents. Being wise, their gifts were no doubt wise ones, possibly bearing the privilege of exchange in case of duplication. And here I have lamely related to you the uneventful chronicle of two foolish children in a flat who most unwisely sacrificed for each other the greatest treasures of their house. But in a last word to the wise of these

5

days let it be said that of all who give gifts these two were the wisest. Of all who give and receive gifts, such as they are wisest. Everywhere they are wisest. They are the magi.

O. Henry was the pen name of William Sydney Porter (1862–1910), who was born in Greensboro, North Carolina, and worked as a pharmacist, rancher, draughtsman and bank teller before establishing a reputation as a writer of witty short stories and satirical newspaper columns. Like the Dillingham Youngs in 'The Gift of the Magi', Henry himself well knew what it felt like to be driven to desperate measures to remain financially afloat: some of his early stories were written while he was serving a prison sentence for embezzlement from the bank in which he formerly worked.

The Haunted Inheritance
Edith Nesbit

The most extraordinary thing that ever happened to me was my going back to town on that day. I am a reasonable being; I do not do such things. I was on a bicycling tour with another man. We were far from the mean cares of an unremunerative profession; we were men not fettered by any given address, any pledged date, any preconcerted route. I went to bed weary and cheerful, fell asleep a mere animal—a tired dog after a day's hunting—and awoke at four in the morning that creature of nerves and fancies which is my other self, and which has driven me to all the follies I have ever kept company with. But even that second self of mine, whining beast and traitor as it is, has never played me such a trick as it played then. Indeed, something in the result of that day's rash act sets me wondering whether after all it could have been I, or even my other self, who moved in the adventure; whether it was not rather some power outside both of us... but this is a speculation as idle in me as uninteresting to you, and so enough of it.

From four to seven I lay awake, the prey of a growing detestation of bicycling tours, friends, scenery, physical exertion, holidays. By seven o'clock I felt that I would rather perish than spend another day in the society of the other man—an excellent fellow, by the way, and the best of company.

At half-past seven the post came. I saw the postman through my window as I shaved. I went down to get my letters—there were none, naturally.

At breakfast I said: 'Edmundson, my dear fellow, I am extremely sorry; but my letters this morning compel me to return to town at once.'

'But I thought,' said Edmundson—then he stopped, and I saw that he had perceived in time that this was no moment for reminding me that, having left no address, I could have had no letters.

He looked sympathetic, and gave me what there was left of the bacon. I suppose he thought that it was a love affair or some such folly. I let him think so; after all, no love affair but would have seemed wise compared with the blank idiocy of this sudden determination to cut short a delightful holiday and go back to those dusty, stuffy rooms in Gray's Inn.

After that first and almost pardonable lapse, Edmundson behaved beautifully. I caught the 9.17 train, and by half-past eleven I was climbing my dirty staircase.

I let myself in and waded through a heap of envelopes and wrappered circulars that had drifted in through the letter-box, as dead leaves drift into the areas of houses in squares. All the windows were shut. Dust lay thick on everything. My laundress had evidently chosen this as a good time for her holiday. I wondered idly where she spent it. And now the close, musty smell of the rooms caught at my senses, and I remembered with a positive pang the sweet scent of the earth and the dead leaves in that wood through which, at this very moment, the sensible and fortunate Edmundson would be riding.

The thought of dead leaves reminded me of the heap of correspondence. I glanced through it. Only one of all those letters interested me in the least. It was from my mother:—

'ELLIOT'S BAY, NORFOLK,
17th August.

DEAR LAWRENCE,—I have wonderful news for you. Your great-uncle Sefton has died, and left you half his immense property. The other half is left to your second cousin Selwyn. You must come home at once. There are heaps of letters here for you, but I dare not send them on, as goodness only knows where you may be. I do wish you would remember to leave an address. I send this to your rooms, in case you have had the forethought to instruct your charwoman to send your letters on to you. It is a most handsome fortune, and I am too happy about your accession to it to scold you as you deserve, but I hope this will be a lesson to you to leave an address when next you go away. Come home at once.—Your loving Mother,

MARGARET SEFTON.

P.S.—It is the maddest will; everything divided evenly between you two except the house and estate. The will says you and your cousin Selwyn are to meet there on the 1st September following his death, in presence of the family, and decide which of you is to have the house. If you can't agree, it's to be presented to the county for a lunatic asylum. I should think so! He was always so eccentric. The one who doesn't have the house, etc., gets £20,000 extra. Of course you will choose *that*.

P.P.S.—Be sure to bring your under-shirts with you—the air here is very keen of an evening.'

I opened both the windows and lit a pipe. Sefton Manor, that gorgeous old place,—I knew its picture in Hasted, cradle of our race, and so on—and a big fortune. I hoped my cousin Selwyn would want the £20,000 more than he wanted the house. If he didn't—well, perhaps my fortune might be large enough to increase that £20,000 to a sum that he *would* want.

And then, suddenly, I became aware that this was the 31st of August, and that to-morrow was the day on which I was to meet my cousin Selwyn and 'the family', and come to a decision about the house. I had never, to my knowledge, heard of my cousin Selwyn. We were a family rich in collateral branches. I hoped he would be a reasonable young man. Also, I had never seen Sefton Manor House, except in a print. It occurred to me that I would rather see the house before I saw the cousin.

I caught the next train to Sefton.

'It's but a mile by the field way,' said the railway porter. 'You take the stile—the first on the left—and follow the path till you come to the wood. Then skirt along the left of it, cater across the meadow at the end, and you'll see the place right below you in the vale.'

'It's a fine old place, I hear,' said I.

'All to pieces, though,' said he. 'I shouldn't wonder if it cost a couple o' hundred to put it to rights. Water coming through the roof and all.'

'But surely the owner—'

'Oh, he never lived there; not since his son was taken. He lived in the lodge; it's on the brow of the hill looking down on the Manor House.'

'Is the house empty?'

'As empty as a rotten nutshell, except for the old sticks o' furniture. Anyone who likes,' added the porter, 'can lie there o' nights. But it wouldn't be me!'

9

'Do you mean there's a ghost?' I hope I kept any note of undue elation out of my voice.

'I don't hold with ghosts,' said the porter firmly, 'but my aunt was in service at the lodge, and there's no doubt but *something* walks there.'

'Come,' I said, 'this is very interesting. Can't you leave the station, and come across to where beer is?'

'I don't mind if I do,' said he. 'That is so far as your standing a drop goes. But I can't leave the station, so if you pour my beer you must pour it dry, sir, as the saying is.'

So I gave the man a shilling, and he told me about the ghost at Sefton Manor House. Indeed, about the ghosts, for there were, it seemed, two; a lady in white, and a gentleman in a slouch hat and black riding cloak.

'They do say,' said my porter, 'as how one of the young ladies once on a time was wishful to elope, and started so to do—not getting further than the hall door; her father, thinking it to be burglars, fired out of the window, and the happy pair fell on the doorstep, corpses.'

'Is it true, do you think?'

The porter did not know. At any rate there was a tablet in the church to Maria Sefton and George Ballard—'and something about in their death them not being divided.'

I took the stile, I skirted the wood, I 'catered' across the meadow—and so I came out on a chalky ridge held in a net of pine roots, where dog violets grew. Below stretched the green park, dotted with trees. The lodge, stuccoed but solid, lay below me. Smoke came from its chimneys. Lower still lay the Manor House—red brick with grey lichened mullions, a house in a thousand, Elizabethan—and from its twisted beautiful chimneys no smoke arose. I hurried across the short turf towards the Manor House.

I had no difficulty in getting into the great garden. The bricks of the wall were everywhere displaced or crumbling. The ivy had forced the coping stones away; each red buttress offered a dozen spots for foothold. I climbed the wall and found myself in a garden—oh! but such a garden. There are not half a dozen such in England—ancient box hedges, rosaries, fountains, yew tree avenues, bowers of clematis (now feathery in its seeding time), great trees, grey-grown marble balustrades and steps, terraces, green lawns, one green lawn, in especial, girt round with a sweet briar hedge, and in the middle of this lawn a sundial. All this was mine, or, to be more exact, might be mine, should my cousin Selwyn prove to be a person of sense. How I prayed that he might not be a person of taste! That he might be a person who liked yachts or racehorses or diamonds, or motor-cars, or anything that money can buy, not a person who liked beautiful Elizabethan houses, and gardens old beyond belief.

The sundial stood on a mass of masonry, too low and wide to be called a pillar. I mounted the two brick steps and leaned over to read the date and the motto:

'Tempus fugit manet amor.'

The date was 1617, the initials S.S. surmounted it. The face of the dial was unusually ornate—a wreath of stiffly drawn roses was traced outside the circle of the numbers. As I leaned there a sudden movement on the other side of the pedestal compelled my attention. I leaned over a little further to see what had rustled—a rat—a rabbit? A flash of pink struck at my eyes. A lady in a pink dress was sitting on the step at the other side of the sundial.

I suppose some exclamation escaped me—the lady looked up. Her hair was dark, and her eyes; her face was pink and white, with a few little gold-coloured freckles on nose and on cheek bones. Her dress was of pink cotton stuff, thin and soft. She looked like a beautiful pink rose.

Our eyes met.

'I beg your pardon,' said I, 'I had no idea–' there I stopped and tried to crawl back to firm ground. Graceful explanations are not best given by one sprawling on his stomach across a sundial.

By the time I was once more on my feet she too was standing.

'It is a beautiful old place,' she said gently, and, as it seemed, with a kindly wish to relieve my embarrassment. She made a movement as if to turn away.

'Quite a show place,' said I stupidly enough, but I was still a little embarrassed, and I wanted to say something—anything—to arrest her departure. You have no idea how pretty she was. She had a straw hat in her hand, dangling by soft black ribbons. Her hair was all fluffy-soft—like a child's. 'I suppose you have seen the house?' I asked.

She paused, one foot still on the lower step of the sundial, and her face seemed to brighten at the touch of some idea as sudden as welcome.

'Well—no,' she said. 'The fact is—I wanted frightfully to see the house; in fact, I've come miles and miles on purpose, but there's no one to let me in.'

'The people at the lodge?' I suggested.

'Oh no,' she said. 'I—the fact is I—I don't want to be shown round. I want to explore!'

She looked at me critically. Her eyes dwelt on my right hand, which lay on the sundial. I have always taken reasonable care of my hands, and I wore a good ring, a sapphire, cut with the Sefton arms: an heirloom, by the way. Her glance at my hand preluded a longer glance at my face. Then she shrugged her pretty shoulders.

'Oh well,' she said, and it was as if she had said plainly, 'I see that you are a gentleman and a decent fellow. Why should I not look over the house in your company? Introductions? Bah!'

All this her shrug said without ambiguity as without words.

'Perhaps,' I hazarded, 'I could get the keys.'

'Do you really care very much for old houses?'

'I do,' said I; 'and you?'

'I care so much that I nearly broke into this one. I should have done it quite if the windows had been an inch or two lower.'

'I am an inch or two higher,' said I, standing squarely so as to make the most of my six-feet beside her five-feet-five or thereabouts.

'Oh—if you only would!' said she.

'Why not?' said I.

She led the way past the marble basin of the fountain, and along the historic yew avenue, planted, like all old yew avenues, by that industrious gardener our Eighth Henry. Then across a lawn, through a winding, grassy, shrubbery path, that ended at a green door in the garden wall.

'You can lift this latch with a hairpin,' said she, and therewith lifted it.

We walked into a courtyard. Young grass grew green between the grey flags on which our steps echoed.

'This is the window,' said she. 'You see there's a pane broken. If you could get on to the window-sill, you could get your hand in and undo the hasp, and–'

'And you?'

'Oh, you'll let me in by the kitchen door.'

I did it. My conscience called me a burglar—in vain. Was it not my own, or as good as my own house?

I let her in at the back door. We walked through the big dark kitchen where the old three-legged pot towered large on the hearth, and the old spits and firedogs still kept their ancient place. Then through another kitchen where red rust was making its full meal of a comparatively modern range.

Then into the great hall, where the old armour and the buff-coats and round-caps hang on the walls, and where the carved stone staircases run at each side up to the gallery above.

The long tables in the middle of the hall were scored by the knives of the many who had eaten meat there—initials and dates were cut into them. The roof was groined, the windows low-arched.

'Oh, but what a place!' said she; 'this must be much older than the rest of it–'

'Evidently. About 1300, I should say.'

'Oh, let us explore the rest,' she cried; 'it is really a comfort not to have a guide, but only a person like you who just guesses comfortably at dates. I should hate to be told *exactly* when this hall was built.'

We explored ball-room and picture gallery, white parlour and library. Most of the rooms were furnished—all heavily, some magnificently—but everything was dusty and faded.

It was in the white parlour, a spacious panelled room on the first floor, that she told me the ghost story, substantially the same as my porter's tale, only in one respect different.

'And so, just as she was leaving this very room—yes, I'm sure it's this room, because the woman at the inn pointed out this double window and told me so—just as the poor lovers were creeping out of the door, the cruel father came quickly out of some dark place and killed them both. So now they haunt it.'

'It is a terrible thought,' said I gravely. 'How would you like to live in a haunted house?'

'I couldn't,' she said quickly.

'Nor I; it would be too–' my speech would have ended

13

flippantly, but for the grave set of her features.

'I wonder who *will* live here?' she said. 'The owner is just dead. They say it is an awful house, full of ghosts. Of course one is not afraid now'—the sunlight lay golden and soft on the dusty parquet of the floor—'but at night, when the wind wails, and the doors creak, and the things rustle, oh, it must be awful!'

'I hear the house has been left to two people, or rather one is to have the house, and the other a sum of money,' said I. 'It's a beautiful house, full of beautiful things, but I should think at least one of the heirs would rather have the money.'

'Oh yes, I should think so. I wonder whether the heirs know about the ghost? The lights can be seen from the inn, you know, at twelve o'clock, and they see the ghost in white at the window.'

'Never the black one?'

'Oh yes, I suppose so.'

'The ghosts don't appear together?'

'No.'

'I suppose,' said I, 'whoever it is that manages such things knows that the poor ghosts would like to be together, so it won't let them.'

She shivered.

'Come,' she said, 'we have seen all over the house; let us get back into the sunshine. Now I will go out, and you shall bolt the door after me, and then you can come out by the window. Thank you so much for all the trouble you have taken. It has really been quite an adventure...'

I rather liked that expression, and she hastened to spoil it.

'...Quite an adventure going all over this glorious old place, and looking at everything one wanted to see, and not just at what the housekeeper didn't mind one's looking at.'

She passed through the door, but when I had closed it and prepared to lock it, I found that the key was no longer in the lock. I looked on the floor—I felt in my pockets, and at last, wandering back into the kitchen, discovered it on the table, where I swear I never put it.

When I had fitted that key into the lock and turned it, and got out of the window and made that fast, I dropped into the yard. No one shared its solitude with me. I searched garden and pleasure grounds, but never a glimpse of pink rewarded my anxious eyes. I found the sundial again, and stretched myself along the warm brick of the wide step where she had sat: and called myself a fool.

I had let her go. I did not know her name; I did not know where she lived; she had been at the inn, but probably only for lunch. I should never see her again, and certainly in that event I should never see again such dark, soft eyes, such hair, such a contour of cheek and chin, such a frank smile—in a word, a girl with whom it would be so delightfully natural for me to fall in love. For all the time she had been talking to me of architecture and archæology, of dates and periods, of carvings and mouldings, I had been recklessly falling in love with the idea of falling in love with her. I had cherished and adored this delightful possibility, and now my chance was over. Even I could not definitely fall in love after one interview with a girl I was never to see again! And falling in love is so pleasant! I cursed my lost chance, and went back to the inn. I talked to the waiter.

'Yes, a lady in pink had lunched there with a party. Had gone on to the Castle. A party from Tonbridge it was.'

Barnhurst Castle is close to Sefton Manor. The inn lays itself out to entertain persons who come in brakes and carve their names on the walls of the Castle keep. The inn has a visitors' book. I examined it. Some twenty feminine names. Any one might be hers. The waiter looked over my shoulder. I turned the pages.

'Only parties staying in the house in this part of the book,' said the waiter.

My eye caught one name. 'Selwyn Sefton,' in a clear, round, black hand-writing.

'Staying here?' I pointed to the name.

'Yes, sir; came to-day, sir.'

'Can I have a private sitting-room?'

I had one. I ordered my dinner to be served in it, and I sat down and considered my course of action. Should I invite my cousin Selwyn to dinner, ply him with wine, and exact promises? Honour forbade. Should I seek him out and try to establish friendly relations? To what end?

Then I saw from my window a young man in a light-checked suit, with a face at once pallid and coarse. He strolled along the gravel path, and a woman's voice in the garden called 'Selwyn'.

He disappeared in the direction of the voice. I don't think I ever disliked a man so much at first sight.

'Brute,' said I, 'why should he have the house? He'd stucco it all over as likely as not; perhaps let it! He'd never stand the ghosts, either–'

Then the inexcusable, daring idea of my life came to me, striking me rigid—a blow from my other self. It must have been a minute or two before my muscles relaxed and my arms fell at my sides.

'I'll do it,' I said.

I dined. I told the people of the house not to sit up for me. I was going to see friends in the neighbourhood, and might stay the night with them. I took my Inverness cape with me on my arm and my soft felt hat in my pocket. I wore a light suit and a straw hat.

Before I started I leaned cautiously from my window. The lamp at the bow window next to mine showed me the pallid young man, smoking a fat, reeking cigar. I hoped he would continue to sit there smoking. His window looked the right way; and if he didn't see what I wanted him to see someone else in the inn would. The landlady had assured me that I should disturb no one if I came in at half-past twelve.

'We hardly keep country hours here, sir,' she said, 'on account of so much excursionist business.'

I bought candles in the village, and, as I went down across the park in the soft darkness, I turned again and again to be sure that the light and the pallid young man were still at that window. It was now past eleven.

I got into the house and lighted a candle, and crept through the dark kitchens, whose windows, I knew, did not look towards the inn. When I came to the hall I blew out my candle. I dared not show light prematurely, and in the unhaunted part of the house.

I gave myself a nasty knock against one of the long tables, but it helped me to get my bearings, and presently I laid my hand on the stone balustrade of the great staircase. You would hardly believe me if I were to tell you truly of my sensations as I began to go up these stairs. I am not a coward—at least, I had never thought so till then—but the absolute darkness unnerved me. I had to go slowly, or I should have lost my head and blundered up the stairs three at a time, so strong was the feeling of something—something uncanny—just behind me.

I set my teeth. I reached the top of the stairs, felt along the walls, and after a false start, which landed me in the great picture gallery, I found the white parlour, entered it, closed the door, and felt my way to a little room without a window, which we had decided must have been a powdering-room.

Here I ventured to re-light my candle.

The white parlour, I remembered, was fully furnished. Returning to it I struck one match, and by its flash determined the way to the mantelpiece.

Then I closed the powdering-room door behind me. I felt my way to the mantelpiece and took down the two brass twenty-lighted candelabra. I placed these on a table a yard or two from the window, and in them set up my candles. It is astonishingly difficult in the dark to do anything, even a thing so simple as the setting up of a candle.

Then I went back into my little room, put on the Inverness cape and the slouch hat, and looked at my watch. Eleven-thirty. I must wait. I sat down and waited. I thought how rich I was—the thought fell flat; I wanted this house. I thought of my beautiful pink lady; but I put that thought aside; I had an inward consciousness that my conduct, more heroic than enough in one sense, would seem mean and crafty in her eyes. Only ten minutes had passed. I could not wait till twelve. The chill of the night and of the damp, unused house, and, perhaps, some less material influence, made me shiver.

I opened the door, crept on hands and knees to the table, and, carefully keeping myself below the level of the window, I reached up a trembling arm, and lighted, one by one, my forty candles. The room was a blaze of light. My courage came back to me with the retreat of the darkness. I was far too excited to know what a fool I was making of myself. I rose boldly, and struck an attitude over against the window, where the candle-light shone upon as well as behind me. My Inverness was flung jauntily over my shoulder, my soft, black felt twisted and slouched over my eyes.

There I stood for the world, and particularly for my cousin Selwyn, to see, the very image of the ghost that haunted that chamber. And from my window I could see the light in that other window, and indistinctly the lounging figure there. Oh, my cousin Selwyn, I wished many things to your address in that moment! For it was only a moment that I had to feel brave and daring in. Then I heard, deep down in the house, a sound, very slight, very faint. Then came silence. I drew a deep breath. The silence endured. And I stood by my lighted window.

After a very long time, as it seemed, I heard a board crack, and then a soft rustling sound that drew near and seemed to pause outside the very door of my parlour.

Again I held my breath, and now I thought of the most horrible story Poe ever wrote—'The Fall of the House of Usher'—and I fancied I saw the handle of that door move. I fixed my eyes on it. The fancy passed: and returned.

Then again there was silence. And then the door opened with a soft, silent suddenness, and I saw in the doorway a figure in trailing white. Its eyes blazed in a death-white face. It made two ghostly, gliding steps forward, and my heart stood still. I had not thought it possible for a man to experience so sharp a pang of sheer terror. I had masqueraded as one of the ghosts in this accursed house. Well, the other ghost—the real one—had come to meet me. I do not like to dwell on that moment. The only thing which it pleases me to remember is that I did not scream or go mad. I think I stood on the verge of both.

The ghost, I say, took two steps forward; then it threw up its arms, the lighted taper it carried fell on the floor, and it reeled back against the door with its arms across its face.

The fall of the candle woke me as from a nightmare. It fell solidly, and rolled away under the table.

I perceived that my ghost was human. I cried incoherently: 'Don't, for Heaven's sake—it's all right.'

The ghost dropped its hands and turned agonised eyes on me. I tore off my cloak and hat.

'I—didn't—scream,' she said, and with that I sprang forward and caught her in my arms—my poor, pink lady—white now as a white rose.

I carried her into the powdering-room, and left one candle with her, extinguishing the others hastily, for now I saw what in my extravagant folly had escaped me before, that my ghost exhibition might bring the whole village down on the house. I tore down the long corridor and double locked the doors leading from it to the staircase, then back to the powdering-room and the prone white rose. How, in the madness of that night's folly, I had thought to bring a brandy-flask passes my understanding. But I had done it. Now I rubbed her hands with the spirit.

I rubbed her temples, I tried to force it between her lips, and at last she sighed and opened her eyes.

'Oh—thank God—thank God!' I cried, for indeed I had almost feared that my mad trick had killed her. 'Are you better? oh, poor little lady, are you better?'

She moved her head a little on my arm.

Again she sighed, and her eyes closed. I gave her more brandy. She took it, choked, raised herself against my shoulder.

'I'm all right now,' she said faintly. 'It served me right. How silly it all is!' Then she began to laugh, and then she began to cry.

It was at this moment that we heard voices on the terrace below. She clutched at my arm in a frenzy of terror, the bright tears glistening on her cheeks.

'Oh! not any more, not any more,' she cried. 'I can't bear it.'

'Hush,' I said, taking her hands strongly in mine. 'I've played the fool; so have you. We must play the man now. The people in the village have seen the lights—that's all. They think we're burglars. They can't get in. Keep quiet, and they'll go away.'

But when they did go away they left the local constable on guard. He kept guard like a man till daylight began to creep over the hill, and then he crawled into the hayloft and fell asleep, small blame to him.

But through those long hours I sat beside her and held her hand. At first she clung to me as a frightened child clings, and her tears were the prettiest, saddest things to see. As we grew calmer we talked.

'I did it to frighten my cousin,' I owned. 'I meant to have told you to-day, I mean yesterday, only you went away. I am Lawrence Sefton, and the place is to go either to me or to my cousin Selwyn. And I wanted to frighten him off it. But you, why did you–?'

Even then I couldn't see. She looked at me.

'I don't know how I ever could have thought I was brave enough to do it, but I did want the house so, and I wanted to frighten you–'

'To frighten *me*. Why?'

'Because I am your cousin Selwyn,' she said, hiding her face in her hands.

'And you knew me?' I asked.

'By your ring,' she said. 'I saw your father wear it when I was a little girl. Can't we get back to the inn now?'

'Not unless you want everyone to know how silly we have been.'

'I wish you'd forgive me,' she said when we had talked awhile, and she had even laughed at the description of the pallid young man on whom I had bestowed, in my mind, her name.

'The wrong is mutual,' I said; 'we will exchange forgivenesses.'

'Oh, but it isn't,' she said eagerly. 'Because I knew it was you, and you didn't know it was me: you wouldn't have tried to frighten *me*.'

'You know I wouldn't.' My voice was tenderer than I meant it to be.

She was silent.

'And who is to have the house?' she said.

'Why you, of course.'

'I never will.'

'Why?'

'Oh, because!'

'Can't we put off the decision?' I asked.

'Impossible. We must decide to-morrow—to-day I mean.'

'Well, when we meet to-morrow—I mean to-day—with lawyers and chaperones and mothers and relations, give me one word alone with you.'

'Yes,' she answered, with docility.

'Do you know,' she said presently, 'I can never respect myself again? To undertake a thing like that, and then be so horribly frightened. Oh! I thought you really *were* the other ghost.'

'I will tell you a secret,' said I. 'I thought *you* were, and I was much more frightened than you.'

'Oh well,' she said, leaning against my shoulder as a tired child might have done, 'if you were frightened too, Cousin Lawrence, I don't mind so very, very much.'

It was soon afterwards that, cautiously looking out of the parlour window for the twentieth time, I had the happiness of seeing the local policeman disappear into the stable rubbing his eyes.

We got out of the window on the other side of the house, and went back to the inn across the dewy park. The French window of the sitting-room which had let her out let us both in. No one was stirring, so no one save she and I were any the wiser as to that night's work.

It was like a garden party next day, when lawyers and executors and aunts and relations met on the terrace in front of Sefton Manor House.

Her eyes were downcast. She followed her Aunt demurely over the house and the grounds.

'Your decision,' said my great-uncle's solicitor, 'has to be given within the hour.'

'My cousin and I will announce it within that time,' I said and I at once gave her my arm.

Arrived at the sundial we stopped.

'This is my proposal,' I said: 'we will say that we decide that the house is yours—we will spend the £20,000 in restoring it and the grounds. By the time that's done we can decide who is to have it.'

'But how?'

'Oh, we'll draw lots, or toss a halfpenny, or anything you like.'

'I'd rather decide now,' she said; '*you* take it.'

'No, *you* shall.'

'I'd rather you had it. I—I don't feel so greedy as I did yesterday,' she said.

'Neither do I. Or at any rate not in the same way.'

'Do—do take the house,' she said very earnestly.

Then I said: 'My cousin Selwyn, unless you take the house, I shall make you an offer of marriage.'

'*Oh!*' she breathed.

'And when you have declined it, on the very proper ground of our too slight acquaintance, I will take my turn at declining. I will decline the house. Then, if you are obdurate, it will become an asylum. Don't be obdurate. Pretend to take the house and–'

She looked at me rather piteously.

'Very well,' she said, 'I will pretend to take the house, and when it is restored–'

'We'll spin the penny.'

So before the waiting relations the house was adjudged to my cousin Selwyn. When the restoration was complete I met Selwyn at the sundial. We had met there often in the course of the restoration, in which business we both took an extravagant interest.

'Now,' I said, 'we'll spin the penny. Heads you take the house, tails it comes to me.'

I spun the coin—it fell on the brick steps of the sundial, and stuck upright there, wedged between two bricks. She laughed; I laughed.

'It's not *my* house,' I said.

'It's not *my* house,' said she.

'Dear,' said I, and we were neither of us laughing then, 'can't it be *our* house?'

And, thank God, our house it is.

Edith Nesbit (1858–1924) was born in Surrey but as a child spent time in Brighton, Buckinghamshire, France, Spain, Germany, and Kent before settling in London. She is usually remembered for such children's classics as The Railway Children *and* Five Children and It, *but her many short stories are also much admired. Her own (first) marriage, to Hubert Bland, was less than idyllic, complicated as it was by Bland's affairs. To keep the marriage going, Nesbit adopted her husband's two children by Alice Hoatson, who moved in with them, and brought them up as her own.*

The Lady with the Dog
Anton Chekhov

I

It was said that a new person had appeared on the sea-front: a lady with a little dog. Dmitri Dmitritch Gurov, who had by then been a fortnight at Yalta, and so was fairly at home there, had begun to take an interest in new arrivals. Sitting in Verney's pavilion, he saw, walking on the sea-front, a fair-haired young lady of medium height, wearing a *béret*; a white Pomeranian dog was running behind her.

And afterwards he met her in the public gardens and in the square several times a day. She was walking alone, always wearing the same *béret*, and always with the same white dog; no one knew who she was, and everyone called her simply 'the lady with the dog'.

'If she is here alone without a husband or friends, it wouldn't be amiss to make her acquaintance,' Gurov reflected.

He was under forty, but he had a daughter already twelve years old, and two sons at school. He had been married young, when he was a student in his second year, and by now his wife seemed half as old again as he. She was a tall, erect woman with dark eyebrows, staid and dignified, and, as she said of herself, intellectual. She read a great deal, used phonetic spelling, called her husband, not Dmitri, but Dimitri, and he secretly considered her unintelligent, narrow, inelegant, was afraid of her, and did not like to be at home. He had begun being unfaithful to her long ago—had been unfaithful to her often, and, probably on that account, almost always spoke ill of women, and when they were talked about in his presence, used to call them 'the lower race'.

It seemed to him that he had been so schooled by bitter experience that he might call them what he liked, and yet he could not get on for two days together without 'the lower race'. In the society of men he was bored and not himself, with them he was cold and uncommunicative; but when he was in the company of women he felt

23

free, and knew what to say to them and how to behave; and he was at ease with them even when he was silent. In his appearance, in his character, in his whole nature, there was something attractive and elusive which allured women and disposed them in his favour; he knew that, and some force seemed to draw him, too, to them.

Experience often repeated, truly bitter experience, had taught him long ago that with decent people, especially Moscow people—always slow to move and irresolute—every intimacy, which at first so agreeably diversifies life and appears a light and charming adventure, inevitably grows into a regular problem of extreme intricacy, and in the long run the situation becomes unbearable. But at every fresh meeting with an interesting woman this experience seemed to slip out of his memory, and he was eager for life, and everything seemed simple and amusing.

One evening he was dining in the gardens, and the lady in the *béret* came up slowly to take the next table. Her expression, her gait, her dress, and the way she did her hair told him that she was a lady, that she was married, that she was in Yalta for the first time and alone, and that she was dull there... The stories told of the immorality in such places as Yalta are to a great extent untrue; he despised them, and knew that such stories were for the most part made up by persons who would themselves have been glad to sin if they had been able; but when the lady sat down at the next table three paces from him, he remembered these tales of easy conquests, of trips to the mountains, and the tempting thought of a swift, fleeting love affair, a romance with an unknown woman, whose name he did not know, suddenly took possession of him.

He beckoned coaxingly to the Pomeranian, and when the dog came up to him he shook his finger at it. The Pomeranian growled: Gurov shook his finger at it again.

The lady looked at him and at once dropped her eyes.

'He doesn't bite,' she said, and blushed.

'May I give him a bone?' he asked; and when she nodded he asked courteously, 'Have you been long in Yalta?'

'Five days.'

'And I have already dragged out a fortnight here.'

There was a brief silence.

'Time goes fast, and yet it is so dull here!' she said, not looking at him.

'That's only the fashion to say it is dull here. A provincial will live in Belyov or Zhidra and not be dull, and when he comes here it's "Oh, the dullness! Oh, the dust!" One would think he came from Grenada.'

She laughed. Then both continued eating in silence, like strangers, but after dinner they walked side by side; and there sprang up between them the light jesting conversation of people who are free and satisfied, to whom it does not matter where they go or what they talk about. They walked and talked of the strange light on the sea: the water was of a soft warm lilac hue, and there was a golden streak from the moon upon it. They talked of how sultry it was after a hot day. Gurov told her that he came from Moscow, that he had taken his degree in Arts, but had a post in a bank; that he had trained as an opera-singer, but had given it up, that he owned two houses in Moscow... And from her he learnt that she had grown up in Petersburg, but had lived in S—— since her marriage two years before, that she was staying another month in Yalta, and that her husband, who needed a holiday too, might perhaps come and fetch her. She was not sure whether her husband had a post in a Crown Department or under the Provincial Council—and was amused by her own ignorance. And Gurov learnt, too, that she was called Anna Sergeyevna.

Afterwards he thought about her in his room at the hotel— thought she would certainly meet him next day; it would be sure to happen. As he got into bed he thought how lately she had been a girl at school, doing lessons like his own daughter; he recalled the diffidence, the angularity, that was still manifest in her laugh and her manner of talking with a stranger. This must have been the first time in her life she had been alone in surroundings in which she was followed, looked at, and spoken to merely from a secret motive which she could hardly fail to guess. He recalled her slender, delicate neck, her lovely grey eyes.

'There's something pathetic about her, anyway,' he thought, and fell asleep.

II

A week had passed since they had made acquaintance. It was a holiday. It was sultry indoors, while in the street the wind whirled the dust round and round, and blew people's hats off. It was a thirsty day, and Gurov often went into the pavilion, and pressed Anna Sergeyevna to have syrup and water or an ice. One did not know what to do with oneself.

In the evening when the wind had dropped a little, they went out on the groyne to see the steamer come in. There were a great many people walking about the harbour; they had gathered to welcome someone, bringing bouquets. And two peculiarities of a well-dressed Yalta crowd were very conspicuous: the elderly ladies were dressed like young ones, and there were great numbers of generals.

Owing to the roughness of the sea, the steamer arrived late, after the sun had set, and it was a long time turning about before it reached the groyne. Anna Sergeyevna looked through her lorgnette at the steamer and the passengers as though looking for acquaintances, and when she turned to Gurov her eyes were shining. She talked a great deal and asked disconnected questions, forgetting next moment what she had asked; then she dropped her lorgnette in the crush.

The festive crowd began to disperse; it was too dark to see people's faces. The wind had completely dropped, but Gurov and Anna Sergeyevna still stood as though waiting to see someone else come from the steamer. Anna Sergeyevna was silent now, and sniffed the flowers without looking at Gurov.

'The weather is better this evening,' he said. 'Where shall we go now? Shall we drive somewhere?'

She made no answer.

Then he looked at her intently, and all at once put his arm round her and kissed her on the lips, and breathed in the moisture and the fragrance of the flowers; and he immediately looked round him, anxiously wondering whether anyone had seen them.

'Let us go to your hotel,' he said softly. And both walked quickly.

The room was close and smelt of the scent she had bought at the Japanese shop. Gurov looked at her and thought: 'What different people one meets in the world!' From the past he preserved memories of careless, good-natured women, who loved cheerfully and were grateful to him for the happiness he gave them, however brief it might be; and of women like his wife who loved without any genuine feeling, with superfluous phrases, affectedly, hysterically, with an expression that suggested that it was not love nor passion, but something more significant; and of two or three others, very beautiful, cold women, on whose faces he had caught a glimpse of a rapacious expression—an obstinate desire to snatch from life more than it could give, and these were capricious, unreflecting, domineering, unintelligent women not in their first youth, and when Gurov grew cold to them their beauty excited his hatred, and the lace on their linen seemed to him like scales.

But in this case there was still the diffidence, the angularity of inexperienced youth, an awkward feeling; and there was a sense of consternation as though someone had suddenly knocked at the door. The attitude of Anna Sergeyevna—'the lady with the dog'—to what had happened was somehow peculiar, very grave, as though it were her fall—so it seemed, and it was strange and inappropriate. Her face dropped and faded, and on both sides of it her long hair hung down mournfully; she mused in a dejected attitude like 'the woman who was a sinner' in an old-fashioned picture.

'It's wrong,' she said. 'You will be the first to despise me now.'

There was a water-melon on the table. Gurov cut himself a slice and began eating it without haste. There followed at least half an hour of silence.

Anna Sergeyevna was touching; there was about her the purity of a good, simple woman who had seen little of life. The solitary candle burning on the table threw a faint light on her face, yet it was clear that she was very unhappy.

'How could I despise you?' asked Gurov. 'You don't know what you are saying.'

'God forgive me,' she said, and her eyes filled with tears. 'It's awful.'

'You seem to feel you need to be forgiven.'

'Forgiven? No. I am a bad, low woman; I despise myself and don't attempt to justify myself. It's not my husband but myself I have deceived. And not only just now; I have been deceiving myself for a long time. My husband may be a good, honest man, but he is a flunkey! I don't know what he does there, what his work is, but I know he is a flunkey! I was twenty when I was married to him. I have been tormented by curiosity; I wanted something better. "There must be a different sort of life," I said to myself. I wanted to live! To live, to live!... I was fired by curiosity... you don't understand it, but, I swear to God, I could not control myself; something happened to me: I could not be restrained. I told my husband I was ill, and came here... And here I have been walking about as though I were dazed, like a mad creature; ...and now I have become a vulgar, contemptible woman whom anyone may despise.'

Gurov felt bored already, listening to her. He was irritated by the naïve tone, by this remorse, so unexpected and inopportune; but for the tears in her eyes, he might have thought she was jesting or playing a part.

'I don't understand,' he said softly. 'What is it you want?'

She hid her face on his breast and pressed close to him.

'Believe me, believe me, I beseech you...' she said. 'I love a pure, honest life, and sin is loathsome to me. I don't know what I am doing. Simple people say: "The Evil One has beguiled me." And I may say of myself now that the Evil One has beguiled me.'

'Hush, hush!...' he muttered.

He looked at her fixed, scared eyes, kissed her, talked softly and affectionately, and by degrees she was comforted, and her gaiety returned; they both began laughing.

Afterwards when they went out there was not a soul on the sea-front. The town with its cypresses had quite a deathlike air, but the sea still broke noisily on the shore; a single barge was rocking on the waves, and a lantern was blinking sleepily on it.

They found a cab and drove to Oreanda.

'I found out your surname in the hall just now: it was written on the board—Von Diderits,' said Gurov. 'Is your husband a German?'

'No; I believe his grandfather was a German, but he is an Orthodox Russian himself.'

At Oreanda they sat on a seat not far from the church, looked down at the sea, and were silent. Yalta was hardly visible through the morning mist; white clouds stood motionless on the mountain-tops. The leaves did not stir on the trees, grasshoppers chirruped, and the monotonous hollow sound of the sea rising up from below, spoke of the peace, of the eternal sleep awaiting us. So it must have sounded when there was no Yalta, no Oreanda here; so it sounds now, and it will sound as indifferently and monotonously when we are all no more. And in this constancy, in this complete indifference to the life and death of each of us, there lies hid, perhaps, a pledge of our eternal salvation, of the unceasing movement of life upon earth, of unceasing progress towards perfection. Sitting beside a young woman who in the dawn seemed so lovely, soothed and spellbound in these magical surroundings—the sea, mountains, clouds, the open sky—Gurov thought how in reality everything is beautiful in this world when one reflects: everything except what we think or do ourselves when we forget our human dignity and the higher aims of our existence.

A man walked up to them—probably a keeper—looked at them and walked away. And this detail seemed mysterious and beautiful, too. They saw a steamer come from Theodosia, with its lights out in the glow of dawn.

'There is dew on the grass,' said Anna Sergeyevna, after a silence.

'Yes. It's time to go home.'

They went back to the town.

Then they met every day at twelve o'clock on the sea-front, lunched and dined together, went for walks, admired the sea. She complained that she slept badly, that her heart throbbed violently; asked the same questions, troubled now by jealousy and now by the fear that he did not respect her sufficiently. And often in the square or gardens, when there was no one near them, he suddenly drew her to him and kissed her passionately. Complete idleness, these kisses in broad daylight while he looked round in dread of someone's seeing them, the heat, the smell of the sea, and the continual passing to and fro before him of idle, well-dressed, well-fed people, made a new man of him; he told Anna Sergeyevna how beautiful she was, how fascinating. He was impatiently passionate, he would not move a step away from her, while she was often pensive and continually urged him to confess that he did not respect her, did not love her in the least, and thought of her as nothing but a common woman. Rather late almost every evening they drove somewhere out of town, to Oreanda or to the waterfall; and the expedition was always a success, the scenery invariably impressed them as grand and beautiful.

They were expecting her husband to come, but a letter came

from him, saying that there was something wrong with his eyes, and he entreated his wife to come home as quickly as possible. Anna Sergeyevna made haste to go.

'It's a good thing I am going away,' she said to Gurov. 'It's the finger of destiny!'

She went by coach and he went with her. They were driving the whole day. When she had got into a compartment of the express, and when the second bell had rung, she said:

'Let me look at you once more... look at you once again. That's right.'

She did not shed tears, but was so sad that she seemed ill, and her face was quivering.

'I shall remember you... think of you,' she said. 'God be with you; be happy. Don't remember evil against me. We are parting forever—it must be so, for we ought never to have met. Well, God be with you.'

The train moved off rapidly, its lights soon vanished from sight, and a minute later there was no sound of it, as though everything had conspired together to end as quickly as possible that sweet delirium, that madness. Left alone on the platform, and gazing into the dark distance, Gurov listened to the chirrup of the grasshoppers and the hum of the telegraph wires, feeling as though he had only just waked up. And he thought, musing, that there had been another episode or adventure in his life, and it, too, was at an end, and nothing was left of it but a memory... He was moved, sad, and conscious of a slight remorse. This young woman whom he would never meet again had not been happy with him; he was genuinely warm and affectionate with her, but yet in his manner, his tone, and his caresses there had been a shade of light irony, the coarse condescension of a happy man who was, besides, almost twice her age. All the time she had called him kind, exceptional, lofty; obviously he had seemed to her different from what he really was, so he had unintentionally deceived her...

Here at the station was already a scent of autumn; it was a cold evening.

'It's time for me to go north,' thought Gurov as he left the platform. 'High time!'

III

At home in Moscow everything was in its winter routine; the stoves were heated, and in the morning it was still dark when the children were having breakfast and getting ready for school, and the nurse would light the lamp for a short time. The frosts had begun already. When the first snow has fallen, on the first day of sledge-driving it is pleasant to see the white earth, the white roofs, to draw soft, delicious breath, and the season brings back the days of one's youth. The old limes and birches, white with hoar-frost, have a good-natured expression; they are nearer to one's heart than cypresses and palms, and near them one doesn't want to be thinking of the sea and the mountains.

Gurov was Moscow born; he arrived in Moscow on a fine frosty day, and when he put on his fur coat and warm gloves, and walked along Petrovka, and when on Saturday evening he heard the ringing of the bells, his recent trip and the places he had seen lost all charm for him. Little by little he became absorbed in Moscow life, greedily read three newspapers a day, and declared he did not read the Moscow papers on principle! He already felt a longing to go to restaurants, clubs, dinner-parties, anniversary celebrations, and he felt flattered at entertaining distinguished lawyers and artists, and at playing cards with a professor at the doctors' club. He could already eat a whole plateful of salt fish and cabbage.

In another month, he fancied, the image of Anna Sergeyevna would be shrouded in a mist in his memory, and only from time to time would visit him in his dreams with a touching smile as others did. But more than a month passed, real winter had come, and everything was still clear in his memory as though he had parted with Anna Sergeyevna only the day before. And his memories glowed more and more vividly. When in the evening stillness he heard from his study the voices of his children, preparing their lessons, or when he listened to a song or the organ at the restaurant, or the storm howled in the chimney, suddenly everything would rise up in his memory: what had happened on the groyne, and the early morning with the mist on the mountains, and the steamer coming from Theodosia, and the kisses. He would pace a long time about his room, remembering it all and smiling; then his memories passed into dreams, and in his fancy the past was mingled with what was to come.

Anna Sergeyevna did not visit him in dreams, but followed him about everywhere like a shadow and haunted him. When he shut his eyes he saw her as though she were living before him, and she seemed to him lovelier, younger, tenderer than she was; and he imagined himself finer than he had been in Yalta. In the evenings she peeped out at him from the bookcase, from the fireplace, from the corner—he heard her breathing, the caressing rustle of her dress. In the street he watched the women, looking for someone like her.

He was tormented by an intense desire to confide his memories to someone. But in his home it was impossible to talk of his love, and he had no one outside; he could not talk to his tenants nor to anyone at the bank. And what had he to talk of? Had he been in love, then? Had there been anything beautiful, poetical, or edifying or simply interesting in his relations with Anna Sergeyevna? And there was nothing for him but to talk vaguely of love, of woman, and no one guessed what it meant; only his wife twitched her black eyebrows, and said:

'The part of a lady-killer does not suit you at all, Dimitri.'

One evening, coming out of the doctors' club with an official with whom he had been playing cards, he could not resist saying:

'If only you knew what a fascinating woman I made the acquaintance of in Yalta!'

The official got into his sledge and was driving away, but turned suddenly and shouted:

'Dmitri Dmitritch!'

'What?'

'You were right this evening: the sturgeon was a bit too strong!'

These words, so ordinary, for some reason moved Gurov to indignation, and struck him as degrading and unclean. What savage manners, what people! What senseless nights, what uninteresting, uneventful days! The rage for card-playing, the gluttony, the drunkenness, the continual talk always about the same thing. Useless pursuits and conversations always about the same things absorb the better part of one's time, the better part of one's strength, and in the end there is left a life grovelling and curtailed, worthless and trivial, and there is no escaping or getting away from it—just as though one were in a madhouse or a prison.

Gurov did not sleep all night, and was filled with indignation.

And he had a headache all next day. And the next night he slept badly; he sat up in bed, thinking, or paced up and down his room. He was sick of his children, sick of the bank; he had no desire to go anywhere or to talk of anything.

In the holidays in December he prepared for a journey, and told his wife he was going to Petersburg to do something in the interests of a young friend—and he set off for S——. What for? He did not very well know himself. He wanted to see Anna Sergeyevna and to talk with her—to arrange a meeting, if possible.

He reached S—— in the morning, and took the best room at the hotel, in which the floor was covered with grey army cloth, and on the table was an inkstand, grey with dust and adorned with a figure on horseback, with its hat in its hand and its head broken off. The hotel porter gave him the necessary information; Von Diderits lived in a house of his own in Old Gontcharny Street—it was not far from the hotel: he was rich and lived in good style, and had his own horses; everyone in the town knew him. The porter pronounced the name 'Dridirits'.

Gurov went without haste to Old Gontcharny Street and found the house. Just opposite the house stretched a long grey fence adorned with nails.

'One would run away from a fence like that,' thought Gurov, looking from the fence to the windows of the house and back again.

He considered: today was a holiday, and the husband would probably be at home. And in any case it would be tactless to go into the house and upset her. If he were to send her a note it might fall into her husband's hands, and then it might ruin everything. The best thing was to trust to chance. And he kept walking up and down the street by the fence, waiting for the chance. He saw a beggar go in at the gate and dogs fly at him; then an hour later he heard a piano, and the sounds were faint and indistinct. Probably it was Anna Sergeyevna playing. The front door suddenly opened, and an old woman came out, followed by the familiar white Pomeranian. Gurov was on the point of calling to the dog, but his heart began beating violently, and in his excitement he could not remember the dog's name.

He walked up and down, and loathed the grey fence more and more, and by now he thought irritably that Anna Sergeyevna had forgotten him, and was perhaps already amusing herself with someone else, and that that was very natural in a young woman who had nothing to look at from morning till night but that confounded fence. He went back to his hotel room and sat for a long while on the sofa, not knowing what to do, then he had dinner and a long nap.

'How stupid and worrying it is!' he thought when he woke and looked at the dark windows: it was already evening. 'Here I've had a good sleep for some reason. What shall I do in the night?'

He sat on the bed, which was covered by a cheap grey blanket, such as one sees in hospitals, and he taunted himself in his vexation:

'So much for the lady with the dog... so much for the adventure... You're in a nice fix...'

That morning at the station a poster in large letters had caught his eye. 'The Geisha' was to be performed for the first time. He thought of this and went to the theatre.

'It's quite possible she may go to the first performance,' he thought.

The theatre was full. As in all provincial theatres, there was a fog above the chandelier, the gallery was noisy and restless; in the front row the local dandies were standing up before the beginning of the performance, with their hands behind them; in the Governor's box the Governor's daughter, wearing a boa, was sitting in the front seat, while the Governor himself lurked modestly behind the curtain with only his hands visible; the orchestra was a long time tuning up; the stage curtain swayed. All the time the audience were coming in and taking their seats Gurov looked at them eagerly.

Anna Sergeyevna, too, came in. She sat down in the third row, and when Gurov looked at her his heart contracted, and he understood clearly that for him there was in the whole world no creature so near, so precious, and so important to him; she, this little woman, in no way remarkable, lost in a provincial crowd, with a vulgar lorgnette in her hand, filled his whole life now, was his sorrow and his joy, the one happiness that he now desired for himself, and to the sounds of the inferior orchestra, of the wretched provincial violins, he thought how lovely she was. He thought and dreamed.

A young man with small side-whiskers, tall and stooping, came in with Anna Sergeyevna and sat down beside her; he bent his head at every step and seemed to be continually bowing. Most likely this was the husband whom at Yalta, in a rush of bitter feeling, she had called a flunkey. And there really was in his long figure, his side-whiskers, and the small bald patch on his head, something of the flunkey's obsequiousness; his smile was sugary, and in his buttonhole there was some badge of distinction like the number on a waiter.

During the first interval the husband went away to smoke; she remained alone in her stall. Gurov, who was sitting in the stalls, too, went up to her and said in a trembling voice, with a forced smile:

'Good-evening.'

She glanced at him and turned pale, then glanced again with horror, unable to believe her eyes, and tightly gripped the fan and the lorgnette in her hands, evidently struggling with herself not to faint. Both were silent. She was sitting, he was standing, frightened by her confusion and not venturing to sit down beside her. The violins and the flute began tuning up. He felt suddenly frightened; it seemed as though all the people in the boxes were looking at them. She got up and went quickly to the door; he followed her, and both walked senselessly along passages, and up and down stairs, and figures in legal, scholastic, and civil service uniforms, all wearing badges, flitted before their eyes. They caught glimpses of ladies, of fur coats hanging on pegs; the draughts blew on them, bringing a smell of stale tobacco. And Gurov, whose heart was beating violently, thought:

'Oh, heavens! Why are these people here and this orchestra!...'

And at that instant he recalled how when he had seen Anna Sergeyevna off at the station he had thought that everything was over and they would never meet again. But how far they were still from the end!

On the narrow, gloomy staircase over which was written 'To the Amphitheatre,' she stopped.

'How you have frightened me!' she said, breathing hard, still pale and overwhelmed. 'Oh, how you have frightened me! I am half dead. Why have you come? Why?'

'But do understand, Anna, do understand...' he said hastily in a low voice. 'I entreat you to understand...'

She looked at him with dread, with entreaty, with love; she looked at him intently, to keep his features more distinctly in her memory.

'I am so unhappy,' she went on, not heeding him. 'I have

thought of nothing but you all the time; I live only in the thought of you. And I wanted to forget, to forget you; but why, oh, why, have you come?'

On the landing above them two schoolboys were smoking and looking down, but that was nothing to Gurov; he drew Anna Sergeyevna to him, and began kissing her face, her cheeks, and her hands.

'What are you doing, what are you doing!' she cried in horror, pushing him away. 'We are mad. Go away to-day; go away at once... I beseech you by all that is sacred, I implore you... There are people coming this way!'

Someone was coming up the stairs.

'You must go away,' Anna Sergeyevna went on in a whisper. 'Do you hear, Dmitri Dmitritch? I will come and see you in Moscow. I have never been happy; I am miserable now, and I never, never shall be happy, never! Don't make me suffer still more! I swear I'll come to Moscow. But now let us part. My precious, good, dear one, we must part!'

She pressed his hand and began rapidly going downstairs, looking round at him, and from her eyes he could see that she really was unhappy. Gurov stood for a little while, listened, then, when all sound had died away, he found his coat and left the theatre.

IV

And Anna Sergeyevna began coming to see him in Moscow. Once in two or three months she left S——, telling her husband that she was going to consult a doctor about an internal complaint—and her husband believed her, and did not believe her. In Moscow she stayed at the Slaviansky Bazaar hotel, and at once sent a man in a red cap to Gurov. Gurov went to see her, and no one in Moscow knew of it.

Once he was going to see her in this way on a winter morning (the messenger had come the evening before when he was out). With him walked his daughter, whom he wanted to take to school: it was on the way. Snow was falling in big wet flakes.

'It's three degrees above freezing-point, and yet it is snowing,' said Gurov to his daughter. 'The thaw is only on the surface of the earth;

there is quite a different temperature at a greater height in the atmosphere.'

'And why are there no thunderstorms in the winter, father?'

He explained that, too. He talked, thinking all the while that he was going to see her, and no living soul knew of it, and probably never would know. He had two lives: one, open, seen and known by all who cared to know, full of relative truth and of relative falsehood, exactly like the lives of his friends and acquaintances; and another life running its course in secret. And through some strange, perhaps accidental, conjunction of circumstances, everything that was essential, of interest and of value to him, everything in which he was sincere and did not deceive himself, everything that made the kernel of his life, was hidden from other people; and all that was false in him, the sheath in which he hid himself to conceal the truth—such, for instance, as his work in the bank, his discussions at the club, his 'lower race', his presence with his wife at anniversary festivities—all that was open. And he judged of others by himself, not believing in what he saw, and always believing that every man had his real, most interesting life under the cover of secrecy and under the cover of night. All personal life rested on secrecy, and possibly it was partly on that account that civilised man was so nervously anxious that personal privacy should be respected.

After leaving his daughter at school, Gurov went on to the Slaviansky Bazaar. He took off his fur coat below, went upstairs, and softly knocked at the door. Anna Sergeyevna, wearing his favourite grey dress, exhausted by the journey and the suspense, had been expecting him since the evening before. She was pale; she looked at him, and did not smile, and he had hardly come in when she fell on his breast. Their kiss was slow and prolonged, as though they had not met for two years.

'Well, how are you getting on there?' he asked. 'What news?'

'Wait; I'll tell you directly... I can't talk.'

She could not speak; she was crying. She turned away from him, and pressed her handkerchief to her eyes.

'Let her have her cry out. I'll sit down and wait,' he thought, and he sat down in an arm-chair.

Then he rang and asked for tea to be brought him, and while he drank his tea she remained standing at the window with her back to him. She was crying from emotion, from the miserable consciousness that their life was so hard for them; they could only meet in secret, hiding themselves from people, like thieves! Was not their life shattered?

'Come, do stop!' he said.

It was evident to him that this love of theirs would not soon be over, that he could not see the end of it. Anna Sergeyevna grew more and more attached to him. She adored him, and it was unthinkable to say to her that it was bound to have an end some day; besides, she would not have believed it!

He went up to her and took her by the shoulders to say something affectionate and cheering, and at that moment he saw himself in the looking-glass.

His hair was already beginning to turn grey. And it seemed strange to him that he had grown so much older, so much plainer during the last few years. The shoulders on which his hands rested were warm and quivering. He felt compassion for this life, still so warm and lovely, but probably already not far from beginning to fade and wither like his own. Why did she love him so much? He always seemed to women different from what he was, and they loved in him not himself, but the man created by their imagination, whom they had been eagerly seeking all their lives; and afterwards, when they noticed their mistake, they loved him all the same. And not one of them had been happy with him. Time passed, he had made their acquaintance, got on with them, parted, but he had never once loved; it was anything you like, but not love.

And only now when his head was grey he had fallen properly, really in love—for the first time in his life.

Anna Sergeyevna and he loved each other like people very close and akin, like husband and wife, like tender friends; it seemed to them that fate itself had meant them for one another, and they could not understand why he had a wife and she a husband; and it was as though they were a pair of birds of passage, caught and forced to live in different cages. They forgave each other for what they were ashamed of in their past, they forgave everything in the present, and felt that this love of theirs had changed them both.

In moments of depression in the past he had comforted himself with any arguments that came into his mind, but now he no longer cared for arguments; he felt profound compassion, he wanted to be sincere and tender...

'Don't cry, my darling,' he said. 'You've had your cry; that's enough... Let us talk now, let us think of some plan.'

Then they spent a long while taking counsel together, talked of how to avoid the necessity for secrecy, for deception, for living in different towns and not seeing each other for long at a time. How could they be free from this intolerable bondage?

'How? How?' he asked, clutching his head. 'How?'

And it seemed as though in a little while the solution would be found, and then a new and splendid life would begin; and it was clear to both of them that they had still a long, long road before them, and that the most complicated and difficult part of it was only just beginning.

Anton Pavlovich Chekhov (1860–1904) was born in Taganrog in southern Russia, the son of a former serf, and grew up to become not only a physician but one of the most admired playwrights and authors in world literature, renowned for such masterpieces as the plays The Seagull *and* The Cherry Orchard. *In short stories like 'The Lady with the Dog', which was published in 1899, he rejected the conventions of contemporary story-telling to pose questions to his readers rather than offer them easy answers. He wrote this story while staying in Yalta, where his doctors had sent him in the hope that the warm climate there would alleviate the tuberculosis that would eventually kill him at the early age of 44.*

Cupid's Arrows
Rudyard Kipling

Pit where the buffalo cooled his hide,
By the hot sun emptied, and blistered and dried;
Log in the reh-grass, hidden and alone;
Bund where the earth-rat's mounds are strown:
Cave in the bank where the sly stream steals;
Aloe that stabs at the belly and heels,
Jump if you dare on a steed untried—
Safer it is to go wide—go wide!
Hark, from in front where the best men ride:—
'Pull to the off, boys! Wide! Go wide!'

The Peora Hunt.

Once upon a time there lived at Simla a very pretty girl, the daughter of a poor but honest District and Sessions Judge. She was a good girl, but could not help knowing her power and using it. Her Mamma was very anxious about her daughter's future, as all good Mammas should be.

When a man is a Commissioner and a bachelor and has the right of wearing open-work jam-tart jewels in gold and enamel on his clothes, and of going through a door before everyone except a Member of Council, a Lieutenant-Governor, or a Viceroy, he is worth marrying. At least, that is what ladies say. There was a Commissioner in Simla, in those days, who was, and wore, and did, all I have said. He was a plain man—an ugly man—the ugliest man in Asia, with two exceptions. His was a face to dream about and try to carve on a pipe-head afterwards. His name was Saggott—Barr-Saggott—Anthony Barr-Saggott and six letters to follow. Departmentally, he was one of the best men the Government of India owned. Socially, he was like a blandishing gorilla.

When he turned his attentions to Miss Beighton, I believe that Mrs Beighton wept with delight at the reward Providence had sent her in her old age.

Mr Beighton held his tongue. He was an easy-going man.

Now a Commissioner is very rich. His pay is beyond the dreams of avarice—is so enormous that he can afford to save and scrape in a way that would almost discredit a Member of Council. Most Commissioners are mean; but Barr-Saggott was an exception. He entertained royally; he horsed himself well; he gave dances; he was a power in the land; and he behaved as such.

Consider that everything I am writing of took place in an almost pre-historic era in the history of British India. Some folk may remember the years before lawn-tennis was born when we all played croquet. There were seasons before that, if you will believe me, when even croquet had not been invented, and archery—which was revived in England in 1844—was as great a pest as lawn-tennis is now. People talked learnedly about 'holding' and 'loosing', 'steles', 'reflexed bows', '56-pound bows', 'backed' or 'self-yew bows', as we talk about 'rallies', 'volleys', 'smashes', 'returns', and '16-ounce rackets'.

Miss Beighton shot divinely over ladies' distance—60 yards, that is—and was acknowledged the best lady archer in Simla. Men called her 'Diana of Tara-Devi'.

Barr-Saggott paid her great attention; and, as I have said, the heart of her mother was uplifted in consequence. Kitty Beighton took matters more calmly. It was pleasant to be singled out by a Commissioner with letters after his name, and to fill the hearts of other girls with bad feelings. But there was no denying the fact that Barr-Saggott was phenomenally ugly; and all his attempts to adorn himself only made him more grotesque. He was not christened 'The Langur'—which means grey ape—for nothing. It was pleasant, Kitty thought, to have him at her feet, but it was better to escape from him and ride with the graceless Cubbon—the man in a Dragoon Regiment at Umballa—the boy with a handsome face, and no prospects. Kitty liked Cubbon more than a little. He never pretended for a moment that he was anything less than head over heels in love with her; for he was an honest boy. So Kitty fled, now and again, from the stately wooings of Barr-Saggott to the company of young Cubbon, and was scolded by her Mamma in consequence. 'But, Mother,' she said, 'Mr Saggot is such—such a—is so *fearfully* ugly, you know!'

'My dear,' said Mrs Beighton, piously, 'we cannot be other than an all-ruling Providence has made us. Besides, you will take precedence of your own Mother, you know! Think of that and be reasonable.'

Then Kitty put up her little chin and said irreverent things about precedence, and Commissioners, and matrimony. Mr Beighton rubbed the top of his head; for he was an easy-going man.

Late in the season, when he judged that the time was ripe, Barr-Saggott developed a plan which did great credit to his administrative powers. He arranged an archery tournament for ladies, with a most sumptuous diamond-studded bracelet as prize. He drew up his terms skilfully, and everyone saw that the bracelet was a gift to Miss Beighton; the acceptance carrying with it the hand and the heart of Commissioner Barr-Saggott. The terms were a St Leonard's Round—thirty-six shots at sixty yards—under the rules of the Simla Toxophilite Society.

All Simla was invited. There were beautifully arranged tea-tables under the deodars at Annandale, where the Grand Stand is now; and, alone in its glory, winking in the sun, sat the diamond bracelet in a blue velvet case. Miss Beighton was anxious—almost too anxious to compete. On the appointed afternoon, all Simla rode down to Annandale to witness the Judgement of Paris turned upside down. Kitty rode with young Cubbon, and it was easy to see that the boy was troubled in his mind. He must be held innocent of everything that followed. Kitty was pale and nervous, and looked long at the bracelet. Barr-Saggott was gorgeously dressed, even more nervous than Kitty, and more hideous than ever.

Mrs Beighton smiled condescendingly, as befitted the mother of a potential Commissioneress, and the shooting began; all the world standing in a semicircle as the ladies came out one after the other.

Nothing is so tedious as an archery competition. They shot, and they shot, and they kept on shooting, till the sun left the valley, and little breezes got up in the deodars, and people waited for Miss Beighton to shoot and win. Cubbon was at one horn of the semicircle round the shooters, and Barr-Saggott at the other. Miss Beighton was last on the list. The scoring had been weak, and the bracelet, *plus* Commissioner Barr-Saggott, was hers to a certainty.

The Commissioner strung her bow with his own sacred hands. She stepped forward, looked at the bracelet, and her first arrow went true to a hair—full into the heart of the 'gold'—counting nine points.

Young Cubbon on the left turned white, and his Devil prompted

Barr-Saggott to smile. Now horses used to shy when Barr-Saggott smiled. Kitty saw that smile. She looked to her left-front, gave an almost imperceptible nod to Cubbon, and went on shooting.

I wish I could describe the scene that followed. It was out of the ordinary and most improper. Miss Kitty fitted her arrows with immense deliberation, so that everyone might see what she was doing. She was a perfect shot; and her 46-pound bow suited her to a nicety. She pinned the wooden legs of the target with great care four successive times. She pinned the wooden top of the target once, and all the ladies looked at each other. Then she began some fancy shooting at the white, which, if you hit it, counts exactly one point. She put five arrows into the white. It was wonderful archery; but, seeing that her business was to make 'golds' and win the bracelet, Barr-Saggott turned a delicate green like young water-grass. Next, she shot over the target twice, then wide to the left twice—always with the same deliberation—while a chilly hush fell over the company, and Mrs Beighton took out her handkerchief. Then Kitty shot at the ground in front of the target, and split several arrows. Then she made a red—or seven points—just to show what she could do if she liked, and finished up her amazing performance with some more fancy shooting at the target-supports. Here is her score as it was picked off:—

	Gold	Red	Blue	Black	White	Total Hits	Total Score
Miss Beighton	1	1	0	0	5	7	21

Barr-Saggott looked as if the last few arrowheads had been driven into his legs instead of the target's, and the deep stillness was broken by a little snubby, mottled, half-grown girl saying in a shrill voice of triumph: 'Then *I've* won!'

Mrs Beighton did her best to bear up; but she wept in the presence of the people. No training could help her through such a disappointment. Kitty unstrung her bow with a vicious jerk, and went back to her place, while Barr-Saggott was trying to pretend that he enjoyed snapping the bracelet on the snubby girl's raw, red wrist. It was an awkward scene—most awkward. Everyone tried to depart in a body and leave Kitty to the mercy of her Mamma.

But Cubbon took her away instead, and—the rest isn't worth printing.

*Joseph Rudyard Kipling (1865–1936) was born in Bombay (Mumbai),
India, and, although he was educated in England and spent much of his
life in London, the USA and South Africa, always considered himself to
be Anglo-Indian and set many of his tales in India. Winner of the Nobel
Prize for Literature in 1907, he is remembered today as the author of
such classics as* The Jungle Book *(1894),* The Just So Stories *(1902) and*
Kim *(1901). 'Cupid's Arrows' was one of the stories included in* Plain
Tales from the Hills *(1888). Kipling knew Simla well from his regular
visits there in the 1880s, and it was while staying there that he wrote
many of his 'Plain Tales', which were first published in Calcutta when
he was just 22.*

An Elixir of Love

W.S. Gilbert

CHAPTER I

Ploverleigh was a picturesque little village in Dorsetshire, ten miles from anywhere. It lay in a pretty valley nestling amid clumps of elm trees, and a pleasant little trout stream ran right through it from end to end. The vicar of Ploverleigh was the Hon. and Rev. Mortimer De Becheville, third son of the forty-eighth Earl of Caramel. He was an excellent gentleman, and his living was worth £1,200 a-year. He was a graduate of Cambridge, and held a College Fellowship, besides which his father allowed him £500 a-year. So he was very comfortably 'off'.

Mr De Becheville had a very easy time of it, for he spent eleven-twelfths of the year away from the parish, delegating his duties to the Rev. Stanley Gay, an admirable young curate to whom he paid a stipend of £120 a-year, pocketing by this means a clear annual profit of £1,080. It was said by unkind and ungenerous people, that, as Mr De Becheville had (presumably) been selected for his sacred duties at a high salary on account of his special and exceptional qualifications for their discharge, it was hardly fair to delegate them to a wholly inexperienced young gentleman of two-and-twenty. It was argued that if a colonel, or a stipendiary magistrate, or a superintendent of a county lunatic asylum, or any other person holding a responsible office (outside the Church of England), for which he was handsomely paid, were to do his work by cheap deputy, such a responsible official would be looked upon as a swindler. But this line of reasoning is only applied to the cure of souls by uncharitable and narrow-minded people who never go to church, and consequently can't know anything about it. Besides, who cares what people who never go to church think? If it comes to that, Mr De Becheville was *not* selected (as it happens) on account of his special and exceptional fitness for the cure of souls, inasmuch as the living was a family one, and went to De Becheville because his two elder brothers preferred the Guards. So that argument falls to the ground.

The Rev. Stanley Gay was a Leveller. I don't mean to say that he was a mere I'm-as-good-as-you Radical spouter, who advocated a redistribution of property from mere sordid motives. Mr Gay was an aesthetic Leveller. He held that as Love is the great bond of union between man and woman, no arbitrary obstacle should be allowed to interfere with its progress. He did not desire to abolish Rank, but he *did* desire that a mere difference in rank should not be an obstacle in the way of making two young people happy. He could prove to you by figures (for he was a famous mathematician) that, rank notwithstanding, all men are equal, and this is how he did it.

He began, as a matter of course, with x, because, as he said, x, whether it represents one or one hundred thousand, is always x, and do what you will, you cannot make w or y of it by any known process.

Having made this quite clear to you, he carried on his argument by means of algebra, until he got right through algebra to the 'cases' at the end of the book, and then he slid by gentle and imperceptible degrees into conic sections, where x, although you found it masquerading as the equation to the parabola, was still as much x as ever. Then if you were not too tired to follow him, you found yourself up to the eyes in plane and spherical trigonometry, where x again turned up in a variety of assumed characters, sometimes as '$\cos a$', sometimes as '$\sin \beta$', but generally with a $\sqrt{}$ over it, and none the less x on that account. This singular character then made its appearance in a quaint binomial disguise, and was eventually run to earth in the very heart of differential and integral calculus, looking less like x, but being, in point of fact, more like x than ever. The force of his argument went to show that, do what you would, you could not stamp x out, and therefore it was better and wiser and more straightforward to call him x at once than to invest him with complicated sham dignities which meant nothing, and only served to bother and perplex people who met him for the first time. It's a very easy problem—anybody can do it.

Mr Gay was, as a matter of course, engaged to be married. He loved a pretty little girl of eighteen, with soft brown eyes, and bright silky brown hair. Her name was Jessie Lightly, and she was the only daughter of Sir Caractacus Lightly, a wealthy baronet who had a large place in the neighbourhood of Ploverleigh. Sir Caractacus was a very dignified old gentleman, whose wife had died two years after Jessie's birth. A well-bred, courtly old gentleman, too, with a keen sense of honour. He was very fond of Mr Gay, though he had no sympathy with his levelling views.

One beautiful moonlit evening Mr Gay and Jessie were sitting together on Sir Caractacus's lawn. Everything around them was pure and calm and still, so they grew sentimental.

'Stanley,' said Jessie, 'we are very, very happy, are we not?'

'Unspeakably happy,' said Gay. 'So happy that when I look around me, and see how many there are whose lives are embittered by disappointment—by envy, by hatred, and by malice (when he grew oratorical he generally lapsed into the Litany) 'I turn to the tranquil and unruffled calm of my own pure and happy love for you with gratitude unspeakable.'

He really meant all this, though he expressed himself in rather flatulent periods.

'I wish with all my heart,' said Jessie, 'that every soul on earth were as happy as we two.'

'And why are they not?' asked Gay, who hopped on to his hobby whenever it was, so to speak, brought round to the front door. 'And why are they not, Jessie? I will tell you why they are not. Because–'

'Yes, darling,' said Jessie, who had often heard his argument before. 'I know why. It's dreadful.'

'It's as simple as possible,' said Gay. 'Take x to represent the abstract human being–'

'Certainly, dear,' said Jessie, who agreed with his argument heart and soul, but didn't want to hear it again. 'We took it last night.'

'Then,' said Gay, not heeding the interruption, 'let $x + 1$, $x + 2$, $x + 3$, represent three grades of high rank.'

'Exactly, it's contemptible,' said Jessie. 'How softly the wind sighs among the trees.'

'What is a duke?' asked Gay—not for information, but oratorically, with a view to making a point.

'A mere $x + 3$,' said Jessie. 'Could anything be more hollow. What a lovely evening!'

'The Duke of Buckingham and Chandos—it sounds well, I grant you,' continued Gay, 'but call him the $x + 3$ of Buckingham and Chandos, and you reduce him at once to–'

'I know,' said Jessie, 'to his lowest common denominator,' and her little upper lip curled with contempt.

'Nothing of the kind,' said Gay, turning red. 'Either hear me out, or let me drop the subject. At all events don't make ridiculous suggestions.'

'I'm very sorry, dear,' said Jessie, humbly. 'Go on, I'm listening, and I won't interrupt any more.'

But Gay was annoyed and wouldn't go on. So they returned to the house together. It was their first tiff.

CHAPTER II

In St Martin's Lane lived Baylis and Culpepper, magicians, astrologers, and professors of the Black Art. Baylis had sold himself to the Devil at a very early age, and had become remarkably proficient in all kinds of enchantment. Culpepper had been his apprentice, and having also acquired considerable skill as a necromancer, was taken into partnership by the genial old magician, who from the first had taken a liking to the frank and fair-haired boy. Ten years ago (the date of my story) the firm of Baylis and Culpepper stood at the very head of the London family magicians. They did what is known as a pushing trade, but although they advertised largely, and never neglected a chance, it was admitted even by their rivals, that the goods they supplied could be relied on as sound useful articles. They had a special reputation for a class of serviceable family nativity, and they did a very large and increasing business in love philtres, 'The Patent Oxy-Hydrogen Love-at-First-Sight Draught' in bottles at 1s. 1½d. and 2s. 3d. ('our leading article', as Baylis called it) was strong enough in itself to keep the firm going, had all its other resources failed them. But the establishment in St Martin's Lane was also a 'Noted House for Amulets', and if you wanted a neat, well-finished divining-rod, I don't know any place to which I would sooner recommend you. Their Curses at a shilling per dozen were the cheapest things in the trade, and they sold thousands of them in the course of the year. Their Blessings—also very cheap indeed, and quite effective— were not much asked for. 'We always keep a few on hand as curiosities and for completeness, but we don't sell two in the twelvemonth,' said Mr

Baylis. 'A gentleman bought one last week to send to his mother-in-law, but it turned out that he was afflicted in the head, and the persons who had charge of him declined to pay for it, and it's been returned to us. But the sale of penny curses, especially on Saturday nights, is tremendous. We can't turn 'em out fast enough.'

As Baylis and Culpepper were making up their books one evening, just at closing time, a gentle young clergyman with large violet eyes, and a beautiful girl of eighteen, with soft brown hair, and a Madonna-like purity of expression, entered the warehouse. These were Stanley Gay and Jessie Lightly. And this is how it came to pass that they found themselves in London, and in the warehouse of the worthy magicians.

As the reader knows, Stanley Gay and Jessie had for many months given themselves up to the conviction that it was their duty to do all in their power to bring their fellow men and women together in holy matrimony, without regard to distinctions of age or rank. Stanley gave lectures on the subject at mechanics' institutes, and the mechanics were unanimous in their approval of his views. He preached his doctrine in workhouses, in beer-shops, and in lunatic asylums, and his listeners supported him with enthusiasm. He addressed navvies at the roadside on the humanising advantages that would accrue to them if they married refined and wealthy ladies of rank, and not a navvy dissented. In short, he felt more and more convinced every day that he had at last discovered the secret of human happiness. Still he had a formidable battle to fight with class prejudice, and he and Jessie pondered gravely on the difficulties that were before them, and on the best means of overcoming them.

'It's no use disguising the fact, Jessie,' said Mr Gay, 'that the Countesses won't like it.' And little Jessie gave a sigh, and owned that she expected some difficulty with the Countesses. 'We must look these things in the face, Jessie, it won't do to ignore them. We have convinced the humble mechanics and artisans, but the aristocracy hold aloof.'

'The working-man is the true Intelligence after all,' said Jessie.

'He is a noble creature when he is quite sober,' said Gay. 'God bless him.'

Stanley Gay and Jessie were in this frame of mind when they came across Baylis and Culpepper's advertisement in the *Connubial*

Chronicle.

'My dear Jessie,' said Gay, 'I see a way out of our difficulty.'

And dear little Jessie's face beamed with hope.

'These Love Philtres that Baylis and Culpepper advertise—they are very cheap indeed, and if we may judge by the testimonials, they are very effective. Listen, darling.'

And Stanley Gay read as follows:—

'From the Earl of Market Harborough. "I am a hideous old man of eighty, and everyone avoided me. I took a family bottle of your philtre, immediately on my accession to the title and estates a fortnight ago, and I can't keep the young women off. Please send me a pipe of it to lay down."

'From Amelia Orange Blossom.—"I am a very pretty girl of fifteen. For upwards of fourteen years past I have been without a definitely declared admirer. I took a large bottle of your philtre yesterday, and within fourteen hours a young nobleman winked at me in church. Send me a couple of dozen."'

'What can the girl want with a couple of dozen young noblemen, darling?' asked Jessie.

'I don't know—perhaps she took it too strong. Now these men,' said Gay, laying down the paper, 'are benefactors indeed, if they can accomplish all they undertake. I would ennoble these men. They should have statues. I would enthrone them in high places. They would be $x + 3$.'

'My generous darling,' said Jessie, gazing into his eyes in a fervid ecstasy.

'Not at all,' replied Gay. 'They deserve it. We confer peerages on generals who plunge half a nation into mourning—shall we deny them to men who bring a life's happiness home to every door? Always supposing,' added the cautious clergyman, 'that they can really do what they profess.'

The upshot of this conversation was that Gay determined to lay in a stock of philtres for general use among his parishioners. If the effect upon them was satisfactory he would extend the sphere of their operations. So when Sir Caractacus and his daughter went to town for the season, Stanley Gay spent a fortnight with them, and thus it came to pass that he and Jessie went together to Baylis and Culpepper's.

'Have you any fresh Love Philtres to day?' said Gay.

'Plenty, sir,' said Mr Culpepper. 'How many would you like?'

'Well—let me see,' said Gay. 'There are a hundred and forty souls in my parish,—say twelve dozen.'

'I think, dear,' said little Jessie, 'you are better to take a few more than you really want, in case of accidents.'

'In purchasing a large quantity, sir,' said Mr Culpepper, 'we would strongly advise you taking it in the wood, and drawing it off as you happen to want it. We have it in four-and-a-half and nine-gallon casks, and we deduct ten per cent, for cash payments.'

'Then, Mr Culpepper, be good enough to let me have a nine-gallon cask of Love Philtre as soon as possible. Send it to the Rev. Stanley Gay, Ploverleigh.'

He wrote a cheque for the amount, and so the transaction ended.

'Is there any other article?' said Mr Culpepper.

'Nothing to-day. Good afternoon.'

'Have you seen our new wishing-caps? They are lined with silk and very chastely quilted, sir. We sold one to the Archbishop of Canterbury not an hour ago. Allow me to put you up a wishing-cap.'

'I tell you that I want nothing more,' said Gay, going.

'Our Flying Carpets are quite the talk of the town, sir,' said Culpepper, producing a very handsome piece of Persian tapestry. 'You spread it on the ground and sit on it, and then you think of a place and you find yourself there before you can count ten. Our Abudah chests, sir, each chest containing a patent Hag, who comes out and prophesies disasters whenever you touch this spring, are highly spoken of. We can sell the Abudah chest complete for fifteen guineas.'

'I think you tradespeople make a great mistake in worrying people to buy things they don't want,' said Gay.

'You'd be surprised if you knew the quantity of things we get rid of by this means, sir.'

'No doubt, but I think you keep a great many people out of your shop. If x represents the amount you gain by it, and y the amount you lose by it, then if $x/2 = y$ you are clearly out of pocket by it at the end of the year. Think this over. Good evening.'

And Mr Gay left the shop with Jessie.

'Stanley,' said she, 'what a blessing you are to mankind. You do good wherever you go.'

'My dear Jessie,' replied Gay, 'I have had a magnificent education, and if I can show these worthy but half-educated tradesmen that their ignorance of the profounder mathematics is misleading them, I am only dealing as I should deal with the blessings that have been entrusted to my care.'

As Messrs Baylis & Culpepper have nothing more to do with this story, it may be stated at once that Stanley Gay's words had a marked effect upon them. They determined never to push an article again, and within two years of this resolve they retired on ample fortunes, Baylis to a beautiful detached house on Clapham Common, and Culpepper to a handsome chateau on the Mediterranean, about four miles from Nice.

CHAPTER III

We are once more at Ploverleigh, but this time at the Vicarage. The scene is Mr Gay's handsome library, and in this library three persons are assembled—Mr Gay, Jessie, and old Zorah Clarke. It should be explained that Zorah is Mr Gay's cook and housekeeper, and it is understood between him and Sir Caractacus Lightly that Jessie may call on the curate whenever she likes, on condition that Zorah is present during the whole time of the visit. Zorah is stone deaf and has to be communicated with through the medium of pantomime, so that while she is really no impediment whatever to the free flow of conversation, the chastening influence of her presence would suffice of itself to silence ill-natured comments, if such articles had an existence among the primitive and innocent inhabitants of Ploverleigh.

The nine-gallon cask of Love Philtre had arrived in due course, and Mr Gay had decided that it should be locked up in a cupboard in his library, as he thought it would scarcely be prudent to trust it to Zorah, whose curiosity might get the better of her discretion. Zorah (who believed that the cask contained sherry) was much scandalised at her master's action in keeping it in his library, and looked upon it as an evident and unmistakeable sign that he had deliberately made up his mind to take to a steady course of drinking. However, Mr Gay partly reassured the good old lady by informing her in pantomime (an art of expression in which long practice had made him singularly expert) that the liquid was not intoxicating in the ordinary sense of the word, but that it was a cunning and subtle essence, concocted from innocent herbs by learned gentlemen who had devoted a lifetime to the study of its properties. He added (still in pantomime) that he did not propose to drink a single drop of it himself, but that he intended to distribute it among his parishioners, whom it would benefit socially, mentally, and morally to a considerable extent. Master as he was of the art of expression by gesture, it took two days' hard work to make this clear to her, and even then she had acquired but a faint and feeble idea of its properties, for she always referred to it as sarsaparilla.

'Jessie,' said Gay, 'the question now arises,—How shall we most effectually dispense the great boon we have at our command? Shall we give a party to our friends, and put the Love Philtre on the table in decanters, and allow them to help themselves?'

'We must be very careful, dear,' said Jessie, 'not to allow any married people to taste it.'

'True,' said Gay, 'quite true. I never thought of that. It wouldn't do at all. I am much obliged to you for the suggestion. It would be terrible—quite terrible.'

And Stanley Gay turned quite pale and faint at the very thought of such a contretemps.

'Then,' said Jessie, 'there are the engaged couples. I don't think we ought to do anything to interfere with the prospects of those who have already plighted their troth.'

'Quite true,' said Gay, 'we have no right, as you say, to interfere with the arrangements of engaged couples. That narrows our sphere of action very considerably.'

'Then the widows and the widowers of less than one year's standing should be exempted from its influence.'

'Certainly, most certainly. That reflection did not occur to me, I confess. It is clear that the dispensing of the philtre will be a very delicate operation: it will have to be conducted with the utmost tact. Can you think of any more exceptions?'

'Let me see,' said Jessie. 'There's Tibbits, our gardener, who has fits; and there's Williamson, papa's second groom, who drinks, oughtn't to be allowed to marry; and Major Crump, who uses dreadful language before ladies; and Dame Parboy, who is bed-ridden; and the old ladies in the almshouses—and little Tommy, the idiot—and, indeed, all children under—under what age shall we say?'

'All children who have not been confirmed,' said Gay. 'Yes, these exceptions never occurred to me.'

'I don't think we shall ever use the nine gallons, dear,' said Jessie. 'One tablespoonful is a dose.'

'I have just thought of another exception,' said Gay. 'Your papa.'

'Oh! papa *must* marry again! Poor dear old papa! Oh! You *must* let *him* marry.'

'My dear Jessie,' said Gay, 'Heaven has offered me the chance of entering into the married state unencumbered with a mother-in-law. And I am content to accept the blessing as I find it. Indeed, I prefer it so.'

'Papa *does* so want to marry—he is always talking of it,' replied the poor little woman, with a pretty pout. 'O indeed, *indeed*, my new mamma, whoever she may be, shall never interfere with us. Why, how thankless you are! My papa is about to confer upon you the most inestimable treasure in the world, a young, beautiful and devoted wife, and you withhold from him a priceless blessing that you are ready to confer on the very meanest of your parishioners.'

'Jessie,' said Gay, 'you have said enough. Sir Caractacus *shall* marry. I was wrong. If a certain burden to which I will not more particularly refer is to descend upon my shoulders, I will endeavour to bear it without repining.'

It was finally determined that there was only one way in which the philtre could be safely and properly distributed. Mr Gay was to give out that he was much interested in the sale of a very peculiar and curious old Amontillado, and small sample bottles of the wine were to be circulated among such of his parishioners as were decently eligible as brides and bridegrooms. The scheme was put into operation as soon as it was decided upon. Mr Gay sent to the nearest market-town for a gross of two-ounce phials, and Jessie and he spent a long afternoon bottling the elixir into these convenient receptacles. They then rolled them up in papers, and addressed them to the persons who were destined to be operated upon. And when all this was done Jessie returned to her papa, and Mr Gay sat up all night explaining in pantomime to Zorah that a widowed aunt of his, in somewhat straitened circumstances, who resided in a small but picturesque villa in the suburbs of Montilla, had been compelled to take a large quantity of the very finest sherry from a bankrupt wine-merchant, in satisfaction of a year's rent of her second floor, and that he had undertaken to push its sale in Ploverleigh in consideration of a commission of two-and-a-half per cent, on the sales effected—which commission was to be added to the fund for the restoration of the church steeple. He began his explanation at 9 p.m., and at 6 a.m. Zorah thought she began to understand him, and Stanley Gay, quite exhausted with his pantomimic exertions, retired, dead beat, to his chamber.

CHAPTER IV

The next morning as Sir Caractacus Lightly sat at breakfast with Jessie, the footman informed him that Mr Gay's housekeeper wished to speak to him on very particular business. The courtly old Baronet directed that she should be shown into the library, and at once proceeded to ask what she wanted.

'If you please Sir Caractacus, and beggin' your pardon,' said Zorah as he entered, 'I've come with a message from my master.'

'Pray be seated,' said Sir Caractacus. But the poor old lady could not hear him, so he explained his meaning to her in the best dumb show he could command. He pointed to a chair—walked to it—sat down in it—leant back, crossed his legs cosily, got up, and waved his hand to her in a manner that clearly conveyed to her that she was expected to do as he had done.

'My master's compliments and he's gone into the wine trade, and would you accept a sample?'

After all, Mr Gay's exertions had failed to convey his exact meaning to the deaf old lady.

'You astonish me,' said Sir Caractacus; then, finding that she did not understand him, he rumpled his hair, opened his mouth, strained his eye-balls, and threw himself into an attitude of the most horror-struck amazement. Having made his state of mind quite clear to her, he smiled pleasantly, and nodded to her to proceed.

'If you'll kindly taste it, sir, I'll take back any orders with which you may favour me.'

Sir Caractacus rang for a wineglass and proceeded to taste the sample.

'I don't know what it is, but it's not Amontillado,' said he, smacking his lips ; 'still it is a pleasant cordial. Taste it.'

The old lady seemed to gather his meaning at once. She nodded, bobbed a curtsey, and emptied the glass.

Baylis and Culpepper had not over-stated the singular effects of the 'Patent Oxy-Hydrogen Love-at-First-Sight Draught'. Sir Caractacus's hard and firmly-set features gradually relaxed as the old lady sipped the contents of her glass. Zorah set it down when she had quite emptied it, and as she did so her eyes met those of the good old Baronet. She blushed under the ardour of his gaze, and a tear trembled on her old eyelid.

'You're a remarkably fine woman,' said Sir Caractacus, 'and singularly well preserved for your age.'

'Alas, kind sir,' said Zorah, 'I'm that hard of hearin' that cannons is whispers.'

Sir Caractacus stood up, stroked his face significantly, smacked his hands together, slapped them both upon his heart, and sank on one knee at her feet. He then got up and nodded smilingly at her to imply that he really meant it.

Zorah turned aside and trembled.

'I ain't no scollard, Sir Caractacus, and I don't rightly know how a poor old 'ooman like me did ought to own her likings for a lordly barrownight—but a true 'art is more precious than diamonds they do say, and a lovin' wife is a crown of gold to her husband. I ain't fashionable, but I'm a respectable old party, and can make you comfortable if nothing else.'

'Zorah, you are the very jewel of my hopes. My dear daughter will soon be taken from me. It lies with you to brighten my desolate old age. Will you be Lady Lightly?'

And he pointed to a picture of his late wife, and went through the pantomime of putting a ring on Zorah's finger. He then indicated the despair that would possess him if she refused to accept his offer. Having achieved these feats of silent eloquence, he smiled and nodded at her reassuringly, and waited for a reply with an interrogative expression of countenance.

'Yes, dearie,' murmured Zorah, as she sank into the Baronet's arms.

After a happy half-hour Zorah felt it was her duty to return to her master, so the lovers took a fond farewell of each other, and Sir Caractacus returned to the breakfast-room.

'Jessie,' said Sir Caractacus, 'I think you really love your poor old father?'

'Indeed, papa, I do.'

'Then you will, I trust, be pleased to hear that my declining years are not unlikely to be solaced by the companionship of a good, virtuous, and companionable woman.'

'My dear papa,' said Jessie, 'do you really mean that—that you are likely to be married?'

'Indeed, Jessie, I think it is more than probable! You know you are going to leave me very soon, and my dear little nurse must be replaced, or what will become of me?'

Jessie's eyes filled with tears—but they were tears of joy–

'I cannot tell you papa—dear, dear, papa—how happy you have made me.'

'And you will, I am sure, accept your new mamma with every feeling of respect and affection.'

'Any wife of yours is a mamma of mine,' said Jessie.

'My darling! Yes, Jessie, before very long I hope to lead to the altar a bride who will love and honour me as I deserve. She is no light and giddy girl, Jessie. She is a woman of sober age and staid demeanour, yet easy and comfortable in her ways. I am going to marry Mr Gay's cook, Zorah.'

'Zorah,' cried Jessie, 'dear, dear old Zorah! Oh, indeed, I am very, very glad and happy!'

'Bless you, my child,' said the Baronet. 'I knew my pet would not blame her poor old father for acting on the impulse of a heart that has never misled him. Yes, I think—nay, I am sure—that I have taken a wise and prudent step. Zorah is not what the world calls beautiful.'

'Zorah is very good, and very clean and honest, and quite, quite sober in her habits,' said Jessie warmly, 'and that is worth more—far more than beauty, dear papa. Beauty will fade and perish, but personal cleanliness is practically undying, for it can be renewed whenever it discovers symptoms of decay. Oh, I am sure you will be happy!' And Jessie hurried off to tell Stanley Gay how nobly the potion had done its work.

'Stanley, dear Stanley,' said she, 'I have such news—Papa and Zorah are engaged!'

'I am very glad to hear it. She will make him an excellent wife; it is a very auspicious beginning.'

'And have *you* any news to tell me?'

'None, except that all the bottles are distributed, and I am now waiting to see their effect. By the way, the Bishop has arrived unexpectedly, and is stopping at the Rectory, and I have sent him a bottle. I should like to find a nice little wife for the Bishop, for he has Crawleigh in his gift—the present incumbent is at the point of death, and the living is worth £1,800 a year. The duty is extremely light, and the county society unexceptional. I think I could be truly useful in such a sphere of action.'

CHAPTER V

The action of the 'Patent Oxy-Hydrogen Love-at-First-Sight Philtre' was rapid and powerful, and before evening there was scarcely a disengaged person (over thirteen years of age) in Ploverleigh. The Dowager Lady Fitz-Saracen, a fierce old lady of sixty, had betrothed herself to Alfred Creeper, of the 'Three Fiddlers', a very worthy man, who had been engaged in the public trade all his life, and had never yet had a mark on his licence. Colonel Pemberton, of The Grove, had fixed his affections on dear little Bessie Lane, the pupil teacher, and his son Willie (who had returned from Eton only the day before) had given out his engagement to kind old Mrs Partlet, the widow of the late sexton. In point of fact there was only one disengaged person in the village—the good and grave old Bishop. He was in the position of the odd player who can't find a seat in the 'Family Coach'. But, on the whole, Stanley Gay was rather glad of this, as he venerated the good old prelate, and in his opinion there was no one in the village at that time who was really good enough to be a Bishop's wife, except, indeed, the dear little brown-haired, soft-eyed maiden to whom Stanley himself was betrothed.

So far everything had worked admirably, and the unions effected through the agency of the philtre, if they were occasionally ill-assorted as regards the stations in life of the contracting parties, were all that could be desired in every other respect. Good, virtuous straightforward, and temperate men were engaged to blameless women who were calculated to make admirable wives and mothers, and there was every prospect that Ploverleigh would become celebrated as the only Home of Perfect Happiness. There was but one sad soul in the village. The good old Bishop had drunk freely of the philtre, but there was no one left to love him. It was pitiable to see the poor love-lorn prelate as he wandered disconsolately through the smiling meadows of Ploverleigh, pouring out the accents of his love to an incorporeal abstraction.

'Something must be done for the Bishop,' said Stanley, as he watched him sitting on a stile in the distance. 'The poor old gentleman is wasting to a shadow.'

The next morning as Stanley was carefully reading through the manuscript sermon which had been sent to him by a firm in Paternoster Row for delivery on the ensuing Sabbath, little Jessie entered his library (with Zorah) and threw herself on a sofa, sobbing as if her heart would break.

'Why, Jessie—my own little love,' exclaimed Stanley. 'What in the world is the matter?'

And he put his arms fondly round her waist, and endeavoured to raise her face to his.

'Oh, no—no—Stanley—don't—you musn't—indeed, indeed, you musn't.'

'Why, my pet, what can you mean?'

'Oh, Stanley, Stanley—you will never, never forgive me.'

'Nonsense, child,' said he. 'My dear little Jessie is incapable of an act which is beyond the pale of forgiveness.' And he gently kissed her forehead.

'Stanley, you musn't do it—indeed you musn't.'

'No, you musn't do it, Muster Gay,' said Zorab.

'Why, confound you, what do you mean by interfering?' said Stanley in a rage.

'Ah, it's all very fine, I dare say, but I don't know what you're a-talking about.'

And Stanley, recollecting her infirmity, explained in pantomime the process of confounding a person, and intimated that it would be put into operation upon her if she presumed to cut in with impertinent remarks.

'Stanley—Mr Gay–' said Jessie.

'*Mr* Gay!' ejaculated Stanley.

'I musn't call you Stanley any more.'

'Great Heaven, why not?'

'I'll tell you all about it if you promise not to be violent.'

And Gay, prepared for some terrible news, hid his head in his hands, and sobbed audibly.

'I loved you—oh so, so much—you were my life—my heart,' said the poor little woman. 'By day and by night my thoughts were with you, and the love came from my heart as the water from a well!'

Stanley groaned.

'When I rose in the morning it was to work for your happiness, and when I lay down in my bed at night it was to dream of the love that was to weave itself through my life.'

He kept his head between his hands and moved not.

'My life was for your life—my soul for yours! I drew breath but for one end—to love, to honour, to reverence you.'

He lifted his head at last. His face was ashy pale.

'Come to the point,' he gasped.

'Last night,' said Jessie, 'I was tempted to taste a bottle of the Elixir. It was but a drop I took on the tip of my finger. I went to bed thinking but of you. I rose to-day, still with you in my mind. Immediately after breakfast I left home to call upon you, and as I crossed Bullthorn's meadow I saw the Bishop of Chelsea seated on a stile. At once I became conscious that I had placed myself unwittingly under the influence of the fatal potion. Horrified at my involuntary faithlessness—loathing my miserable weakness—hating myself for the misery I was about to weave around the life of a saint I had so long adored—I could not but own to myself that the love of my heart was given over, for ever, to that solitary and love-lorn prelate. Mr Gay (for by that name I must call you to the end), I have told you nearly all that you need care to know. It is enough to add that my love is, as a matter of course, reciprocated, and, but for the misery I have caused you, I am happy. But, full as my cup of joy may be, it will never be without a bitter after-taste, for I cannot forget that my folly—my wicked folly—has blighted the life of a man who, an hour ago, was dearer to me than the whole world!'

And Jessie fell sobbing on Zorah's bosom. Stanley Gay, pale and haggard, rose from his chair, and staggered to a side table. He tried to pour out a glass of water, but as he was in the act of doing so the venerable Bishop entered the room.

'Mr Gay, I cannot but feel that I owe you some apology for having gained the affections of a young lady to whom you were attached—Jessie, my love, compose yourself.'

And the Bishop gently removed Jessie's arms from Zorah's neck, and placed them about his own.

'My Lord,' said Mr Gay, 'I am lost in amazement. When I have more fully realised the unparalleled misfortune that has overtaken me I shall perhaps be able to speak and act with calmness. At the present moment I am unable to trust myself to do either. I am stunned—quite, quite stunned.'

'Do not suppose, my dear Mr Gay,' said the Bishop, 'that I came here this morning to add to your reasonable misery by presenting myself before you in the capacity of a successful rival. No. I came to tell you that poor old Mr Chudd, the vicar of Crawleigh has been mercifully removed. He is no more, and as the living is in my gift, I have come to tell you that, if it can compensate in any way for the terrible loss I have been the unintentional means of inflicting upon you, it is entirely at your disposal. It is worth £1,800 per annum—the duty is extremely light, and the local society is unexceptional.'

Stanley Gay pressed the kind old bishop's hand.

'Eighteen hundred a year will not entirely compensate me for Jessie.'

'For Miss Lightly,' murmured the bishop, gently.

'For Miss Lightly—but it will go some way towards doing so. I accept your lordship's offer with gratitude.'

'We shall always take an interest in you,' said the Bishop.

61

'Always—always,' said Jessie. 'And we shall be so glad to see you at the Palace—shall we not Frederick?'

'Well—ha—hum—yes—oh, yes, of course. Always,' said the Bishop. 'That is—oh, yes—always.'

The 14th of February was a great day for Ploverleigh, for on that date all the couples that had been brought together through the agency of the philtre were united in matrimony by the only bachelor in the place, the Rev. Stanley Gay. A week afterwards he took leave of his parishioners in an affecting sermon, and 'read himself in' at Crawleigh. He is still unmarried, and likely to remain so. He has quite got over his early disappointment, and he and the Bishop and Jessie have many a hearty laugh together over the circumstances under which the good old prelate wooed and won the bright-eyed little lady. Sir Caractacus died within a year of his marriage, and Zorah lives with her daughter-in-law at the Palace. The Bishop works hard at the art of pantomimic expression, but as yet with qualified success. He has lately taken to conversing with her through the medium of diagrams, many of which are very spirited in effect, though crude in design. It is not unlikely that they may be published before long. The series of twelve consecutive sketches, by which the Bishop informed his mother-in-law that, if she didn't mind her own business, and refrain from interfering between his wife and himself, he should be under the necessity of requiring her to pack up and be off, is likely to have a very large sale.

William Schwenck Gilbert (1836–1911) was born in London and as an adult carved out a career as a popular playwright, librettist, poet and illustrator. He is celebrated chiefly for his highly successful partnership with composer Sir Arthur Sullivan on such 'Savoy Operas' as The Pirates of Penzance *(1879) and* The Mikado *(1885). The short story 'An Elixir of Love' was written for* The Graphic *magazine in 1876 but subsequently provided the basis for the comic opera* The Sorcerer *(1877), Gilbert's third collaboration with Sullivan. The circumstances of Gilbert's death rank among the most romantic of literary demises, the 74-year-old writer suffering a heart attack while trying to save the life of a 17-year-old girl who had got into difficulties while learning to swim.*

Scarlet Stockings
Louisa M. Alcott

Chapter 1
How They Walked into Lennox's Life

'Come out for a drive, Harry?'

'Too cold.'

'Have a game of billiards?'

'Too tired.'

'Go and call on the Fairchilds?'

'Having an unfortunate prejudice against country girls, I respectfully decline.'

'What will you do, then?'

'Nothing, thank you.'

And, settling himself more luxuriously upon the couch, Lennox closed his eyes, and appeared to slumber tranquilly. Kate shook her head, and stood regarding her brother despondently, till a sudden idea made her turn toward the window, exclaiming abruptly,–

'Scarlet stockings, Harry!'

'Where?' and, as if the words were a spell to break the deepest day-dream, Lennox hurried to the window, with an unusual expression of interest in his listless face.

'I thought that would succeed! She isn't there, but I've got you up, and you are not to go down again,' laughed Kate, taking possession of the sofa.

'Not a bad manœuvre. I don't mind: it's about time for the one interesting event of the day to occur, so I'll watch for myself, thank you,' and Lennox took the easy chair by the window with a shrug and a yawn.

'I'm glad any thing does interest you,' said Kate, petulantly. 'I don't think it amounts to much, for, though you perch yourself at the window every day to see that girl pass, you don't care enough about it to ask her name.'

'I've been waiting to be told.'

'It's Belle Morgan, the doctor's daughter, and my dearest friend.'

'Then, of course, she is a blue-belle?'

'Don't try to be witty or sarcastic with her, for she will beat you at that.'

'Not a dumb-belle, then?'

'Quite the reverse: she talks a good deal, and very well, too, when she likes.'

'She is very pretty: has anybody the right to call her "Ma belle"?'

'Many would be glad to do so, but she won't have anything to say to them.'

'A Canterbury belle, in every sense of the word, then?'

'She might be, for all Canterbury loves her; but she isn't fashionable, and has more friends among the poor than among the rich.'

'Ah, I see, a diving-bell, who knows how to go down into a sea of troubles, and bring up the pearls worth having.'

'I'll tell her that, it will please her. You are really waking up, Harry,' and Kate smiled approvingly upon him.

'This page of "Belle's Life" is rather amusing, so read away,' said Lennox, glancing up the street, as if he awaited the appearance of the next edition with pleasure.

'There isn't much to tell; she is a nice, bright, energetic, warm-hearted dear; the pride of the doctor's heart, and a favourite with everyone, though she is odd.'

'How odd?'

'Does and says what she likes, is very blunt and honest, has ideas and principles of her own, goes to parties in high dresses, won't dance round dances, and wears red stockings, though Mrs Plantagenet says it's fast.'

'Rather a jolly little person, I fancy. Why haven't we met her at some of the tea-fights and muffin-worries we've been to lately?'

'It may make you angry, but it will do you good, so I'll tell. She didn't care enough about seeing the distinguished stranger to come; that's the truth.'

'Sensible girl, to spare herself hours of mortal dullness, gossip, and dyspepsia,' was the placid reply.

'She has seen you, though, at church, and dawdling about town, and she called you "Sir Charles Coldstream", on the spot. How does that suit?' asked Kate, maliciously.

'Not bad; I rather like that. Wish she'd call some day, and stir us up.'

'She won't; I asked her, but she said she was very busy, and told Jessy Tudor she wasn't fond of peacocks.'

'I don't exactly see the connection.'

'Stupid boy! she meant you, of course.'

'Oh, I'm peacocks, am I?'

'I don't wish to be rude, but I really do think you *are* vain of your good looks, elegant accomplishments, and the impression you make wherever you go. When it's worthwhile, you exert yourself, and are altogether fascinating; but the "I come-see-and-conquer" air you put on spoils it all for sensible people.'

'It strikes me that Miss Morgan has slightly infected you with her oddity, as far as bluntness goes. Fire away! it's rather amusing to be abused when one is dying of ennui.'

'That's grateful and complimentary to me, when I have devoted myself to you ever since you came. But everything bores you, and the only sign of interest you've shown is in those absurd red hose. I *should* like to know what the charm is,' said Kate, sharply.

'Impossible to say; accept the fact calmly as I do, and be grateful that there is one glimpse of colour, life, and spirit in this aristocratic tomb of a town.'

'You are not obliged to stay in it!' fiercely.

'Begging your pardon, my dove, but I am. I promised to give you my enlivening society for a month, and a Lennox keeps his word, even at the cost of his life.'

'I'm sorry I asked such a sacrifice; but I innocently thought that, after being away for five long years, you might care to see your orphan sister,' and the dove produced her handkerchief with a plaintive sniff.

'Now, my dear creature, don't be melodramatic, I beg of you!' cried her brother, imploringly. 'I wished to come, I pined to embrace you, and, I give you my word, I don't blame you for the stupidity of this confounded place.'

'It never was so gay as since you came, for everyone has tried to make it pleasant for you,' cried Kate, ruffled at his indifference to the hospitable efforts of herself and friends. 'But you don't care for any of our simple amusements, because you are spoilt by the flattery, gaiety, and nonsense of foreign society. If I didn't know it was half affectation, I should be in despair, you are so *blasé* and absurd. It's always the way with men: if one happens to be handsome, accomplished, and talented, he puts on as many airs, and is as vain as any silly girl.'

'Don't you think if you took breath you'd get on faster, my dear?' asked the imperturbable gentleman, as Kate paused with a gasp.

'I know it's useless for me to talk, as you don't care a straw what I say; but it's true, and some day you'll wish you had done something worth doing all these years. I was so proud of you, so fond of you, that I can't help being disappointed to find you with no more ambition than to kill time comfortably, no interest in anything but your own pleasures, and only energy enough to amuse yourself with a pair of scarlet stockings.'

Pathetic as poor Kate's face and voice were, it was impossible to help laughing at the comical conclusion of her lament. Lennox tried to hide the smile on his lips by affecting to curl his moustache with care, and to gaze pensively out as if touched by her appeal. But he wasn't,— oh, bless you, no! she was only his sister, and, though she might have talked with the wisdom of Solomon and the eloquence of Demosthenes, it wouldn't have done a particle of good. Sisters do very well to work for one, to pet one, and play confidante when one's love affairs need feminine wit to conduct them; but when they begin to reprove, or criticise, or moralize, it won't do, and can't be allowed, of course. Lennox never snubbed anybody, but blandly extinguished them by a polite acquiescence in all their affirmations, for the time being, and then went on in his own way as if nothing had been said.

'I dare say you are right; I'll go and think over your very sensible advice,' and, as if roused to unwonted exertion by the stings of an accusing conscience, he left the room abruptly.

'I do believe I've made an impression at last! He's actually gone out to think over what I've said. Dear Harry, I was sure he had a heart, if one only knew how to get at it!' and with a sigh of satisfaction Kate went to the window to behold the "Dear Harry" going briskly down the street after a pair of scarlet stockings. A spark of anger kindled in her eyes as she watched him, and when he vanished she still stood knitting her brows in deep thought, for a grand idea was dawning upon her.

It *was* a dull town; no one could deny that, for everybody was so intensely proper and well-born that nobody dared to be jolly. All the houses were square, aristocratic mansions with Revolutionary elms in front and spacious coach-houses behind. The knockers had a supercilious perk to their bronze or brass noses, the dandelions on the lawns had a highly connected air, and the very pigs were evidently descended from 'our first families'. Stately dinner-parties, decorous dances, moral picnics, and much tea-pot gossiping were the social resources of the place. Of course, the young people flirted, for that diversion is apparently irradicable even in the 'best society', but it was done with a propriety which was edifying to behold.

One can easily imagine that such a starched state of things would not be particularly attractive to a travelled young gentleman like Lennox, who, as Kate very truly said, *had* been spoilt by the flattery, luxury, and gaiety of foreign society. He did his best, but by the end of the first week ennui claimed him for its own, and passive endurance was all that was left him. From perfect despair he was rescued by the scarlet stockings, which went tripping by one day as he stood at the window, planning some means of escape.

A brisk, blithe-faced girl passed in a grey walking suit with a distracting pair of high-heeled boots and glimpses of scarlet at the ankle. Modest, perfectly so, I assure you, were the glimpses; but the feet were so decidedly pretty that one forgot to look at the face appertaining thereunto. It wasn't a remarkably lovely face, but it was a happy, wholesome one, with all sorts of good little dimples in cheek and chin, sunshiny twinkles in the black eyes, and a decided yet lovable look about the mouth that was quite satisfactory. A busy, bustling little body she seemed to be, for sack-pockets and muff were full of bundles, and the trim boots tripped briskly over the ground, as if the girl's heart were as light as her heels. Somehow this active, pleasant figure seemed to wake up the whole street, and leave a streak of sunshine behind it, for everyone nodded as it passed, and the primmest faces relaxed into smiles, which lingered when the girl had gone.

'Uncommonly pretty feet,—she walks well, which American

girls seldom do,—all waddle or prance,—nice face, but the boots are French, and it does my heart good to see them.'

Lennox made these observations to himself as the young lady approached, nodded to Kate at another window, gave a quick but comprehensive glance at himself and trotted round the corner, leaving the impression on his mind that a whiff of fresh spring air had blown through the street in spite of the December snow. He didn't trouble himself to ask who it was, but fell into the way of lounging in the bay-window at about three P.M., and watching the grey and scarlet figure pass with its blooming cheeks, bright eyes, and elastic step. Having nothing else to do, he took to petting this new whim, and quite depended on the daily stirring up which the sight of the energetic damsel gave him. Kate saw it all, but took no notice till the day of the little tiff above recorded; after that she was as soft as a summer sea, and by some clever stroke had Belle Morgan to tea that very week.

Lennox was one of the best-tempered fellows in the world, but the 'peacocks' did rather nettle him, because there was some truth in the insinuation; so he took care to put on no airs or try to be fascinating in the presence of Miss Belle. In truth, he soon forgot himself entirely, and enjoyed her oddities with a relish, after the prim proprieties of the other young ladies who had simpered and sighed before him. For the first time in his life, the 'Crusher', as his male friends called him, got crushed; for Belle, with the subtle skill of a quick-witted, keen-sighted girl, soon saw and condemned the elegant affectations which others called foreign polish. A look, a word, a gesture from a pretty woman, is often more eloquent and impressive than moral essays or semi-occasional twinges of conscience; and in the presence of one satirical little person Sir Charles Coldstream soon ceased to deserve the name.

Belle seemed to get over her hurry and to find time for occasional relaxation, but one never knew in what mood he might find her, for the weathercock was not more changeable than she. Lennox liked that, and found the muffin-worries quite endurable with this *sauce piquante* to relieve their insipidity. Presently he discovered that he was suffering for exercise, and formed the wholesome habit of promenading the town about three P.M.; Kate said, to follow the scarlet stockings.

Chapter 2

Where They Led Him

'Whither away, Miss Morgan?' asked Lennox, as he overtook her one bitter cold day.

'I'm taking my constitutional.'

'So am I.'

'With a difference,' and Belle glanced at the blue-nosed, muffled-up gentleman strolling along beside her with an occasional shiver and shrug.

'After a winter in the south of France, one does not find arctic weather like this easy to bear,' he said, with a disgusted air.

'I like it, and do my five or six miles a day, which keeps me in what fine ladies call "rude health",' answered Belle, walking him on at a pace which soon made his furs a burden.

She was a famous pedestrian, and a little proud of her powers; but she outdid all former feats that day, and got over the ground in gallant style. Something in her manner put her escort on his mettle; and his usual lounge was turned into a brisk march, which set his blood dancing, face glowing, and spirits effervescing as they had not done for many a day.

'There! you look more like your real self now,' said Belle, with the first sign of approval she had ever vouchsafed him, as he rejoined her after a race to recover her veil, which the wind whisked away over hedge and ditch.

'Are you sure you know what my real self is?' he asked, with a touch of the 'conquering hero' air.

'Not a doubt of it. I always know a soldier when I see one,' returned Belle, decidedly.

'A soldier! that's the last thing I should expect to be accused of,' and Lennox looked both surprised and gratified.

'There's a flash in your eye and a ring to your voice, occasionally, which made me suspect that you had fire and energy enough if you only chose to show it, and the spirit with which you have just executed the "Morgan Quickstep" proves that I was right,' returned Belle, laughing.

'Then I am not altogether a "peacock"?' said Lennox,

significantly, for during the chat, which had been as brisk as the walk, Belle had given his besetting sins several sly hits, and he couldn't resist one return shot, much as her unexpected compliment pleased him.

Poor Belle blushed up to her forehead, tried to look as if she did not understand, and gladly hid her confusion behind the recovered veil without a word.

There was a decided display both of the 'flash' and the 'ring', as Lennox looked at the suddenly subdued young lady, and, quite satisfied with his retaliation, gave the order, 'Forward, march!' which brought them to the garden-gate breathless, but better friends than before.

The next time the young people met, Belle was in such a hurry that she went round the corner with an abstracted expression which was quite a triumph of art. Just then, off tumbled the lid of the basket she carried; and Lennox, rescuing it from a puddle, obligingly helped readjust it over a funny collection of bottles, dishes, and tidy little rolls of all sorts.

'It's very heavy, mayn't I carry it for you?' he asked, in an insinuating manner.

'No, thank you,' was on Belle's lips; but, observing that he was dressed with unusual elegance to pay calls, she couldn't resist the temptation of making a beast of burden of him, and took him at his word.

'You may, if you like. I've got more bundles to take from the store, and another pair of hands won't come amiss.'

Lennox lifted his eyebrows, also the basket; and they went on again, Belle very much absorbed in her business, and her escort wondering where she was going with all that rubbish. Filling his unoccupied hand with sundry brown paper parcels, much to the detriment of the light glove that covered it, Belle paraded him down the main street before the windows of the most aristocratic mansions, and then dived into a dirty back-lane, where the want and misery of the town was decorously kept out of sight.

'You don't mind scarlet fever, I suppose?' observed Belle, as they approached the unsavoury residence of Biddy O'Brien.

'Well, I'm not exactly partial to it,' said Lennox, rather taken aback.

'You needn't go in if you are afraid, or speak to me afterwards, so no harm will be done—except to your gloves.'

'Why do *you* come here, if I may ask? It isn't the sort of amusement I should recommend,' he began, evidently disapproving of the step.

'Oh, I'm used to it, and like to play nurse where father plays doctor. I'm fond of children and Mrs O'Brien's are little dears,' returned Belle, briskly, threading her way between ash-heaps and mud-puddles as if bound to a festive scene.

'Judging from the row in there, I should infer that Mrs O'Brien had quite a herd of little dears.'

'Only nine.'

'And all sick?'

'More or less.'

'By Jove! it's perfectly heroic in you to visit this hole in spite of dirt, noise, fragrance, and infection,' cried Lennox, who devoutly wished that the sense of smell if not of hearing were temporarily denied him.

'Bless you, it's the sort of thing I enjoy, for there's no nonsense here; the work you do is pleasant if you do it heartily, and the thanks you get are worth having, I assure you.'

She put out her hand to relieve him of the basket, but he gave it an approving little shake, and said briefly,—

'Not yet, I'm coming in.'

It's all very well to rhapsodize about the exquisite pleasure of doing good, to give carelessly of one's abundance, and enjoy the delusion of having remembered the poor. But it is a cheap charity, and never brings the genuine satisfaction which those know who give their mite with heart as well as hand, and truly love their neighbour as themselves. Lennox had seen much fashionable benevolence, and laughed at it even while he imitated it, giving generously when it wasn't inconvenient. But this was a new sort of thing entirely; and in spite of the dirt, the noise, and the smells, he forgot the fever, and was glad he came when poor Mrs O'Brien turned from her sick babies, exclaiming, with Irish fervour at sight of Belle,—

'The Lord love ye, darlin, for remimberin us when ivery one, barrin' the doctor, and the praste, turns the cowld shouldther in our throuble!'

'Now if you really want to help, just keep this child quiet while I see to the sickest ones,' said Belle, dumping a stout infant on to his knee,

71

thrusting an orange into his hand, and leaving him aghast while she unpacked her little messes, and comforted the maternal bird.

With the calmness of desperation, her aide-de-camp put down his best beaver on the rich soil which covered the floor, pocketed his gloves, and, making a bib of his cambric handkerchief, gagged young Pat deliciously with bits of orange whenever he opened his mouth to roar. At her first leisure moment, Belle glanced at him to see how he was getting on, and found him so solemnly absorbed in his task that she went off into a burst of such infectious merriment that the O'Briens, sick and well, joined in it to a man.

'Good fun, isn't it?' she asked, turning down her cuffs when the last spoonful of gruel was administered.

'I've no doubt of it, when one is used to the thing. It comes a little hard at first, you know,' returned Lennox, wiping his forehead, with a long breath, and seizing his hat as if quite ready to tear himself away.

'You've done very well for a beginner; so kiss the baby and come home,' said Belle approvingly.

'No, thank you,' muttered Lennox, trying to detach the bedaubed innocent. But little Pat had a grateful heart, and, falling upon his new nurse's neck with a rapturous crow, clung there like a burr.

'Take him off! Let me out of this! He's one too many for me!' cried the wretched young man in comic despair.

Being freed with much laughter, he turned and fled, followed by a shower of blessings from Mrs O'Brien.

As they came up again into the pleasant highways, Lennox said, awkwardly for him,—

'The thanks of the poor *are* excellent things to have, but I think I'd rather receive them by proxy. Will you kindly spend this for me in making that poor soul comfortable?'

But Belle wouldn't take what he offered her; she put it back, saying earnestly,—

'Give it yourself; one can't buy blessings,—they must be *earned* or they are not worth having. Try it, please, and, if you find it a failure, then I'll gladly be your almoner.'

There was a significance in her words which he could not fail to understand. He neither shrugged, drawled, nor sauntered now, but gave her a look in which respect and self-reproach were mingled, and left her, simply saying, 'I'll try it, Miss Morgan.'

'Now isn't she odd?' whispered Kate to her brother, as Belle appeared at a little dance at Mrs Plantagenet's in a high-necked dress, knitting away on an army-sock, as she greeted the friends who crowded round her.

'Charmingly so. Why don't you do that sort of thing when you can?' answered her brother, glancing at her thin, bare shoulders, and hands rendered nearly useless by the tightness of the gloves.

'Gracious, no! It's natural to her to do so, and she carries it off well; I couldn't, therefore I don't try, though I admire it in her. Go and ask her to dance, before she is engaged.'

'She doesn't dance round dances, you know.'

'She is dreadfully prim about some things, and so free and easy about others: I can't understand it, do you?'

'Well, yes, I think I do. Here's Forbes coming for you, I'll go and entertain Belle by a quarrel.'

He found her in a recess out of the way of the rushing and romping, busy with her work, yet evidently glad to be amused.

'I admire your adherence to principle, Miss Belle; but don't you find it a little hard to sit still while your friends are enjoying themselves?' he asked, sinking luxuriously into the lounging chair beside her.

'Yes, very,' answered Belle with characteristic candour. 'But father does not approve of that sort of exercise, so I console myself with something useful till my chance comes.'

'Your work can't exactly be called ornamental,' said Lennox, looking at the big sock.

'Don't laugh at it, sir; it is for the foot of the brave fellow who is going to fight for me and his country.'

'Happy fellow! May I ask who he is?' and Lennox sat up with an air of interest.

'My substitute: I don't know his name, for father has not got him yet; but I'm making socks, and towels, and a comfort-bag for him, so that when found he may be off at once.'

'You really mean it?' cried Lennox.

'Of course I do; I can't go myself, but I *can* buy a pair of strong arms to fight for me, and I intend to do it. I only hope he'll have the right sort of courage, and be a credit to me.'

'What do you call the right sort of courage?' asked Lennox, soberly.

'That which makes a man ready and glad to live or die for a principle. There's a chance for heroes now, if there ever was. When do you join your regiment?' she added, abruptly.

'Haven't the least idea,' and Lennox subsided again.

'But you intend to do so, of course?'

'Why should I?'

Belle dropped her work. 'Why should you? What a question! Because you have health, and strength, and courage, and money to help on the good cause, and every man should give his best, and not *dare* to stay at home when he is needed.'

'You forget that I am an Englishman, and we rather prefer to be strictly neutral just now.'

'You are only half English; and for your mother's sake you should be proud and glad to fight for the North,' cried Belle warmly.

'I don't remember my mother,—'

'That's evident!'

'But, I was about to add, I've no objection to lend a hand if it isn't too much trouble to get off,' said Lennox indifferently, for he liked to see Belle's colour rise, and her eyes kindle while he provoked her.

'Do you expect to go South in a bandbox? You'd better join one of the kid-glove regiments; they say the dandies fight well when the time comes.'

'I've been away so long, the patriotic fever hasn't seized me yet; and, as the quarrel is none of mine, I think perhaps I'd better take care of Kate, and let you fight it out among yourselves. Here's the Lancers, may I have the honour?'

But Belle, being very angry at this lukewarmness, answered in her bluntest manner,—

'Having reminded me that you are a "strictly neutral" Englishman, you must excuse me if I decline; *I* dance only with loyal Americans,' and, rolling up her work with a defiant flourish, she walked away, leaving him to lament his loss and wonder how he could retrieve it. She did not speak to him again till he stood in the hall waiting for Kate; then Belle came down in a charming little red hood, and going straight up to him with her hand out, a repentant look and a friendly smile, said frankly,—

'I was very rude; I want to beg pardon of the English, and shake hands with the American, half.'

So peace was declared, and lasted unbroken for the remaining week of his stay, when he proposed to take Kate to the city for a little gaiety. Miss Morgan openly approved the plan, but secretly felt as if the town was about to be depopulated, and tried to hide her melancholy in her substitute's socks. They were not large enough, however, to absorb it all; and, when Lennox went to make his adieu, it was perfectly evident that the Doctor's Belle was out of tune. The young gentleman basely exulted over this, till she gave him something else to think about by saying gravely:

'Before you go, I feel as if I ought to tell you something, since Kate won't. If you are offended about it please don't blame her; she meant it kindly, and so did I.' Belle paused as if it was not an easy thing to tell and then went on quickly, with her eyes upon her work.

'Three weeks ago Kate asked me to help her in a little plot; and I consented, for the fun of the thing. She wanted something to amuse and stir you up, and, finding that my queer ways diverted you, she begged me to be neighbourly and let you do what you liked. I didn't care particularly about amusing you, but I did think you needed rousing; so for her sake I tried to do it, and you very good-naturedly bore my lecturing. I don't like deceit of any kind, so I confess; but I can't say I'm sorry, for I really think you are none the worse for the teasing and teaching you've had.'

Belle didn't see him flush and frown as she made her confession, and when she looked up he only said, half gratefully, half reproachfully,—

'I'm a good deal the better for it, I dare say, and ought to be very thankful for your friendly exertions. But two against one was hardly fair, now, was it?'

'No, it was sly and sinful in the highest degree, but we did it for your good; so I know you'll forgive us, and as a proof of it sing one or two of my favourites for the last time.'

'You don't deserve any favour; but I'll do it, to show you how much more magnanimous men are than women.'

Not at all loth to improve his advantages, Lennox warbled his most melting lays *con amore*, watching, as he sung, for any sign of sentiment in the girlish face opposite. But Belle wouldn't be sentimental; and sat rattling her knitting-needles industriously, though 'The Harbour Bar was moaning' dolefully, though 'Douglas' was touchingly 'tender and true', and the 'Wind of the Summer Night' sighed romantically through the sitting-room.

'Much obliged. Must you go?' she said, without a sign of soft confusion as he rose.

'I must; but I shall come again before I leave the country. May I?' he asked, holding her hand.

'If you come in a uniform.'

'Good night, Belle,' tenderly.—'Good-by, Sir Charles,' with a wicked twinkle of the eye, which lasted till he closed the hall-door, growling irefully,—

'I thought I'd had some experience, but one never *can* understand these women!'

Canterbury did become a desert to Belle after her dear friend had gone (of course the dear friend's brother had nothing to do with the desolation); and as the weeks dragged slowly Belle took to reading poetry, practising plaintive ballads, and dawdling over her work at a certain window which commanded a view of the railway station and hotel.

'You're dull, my dear; run up to town with me to-morrow, and see your young man off,' said the Doctor one evening, as Belle sat musing with a half-mended red stocking in her hand.

'My young man?' she ejaculated, turning with a start and a blush.

'Your substitute, child. Stephens attended to the business for me, and he's off to-morrow. I began to tell you about the fellow last week, but you were wool-gathering, so I stopped.'

'Yes, I remember, it was all very nice. Goes to-morrow, does he? I'd like to see him; but do you think we can both leave home at once? Someone might come you know, and I fancy it's going to snow,' said Belle, putting her face behind the curtain to inspect the weather.

'You'd better go, the trip will do you good; you can take your things to Tom Jones, and see Kate on the way: she's got back from Philadelphia.'

'Has she? I'll go, then; it will please her, and I do need change. You are a dear, to think of it;' and, giving her father a hasty glimpse of a suddenly excited countenance, Belle slipped out of the room to prepare her best array, with a most reckless disregard of the impending storm.

It did not snow on the morrow, and up they went to see the —th regiment off. Belle did not see 'her young man', however, for while her father went to carry him her comforts and a patriotic nosegay of red and white flowers, tied up with a smart blue ribbon, she called on Kate. But Miss Lennox was engaged, and sent an urgent request that her friend would call in the afternoon. Much disappointed and a little hurt, Belle then devoted herself to the departing regiment, wishing she was going with it, for she felt in a warlike mood. It was past noon when a burst of martial music, the measured tramp of many feet, and enthusiastic cheers announced that 'the boys' were coming. From the balcony where she stood with her father, Belle looked down upon the living stream that flowed by like a broad river, with a steely glitter above the blue. All her petty troubles vanished at the sight; her heart beat high, her face glowed, her eyes filled, and she waved her handkerchief as zealously as if she had a dozen friends and lovers in the ranks below.

'Here comes your man; I told him to stick the posy where it would catch my eye, so I could point him out to you. Look, it's the tall fellow at the end of the front line,' said the Doctor in an excited tone, as he pointed and beckoned.

Belle looked and gave a little cry, for there, in a private's uniform, with her nosegay at his button-hole, and on his face a smile she never forgot, was Lennox! For an instant she stood staring at him as pale and startled as if he were a ghost; then the colour rushed into her face, she kissed both hands to him, and cried bravely, 'Good-by, good-by; God bless you, Harry!' and immediately laid her head on her father's shoulder, sobbing as if her heart was broken.

When she looked up, her substitute was lost in the undulating mass below, and for her the spectacle was over.

'Was it really he? Why wasn't I told? What does it all mean?' she demanded, looking bewildered, grieved, and ashamed.

'He's really gone, my dear. It's a surprise of his, and I was bound over to silence. Here, this will explain the joke, I suppose,' and the Doctor handed her a cocked-hat note, done up like a military order.

'A Roland for your Oliver, Mademoiselle! I came home for the express purpose of enlisting, and only delayed a month on Kate's account. If I ever return, I will receive my bounty at your hands. Till then please comfort Kate, think as kindly as you can of "Sir Charles", and sometimes pray a little prayer for

Your unworthy

Substitute.'

Belle looked very pale and meek when she put the note in her pocket, but she only said, 'I must go and comfort Kate;' and the Doctor gladly obeyed, feeling that the joke was more serious than he had imagined.

The moment her friend appeared, Miss Lennox turned on her tears, and 'played away', pouring forth lamentations, reproaches, and regrets in a steady stream.

'I hope you are satisfied now, you cruel girl!' she began, refusing to be kissed. 'You've sent him off with a broken heart to rush into danger and be shot, or get his arms and legs spoiled. You know he loved you and wanted to tell you so, but you wouldn't let him; and now you've driven him away, and he's gone as an insignificant private with his head shaved, and a heavy knapsack breaking his back, and a horrid gun that will be sure to explode: and he *would* wear those immense blue socks you sent, for he adores you, and you only teased and laughed at him, my poor, deluded, deserted brother!' And, quite overwhelmed by the afflicting picture, Kate lifted up her voice and wept again.

'I *am* satisfied, for he's done what I hoped he would; and he's none the less a gentleman because he's a private and wears my socks. I pray they will keep him safe, and bring him home to us when he has done his duty like a man, as I know he will. I'm proud of my brave substitute, and I'll try to be worthy of him,' cried Belle, kindling beautifully as she looked out into the wintry sunshine with a new softness in the eyes that still seemed watching that blue-coated figure marching away to danger, perhaps death.

'It's ill playing with edged tools; we meant to amuse him, and we may have sent him to destruction. I'll never forgive you for your part, never!' said Kate, with the charming inconsistency of her sex.

But Belle turned away her wrath by a soft answer, as she

whispered, with a tender choke in her voice,—

'We both loved him, dear; let's comfort one another.'

Chapter 3
What Became of Them

Private Lennox certainly *had* chosen pretty hard work, for the —th was not a 'kid-glove' regiment by any means; fighting in mid-winter was not exactly festive, and camps do not abound in beds of roses even at the best of times. But Belle was right in saying she knew a soldier when she saw him, for, now that he was thoroughly waked up, he proved that there was plenty of courage, energy, and endurance in him.

It is my private opinion that he might now and then have slightly regretted the step he had taken, had it not been for certain recollections of a sarcastic tongue and a pair of keen eyes, not to mention the influence of one of the most potent rulers of the human heart; namely, the desire to prove himself worthy the respect, if nothing more, of somebody at home. Belle's socks did seem to keep him safe, and lead him straight in the narrow path of duty. Belle's comfort-bag was such in very truth, for not one of the stout needles on the tri-coloured cushion but what seemed to wink its eye approvingly at him; not one of the tidy balls of thread that did not remind him of the little hand he coveted, and the impracticable scissors were cherished as a good omen, though he felt that the sharpest steel that ever came from Sheffield couldn't cut his love in twain. And Belle's lessons, short as they had been, were not forgotten, but seemed to have been taken up by a sterner mistress, whose rewards were greater, if not so sweet, as those the girl could give. There was plenty of exercise nowadays, and of hard work that left many a tired head asleep for ever under the snow. There were many opportunities for diving 'into the depths and bringing up pearls worth having' by acts of kindness among the weak, the wicked, and the suffering all about him. He learned now how to earn, not buy, the thanks of the poor, and unconsciously proved in the truest way that a private *could* be a gentleman. But best of all was the steadfast purpose 'to live and die for a principle', which grew and strengthened with each month of bitter hardship, bloody strife, and dearly bought success. Life grew earnest to him, time seemed precious, self was

79

forgotten, and all that was best and bravest rallied round the flag on which his heart inscribed the motto, 'Love and Liberty'.

Praise and honour he could not fail to win, and had he never gone back to claim his bounty he would have earned the great 'Well done', for he kept his oath loyally, did his duty manfully, and loved his lady faithfully, like a knight of the chivalrous times. He knew nothing of her secret, but wore her blue ribbon like an order, never went into battle without first, like many another poor fellow, kissing something which he carried next his heart, and with each day of absence felt himself a better man, and braver soldier, for the fondly foolish romance he had woven about the scarlet stockings.

Belle and Kate did comfort one another, not only with tears and kisses, but with womanly work which kept hearts happy and hands busy. How Belle bribed her to silence will always remain the ninth wonder of the world; but, though reams of paper passed between brother and sister during those twelve months, not a hint was dropped on one side in reply to artful inquiries from the other. Belle never told her love in words; but she stowed away an unlimited quantity of the article in the big boxes that went to gladden the eyes and—alas for romance!—the stomach of Private Lennox. If pickles could typify passion, cigars prove constancy, and gingerbread reveal the longings of the soul, then would the above-mentioned gentleman have been the happiest of lovers. But camp-life had doubtless dulled his finer intuitions: for he failed to understand the new language of love, and gave away these tender tokens with lavish prodigality. Concealment preyed a trifle on Belle's damask cheek, it must be confessed, and the keen eyes grew softer with the secret tears that sometimes dimmed them; the sharp tongue seldom did mischief now, but uttered kindly words to everyone, as if doing penance for the past; and a sweet seriousness toned down the lively spirit, which was learning many things in the sleepless nights that followed when the 'little prayer' for the beloved substitute was done.

'I'll wait and see if he is all I hope he will be, before I let him know. I shall read the truth the instant I see him, and if he has stood the test I'll run into his arms and tell him everything,' she said to herself, with delicious thrills at the idea; but you may be sure she did nothing of the sort when the time came.

A rumour flew through the town one day that Lennox had

arrived; upon receipt of which joyful tidings, Belle had a panic and hid herself in the garret. But when she had quaked, and cried, and peeped, and listened for an hour or two, finding that no one came to hunt her up, she composed her nerves and descended to pass the afternoon in the parlour and a high state of dignity. All sorts of reports reached her: he was mortally wounded; he had been made a major or a colonel or a general, no one knew exactly which; he was dead, was going to be married, and hadn't come at all. Belle fully expiated all her small sins by the agonies of suspense she suffered that day, and when at last a note came from Kate, begging her 'to drop over to see Harry', she put her pride in her pocket and went at once.

The drawing-room was empty and in confusion, there was a murmur of voices upstairs, a smell of camphor in the air, and an empty wine-glass on the table where a military cap was lying. Belle's heart sunk, and she covertly kissed the faded blue coat as she stood waiting breathlessly, wondering if Harry had any arms for her to run into. She heard the chuckling Biddy lumber up and announce her, then a laugh, and a half-fond, half-exulting, 'Ah, ha, I thought she'd come!'

That spoilt it all; Belle took out her pride instanter, rubbed a quick colour into her white cheeks, and, snatching up a newspaper, sat herself down with as expressionless a face as it was possible for an excited young woman to possess. Lennox came running down. 'Thank Heaven, his legs are safe!' sighed Belle, with her eyes glued to the price of beef. He entered with both hands extended, which relieved her mind upon another point; and he beamed upon her, looking so vigorous, manly, and martial, that she cried within herself, 'My beautiful brown soldier!' even while she greeted him with an unnecessarily brief, 'How do you do, Mr Lennox?'

The sudden eclipse which passed over his joyful countenance would have been ludicrous, if it hadn't been pathetic; but he was used to hard knocks now, and bore this, his hardest, like a man. He shook hands heartily; and, as Belle sat down again (not to betray that she was trembling a good deal), he stood at ease before her, talking in a way which soon satisfied her that he *had* borne the test, and that bliss was waiting for her round the corner. But she had made it such a very sharp corner she couldn't turn it gracefully, and while she pondered how to do so he helped her with a cough. She looked up quickly, discovering all at once that he was very thin, rather pale in spite of the nice tan, and breathed hurriedly as he stood with one hand in his breast.

'Are you ill, wounded, in pain?' she asked, forgetting herself entirely.

'Yes, all three,' he answered, after a curious look at her changing colour and anxious eyes.

'Sit down—tell me about it—can I do anything?' and Belle began to plump up the pillows on the couch with nervous eagerness.

'Thank you, I'm past help,' was the mournful reply accompanied by a hollow cough which made her shiver.

'Oh, don't say so! Let me bring father; he is very skilful. Shall I call Kate?'

'He can do nothing; Kate doesn't know this, and I beg you won't tell her. I got a shot in the breast and made light of it, but it will finish me sooner or later. I don't mind telling you, for you are one of the strong, cool sort, you know, and are not affected by such things. But Kate is so fond of me, I don't want to shock and trouble her yet awhile. Let her enjoy my little visit, and after I'm gone you can tell her the truth.'

Belle had sat like a statue while he spoke with frequent pauses and an involuntary clutch or two at the suffering breast. As he stopped and passed his hand over his eyes, she said slowly, as if her white lips were stiff,—

'Gone! where?'

'Back to my place. I'd rather die fighting than fussed and wailed over by a parcel of women. I expected to stay a week or so, but a battle is coming off sooner than we imagined, so I'm away again to-morrow. As I'm not likely ever to come back, I just wanted to ask you to stand by poor Kate when I'm finished, and to say good-by to you, Belle, before I go.' He put out his hand, but, holding it fast in both her own, she laid her tearful face down on it, whispering imploringly,—

'Oh, Harry, stay!'

Never mind what happened for the next ten minutes; suffice it to say that the enemy having surrendered, the victor took possession with great jubilation and showed no quarter.

'Bang the field-piece, toot the fife, and beat the rolling drum, for ruse number three has succeeded. Come down, Kate, and give us your blessing!' called Lennox, taking pity on his sister, who was anxiously awaiting the *dénouement* on the stairs.

In she rushed, and the young ladies laughed and cried, kissed and talked tumultuously, while their idol benignantly looked on, vainly endeavouring to repress all vestiges of unmanly emotion.

'And you are not dying, really, truly?' cried Belle, when fair weather set in after the flurry.

'Bless your dear heart, no! I'm as sound as a nut, and haven't a wound to boast of, except this ugly slash on the head.'

'It's a splendid wound, and I'm proud of it,' and Belle set a rosy little seal on the scar, which quite reconciled her lover to the disfigurement of his handsome forehead. 'You've learned to fib in the army, and I'm disappointed in you,' she added, trying to look reproachful and failing entirely.

'No, only the art of strategy. You quenched me by your frosty reception, and I thought it was all up till you put the idea of playing invalid into my head. It succeeded so well that I piled on the agony, resolving to fight it out on that line, and if I failed again to make a masterly retreat. You gave me a lesson in deceit once, so don't complain if I turned the tables and made your heart ache for a minute, as you've made mine for a year.'

Belle's spirit was rapidly coming back, so she gave him a capital imitation of his French shrug, and drawled out in his old way,—

'I have my doubts about that, *mon ami.*'

'What do you say to this—and this—and this?' he retorted, pulling out and laying before her with a triumphant flourish a faded blue ribbon, a fat pincushion with a hole through it, and a daintily painted little picture of a pretty girl in scarlet stockings.

'There, I've carried those treasures in my breast-pocket for a year, and I'm firmly convinced that they have all done their part toward keeping me safe. The blue ribbon bound me fast to you, Belle; the funny cushion caught the bullet that otherwise might have finished me; and the blessed little picture was my comfort during those dreadful marches, my companion on picket-duty with treachery and danger all about me, and my inspiration when the word "Charge!" went down the line, for in the thickest of the fight I always saw the little grey figure beckoning me on to my duty.'

'Oh, Harry, you won't go back to all those horrors, will you? I'm sure you've done enough, and may rest now and enjoy your reward,' said Kate, trying not to feel that 'two is company, and three is none'.

'I've enlisted for the war, and shall not rest till either it or I come to an end. As for my reward, I had it when Belle kissed me.'

'You are right, I'll wait for you, and love you all the better for the sacrifice,' whispered Belle. 'I only wish I could share your hardships, dear, for while you fight and suffer I can only love and pray.'

'Waiting is harder than working to such as you; so be contented with your share, for the thought of you will glorify the world generally for me. I'll tell you what you *can* do while I'm away: it's both useful and amusing, so it will occupy and cheer you capitally. Just knit lots of red hose, because I don't intend you to wear any others hereafter, Mrs Lennox.'

'Mine are not worn out yet,' laughed Belle, getting merry at the thought.

'No matter for that; those are sacred articles, and henceforth must be treasured as memorials of our love. Frame and hang them up; or, if the prejudices of society forbid that flight of romance, lay them carefully away where moths can't devour nor thieves steal them, so that years hence, when my descendants praise me for any virtues I may possess, any good I may have done, or any honour I may have earned, I can point to those precious relics and say proudly,—

'My children, for all that I am, or hope to be, you must thank your honoured mother's scarlet stockings.'

Louisa May Alcott (1832–88) was born and raised in New England and is remembered today as the author of such celebrated period novels as Little Women *(1868),* Good Wives *(1869) and* Little Men *(1871). An abolitionist and feminist, whose family once sheltered a runaway slave for a week, Alcott herself never married and once declared that although she had fallen in love with many pretty girls, she had never once fallen in love with a man.*

The Pride of the Village
Washington Irving

May no wolfe howle; no screcch owle stir
A wing about thy sepulchre!
No boysterous winds or stormes come hither,
To starve or wither
Thy soft sweet earth! but, like a spring,
Love kept it ever flourishing.

HERRICK.

In the course of an excursion through one of the remote counties of England, I had struck into one of those cross-roads that lead through the more secluded parts of the country, and stopped one afternoon at a village the situation of which was beautifully rural and retired. There was an air of primitive simplicity about its inhabitants not to be found in the villages which lie on the great coach-roads. I determined to pass the night there, and, having taken an early dinner, strolled out to enjoy the neighbouring scenery.

My ramble, as is usually the case with travellers, soon led me to the church, which stood at a little distance from the village. Indeed, it was an object of some curiosity, its old tower being completely overrun with ivy so that only here and there a jutting buttress, an angle of grey wall, or a fantastically carved ornament peered through the verdant covering. It was a lovely evening. The early part of the day had been dark and showery, but in the afternoon it had cleared up, and, though sullen clouds still hung overhead, yet there was a broad tract of golden sky in the west, from which the setting sun gleamed through the dripping leaves and lit up all Nature into a melancholy smile. It seemed like the parting hour of a good Christian smiling on the sins and sorrows of the world, and giving, in the serenity of his decline, an assurance that he will rise again in glory.

I had seated myself on a half-sunken tombstone, and was musing, as one is apt to do at this sober-thoughted hour, on past scenes and early friends—on those who were distant and those who were dead—and indulging in that kind of melancholy fancying which has in it something sweeter even than pleasure. Every now and then the stroke of a bell from the neighbouring tower fell on my ear; its tones were in unison with the scene, and, instead of jarring, chimed in with my feelings; and it was some time before I recollected that it must be tolling the knell of some new tenant of the tomb.

Presently I saw a funeral train moving across the village green; it wound slowly along a lane, was lost, and reappeared through the breaks of the hedges, until it passed the place where I was sitting. The pall was supported by young girls dressed in white, and another, about the age of seventeen, walked before, bearing a chaplet of white flowers—a token that the deceased was a young and unmarried female. The corpse was followed by the parents. They were a venerable couple of the better order of peasantry. The father seemed to repress his feelings, but his fixed eye, contracted brow, and deeply-furrowed face showed the struggle that was passing within. His wife hung on his arm, and wept aloud with the convulsive bursts of a mother's sorrow.

I followed the funeral into the church. The bier was placed in the centre aisle, and the chaplet of white flowers, with a pair of white gloves, was hung over the seat which the deceased had occupied.

Everyone knows the soul-subduing pathos of the funeral service, for who is so fortunate as never to have followed someone he has loved to the tomb? But when performed over the remains of innocence and beauty, thus laid low in the bloom of existence, what can be more affecting? At that simple but most solemn consignment of the body to the grave—'Earth to earth, ashes to ashes, dust to dust!'—the tears of the youthful companions of the deceased flowed unrestrained. The father still seemed to struggle with his feelings, and to comfort himself with the assurance that the dead are blessed which die in the Lord; but the mother only thought of her child as a flower of the field cut down and withered in the midst of its sweetness; she was like Rachel, 'mourning over her children, and would not be comforted'.

On returning to the inn I learnt the whole story of the deceased. It was a simple one, and such as has often been told. She had been the beauty and pride of the village. Her father had once been an opulent farmer, but was reduced in circumstances. This was an only child, and brought up entirely at home in the simplicity of rural life. She had been the pupil of the village pastor, the favourite lamb of his little flock. The good man watched over her education with paternal care; it was limited and suitable to the sphere in which she was to move, for he only sought to make her an ornament to her station in life, not to raise her above it. The tenderness and indulgence of her parents and the exemption from all ordinary occupations had fostered a natural grace and delicacy of character that accorded with the fragile loveliness of her form. She appeared like some tender plant of the garden blooming accidentally amid the hardier natives of the fields.

The superiority of her charms was felt and acknowledged by her companions, but without envy, for it was surpassed by the unassuming gentleness and winning kindness of her manners. It might be truly said of her:

> 'This is the prettiest low-born lass, that ever
> Ran on the green-sward: nothing she does or seems
> But smacks of something greater than herself;
> Too noble for this place.'

The village was one of those sequestered spots which still retain some vestiges of old English customs. It had its rural festivals and holiday pastimes, and still kept up some faint observance of the once popular rites of May. These, indeed, had been promoted by its present pastor, who was a lover of old customs and one of those simple Christians that think their mission fulfilled by promoting joy on earth and good-will among mankind. Under his auspices the May-pole stood from year to year in the centre of the village green; on Mayday it was decorated with garlands and streamers, and a queen or lady of the May was appointed, as in former times, to preside at the sports and distribute the prizes and rewards. The picturesque situation of the village and the fancifulness of its rustic fetes would often attract the notice of casual visitors. Among these, on one Mayday, was a young officer whose regiment had been recently quartered in the neighbourhood. He was charmed with the native taste that pervaded this village pageant, but, above all, with the dawning loveliness of the queen of May. It was the village favourite who was crowned with flowers, and blushing and smiling in all the beautiful confusion of girlish diffidence and delight. The artlessness of rural habits enabled him readily to make her acquaintance; he gradually won his way into her intimacy, and paid his court to her in that unthinking way in which young officers are too apt to trifle with rustic simplicity.

There was nothing in his advances to startle or alarm. He never even talked of love, but there are modes of making it more eloquent than language, and which convey it subtilely and irresistibly to the heart. The beam of the eye, the tone of voice, the thousand tendernesses which emanate from every word and look and action,—these form the true eloquence of love, and can always be felt and understood, but never described. Can we wonder that they should readily win a heart young, guileless, and susceptible? As to her, she loved almost unconsciously; she scarcely inquired what was the growing passion that was absorbing every thought and feeling, or what were to be its consequences. She, indeed, looked not to the future. When present, his looks and words occupied her whole attention; when absent, she thought but of what had passed at their recent interview. She would wander with him through the green lanes and rural scenes of the vicinity. He taught her to see new beauties in Nature; he talked in the language of polite and cultivated life, and breathed into her ear the witcheries of romance and poetry.

Perhaps there could not have been a passion between the sexes more pure than this innocent girl's. The gallant figure of her youthful admirer and the splendour of his military attire might at first have charmed her eye, but it was not these that had captivated her heart. Her attachment had something in it of idolatry. She looked up to him as to a being of a superior order. She felt in his society the enthusiasm of a mind naturally delicate and poetical, and now first awakened to a keen perception of the beautiful and grand. Of the sordid distinctions of rank and fortune she thought nothing; it was the difference of intellect, of demeanour, of manners, from those of the rustic society to which she had been accustomed, that elevated him in her opinion. She would listen to him with charmed ear and downcast look of mute delight, and her cheek would mantle with enthusiasm; or if ever she ventured a shy glance of timid admiration, it was as quickly withdrawn, and she would sigh and blush at the idea of her comparative unworthiness.

Her lover was equally impassioned, but his passion was mingled with feelings of a coarser nature. He had begun the connection in levity, for he had often heard his brother-officers boast of their village conquests, and thought some triumph of the kind necessary to his reputation as a man of spirit. But he was too full of youthful fervour. His heart had not yet been rendered sufficiently cold and selfish by a wandering and a dissipated life: it caught fire from the very flame it sought to kindle, and before he was aware of the nature of his situation he became really in love.

What was he to do? There were the old obstacles which so incessantly occur in these heedless attachments. His rank in life, the prejudices of titled connections, his dependence upon a proud and unyielding father, all forbade him to think of matrimony; but when he looked down upon this innocent being, so tender and confiding, there was a purity in her manners, a blamelessness in her life, and a beseeching modesty in her looks that awed down every licentious feeling. In vain did he try to fortify himself by a thousand heartless examples of men of fashion, and to chill the glow of generous sentiment with that cold derisive levity with which he had heard them talk of female virtue: whenever he came into her presence she was still surrounded by that mysterious but impassive charm of virgin purity in whose hallowed sphere no guilty thought can live.

The sudden arrival of orders for the regiment to repair to the Continent completed the confusion of his mind. He remained for a short time in a state of the most painful irresolution; he hesitated to communicate the tidings until the day for marching was at hand, when he gave her the intelligence in the course of an evening ramble.

The idea of parting had never before occurred to her. It broke in at once upon her dream of felicity; she looked upon it as a sudden and insurmountable evil, and wept with the guileless simplicity of a child. He drew her to his bosom and kissed the tears from her soft cheek; nor did he meet with a repulse, for there are moments of mingled sorrow and tenderness which hallow the caresses of affection. He was naturally impetuous, and the sight of beauty apparently yielding in his arms, the confidence of his power over her, and the dread of losing her forever all conspired to overwhelm his better feelings: he ventured to propose that she should leave her home and be the companion of his fortunes.

He was quite a novice in seduction, and blushed and faltered at his own baseness; but so innocent of mind was his intended victim that she was at first at a loss to comprehend his meaning, and why she should leave her native village and the humble roof of her parents. When at last the nature of his proposal flashed upon her pure mind, the effect was withering. She did not weep; she did not break forth into reproach; she said not a word, but she shrunk back aghast as from a viper, gave him a look of anguish that pierced to his very soul, and, clasping her hands in agony, fled, as if for refuge, to her father's cottage.

The officer retired confounded, humiliated, and repentant. It is uncertain what might have been the result of the conflict of his feelings, had not his thoughts been diverted by the bustle of departure. New scenes, new pleasures, and new companions soon dissipated his self-reproach and stifled his tenderness; yet, amidst the stir of camps, the revelries of garrisons, the array of armies, and even the din of battles, his thoughts would sometimes steal back to the scenes of rural quiet and village simplicity—the white cottage, the footpath along the silver brook and up the hawthorn hedge, and the little village maid loitering along it, leaning on his arm and listening to him with eyes beaming with unconscious affection.

The shock which the poor girl had received in the destruction of all her ideal world had indeed been cruel. Faintings and hysterics had at first shaken her tender frame, and were succeeded by a settled and pining melancholy. She had beheld from her window the march of the departing troops. She had seen her faithless lover borne off, as if in triumph, amidst the sound of drum and trumpet and the pomp of arms. She strained a last aching gaze after him as the morning sun glittered about his figure and his plume waved in the breeze; he passed away like a bright vision from her sight, and left her all in darkness.

It would be trite to dwell on the particulars of her after story. It was, like other tales of love, melancholy. She avoided society and wandered out alone in the walks she had most frequented with her lover. She sought, like the stricken deer, to weep in silence and loneliness and brood over the barbed sorrow that rankled in her soul. Sometimes she would be seen late of an evening sitting in the porch of the village church, and the milk-maids, returning from the fields, would now and then overhear her singing some plaintive ditty in the hawthorn walk. She became fervent in her devotions at church, and as the old people saw her approach, so wasted away, yet with a hectic gloom and that hallowed air which melancholy diffuses round the form, they would make way for her as for something spiritual, and looking after her, would shake their heads in gloomy foreboding.

She felt a conviction that she was hastening to the tomb, but looked forward to it as a place of rest. The silver cord that had bound her to existence was loosed, and there seemed to be no more pleasure under the sun. If ever her gentle bosom had entertained resentment against her lover, it was extinguished. She was incapable of angry passions, and in a moment of saddened tenderness she penned him a farewell letter. It was couched in the simplest language, but touching from its very simplicity. She told him that she was dying, and did not conceal from him that his conduct was the cause. She even depicted the sufferings which she had experienced, but concluded with saying that she could not die in peace until she had sent him her forgiveness and her blessing.

By degrees her strength declined that she could no longer leave the cottage. She could only totter to the window, where, propped up in her chair, it was her enjoyment to sit all day and look out upon the landscape. Still she uttered no complaint nor imparted to anyone the malady that was preying on her heart. She never even mentioned her lover's name, but would lay her head on her mother's bosom and weep in silence. Her poor parents hung in mute anxiety over this fading blossom of their hopes, still flattering themselves that it might again revive to freshness and that the bright unearthly bloom which sometimes flushed her cheek might be the promise of returning health.

In this way she was seated between them one Sunday afternoon; her hands were clasped in theirs, the lattice was thrown open, and the soft air that stole in brought with it the fragrance of the clustering honeysuckle which her own hands had trained round the window.

Her father had just been reading a chapter in the Bible: it spoke of the vanity of worldly things and of the joys of heaven: it seemed to have diffused comfort and serenity through her bosom. Her eye was fixed on the distant village church: the bell had tolled for the evening service; the last villager was lagging into the porch, and everything had sunk into that hallowed stillness peculiar to the day of rest. Her parents were gazing on her with yearning hearts. Sickness and sorrow, which pass so roughly over some faces, had given to hers the expression of a seraph's. A tear trembled in her soft blue eye. Was she thinking of her faithless lover? or were her thoughts wandering to that distant churchyard, into whose bosom she might soon be gathered?

Suddenly the clang of hoofs was heard: a horseman galloped to the cottage; he dismounted before the window; the poor girl gave a faint exclamation and sunk back in her chair: it was her repentant lover. He rushed into the house and flew to clasp her to his bosom; but her wasted form, her deathlike countenance—so wan, yet so lovely in its desolation—smote him to the soul, and he threw himself in agony at her feet. She was too faint to rise—she attempted to extend her trembling hand—her lips moved as if she spoke, but no word was articulated; she looked down upon him with a smile of unutterable tenderness, and closed her eyes forever.

Such are the particulars which I gathered of this village story. They are but scanty, and I am conscious have little novelty to recommend them. In the present rage also for strange incident and high-seasoned narrative they may appear trite and insignificant, but they interested me strongly at the time; and, taken in connection with the affecting ceremony which I had just witnessed, left a deeper impression on my mind than many circumstances of a more striking nature. I have passed through the place since, and visited the church again from a better motive than mere curiosity. It was a wintry evening: the trees were stripped of their foliage, the churchyard looked naked and mournful, and the wind rustled coldly through the dry grass. Evergreens, however, had been planted about the grave of the village favourite, and osiers were bent over it to keep the turf uninjured.

The church-door was open and I stepped in. There hung the chaplet of flowers and the gloves, as on the day of the funeral: the flowers were withered, it is true, but care seemed to have been taken that no dust should soil their whiteness. I have seen many monuments where art has exhausted its powers to awaken the sympathy of the spectator, but I have met with none that spoke more touchingly to my heart than this simple but delicate memento of departed innocence.

Washington Irving (1783–1859) was born in New York City and won recognition as an author, biographer and historian after moving with his family to England in 1815. He is celebrated, alongside James Fenimore Cooper, as the first US writer to establish an international reputation. This particular story was first published in The Sketch Book of Geoffrey Crayon, Gent. *(1820), which also included the classic stories 'Rip Van Winkle' and 'The Legend of Sleepy Hollow'. Irving himself was no stranger to ill-fated love: In 1809, when the author was in his mid-twenties, he was grief-stricken by the death, after a short illness, of his seventeen-year-old fiancée Matilda Hoffman. For the rest of his life Irving could not bear to hear her name mentioned, even by his closest friends.*

The Nightingale and the Rose
Oscar Wilde

'She said that she would dance with me if I brought her red roses,' cried the young Student; 'but in all my garden there is no red rose.'

From her nest in the holm-oak tree the Nightingale heard him, and she looked out through the leaves, and wondered.

'No red rose in all my garden!' he cried, and his beautiful eyes filled with tears. 'Ah, on what little things does happiness depend! I have read all that the wise men have written, and all the secrets of philosophy are mine, yet for want of a red rose is my life made wretched.'

'Here at last is a true lover,' said the Nightingale. 'Night after night have I sung of him, though I knew him not: night after night have I told his story to the stars, and now I see him. His hair is dark as the hyacinth-blossom, and his lips are red as the rose of his desire; but passion has made his face like pale ivory, and sorrow has set her seal upon his brow.'

'The Prince gives a ball to-morrow night,' murmured the young Student, 'and my love will be of the company. If I bring her a red rose she will dance with me till dawn. If I bring her a red rose, I shall hold her in my arms, and she will lean her head upon my shoulder, and her hand will be clasped in mine. But there is no red rose in my garden, so I shall sit lonely, and she will pass me by. She will have no heed of me, and my heart will break.'

'Here indeed is the true lover,' said the Nightingale. 'What I sing of, he suffers—what is joy to me, to him is pain. Surely Love is a wonderful thing. It is more precious than emeralds, and dearer than fine opals. Pearls and pomegranates cannot buy it, nor is it set forth in the marketplace. It may not be purchased of the merchants, nor can it be weighed out in the balance for gold.'

'The musicians will sit in their gallery,' said the young Student, 'and play upon their stringed instruments, and my love will dance to the sound of the harp and the violin. She will dance so lightly that her feet will not touch the floor, and the courtiers in their gay dresses will throng round her. But with me she will not dance, for I have no red rose to give her'; and he flung himself down on the grass, and buried his face in his hands, and wept.

'Why is he weeping?' asked a little Green Lizard, as he ran past him with his tail in the air.

'Why, indeed?' said a Butterfly, who was fluttering about after a sunbeam.

'Why, indeed?' whispered a Daisy to his neighbour, in a soft, low voice.

'He is weeping for a red rose,' said the Nightingale.

'For a red rose?' they cried; 'how very ridiculous!' and the little Lizard, who was something of a cynic, laughed outright.

But the Nightingale understood the secret of the Student's sorrow, and she sat silent in the oak-tree, and thought about the mystery of Love.

Suddenly she spread her brown wings for flight, and soared into the air. She passed through the grove like a shadow, and like a shadow she sailed across the garden.

In the centre of the grass-plot was standing a beautiful Rose-tree, and when she saw it she flew over to it, and lit upon a spray.

'Give me a red rose,' she cried, 'and I will sing you my sweetest song.'

But the Tree shook its head.

'My roses are white,' it answered; 'as white as the foam of the sea, and whiter than the snow upon the mountain. But go to my brother who grows round the old sun-dial, and perhaps he will give you what you want.'

So the Nightingale flew over to the Rose-tree that was growing round the old sun-dial.

'Give me a red rose,' she cried, 'and I will sing you my sweetest song.'

But the Tree shook its head.

'My roses are yellow,' it answered; 'as yellow as the hair of the mermaiden who sits upon an amber throne, and yellower than the daffodil that blooms in the meadow before the mower comes with his scythe. But go to my brother who grows beneath the Student's window, and perhaps he will give you what you want.'

So the Nightingale flew over to the Rose-tree that was growing beneath the Student's window.

'Give me a red rose,' she cried, 'and I will sing you my sweetest song.'

But the Tree shook its head.

'My roses are red,' it answered, 'as red as the feet of the dove, and redder than the great fans of coral that wave and wave in the ocean-cavern. But the winter has chilled my veins, and the frost has nipped my buds, and the storm has broken my branches, and I shall have no roses at all this year.'

'One red rose is all I want,' cried the Nightingale, 'only one red rose! Is there no way by which I can get it?'

'There is a way,' answered the Tree; 'but it is so terrible that I dare not tell it to you.'

'Tell it to me,' said the Nightingale, 'I am not afraid.'

'If you want a red rose,' said the Tree, 'you must build it out of music by moonlight, and stain it with your own heart's-blood. You must sing to me with your breast against a thorn. All night long you must sing to me, and the thorn must pierce your heart, and your life-blood must flow into my veins, and become mine.'

'Death is a great price to pay for a red rose,' cried the Nightingale, 'and Life is very dear to all. It is pleasant to sit in the green wood, and to watch the Sun in his chariot of gold, and the Moon in her chariot of pearl. Sweet is the scent of the hawthorn, and sweet are the bluebells that hide in the valley, and the heather that blows on the hill. Yet Love is better than Life, and what is the heart of a bird compared to the heart of a man?'

So she spread her brown wings for flight, and soared into the air. She swept over the garden like a shadow, and like a shadow she sailed through the grove.

The young Student was still lying on the grass, where she had left him, and the tears were not yet dry in his beautiful eyes.

'Be happy,' cried the Nightingale, 'be happy; you shall have your red rose. I will build it out of music by moonlight, and stain it with my own heart's-blood. All that I ask of you in return is that you will be a true lover, for Love is wiser than Philosophy, though she is wise, and mightier than Power, though he is mighty. Flame-coloured are his wings, and coloured like flame is his body. His lips are sweet as honey, and his breath is like frankincense.'

The Student looked up from the grass, and listened, but he could not understand what the Nightingale was saying to him, for he only knew the things that are written down in books.

But the Oak-tree understood, and felt sad, for he was very fond of the little Nightingale who had built her nest in his branches.

'Sing me one last song,' he whispered; 'I shall feel very lonely when you are gone.'

So the Nightingale sang to the Oak-tree, and her voice was like water bubbling from a silver jar.

When she had finished her song the Student got up, and pulled a note-book and a lead-pencil out of his pocket.

'She has form,' he said to himself, as he walked away through the grove—'that cannot be denied to her; but has she got feeling? I am afraid not. In fact, she is like most artists; she is all style, without any sincerity. She would not sacrifice herself for others. She thinks merely of music, and everybody knows that the arts are selfish. Still, it must be admitted that she has some beautiful notes in her voice. What a pity it is that they do not mean anything, or do any practical good.' And he went into his room, and lay down on his little pallet-bed, and began to think of his love; and, after a time, he fell asleep.

And when the Moon shone in the heavens the Nightingale flew to the Rose-tree, and set her breast against the thorn. All night long she sang with her breast against the thorn, and the cold crystal Moon leaned down and listened. All night long she sang, and the thorn went deeper and deeper into her breast, and her life-blood ebbed away from her.

She sang first of the birth of love in the heart of a boy and a girl. And on the top-most spray of the Rose-tree there blossomed a marvellous rose, petal following petal, as song followed song. Pale was it, at first, as the mist that hangs over the river—pale as the feet of the morning, and silver as the wings of the dawn. As the shadow of a rose in a mirror of silver, as the shadow of a rose in a water-pool, so was the rose that blossomed on the topmost spray of the Tree.

But the Tree cried to the Nightingale to press closer against the thorn. 'Press closer, little Nightingale,' cried the Tree, 'or the Day will come before the rose is finished.'

So the Nightingale pressed closer against the thorn, and louder and louder grew her song, for she sang of the birth of passion in the soul of a man and a maid.

And a delicate flush of pink came into the leaves of the rose, like the flush in the face of the bridegroom when he kisses the lips of the bride. But the thorn had not yet reached her heart, so the rose's heart remained white, for only a Nightingale's heart's-blood can crimson the heart of a rose.

And the Tree cried to the Nightingale to press closer against the thorn. 'Press closer, little Nightingale,' cried the Tree, 'or the Day will come before the rose is finished.'

So the Nightingale pressed closer against the thorn, and the thorn touched her heart, and a fierce pang of pain shot through her. Bitter, bitter was the pain, and wilder and wilder grew her song, for she sang of the Love that is perfected by Death, of the Love that dies not in the tomb.

And the marvellous rose became crimson, like the rose of the eastern sky. Crimson was the girdle of petals, and crimson as a ruby was the heart.

But the Nightingale's voice grew fainter, and her little wings began to beat, and a film came over her eyes. Fainter and fainter grew her song, and she felt something choking her in her throat.

Then she gave one last burst of music. The white Moon heard it, and she forgot the dawn, and lingered on in the sky. The red rose heard it, and it trembled all over with ecstasy, and opened its petals to the cold morning air. Echo bore it to her purple cavern in the hills, and woke the sleeping shepherds from their dreams. It floated through the reeds of the river, and they carried its message to the sea.

'Look, look!' cried the Tree, 'the rose is finished now'; but the Nightingale made no answer, for she was lying dead in the long grass, with the thorn in her heart.

And at noon the Student opened his window and looked out.

'Why, what a wonderful piece of luck!' he cried; 'here is a red rose! I have never seen any rose like it in all my life. It is so beautiful that I am sure it has a long Latin name'; and he leaned down and plucked it.

Then he put on his hat, and ran up to the Professor's house with the rose in his hand.

The daughter of the Professor was sitting in the doorway winding blue silk on a reel, and her little dog was lying at her feet.

'You said that you would dance with me if I brought you a red rose,' cried the Student. 'Here is the reddest rose in all the world. You will wear it to-night next your heart, and as we dance together it will tell you how I love you.'

But the girl frowned.

'I am afraid it will not go with my dress,' she answered; 'and, besides, the Chamberlain's nephew has sent me some real jewels, and everybody knows that jewels cost far more than flowers.'

'Well, upon my word, you are very ungrateful,' said the Student angrily; and he threw the rose into the street, where it fell into the gutter, and a cart-wheel went over it.

'Ungrateful!' said the girl. 'I tell you what, you are very rude; and, after all, who are you? Only a Student. Why, I don't believe you have even got silver buckles to your shoes as the Chamberlain's nephew has'; and she got up from her chair and went into the house.

'What I a silly thing Love is,' said the Student as he walked away. 'It is not half as useful as Logic, for it does not prove anything, and it is always telling one of things that are not going to happen, and making one believe things that are not true. In fact, it is quite unpractical, and, as in this age to be practical is everything, I shall go back to Philosophy and study Metaphysics.'

So he returned to his room and pulled out a great dusty book, and began to read.

Oscar Fingal O'Flahertie Wills Wilde (1854–1900) was born in Dublin, Ireland, and became one of the most successful and controversial writers of his generation, celebrated for such popular stage comedies as The Importance of Being Earnest *as well as for the novel* The Picture of Dorian Gray *and for a number of short stories. A trial and imprisonment arising from public allegations about his homosexuality resulted in his disgrace and contributed to his premature death. 'The Nightingale and the Rose' was published in 1888 and ranks among his most touching and romantic stories.*

Head and Shoulders
F. Scott Fitzgerald

In 1915 Horace Tarbox was thirteen years old. In that year he took the examinations for entrance to Princeton University and received the Grade A—excellent—in Cæsar, Cicero, Vergil, Xenophon, Homer, Algebra, Plane Geometry, Solid Geometry, and Chemistry.

Two years later while George M. Cohan was composing 'Over There', Horace was leading the sophomore class by several lengths and digging out theses on 'The Syllogism as an Obsolete Scholastic Form', and during the battle of Château-Thierry he was sitting at his desk deciding whether or not to wait until his seventeenth birthday before beginning his series of essays on 'The Pragmatic Bias of the New Realists'.

After a while some newsboy told him that the war was over, and he was glad, because it meant that Peat Brothers, publishers, would get out their new edition of 'Spinoza's Improvement of the Understanding'. Wars were all very well in their way, made young men self-reliant or something but Horace felt that he could never forgive the President for allowing a brass band to play under his window the night of the false armistice, causing him to leave three important sentences out of his thesis on 'German Idealism'.

The next year he went up to Yale to take his degree as Master of Arts.

He was seventeen then, tall and slender, with near-sighted grey eyes and an air of keeping himself utterly detached from the mere words he let drop.

'I never feel as though I'm talking to him,' expostulated Professor Dillinger to a sympathetic colleague. 'He makes me feel as though I were talking to his representative. I always expect him to say: "Well, I'll ask myself and find out."'

And then, just as nonchalantly as though Horace Tarbox had been Mr Beef the butcher or Mr Hat the haberdasher, life reached in, seized him, handled him, stretched him, and unrolled him like a piece of

Irish lace on a Saturday-afternoon bargain-counter.

To move in the literary fashion I should say that this was all because when way back in colonial days the hardy pioneers had come to a bald place in Connecticut and asked of each other, 'Now, what shall we build here?' the hardiest one among 'em had answered: 'Let's build a town where theatrical managers can try out musical comedies!' How afterward they founded Yale College there, to try the musical comedies on, is a story everyone knows. At any rate one December, 'Home James' opened at the Shubert, and all the students encored Marcia Meadow, who sang a song about the Blundering Blimp in the first act and did a shaky, shivery, celebrated dance in the last.

Marcia was nineteen. She didn't have wings, but audiences agreed generally that she didn't need them. She was a blonde by natural pigment, and she wore no paint on the streets at high noon. Outside of that she was no better than most women.

It was Charlie Moon who promised her five thousand Pall Malls if she would pay a call on Horace Tarbox, prodigy extraordinary. Charlie was a senior in Sheffield, and he and Horace were first cousins. They liked and pitied each other.

Horace had been particularly busy that night. The failure of the Frenchman Laurier to appreciate the significance of the new realists was preying on his mind. In fact, his only reaction to a low, clear-cut rap at his study was to make him speculate as to whether any rap would have actual existence without an ear there to hear it. He fancied he was verging more and more toward pragmatism. But at that moment, though he did not know it, he was verging with astounding rapidity toward something quite different.

The rap sounded—three seconds leaked by—the rap sounded.

'Come in,' muttered Horace automatically.

He heard the door open and then close, but, bent over his book in the big armchair before the fire, he did not look up.

'Leave it on the bed in the other room,' he said absently.

'Leave what on the bed in the other room?'

Marcia Meadow had to talk her songs, but her speaking voice was like byplay on a harp.

'The laundry.'

'I can't.'

Horace stirred impatiently in his chair.

'Why can't you?'

'Why, because I haven't got it.'

'Hm!' he replied testily. 'Suppose you go back and get it.'

Across the fire from Horace was another easychair. He was accustomed to change to it in the course of an evening by way of exercise and variety. One chair he called Berkeley, the other he called Hume. He suddenly heard a sound as of a rustling, diaphanous form sinking into Hume. He glanced up.

'Well,' said Marcia with the sweet smile she used in Act Two ('Oh, so the Duke liked my dancing!') 'Well, Omar Khayyam, here I am beside you singing in the wilderness.'

Horace stared at her dazedly. The momentary suspicion came to him that she existed there only as a phantom of his imagination. Women didn't come into men's rooms and sink into men's Humes. Women brought laundry and took your seat in the street-car and married you later on when you were old enough to know fetters.

This woman had clearly materialised out of Hume. The very froth of her brown gauzy dress was an emanation from Hume's leather arm there! If he looked long enough he would see Hume right through her and then he would be alone again in the room. He passed his fist across his eyes. He really must take up those trapeze exercises again.

'For Pete's sake, don't look so critical!' objected the emanation pleasantly. 'I feel as if you were going to wish me away with that patent dome of yours. And then there wouldn't be anything left of me except my shadow in your eyes.'

Horace coughed. Coughing was one of his two gestures. When he talked you forgot he had a body at all. It was like hearing a phonograph record by a singer who had been dead a long time.

'What do you want?' he asked.

'I want them letters,' whined Marcia melodramatically—'them letters of mine you bought from my grandsire in 1881.'

Horace considered.

'I haven't got your letters,' he said evenly. 'I am only seventeen years old. My father was not born until March 3, 1879. You evidently have me confused with someone else.'

'You're only seventeen?' repeated March suspiciously.

'Only seventeen.'

'I knew a girl,' said Marcia reminiscently, 'who went on the ten-twenty-thirty when she was sixteen. She was so stuck on herself that she could never say "sixteen" without putting the "only" before it. We got to calling her "Only Jessie". And she's just where she was when she started—only worse. "Only" is a bad habit, Omar—it sounds like an alibi.'

'My name is not Omar.'

'I know,' agreed Marcia, nodding—'your name's Horace. I just call you Omar because you remind me of a smoked cigarette.'

'And I haven't your letters. I doubt if I've ever met your grandfather. In fact, I think it very improbable that you yourself were alive in 1881.'

Marcia stared at him in wonder.

'Me—1881? Why sure! I was second-line stuff when the Florodora Sextette was still in the convent. I was the original nurse to Mrs Sol Smith's Juliette. Why, Omar, I was a canteen singer during the War of 1812.'

Horace's mind made a sudden successful leap, and he grinned.

'Did Charlie Moon put you up to this?'

Marcia regarded him inscrutably.

'Who's Charlie Moon?'

'Small—wide nostrils—big ears.'

She grew several inches and sniffed.

'I'm not in the habit of noticing my friends' nostrils.'

'Then it was Charlie?'

Marcia bit her lip—and then yawned. 'Oh, let's change the subject, Omar. I'll pull a snore in this chair in a minute.'

'Yes,' replied Horace gravely, 'Hume has often been considered soporific–'

'Who's your friend—and will he die?'

Then of a sudden Horace Tarbox rose slenderly and began to pace the room with his hands in his pockets. This was his other gesture.

'I don't care for this,' he said as if he were talking to himself—'at all. Not that I mind your being here—I don't. You're quite a pretty little thing, but I don't like Charlie Moon's sending you up here. Am I a laboratory experiment on which the janitors as well as the chemists can make experiments? Is my intellectual development humorous in any way? Do I look like the pictures of the little Boston boy in the comic magazines? Has that callow ass, Moon, with his eternal tales about his week in Paris, any right to–'

'No,' interrupted Marcia emphatically. 'And you're a sweet boy. Come here and kiss me.'

Horace stopped quickly in front of her.

'Why do you want me to kiss you?' he asked intently, 'Do you just go round kissing people?'

'Why, yes,' admitted Marcia, unruffled. ''At's all life is. Just going round kissing people.'

'Well,' replied Horace emphatically, 'I must say your ideas are horribly garbled! In the first place life isn't just that, and in the second place, I won't kiss you. It might get to be a habit and I can't get rid of habits. This year I've got in the habit of lolling in bed until seven-thirty–'

Marcia nodded understandingly.

'Do you ever have any fun?' she asked.

'What do you mean by fun?'

'See here,' said Marcia sternly, 'I like you, Omar, but I wish you'd talk as if you had a line on what you were saying. You sound as if you were gargling a lot of words in your mouth and lost a bet every time you spilled a few. I asked you if you ever had any fun.'

Horace shook his head.

'Later, perhaps,' he answered. 'You see I'm a plan. I'm an experiment. I don't say that I don't get tired of it sometimes—I do. Yet—oh, I can't explain! But what you and Charlie Moon call fun wouldn't be fun to me.'

'Please explain.'

Horace stared at her, started to speak and then, changing his mind, resumed his walk. After an unsuccessful attempt to determine whether or not he was looking at her Marcia smiled at him.

'Please explain.'

Horace turned.

'If I do, will you promise to tell Charlie Moon that I wasn't in?'

'Uh-uh.'

'Very well, then. Here's my history: I was a "why" child. I wanted to see the wheels go round. My father was a young economics professor at Princeton. He brought me up on the system of answering every question I asked him to the best of his ability. My response to that gave him the idea of making an experiment in precocity. To aid in the massacre I had ear trouble—seven operations between the age of nine and twelve. Of course this kept me apart from other boys and made me ripe for forcing. Anyway, while my generation was labouring through Uncle Remus I was honestly enjoying Catullus in the original.

'I passed off my college examinations when I was thirteen because I couldn't help it. My chief associates were professors, and I took a tremendous pride in knowing that I had a fine intelligence, for though I was unusually gifted I was not abnormal in other ways. When I was sixteen I got tired of being a freak; I decided that someone had made a bad mistake. Still as I'd gone that far I concluded to finish it up by taking my degree of Master of Arts. My chief interest in life is the study of modern philosophy. I am a realist of the School of Anton Laurier—with Bergsonian trimmings—and I'll be eighteen years old in two months. That's all.'

'Whew!' exclaimed Marcia. 'That's enough! You do a neat job with the parts of speech.'

'Satisfied?'

'No, you haven't kissed me.'

'It's not in my programme,' demurred Horace. 'Understand that I don't pretend to be above physical things. They have their place, but–'

'Oh, don't be so darned reasonable!'

'I can't help it.'

'I hate these slot-machine people.'

'I assure you I–' began Horace.

'Oh shut up!'

'My own rationality–'

'I didn't say anything about your nationality. You're Amuricun, ar'n't you?'

'Yes.'

'Well, that's O.K. with me. I got a notion I want to see you do something that isn't in your highbrow programme. I want to see if a what-ch-call-em with Brazilian trimmings—that thing you said you were—can be a little human.'

Horace shook his head again.

'I won't kiss you.'

'My life is blighted,' muttered Marcia tragically. 'I'm a beaten woman. I'll go through life without ever having a kiss with Brazilian trimmings.' She sighed. 'Anyways, Omar, will you come and see my show?'

'What show?'

'I'm a wicked actress from "Home James"!'

'Light opera?'

'Yes—at a stretch. One of the characters is a Brazilian rice-planter. That might interest you.'

'I saw "The Bohemian Girl" once,' reflected Horace aloud. 'I enjoyed it—to some extent–'

'Then you'll come?'

'Well, I'm—I'm—'

'Oh, I know—you've got to run down to Brazil for the week-end.'

'Not at all. I'd be delighted to come–'

Marcia clapped her hands.

'Goodyforyou! I'll mail you a ticket—Thursday night?'

'Why, I–'

'Good! Thursday night it is.'

She stood up and walking close to him laid both hands on his shoulders.

'I like you, Omar. I'm sorry I tried to kid you. I thought you'd be sort of frozen, but you're a nice boy.'

He eyed her sardonically.

'I'm several thousand generations older than you are.'

'You carry your age well.'

They shook hands gravely.

'My name's Marcia Meadow,' she said emphatically. ''Member it—Marcia Meadow. And I won't tell Charlie Moon you were in.'

An instant later as she was skimming down the last flight of stairs three at a time she heard a voice call over the upper banister: 'Oh, say–'

She stopped and looked up—made out a vague form leaning over.

'Oh, say!' called the prodigy again. 'Can you hear me?'

'Here's your connection Omar.'

'I hope I haven't given you the impression that I consider kissing intrinsically irrational.'

'Impression? Why, you didn't even give me the kiss! Never fret—so long.'

Two doors near her opened curiously at the sound of a feminine voice. A tentative cough sounded from above. Gathering her skirts, Marcia dived wildly down the last flight, and was swallowed up in the murky Connecticut air outside.

Up-stairs Horace paced the floor of his study. From time to time he glanced toward Berkeley waiting there in suave dark-red reputability, an open book lying suggestively on his cushions. And then he found that his circuit of the floor was bringing him each time nearer to Hume. There was something about Hume that was strangely and inexpressibly different. The diaphanous form still seemed hovering near, and had Horace sat there he would have felt as if he were sitting on a lady's lap. And though Horace couldn't have named the quality of difference, there was such a quality—quite intangible to the speculative mind, but real, nevertheless. Hume was radiating something that in all the two hundred years of his influence he had never radiated before.

Hume was radiating attar of roses.

II

On Thursday night Horace Tarbox sat in an aisle seat in the fifth row and witnessed 'Home James'. Oddly enough he found that he was enjoying himself. The cynical students near him were annoyed at his audible appreciation of time-honoured jokes in the Hammerstein tradition. But Horace was waiting with anxiety for Marcia Meadow singing her song about a Jazz-bound Blundering Blimp. When she did appear, radiant under a floppity flower-faced hat, a warm glow settled over him, and when the song was over he did not join in the storm of applause. He felt somewhat numb.

In the intermission after the second act an usher materialised beside him, demanded to know if he were Mr Tarbox, and then handed him a note written in a round adolescent hand. Horace read it in some confusion, while the usher lingered with withering patience in the aisle.

'Dear Omar: After the show I always grow an awful hunger. If you want to satisfy it for me in the Taft Grill just communicate your answer to the big-timber guide that brought this and oblige.
Your friend,
Marcia Meadow.'

'Tell her,'—he coughed—'tell her that it will be quite all right. I'll meet her in front of the theatre.'

The big-timber guide smiled arrogantly.

'I giss she meant for you to come roun' t' the stage door.'

'Where—where is it?'

'Ou'side. Tunayulef. Down ee alley.'

'What?'

'Ou'side. Turn to y' left! Down ee alley!'

The arrogant person withdrew. A freshman behind Horace snickered.

Then half an hour later, sitting in the Taft Grill opposite the hair that was yellow by natural pigment, the prodigy was saying an odd thing.

'Do you have to do that dance in the last act?' he was asking earnestly—'I mean, would they dismiss you if you refused to do it?'

Marcia grinned.

'It's fun to do it. I like to do it.'

And then Horace came out with a *faux pas*.

'I should think you'd detest it,' he remarked succinctly. 'The people behind me were making remarks about your bosom.'

Marcia blushed fiery red.

'I can't help that,' she said quickly. 'The dance to me is only a sort of acrobatic stunt. Lord, it's hard enough to do! I rub liniment into my shoulders for an hour every night.'

'Do you have—fun while you're on the stage?'

'Uh-huh—sure! I got in the habit of having people look at me, Omar, and I like it.'

'Hm!' Horace sank into a brownish study.

'How's the Brazilian trimmings?'

'Hm!' repeated Horace, and then after a pause: 'Where does the play go from here?'

'New York.'

'For how long?'

'All depends. Winter—maybe.'

'Oh!'

'Coming up to lay eyes on me, Omar, or arcn't you int'rested? Not as nice here, is it, as it was up in your room? I wish we was there now.'

'I feel idiotic in this place,' confessed Horace, looking round him nervously.

'Too bad! We got along pretty well.'

At this he looked suddenly so melancholy that she changed her tone, and reaching over patted his hand.

'Ever take an actress out to supper before?'

'No,' said Horace miserably, 'and I never will again. I don't know why I came to-night. Here under all these lights and with all these people laughing and chattering I feel completely out of my sphere. I don't know what to talk to you about.'

'We'll talk about me. We talked about you last time.'

'Very well.'

'Well, my name really is Meadow, but my first name isn't Marcia—it's Veronica. I'm nineteen. Question—how did the girl make her leap to the footlights? Answer—she was born in Passaic, New Jersey, and up to a year ago she got the right to breathe by pushing Nabiscoes in Marcel's tea-room in Trenton. She started going with a guy named Robbins, a singer in the Trent House cabaret, and he got her to try a song and dance with him one evening. In a month we were filling the supper-room every night. Then we went to New York with meet-my-friend letters thick as a pile of napkins.

'In two days we landed a job at Divinerries', and I learned to shimmy from a kid at the Palais Royal. We stayed at Divinerries' six months until one night Peter Boyce Wendell, the columnist, ate his milk-toast there. Next morning a poem about Marvellous Marcia came out in his newspaper, and within two days I had three vaudeville offers and a chance at the Midnight Frolic. I wrote Wendell a thank-you letter, and he printed it in his column—said that the style was like Carlyle's, only more rugged and that I ought to quit dancing and do North American literature. This got me a coupla more vaudeville offers and a chance as an ingénue in a regular show. I took it—and here I am, Omar.'

When she finished they sat for a moment in silence she draping the last skeins of a Welsh rabbit on her fork and waiting for him to speak.

'Let's get out of here,' he said suddenly.

Marcia's eyes hardened.

'What's the idea? Am I making you sick?'

'No, but I don't like it here. I don't like to be sitting here with you.'

Without another word Marcia signalled for the waiter.

'What's the check?' she demanded briskly 'My part—the rabbit and the ginger ale.'

Horace watched blankly as the waiter figured it.

'See here,' he began, 'I intended to pay for yours too. You're my guest.'

With a half-sigh Marcia rose from the table and walked from the room. Horace, his face a document in bewilderment, laid a bill down and followed her out, up the stairs and into the lobby. He overtook her in front of the elevator and they faced each other.

'See here,' he repeated 'You're my guest. Have I said something to offend you?'

After an instant of wonder Marcia's eyes softened.

'You're a rude fella!' she said slowly. 'Don't you know you're rude?'

'I can't help it,' said Horace with a directness she found quite disarming. 'You know I like you.'

'You said you didn't like being with me.'

'I didn't like it.'

'Why not?' Fire blazed suddenly from the grey forests of his eyes.

'Because I didn't. I've formed the habit of liking you. I've been thinking of nothing much else for two days.'

'Well, if you–'

'Wait a minute,' he interrupted. 'I've got something to say. It's this: in six weeks I'll be eighteen years old. When I'm eighteen years old I'm coming up to New York to see you. Is there some place in New York

110

where we can go and not have a lot of people in the room?'

'Sure!' smiled Marcia. 'You can come up to my 'partment. Sleep on the couch if you want to.'

'I can't sleep on couches,' he said shortly. 'But I want to talk to you.'

'Why, sure,' repeated Marcia, 'in my 'partment.'

In his excitement Horace put his hands in his pockets.

'All right—just so I can see you alone. I want to talk to you as we talked up in my room.'

'Honey boy,' cried Marcia, laughing, 'is it that you want to kiss me?'

'Yes,' Horace almost shouted. 'I'll kiss you if you want me to.'

The elevator man was looking at them reproachfully. Marcia edged toward the grated door.

'I'll drop you a post-card,' she said.

Horace's eyes were quite wild.

'Send me a post-card! I'll come up any time after January first. I'll be eighteen then.'

And as she stepped into the elevator he coughed enigmatically, yet with a vague challenge, at the calling, and walked quickly away.

III

He was there again. She saw him when she took her first glance at the restless Manhattan audience—down in the front row with his head bent a bit forward and his grey eyes fixed on her. And she knew that to him they were alone together in a world where the high-rouged row of ballet faces and the massed whines of the violins were as imperceivable as powder on a marble Venus. An instinctive defiance rose within her.

'Silly boy!' she said to herself hurriedly, and she didn't take her encore.

'What do they expect for a hundred a week—perpetual motion?' she grumbled to herself in the wings.

'What's the trouble? Marcia?'

'Guy I don't like down in front.'

During the last act as she waited for her specialty she had an odd

111

attack of stage fright. She had never sent Horace the promised post-card. Last night she had pretended not to see him—had hurried from the theatre immediately after her dance to pass a sleepless night in her apartment, thinking—as she had so often in the last month—of his pale, rather intent face, his slim, boyish figure, the merciless, unworldly abstraction that made him charming to her.

And now that he had come she felt vaguely sorry—as though an unwonted responsibility was being forced on her.

'Infant prodigy!' she said aloud.

'What?' demanded the negro comedian standing beside her.

'Nothing—just talking about myself.'

On the stage she felt better. This was her dance—and she always felt that the way she did it wasn't suggestive any more than to some men every pretty girl is suggestive. She made it a stunt.

'Uptown, downtown, jelly on a spoon,
After sundown shiver by the moon.'

He was not watching her now. She saw that clearly. He was looking very deliberately at a castle on the back drop, wearing that expression he had worn in the Taft Grill. A wave of exasperation swept over her—he was criticising her.

'That's the vibration that thrills me,
Funny how affection fi-lls me
Uptown, downtown–'

Unconquerable revulsion seized her. She was suddenly and horribly conscious of her audience as she had never been since her first appearance. Was that a leer on a pallid face in the front row, a droop of disgust on one young girl's mouth? These shoulders of hers—these shoulders shaking—were they hers? Were they real? Surely shoulders weren't made for this!

'Then—you'll see at a glance
I'll need some funeral ushers with St Vitus dance
At the end of the world I'll–

The bassoon and two cellos crashed into a final chord. She paused and poised a moment on her toes with every muscle tense, her young face looking out dully at the audience in what one young girl afterward called 'such a curious, puzzled look', and then without bowing rushed from the stage. Into the dressing-room she sped, kicked out of one dress and into another, and caught a taxi outside.

Her apartment was very warm—small, it was, with a row of professional pictures and sets of Kipling and O. Henry which she had bought once from a blue-eyed agent and read occasionally. And there were several chairs which matched, but were none of them comfortable, and a pink-shaded lamp with blackbirds painted on it and an atmosphere of rather stifled pink throughout. There were nice things in it—nice things unrelentingly hostile to each other, offspring of a vicarious, impatient taste acting in stray moments. The worst was typified by a great picture framed in oak bark of Passaic as seen from the Erie Railroad—altogether a frantic, oddly extravagant, oddly penurious attempt to make a cheerful room. Marcia knew it was a failure.

Into this room came the prodigy and took her two hands awkwardly.

'I followed you this time,' he said.

'Oh!'

'I want you to marry me,' he said.

Her arms went out to him. She kissed his mouth with a sort of passionate wholesomeness.

'There!'

'I love you,' he said.

She kissed him again and then with a little sigh flung herself into an armchair and half lay there, shaken with absurd laughter.

'Why, you infant prodigy!' she cried.

'Very well, call me that if you want to. I once told you that I was ten thousand years older than you—I am.'

She laughed again.

'I don't like to be disapproved of.'

'No one's ever going to disapprove of you again.'

'Omar,' she asked, 'why do you want to marry me?'

The prodigy rose and put his hands in his pockets.

'Because I love you, Marcia Meadow.'

And then she stopped calling him Omar.

'Dear boy,' she said, 'you know I sort of love you. There's something about you—I can't tell what—that just puts my heart through the wringer every time I'm round you. But honey–' She paused.

'But what?'

'But lots of things. But you're only just eighteen, and I'm nearly twenty.'

'Nonsense!' he interrupted. 'Put it this way—that I'm in my nineteenth year and you're nineteen. That makes us pretty close—without counting that other ten thousand years I mentioned.'

Marcia laughed.

'But there are some more "buts". Your people–'

'My people!' exclaimed the prodigy ferociously. 'My people tried to make a monstrosity out of me.' His face grew quite crimson at the enormity of what he was going to say. 'My people can go way back and sit down!'

'My heavens!' cried Marcia in alarm. 'All that? On tacks, I suppose.'

'Tacks—yes,' he agreed wildly—'on anything. The more I think of how they allowed me to become a little dried-up mummy–'

'What makes you thank you're that?' asked Marcia quietly— 'me?'

'Yes. Every person I've met on the streets since I met you has made me jealous because they knew what love was before I did. I used to call it the "sex impulse". Heavens!'

'There's more "buts",' said Marcia

'What are they?'

'How could we live?'

'I'll make a living.'

'You're in college.'

'Do you think I care anything about taking a Master of Arts degree?'

'You want to be Master of Me, hey?'

'Yes! What? I mean, no!'

Marcia laughed, and crossing swiftly over sat in his lap. He put his arm round her wildly and implanted the vestige of a kiss somewhere near her neck.

'There's something white about you,' mused Marcia 'but it doesn't sound very logical.'

'Oh, don't be so darned reasonable!'

'I can't help it,' said Marcia.

'I hate these slot-machine people!'

'But we—'

'Oh, shut up!'

And as Marcia couldn't talk through her ears she had to.

IV

Horace and Marcia were married early in February. The sensation in academic circles both at Yale and Princeton was tremendous. Horace Tarbox, who at fourteen had been played up in the Sunday magazines sections of metropolitan newspapers, was throwing over his career, his chance of being a world authority on American philosophy, by marrying a chorus girl—they made Marcia a chorus girl. But like all modern stories it was a four-and-a-half-day wonder.

They took a flat in Harlem. After two weeks' search, during which his idea of the value of academic knowledge faded unmercifully, Horace took a position as clerk with a South American export company—someone had told him that exporting was the coming thing. Marcia was to stay in her show for a few months—anyway until he got on his feet. He was getting a hundred and twenty-five to start with, and though of course they told him it was only a question of months until he would be earning double that, Marcia refused even to consider giving up the hundred and fifty a week that she was getting at the time.

'We'll call ourselves Head and Shoulders, dear,' she said softly, 'and the shoulders'll have to keep shaking a little longer until the old head gets started.'

'I hate it,' he objected gloomily.

'Well,' she replied emphatically, 'Your salary wouldn't keep us in a tenement. Don't think I want to be public—I don't. I want to be yours. But I'd be a half-wit to sit in one room and count the sunflowers on the wall-paper while I waited for you. When you pull down three hundred a month I'll quit.'

And much as it hurt his pride, Horace had to admit that hers was the wiser course.

March mellowed into April. May read a gorgeous riot act to the parks and waters of Manhattan, and they were very happy. Horace, who had no habits whatsoever—he had never had time to form any—proved the most adaptable of husbands, and as Marcia entirely lacked opinions on the subjects that engrossed him there were very few jottings and bumping. Their minds moved in different spheres. Marcia acted as practical factotum, and Horace lived either in his old world of abstract ideas or in a sort of triumphantly earthy worship and adoration of his wife. She was a continual source of astonishment to him—the freshness and originality of her mind, her dynamic, clear-headed energy, and her unfailing good humour.

And Marcia's co-workers in the nine-o'clock show, whither she had transferred her talents, were impressed with her tremendous pride in her husband's mental powers. Horace they knew only as a very slim, tight-lipped, and immature-looking young man, who waited every night to take her home.

'Horace,' said Marcia one evening when she met him as usual at eleven, 'you looked like a ghost standing there against the street lights. You losing weight?'

He shook his head vaguely.

'I don't know. They raised me to a hundred and thirty-five dollars to-day, and–'

'I don't care,' said Marcia severely. 'You're killing yourself working at night. You read those big books on economy–'

'Economics,' corrected Horace.

'Well, you read 'em every night long after I'm asleep. And you're getting all stooped over like you were before we were married.'

'But, Marcia, I've got to–'

'No, you haven't dear. I guess I'm running this shop for the present, and I won't let my fella ruin his health and eyes. You got to get some exercise.'

'I do. Every morning I–'

'Oh, I know! But those dumb-bells of yours wouldn't give a consumptive two degrees of fever. I mean real exercise. You've got to join a gymnasium. 'Member you told me you were such a trick gymnast once that they tried to get you out for the team in college and they couldn't because you had a standing date with Herb Spencer?'

'I used to enjoy it,' mused Horace, 'but it would take up too much time now.'

'All right,' said Marcia. 'I'll make a bargain with you. You join a gym and I'll read one of those books from the brown row of 'em.'

'"Pepys' Diary"? Why, that ought to be enjoyable. He's very light.'

'Not for me—he isn't. It'll be like digesting plate glass. But you been telling me how much it'd broaden my lookout. Well, you go to a gym three nights a week and I'll take one big dose of Sammy.'

Horace hesitated.

'Well—'

'Come on, now! You do some giant swings for me and I'll chase some culture for you.'

So Horace finally consented, and all through a baking summer he spent three and sometimes four evenings a week experimenting on the trapeze in Skipper's Gymnasium. And in August he admitted to Marcia that it made him capable of more mental work during the day.

'*Mens sana in corpore sano*,' he said.

'Don't believe in it,' replied Marcia. 'I tried one of those patent medicines once and they're all bunk. You stick to gymnastics.'

One night in early September while he was going through one of his contortions on the rings in the nearly deserted room he was addressed by a meditative fat man whom he had noticed watching him for several nights.

'Say, lad, do that stunt you were doin' last night.'

Horace grinned at him from his perch.

'I invented it,' he said. 'I got the idea from the fourth proposition of Euclid.'

'What circus he with?'

'He's dead.'

'Well, he must of broke his neck doin' that stunt. I set here last night thinkin' sure you was goin' to break yours.'

'Like this!' said Horace, and swinging onto the trapeze he did his stunt.

'Don't it kill your neck an' shoulder muscles?'

117

'It did at first, but inside of a week I wrote the *quod erat demonstrandum* on it.'

'Hm!'

Horace swung idly on the trapeze.

'Ever think of takin' it up professionally?' asked the fat man.

'Not I.'

'Good money in it if you're willin' to do stunts like 'at an' can get away with it.'

'Here's another,' chirped Horace eagerly, and the fat man's mouth dropped suddenly agape as he watched this pink-jerseyed Prometheus again defy the gods and Isaac Newton.

The night following this encounter Horace got home from work to find a rather pale Marcia stretched out on the sofa waiting for him.

'I fainted twice to-day,' she began without preliminaries.

'What?'

'Yep. You see baby's due in four months now. Doctor says I ought to have quit dancing two weeks ago.'

Horace sat down and thought it over.

'I'm glad of course,' he said pensively—'I mean glad that we're going to have a baby. But this means a lot of expense.'

'I've got two hundred and fifty in the bank,' said Marcia hopefully, 'and two weeks' pay coming.'

Horace computed quickly.

'Inducing my salary, that'll give us nearly fourteen hundred for the next six months.'

Marcia looked blue.

'That all? Course I can get a job singing somewhere this month. And I can go to work again in March.'

'Of course nothing!' said Horace gruffly. 'You'll stay right here. Let's see now—there'll be doctor's bills and a nurse, besides the maid: We've got to have some more money.'

'Well,' said Marcia wearily, 'I don't know where it's coming from. It's up to the old head now. Shoulders is out of business.'

Horace rose and pulled on his coat.

'Where are you going?'

'I've got an idea,' he answered. 'I'll be right back.'

Ten minutes later as he headed down the street toward Skipper's

118

Gymnasium he felt a placid wonder, quite unmixed with humour, at what he was going to do. How he would have gaped at himself a year before! How everyone would have gaped! But when you opened your door at the rap of life you let in many things.

The gymnasium was brightly lit, and when his eyes became accustomed to the glare he found the meditative fat man seated on a pile of canvas mats smoking a big cigar.

'Say,' began Horace directly, 'were you in earnest last night when you said I could make money on my trapeze stunts?'

'Why, yes,' said the fat man in surprise.

'Well, I've been thinking it over, and I believe I'd like to try it. I could work at night and on Saturday afternoons—and regularly if the pay is high enough.'

The fat men looked at his watch.

'Well,' he said, 'Charlie Paulson's the man to see. He'll book you inside of four days, once he sees you work out. He won't be in now, but I'll get hold of him for to-morrow night.'

The fat man was as good as his word. Charlie Paulson arrived next night and put in a wondrous hour watching the prodigy swoop through the air in amazing parabolas, and on the night following he brought two large men with him who looked as though they had been born smoking black cigars and talking about money in low, passionate voices. Then on the succeeding Saturday Horace Tarbox's torso made its first professional appearance in a gymnastic exhibition at the Coleman Street Gardens. But though the audience numbered nearly five thousand people, Horace felt no nervousness. From his childhood he had read papers to audiences—learned that trick of detaching himself.

'Marcia,' he said cheerfully later that same night, 'I think we're out of the woods. Paulson thinks he can get me an opening at the Hippodrome, and that means an all-winter engagement. The Hippodrome you know, is a big–'

'Yes, I believe I've heard of it,' interrupted Marcia, 'but I want to know about this stunt you're doing. It isn't any spectacular suicide, is it?'

'It's nothing,' said Horace quietly. 'But if you can think of any nicer way of a man killing himself than taking a risk for you, why that's the way I want to die.'

Marcia reached up and wound both arms tightly round his neck.

'Kiss me,' she whispered, 'and call me "dear heart". I love to hear you say "dear heart". And bring me a book to read to-morrow. No more Sam Pepys, but something trick and trashy. I've been wild for something to do all day. I felt like writing letters, but I didn't have anybody to write to.'

'Write to me,' said Horace. 'I'll read them.'

'I wish I could,' breathed Marcia. 'If I knew words enough I could write you the longest love-letter in the world—and never get tired.'

But after two more months Marcia grew very tired indeed, and for a row of nights it was a very anxious, weary-looking young athlete who walked out before the Hippodrome crowd. Then there were two days when his place was taken by a young man who wore pale blue instead of white, and got very little applause. But after the two days Horace appeared again, and those who sat close to the stage remarked an expression of beatific happiness on that young acrobat's face even when he was twisting breathlessly in the air an the middle of his amazing and original shoulder swing. After that performance he laughed at the elevator man and dashed up the stairs to the flat five steps at a time—and then tiptoed very carefully into a quiet room.

'Marcia,' he whispered.

'Hello!' She smiled up at him wanly. 'Horace, there's something I want you to do. Look in my top bureau drawer and you'll find a big stack of paper. It's a book—sort of—Horace. I wrote it down in these last three months while I've been laid up. I wish you'd take it to that Peter Boyce Wendell who put my letter in his paper. He could tell you whether it'd be a good book. I wrote it just the way I talk, just the way I wrote that letter to him. It's just a story about a lot of things that happened to me. Will you take it to him, Horace?'

'Yes, darling.'

He leaned over the bed until his head was beside her on the pillow, and began stroking back her yellow hair.

'Dearest Marcia,' he said softly.

'No,' she murmured, 'call me what I told you to call me.'

'Dear heart,' he whispered passionately—'dearest heart.'

'What'll we call her?'

They rested a minute in happy, drowsy content, while Horace

considered.

'We'll call her Marcia Hume Tarbox,' he said at length.

'Why the Hume?'

'Because he's the fellow who first introduced us.'

'That so?' she murmured, sleepily surprised. 'I thought his name was Moon.'

Her eyes dosed, and after a moment the slow lengthening surge of the bedclothes over her breast showed that she was asleep.

Horace tiptoed over to the bureau and opening the top drawer found a heap of closely scrawled, lead-smeared pages. He looked at the first sheet:

Sandra Pepys, Syncopated
By Marcia Tarbox

He smiled. So Samuel Pepys had made an impression on her after all. He turned a page and began to read. His smile deepened—he read on. Half an hour passed and he became aware that Marcia had waked and was watching him from the bed.

'Honey,' came in a whisper.

'What Marcia?'

'Do you like it?'

Horace coughed.

'I seem to be reading on. It's bright.'

'Take it to Peter Boyce Wendell. Tell him you got the highest marks in Princeton once and that you ought to know when a book's good. Tell him this one's a world beater.'

'All right, Marcia,' Horace said gently.

Her eyes closed again and Horace crossing over kissed her forehead—stood there for a moment with a look of tender pity. Then he left the room.

All that night the sprawly writing on the pages, the constant mistakes in spelling and grammar, and the weird punctuation danced before his eyes. He woke several times in the night, each time full of a welling chaotic sympathy for this desire of Marcia's soul to express itself in words. To him there was something infinitely pathetic about it, and for the first time in months he began to turn over in his mind his own half-forgotten dreams.

He had meant to write a series of books, to popularise the new realism as Schopenhauer had popularised pessimism and William James pragmatism.

But life hadn't come that way. Life took hold of people and forced them into flying rings. He laughed to think of that rap at his door, the diaphanous shadow in Hume, Marcia's threatened kiss.

'And it's still me,' he said aloud in wonder as he lay awake in the darkness. 'I'm the man who sat in Berkeley with temerity to wonder if that rap would have had actual existence had my ear not been there to hear it. I'm still that man. I could be electrocuted for the crimes he committed.

'Poor gauzy souls trying to express ourselves in something tangible. Marcia with her written book; I with my unwritten ones. Trying to choose our mediums and then taking what we get—and being glad.'

V

'Sandra Pepys, Syncopated', with an introduction by Peter Boyce Wendell the columnist, appeared serially in *Jordan's Magazine*, and came out in book form in March. From its first published instalment it attracted attention far and wide. A trite enough subject—a girl from a small New Jersey town coming to New York to go on the stage—treated simply, with a peculiar vividness of phrasing and a haunting undertone of sadness in the very inadequacy of its vocabulary, it made an irresistible appeal.

Peter Boyce Wendell, who happened at that time to be advocating the enrichment of the American language by the immediate adoption of expressive vernacular words, stood as its sponsor and thundered his indorsement over the placid bromides of the conventional reviewers.

Marcia received three hundred dollars an instalment for the serial publication, which came at an opportune time, for though Horace's monthly salary at the Hippodrome was now more than Marcia's had ever been, young Marcia was emitting shrill cries which they interpreted as a demand for country air. So early April found them installed in a bungalow in Westchester County, with a place for a lawn, a place for a garage, and a place for everything, including a sound-proof impregnable study, in which Marcia faithfully promised Mr Jordan she would shut herself up when her daughter's demands began to be abated, and compose immortally illiterate literature.

'It's not half bad,' thought Horace one night as he was on his way from the station to his house. He was considering several prospects that had opened up, a four months' vaudeville offer in five figures, a chance to go back to Princeton in charge of all gymnasium work. Odd! He had once intended to go back there in charge of all philosophic work, and now he had not even been stirred by the arrival in New York of Anton Laurier, his old idol.

The gravel crunched raucously under his heel. He saw the lights of his sitting-room gleaming and noticed a big car standing in the drive. Probably Mr Jordan again, come to persuade Marcia to settle down to work.

She had heard the sound of his approach and her form was silhouetted against the lighted door as she came out to meet him. 'There's some Frenchman here,' she whispered nervously. 'I can't pronounce his name, but he sounds awful deep. You'll have to jaw with him.'

'What Frenchman?'

'You can't prove it by me. He drove up an hour ago with Mr Jordan, and said he wanted to meet Sandra Pepys, and all that sort of thing.'

Two men rose from chairs as they went inside.

'Hello Tarbox,' said Jordan. 'I've just been bringing together two celebrities. I've brought M'sieur Laurier out with me. M'sieur Laurier, let me present Mr Tarbox, Mrs Tarbox's husband.'

'Not Anton Laurier!' exclaimed Horace.

'But, yes. I must come. I have to come. I have read the book of Madame, and I have been charmed'—he fumbled in his pocket—'ah I have read of you too. In this newspaper which I read to-day it has your name.'

He finally produced a clipping from a magazine.

'Read it!' he said eagerly. 'It has about you too.'

Horace's eye skipped down the page.

'A distinct contribution to American dialect literature,' it said. 'No attempt at literary tone; the book derives its very quality from this fact, as did "Huckleberry Finn".'

Horace's eyes caught a passage lower down; he became suddenly aghast—read on hurriedly:

'Marcia Tarbox's connection with the stage is not only as a spectator but as the wife of a performer. She was married last year to Horace Tarbox, who every evening delights the children at the Hippodrome with his wondrous flying performance. It is said that the young couple have dubbed themselves Head and Shoulders, referring doubtless to the fact that Mrs Tarbox supplies the literary and mental qualities, while the supple and agile shoulder of her husband contribute their share to the family fortunes.

'Mrs Tarbox seems to merit that much-abused title—"prodigy". Only twenty–'

Horace stopped reading, and with a very odd expression in his eyes gazed intently at Anton Laurier.

'I want to advise you–' he began hoarsely.

'What?'

'About raps. Don't answer them! Let them alone—have a padded door.'

Francis Scott Key Fitzgerald (1896–1940) was born in St Paul, Minnesota, and grew up to become one of the leading American writers of the Jazz Age of the 1920s. As well as such acclaimed novels as The Beautiful and Damned *(1922) and* The Great Gatsby *(1925), he wrote numerous short stories. Parallels have been drawn between the relationship of the couple in 'Head and Shoulders' and that of Fitzgerald himself and his wife Zelda (whom the author similarly came to consider a hindrance to his work). After military service, Fitzgerald worked in advertising but failed to convince Zelda, to whom he was engaged, that he earned enough for them to live on, so she broke off the engagement. Subsequently he worked as a repairer of car roofs before finally selling his first novel and, through his improved prospects, managing to persuade Zelda to renew the engagement.*

An Imaginative Woman
Thomas Hardy

When William Marchmill had finished his inquiries for lodgings at a well-known watering-place in Upper Wessex, he returned to the hotel to find his wife. She, with the children, had rambled along the shore, and Marchmill followed in the direction indicated by the military-looking hall-porter.

'By Jove, how far you've gone! I am quite out of breath,' Marchmill said, rather impatiently, when he came up with his wife, who was reading as she walked, the three children being considerably further ahead with the nurse.

Mrs Marchmill started out of the reverie into which the book had thrown her. 'Yes,' she said, 'you've been such a long time. I was tired of staying in that dreary hotel. But I am sorry if you have wanted me, Will?'

'Well, I have had trouble to suit myself. When you see the airy and comfortable rooms heard of, you find they are stuffy and uncomfortable. Will you come and see if what I've fixed on will do? There is not much room, I am afraid; but I can light on nothing better. The town is rather full.'

The pair left the children and nurse to continue their ramble, and went back together.

In age well-balanced, in personal appearance fairly matched, and in domestic requirements conformable, in temper this couple differed, though even here they did not often clash, he being equable, if not lymphatic, and she decidedly nervous and sanguine. It was to their tastes and fancies, those smallest, greatest particulars, that no common denominator could be applied. Marchmill considered his wife's likes and inclinations somewhat silly; she considered his sordid and material. The husband's business was that of a gunmaker in a thriving city northwards, and his soul was in that business always; the lady was best characterised by that superannuated phrase of elegance 'a votary of the muse'. An impressionable, palpitating creature was Ella, shrinking humanely from detailed knowledge of her husband's trade whenever she reflected that everything he manufactured had for its purpose the destruction of life. She could only recover her equanimity by assuring herself that some, at least, of his weapons were sooner or later used for the extermination of horrid vermin and animals almost as cruel to their inferiors in species as human beings were to theirs.

She had never antecedently regarded this occupation of his as any objection to having him for a husband. Indeed, the necessity of getting life-leased at all cost, a cardinal virtue which all good mothers teach, kept her from thinking of it at all till she had closed with William, had passed the honeymoon, and reached the reflecting stage. Then, like a person who has stumbled upon some object in the dark, she wondered what she had got; mentally walked round it, estimated it; whether it were rare or common; contained gold, silver, or lead; were a clog or a pedestal, everything to her or nothing.

She came to some vague conclusions, and since then had kept her heart alive by pitying her proprietor's obtuseness and want of refinement, pitying herself, and letting off her delicate and ethereal emotions in imaginative occupations, day-dreams, and night-sighs, which perhaps would not much have disturbed William if he had known of them.

Her figure was small, elegant, and slight in build, tripping, or rather bounding, in movement. She was dark-eyed, and had that marvellously bright and liquid sparkle in each pupil which characterises persons of Ella's cast of soul, and is too often a cause of heartache to the possessor's male friends, ultimately sometimes to herself. Her husband was a tall, long-featured man, with a brown beard; he had a pondering regard; and was, it must be added, usually kind and tolerant to her. He spoke in squarely shaped sentences, and was supremely satisfied with a condition of sublunary things which made weapons a necessity.

Husband and wife walked till they had reached the house they were in search of, which stood in a terrace facing the sea, and was fronted by a small garden of wind-proof and salt-proof evergreens, stone steps leading up to the porch. It had its number in the row, but, being rather larger than the rest, was in addition sedulously distinguished as Coburg House by its landlady, though everybody else called it 'Thirteen, New Parade'. The spot was bright and lively now; but in winter it became necessary to place sandbags against the door, and to stuff up the keyhole against the wind and rain, which had worn the paint so thin that the priming and knotting showed through.

The householder, who bad been watching for the gentleman's return, met them in the passage, and showed the rooms. She informed them that she was a professional man's widow, left in needy circumstances by the rather sudden death of her husband, and she spoke anxiously of the conveniences of the establishment.

Mrs Marchmill said that she liked the situation and the house; but, it being small, there would not be accommodation enough, unless she could have all the rooms.

The landlady mused with an air of disappointment. She wanted the visitors to be her tenants very badly, she said, with obvious honesty. But unfortunately two of the rooms were occupied permanently by a bachelor gentleman. He did not pay season prices, it was true; but as he kept on his apartments all the year round, and was an extremely nice and interesting young man, who gave no trouble, she did not like to turn him out for a month's 'let', even at a high figure. 'Perhaps, however,' she added, 'he might offer to go for a time.'

They would not hear of this, and went back to the hotel, intending to proceed to the agent's to inquire further. Hardly had they sat down to tea when the landlady called. Her gentleman, she said, had been so obliging as to offer to give up his rooms for three or four weeks rather than drive the new-comers away.

'It is very kind, but we won't inconvenience him in that way,' said the Marchmills.

'O, it won't inconvenience him, I assure you!' said the landlady eloquently. 'You see, he's a different sort of young man from most— dreamy, solitary, rather melancholy—and he cares more to be here when the south-westerly gales are beating against the door, and the sea washes over the Parade, and there's not a soul in the place, than he does now in the season. He'd just as soon be where, in fact, he's going temporarily, to a little cottage on the Island opposite, for a change.' She hoped therefore that they would come.

The Marchmill family accordingly took possession of the house next day, and it seemed to suit them very well. After luncheon Mr Marchmill strolled out towards the pier, and Mrs Marchmill, having despatched the children to their outdoor amusements on the sands, settled herself in more completely, examining this and that article, and testing the reflecting powers of the mirror in the wardrobe door.

In the small back sitting-room, which had been the young bachelor's, she found furniture of a more personal nature than in the rest. Shabby books, of correct rather than rare editions, were piled up in a queerly reserved manner in corners, as if the previous occupant had not conceived the possibility that any incoming person of the season's bringing could care to look inside them. The landlady hovered on the threshold to rectify anything that Mrs Marchmill might not find to her satisfaction.

'I'll make this my own little room,' said the latter, 'because the books are here. By the way, the person who has left seems to have a good many. He won't mind my reading some of them, Mrs Hooper, I hope?'

'O dear no, ma'am. Yes, he has a good many. You see, he is in the literary line himself somewhat. He is a poet—yes, really a poet—and he has a little income of his own, which is enough to write verses on, but not enough for cutting a figure, even if he cared to.'

'A poet! O, I did not know that.'

Mrs Marchmill opened one of the books, and saw the owner's name written on the title-page. 'Dear me!' she continued; 'I know his name very well—Robert Trewe—of course I do; and his writings! And it is his rooms we have taken, and him we have turned out of his home?'

Ella Marchmill, sitting down alone a few minutes later, thought with interested surprise of Robert Trewe. Her own latter history will best explain that interest. Herself the only daughter of a struggling man of letters, she had during the last year or two taken to writing poems, in an endeavour to find a congenial channel in which to let flow her painfully embayed emotions, whose former limpidity and sparkle seemed departing in the stagnation caused by the routine of a practical household and the gloom of bearing children to a commonplace father. These poems, subscribed with a masculine pseudonym, had appeared in various obscure magazines, and in two cases in rather prominent ones. In the second of the latter the page which bore her effusion at the bottom, in smallish print, bore at the top, in large print, a few verses on the same subject by this very man, Robert Trewe. Both of them had, in fact, been struck by a tragic incident reported in the daily papers, and had used it simultaneously as an inspiration, the editor remarking in a note upon the coincidence, and that the excellence of both poems prompted him to give them together.

After that event Ella, otherwise 'John Ivy', had watched with much attention the appearance anywhere in print of verse bearing the signature of Robert Trewe, who, with a man's unsusceptibility on the question of sex, had never once thought of passing himself off as a woman. To be sure, Mrs Marchmill had satisfied herself with a sort of reason for doing the contrary in her case; that nobody might believe in her inspiration if they found that the sentiments came from a pushing tradesman's wife, from the mother of three children by a matter-of-fact small-arms manufacturer.

Trewe's verse contrasted with that of the rank and file of recent minor poets in being impassioned rather than ingenious, luxuriant rather than finished. Neither symboliste nor decadent, he was a pessimist in so far as that character applies to a man who looks at the worst contingencies as well as the best in the human condition. Being little attracted by excellences of form and rhythm apart from content, he sometimes, when feeling outran his artistic speed, perpetrated sonnets in the loosely rhymed Elizabethan fashion, which every right-minded reviewer said he ought not to have done.

With sad and hopeless envy, Ella Marchmill had often and often scanned the rival poet's work, so much stronger as it always was than her own feeble lines. She had imitated him, and her inability to touch his level would send her into fits of despondency. Months passed away thus, till she observed from the publishers' list that Trewe had collected his fugitive pieces into a volume, which was duly issued, and was much or little praised according to chance, and had a sale quite sufficient to pay for the printing.

This step onward had suggested to John Ivy the idea of collecting her pieces also, or at any rate of making up a book of her rhymes by adding many in manuscript to the few that had seen the light, for she had been able to get no great number into print. A ruinous charge was made for costs of publication; a few reviews noticed her poor little volume; but nobody talked of it, nobody bought it, and it fell dead in a fortnight—if it had ever been alive.

The author's thoughts were diverted to another groove just then by the discovery that she was going to have a third child, and the collapse of her poetical venture had perhaps less effect upon her mind than it might have done if she had been domestically unoccupied. Her husband had paid the publisher's bill with the doctor's, and there it all had ended for the time. But, though less than a poet of her century, Ella was more than a mere multiplier of her kind, and latterly she had begun to feel the old afflatus once more. And now by an odd conjunction she found herself in the rooms of Robert Trewe.

She thoughtfully rose from her chair and searched the apartment with the interest of a fellow-tradesman. Yes, the volume of his own verse was among the rest. Though quite familiar with its contents, she read it here as if it spoke aloud to her, then called up Mrs Hooper, the landlady, for some trivial service, and inquired again about the young man.

'Well, I'm sure you'd be interested in him, ma'am, if you could see him, only he's so shy that I don't suppose you will.' Mrs Hooper seemed nothing loth to minister to her tenant's curiosity about her predecessor. 'Lived here long? Yes, nearly two years. He keeps on his rooms even when he's not here: the soft air of this place suits his chest, and he likes to be able to come back at any time. He is mostly writing or reading, and doesn't see many people, though, for the matter of that, he is such a good, kind young fellow that folks would only be too glad to be friendly with him if they knew him. You don't meet kind-hearted people every day.'

'Ah, he's kind-hearted... and good.'

'Yes; he'll oblige me in anything if I ask him. "Mr Trewe," I say to him sometimes, "you are rather out of spirits." "Well, I am, Mrs Hooper," he'll say, "though I don't know how you should find it out." "Why not take a little change?" I ask. Then in a day or two he'll say that he will take a trip to Paris, or Norway, or somewhere; and I assure you he comes back all the better for it.'

'Ah, indeed! His is a sensitive nature, no doubt.'

'Yes. Still he's odd in some things. Once when he had finished a poem of his composition late at night he walked up and down the room rehearsing it; and the floors being so thin—jerry-built houses, you know, though I say it myself—he kept me awake up above him till I wished him further... But we get on very well.'

This was but the beginning of a series of conversations about the rising poet as the days went on. On one of these occasions Mrs Hooper drew Ella's attention to what she had not noticed before: minute scribblings in pencil on the wall-paper behind the curtains at the head of the bed.

'O! let me look,' said Mrs Marchmill, unable to conceal a rush of tender curiosity as she bent her pretty face close to the wall.

'These,' said Mrs Hooper, with the manner of a woman who knew things, 'are the very beginnings and first thoughts of his verses. He has tried to rub most of them out, but you can read them still. My belief is that he wakes up in the night, you know, with some rhyme in his head, and jots it down there on the wall lest he should forget it by the morning. Some of these very lines you see here I have seen afterwards in print in the magazines. Some are newer; indeed, I have not seen that one before. It must have been done only a few days ago.'

'O yes!...'

Ella Marchmill flushed without knowing why, and suddenly wished her companion would go away, now that the information was imparted. An indescribable consciousness of personal interest rather than literary made her anxious to read the inscription alone; and she accordingly waited till she could do so, with a sense that a great store of emotion would be enjoyed in the act.

Perhaps because the sea was choppy outside the Island, Ella's husband found it much pleasanter to go sailing and steaming about without his wife, who was a bad sailor, than with her. He did not disdain to go thus alone on board the steamboats of the cheap-trippers, where there was dancing by moonlight, and where the couples would come suddenly down with a lurch into each other's arms; for, as he blandly told her, the company was too mixed for him to take her amid such scenes. Thus, while this thriving manufacturer got a great deal of change and sea-air out of his sojourn here, the life, external at least, of Ella was monotonous enough, and mainly consisted in passing a certain number of hours each day in bathing and walking up and down a stretch of shore. But the poetic impulse having again waxed strong, she was possessed by an inner flame which left her hardly conscious of what was proceeding around her.

She had read till she knew by heart Trewe's last little volume of verses, and spent a great deal of time in vainly attempting to rival some

131

of them, till, in her failure, she burst into tears. The personal element in the magnetic attraction exercised by this circumambient, unapproachable master of hers was so much stronger than the intellectual and abstract that she could not understand it. To be sure, she was surrounded noon and night by his customary environment, which literally whispered of him to her at every moment; but he was a man she had never seen, and that all that moved her was the instinct to specialise a waiting emotion on the first fit thing that came to hand did not, of course, suggest itself to Ella.

In the natural way of passion under the too practical conditions which civilisation has devised for its fruition, her husband's love for her had not survived, except in the form of fitful friendship, any more than, or even so much as, her own for him; and, being a woman of very living ardours, that required sustenance of some sort, they were beginning to feed on this chancing material, which was, indeed, of a quality far better than chance usually offers.

One day the children had been playing hide-and-seek in a closet, whence, in their excitement, they pulled out some clothing. Mrs Hooper explained that it belonged to Mr Trewe, and hung it up in the closet again. Possessed of her fantasy, Ella went later in the afternoon, when nobody was in that part of the house, opened the closet, unhitched one of the articles, a mackintosh, and put it on, with the waterproof cap belonging to it.

'The mantle of Elijah!' she said. 'Would it might inspire me to rival him, glorious genius that he is!'

Her eyes always grew wet when she thought like that, and she turned to look at herself in the glass. His heart had beat inside that coat, and his brain had worked under that hat at levels of thought she would never reach. The consciousness of her weakness beside him made her feel quite sick. Before she had got the things off her the door opened, and her husband entered the room.

'What the devil—'

She blushed, and removed them.

'I found them in the closet here,' she said, 'and put them on in a freak. What have I else to do? You are always away!'

'Always away? Well...'

That evening she had a further talk with the landlady, who might herself have nourished a half-tender regard for the poet, so ready was she to discourse ardently about him.

'You are interested in Mr Trewe, I know, ma'am,' she said; 'and he has just sent to say that he is going to call to-morrow afternoon to look up some books of his that he wants, if I'll be in, and he may select them from your room?'

'O yes!'

'You could very well meet Mr Trewe then, if you'd like to be in the way!'

She promised with secret delight, and went to bed musing of him.

Next morning her husband observed: 'I've been thinking of what you said, Ell: that I have gone about a good deal and left you without much to amuse you. Perhaps it's true. To-day, as there's not much sea, I'll take you with me on board the yacht.'

For the first time in her experience of such an offer Ella was not glad. But she accepted it for the moment. The time for setting out drew near, and she went to get ready. She stood reflecting. The longing to see the poet she was now distinctly in love with overpowered all other considerations.

'I don't want to go,' she said to herself. 'I can't bear to be away! And I won't go.'

She told her husband that she had changed her mind about wishing to sail. He was indifferent, and went his way.

For the rest of the day the house was quiet, the children having gone out upon the sands. The blinds waved in the sunshine to the soft, steady stroke of the sea beyond the wall; and the notes of the Green Silesian band, a troop of foreign gentlemen hired for the season, had drawn almost all the residents and promenaders away from the vicinity of Coburg House. A knock was audible at the door.

Mrs Marchmill did not hear any servant go to answer it, and she became impatient. The books were in the room where she sat; but nobody came up. She rang the bell.

'There is some person waiting at the door,' she said.

'O no, ma'am! He's gone long ago. I answered it.'

Mrs Hooper came in herself.

'So disappointing!' she said. 'Mr Trewe not coming after all!'

'But I heard him knock, I fancy!'

'No; that was somebody inquiring for lodgings who came to the wrong house. I forgot to tell you that Mr Trewe sent a note just before lunch to say I needn't get any tea for him, as he should not require the books, and wouldn't come to select them.'

Ella was miserable, and for a long time could not even re-read his mournful ballad on 'Severed Lives', so aching was her erratic little heart, and so tearful her eyes. When the children came in with wet stockings, and ran up to her to tell her of their adventures, she could not feel that she cared about them half as much as usual.

'Mrs Hooper, have you a photograph of—the gentleman who lived here?' She was getting to be curiously shy in mentioning his name.

'Why, yes. It's in the ornamental frame on the mantelpiece in your own bedroom, ma'am.'

'No; the Royal Duke and Duchess are in that.'

'Yes, so they are; but he's behind them. He belongs rightly to that frame, which I bought on purpose; but as he went away he said: 'Cover me up from those strangers that are coming, for God's sake. I don't want them staring at me, and I am sure they won't want me staring at them.' So I slipped in the Duke and Duchess temporarily in front of him, as they had no frame, and Royalties are more suitable for letting furnished than a private young man. If you take 'em out you'll see him under. Lord, ma'am, he wouldn't mind if he knew it! He didn't think the next tenant would be such an attractive lady as you, or he wouldn't have thought of hiding himself; perhaps.'

'Is he handsome?' she asked timidly.

'I call him so. Some, perhaps, wouldn't.'

'Should I?' she asked, with eagerness.

'I think you would, though some would say he's more striking than handsome; a large-eyed thoughtful fellow, you know, with a very electric flash in his eye when he looks round quickly, such as you'd expect a poet to be who doesn't get his living by it.'

'How old is he?'

'Several years older than yourself, ma'am; about thirty-one or two, I think.'

Ella was, as a matter of fact, a few months over thirty herself; but she did not look nearly so much. Though so immature in nature, she was entering on that tract of life in which emotional women begin to suspect that last love may be stronger than first love; and she would soon, alas, enter on the still more melancholy tract when at least the vainer ones of her sex shrink from receiving a male visitor otherwise than with their backs to the window or the blinds half down. She reflected on Mrs Hooper's remark, and said no more about age.

Just then a telegram was brought up. It came from her husband, who had gone down the Channel as far as Budmouth with his friends in the yacht, and would not be able to get back till next day.

After her light dinner Ella idled about the shore with the children till dusk, thinking of the yet uncovered photograph in her room, with a serene sense of something ecstatic to come. For, with the subtle luxuriousness of fancy in which this young woman was an adept, on learning that her husband was to be absent that night she had refrained from incontinently rushing upstairs and opening the picture-frame, preferring to reserve the inspection till she could be alone, and a more romantic tinge be imparted to the occasion by silence, candles, solemn sea and stars outside, than was afforded by the garish afternoon sunlight.

The children had been sent to bed, and Ella soon followed, though it was not yet ten o'clock. To gratify her passionate curiosity she now made her preparations, first getting rid of superfluous garments and putting on her dressing-gown, then arranging a chair in front of the table and reading several pages of Trewe's tenderest utterances. Then she fetched the portrait-frame to the light, opened the back, took out the likeness, and set it up before her.

It was a striking countenance to look upon. The poet wore a luxuriant black moustache and imperial, and a slouched hat which shaded the forehead. The large dark eyes, described by the landlady, showed an unlimited capacity for misery; they looked out from beneath well-shaped brows as if they were reading the universe in the microcosm of the confronter's face, and were not altogether overjoyed at what the spectacle portended.

Ella murmured in her lowest, richest, tenderest tone: 'And it's you who've so cruelly eclipsed me these many times!'

As she gazed long at the portrait she fell into thought, till her eyes filled with tears, and she touched the cardboard with her lips. Then she laughed with a nervous lightness, and wiped her eyes.

She thought how wicked she was, a woman having a husband and three children, to let her mind stray to a stranger in this unconscionable manner. No, he was not a stranger! She knew his thoughts and feelings as well as she knew her own; they were, in fact, the self-same thoughts and feelings as hers, which her husband distinctly lacked; perhaps luckily for himself; considering that he had to provide for family expenses.

'He's nearer my real self, he's more intimate with the real me than Will is, after all, even though I've never seen him,' she said.

She laid his book and picture on the table at the bedside, and when she was reclining on the pillow she re-read those of Robert Trewe's verses which she had marked from time to time as most touching and true. Putting these aside, she set up the photograph on its edge upon the coverlet, and contemplated it as she lay. Then she scanned again by the light of the candle the half-obliterated pencillings on the wall-paper beside her head. There they were—phrases, couplets, bouts-rimes, beginnings and middles of lines, ideas in the rough, like Shelley's scraps, and the least of them so intense, so sweet, so palpitating, that it seemed as if his very breath, warm and loving, fanned her cheeks from those walls, walls that had surrounded his head times and times as they surrounded her own now. He must often have put up his hand so—with the pencil in it. Yes, the writing was sideways, as it would be if executed by one who extended his arm thus.

These inscribed shapes of the poet's world,

'Forms more real than living man,
Nurslings of immortality,'

were, no doubt, the thoughts and spirit-strivings which had come to him in the dead of night, when he could let himself go and have no fear of the frost of criticism. No doubt they had often been written up hastily by the light of the moon, the rays of the lamp, in the blue-grey dawn, in full daylight perhaps never. And now her hair was dragging where his arm had lain when he secured the fugitive fancies; she was sleeping on a poet's lips, immersed in the very essence of him, permeated by his spirit as by an ether.

While she was dreaming the minutes away thus, a footstep came upon the stairs, and in a moment she heard her husband's heavy step on the landing immediately without.

'Ell, where are you?'

What possessed her she could not have described, but, with an instinctive objection to let her husband know what she had been doing, she slipped the photograph under the pillow just as he flung open the door, with the air of a man who had dined not badly.

'O, I beg pardon,' said William Marchmill. 'Have you a headache? I am afraid I have disturbed you.'

'No, I've not got a headache,' said she. 'How is it you've come?'

'Well, we found we could get back in very good time after all, and I didn't want to make another day of it, because of going somewhere else to-morrow.'

'Shall I come down again?'

'O no. I'm as tired as a dog. I've had a good feed, and I shall turn in straight off. I want to get out at six o'clock to-morrow if I can... I shan't disturb you by my getting up; it will be long before you are awake.' And he came forward into the room.

While her eyes followed his movements, Ella softly pushed the photograph further out of sight.

'Sure you're not ill?' he asked, bending over her.

'No, only wicked!'

'Never mind that.' And he stooped and kissed her.

Next morning Marchmill was called at six o'clock; and in waking and yawning she heard him muttering to himself: 'What the deuce is this that's been crackling under me so?' Imagining her asleep he searched round him and withdrew something. Through her half-opened eyes she perceived it to be Mr Trewe.

'Well, I'm damned!' her husband exclaimed.

'What, dear?' said she.

'O, you are awake? Ha! ha!'

'What do you mean?'

'Some bloke's photograph——a friend of our landlady's, I suppose. I wonder how it came here; whisked off the table by accident perhaps when they were making the bed.'

'I was looking at it yesterday, and it must have dropped in then.'

'O, he's a friend of yours? Bless his picturesque heart!'

Ella's loyalty to the object of her admiration could not endure to hear him ridiculed. 'He's a clever man!' she said, with a tremor in her gentle voice which she herself felt to be absurdly uncalled for.

'He is a rising poet—the gentleman who occupied two of these rooms before we came, though I've never seen him.'

'How do you know, if you've never seen him?'

'Mrs Hooper told me when she showed me the photograph.'

'O; well, I must up and be off. I shall be home rather early. Sorry I can't take you to-day, dear. Mind the children don't go getting drowned.'

That day Mrs Marchmill inquired if Mr Trewe were likely to call at any other time.

'Yes,' said Mrs Hooper. 'He's coming this day week to stay with a friend near here till you leave. He'll be sure to call.'

Marchmill did return quite early in the afternoon; and, opening some letters which had arrived in his absence, declared suddenly that he and his family would have to leave a week earlier than they had expected to do—in short, in three days.

'Surely we can stay a week longer?' she pleaded. 'I like it here.'

'I don't. It is getting rather slow.'

'Then you might leave me and the children!'

'How perverse you are, Ell! What's the use? And have to come to fetch you! No: we'll all return together; and we'll make out our time in North Wales or Brighton a little later on. Besides, you've three days longer yet.'

It seemed to be her doom not to meet the man for whose rival talent she had a despairing admiration, and to whose person she was now absolutely attached. Yet she determined to make a last effort; and having gathered from her landlady that Trewe was living in a lonely spot not far from the fashionable town on the Island opposite, she crossed over in the packet from the neighbouring pier the following afternoon.

What a useless journey it was! Ella knew but vaguely where the house stood, and when she fancied she had found it, and ventured to inquire of a pedestrian if he lived there, the answer returned by the man was that he did not know. And if he did live there, how could she call upon him? Some women might have the assurance to do it, but she had not. How crazy he would think her. She might have asked him to call upon her, perhaps; but she had not the courage for that, either. She lingered mournfully about the picturesque seaside eminence till it was time to return to the town and enter the steamer for recrossing, reaching home for dinner without having been greatly missed.

At the last moment, unexpectedly enough, her husband said that he should have no objection to letting her and the children stay on till the end of the week, since she wished to do so, if she felt herself able to get home without him. She concealed the pleasure this extension of time gave her; and Marchmill went off the next morning alone.

But the week passed, and Trewe did not call.

On Saturday morning the remaining members of the Marchmill family departed from the place which had been productive of so much fervour in her. The dreary, dreary train; the sun shining in moted beams upon the hot cushions; the dusty permanent way; the mean rows of wire—these things were her accompaniment: while out of the window the deep blue sea-levels disappeared from her gaze, and with them her poet's home. Heavy-hearted, she tried to read, and wept instead.

Mr Marchmill was in a thriving way of business, and he and his family lived in a large new house, which stood in rather extensive grounds a few miles outside the city wherein he carried on his trade. Ella's life was lonely here, as the suburban life is apt to be, particularly at certain seasons; and she had ample time to indulge her taste for lyric and elegiac composition. She had hardly got back when she encountered a piece by Robert Trewe in the new number of her favourite magazine, which must have been written almost immediately before her visit to Solentsea, for it contained the very couplet she had seen pencilled on the wallpaper by the bed, and Mrs Hooper had declared to be recent. Ella could resist no longer, but seizing a pen impulsively, wrote to him as a brother-poet, using the name of John Ivy, congratulating him in her letter on his triumphant executions in metre and rhythm of thoughts that moved his soul, as compared with her own brow-beaten efforts in the same pathetic trade.

To this address there came a response in a few days, little as she had dared to hope for it—a civil and brief note, in which the young poet stated that, though he was not well acquainted with Mr Ivy's verse, he recalled the name as being one he had seen attached to some very promising pieces; that he was glad to gain Mr Ivy's acquaintance by letter, and should certainly look with much interest for his productions in the future.

There must have been something juvenile or timid in her own epistle, as one ostensibly coming from a man, she declared to herself; for Trewe quite adopted the tone of an elder and superior in this reply. But what did it matter? he had replied; he had written to her with his own hand from that very room she knew so well, for he was now back again in his quarters.

The correspondence thus begun was continued for two months or more, Ella Marchmill sending him from time to time some that she considered to be the best of her pieces, which he very kindly accepted, though he did not say he sedulously read them, nor did he send her any of his own in return. Ella would have been more hurt at this than she was if she had not known that Trewe laboured under the impression that she was one of his own sex.

Yet the situation was unsatisfactory. A flattering little voice told her that, were he only to see her, matters would be otherwise. No doubt she would have helped on this by making a frank confession of womanhood, to begin with, if something had not happened, to her delight, to render it unnecessary. A friend of her husband's, the editor of the most important newspaper in the city and county, who was dining with them one day, observed during their conversation about the poet that his (the editor's) brother the landscape-painter was a friend of Mr Trewe's, and that the two men were at that very moment in Wales together.

Ella was slightly acquainted with the editor's brother. The next morning down she sat and wrote, inviting him to stay at her house for a short time on his way back, and requesting him to bring with him, if practicable, his companion Mr Trewe, whose acquaintance she was anxious to make. The answer arrived after some few days. Her correspondent and his friend Trewe would have much satisfaction in accepting her invitation on their way southward, which would be on such and such a day in the following week.

Ella was blithe and buoyant. Her scheme had succeeded; her beloved though as yet unseen one was coming. 'Behold, he standeth behind our wall; he looked forth at the windows, showing himself through the lattice,' she thought ecstatically. 'And, lo, the winter is past, the rain is over and gone, the flowers appear on the earth, the time of the singing of birds is come, and the voice of the turtle is heard in our land.'

But it was necessary to consider the details of lodging and feeding him. This she did most solicitously, and awaited the pregnant day and hour.

It was about five in the afternoon when she heard a ring at the door and the editor's brother's voice in the hall. Poetess as she was, or as she thought herself, she had not been too sublime that day to dress with infinite trouble in a fashionable robe of rich material, having a faint resemblance to the chiton of the Greeks, a style just then in vogue among ladies of an artistic and romantic turn, which had been obtained by Ella of her Bond Street dressmaker when she was last in London. Her visitor entered the drawing-room. She looked towards his rear; nobody else came through the door. Where, in the name of the God of Love, was Robert Trewe?

'O, I'm sorry,' said the painter, after their introductory words had been spoken. 'Trewe is a curious fellow, you know, Mrs Marchmill. He said he'd come; then he said he couldn't. He's rather dusty. We've been doing a few miles with knapsacks, you know; and he wanted to get on home.'

'He—he's not coming?'

'He's not; and he asked me to make his apologies.'

'When did you p-p-part from him?' she asked, her nether lip starting off quivering so much that it was like a tremolo-stop opened in her speech. She longed to run away from this dreadful bore and cry her eyes out.

'Just now, in the turnpike road yonder there.'

'What! he has actually gone past my gates?'

'Yes. When we got to them—handsome gates they are, too, the finest bit of modern wrought-iron work I have seen—when we came to them we stopped, talking there a little while, and then he wished me good-bye and went on. The truth is, he's a little bit depressed just now, and doesn't want to see anybody. He's a very good fellow, and a warm friend, but a little uncertain and gloomy sometimes; he thinks too much of things. His poetry is rather too erotic and passionate, you know, for some tastes; and he has just come in for a terrible slating from the ——— Review that was published yesterday; he saw a copy of it at the station by accident. Perhaps you've read it?'

'No.'

'So much the better. O, it is not worth thinking of; just one of those articles written to order, to please the narrow-minded set of subscribers upon whom the circulation depends. But he's upset by it. He says it is the misrepresentation that hurts him so; that, though he can stand a fair attack, he can't stand lies that he's powerless to refute and stop from spreading. That's just Trewe's weak point. He lives so much by himself that these things affect him much more than they would if he were in the bustle of fashionable or commercial life. So he wouldn't come here, making the excuse that it all looked so new and monied—if you'll pardon–'

'But—he must have known—there was sympathy here! Has he never said anything about getting letters from this address?'

'Yes, yes, he has, from John Ivy—perhaps a relative of yours, he thought, visiting here at the time?'

'Did he—like Ivy, did he say?'

'Well, I don't know that he took any great interest in Ivy.'

'Or in his poems?'

'Or in his poems—so far as I know, that is.'

Robert Trewe took no interest in her house, in her poems, or in their writer. As soon as she could get away she went into the nursery and tried to let off her emotion by unnecessarily kissing the children, till she had a sudden sense of disgust at being reminded how plain-looking they were, like their father.

The obtuse and single-minded landscape-painter never once perceived from her conversation that it was only Trewe she wanted, and not himself. He made the best of his visit, seeming to enjoy the society of Ella's husband, who also took a great fancy to him, and showed him everywhere about the neighbourhood, neither of them noticing Ella's mood.

The painter had been gone only a day or two when, while sitting upstairs alone one morning, she glanced over the London paper just arrived, and read the following paragraph:—

'SUICIDE OF A POET

'Mr Robert Trewe, who has been favourably known for some years as one of our rising lyrists, committed suicide at his lodgings at Solentsea on Saturday evening last by shooting himself in the right temple with a revolver. Readers hardly need to be reminded that Mr Trewe has recently attracted the attention of a much wider public than had hitherto known him, by his new volume of verse, mostly of an impassioned kind, entitled 'Lyrics to a Woman Unknown', which has been already favourably noticed in these pages for the extraordinary gamut of feeling it traverses, and which has been made the subject of a severe, if not ferocious, criticism in the —— Review. It is supposed, though not certainly known, that the article may have partially conduced to the sad act, as a copy of the review in question was found on his writing-table; and he has been observed to be in a somewhat depressed state of mind since the critique appeared.'

Then came the report of the inquest, at which the following letter was read, it having been addressed to a friend at a distance:—

'Dear ——,
Before these lines reach your hands I shall be delivered from the inconveniences of seeing, hearing, and knowing more of the things around me. I will not trouble you by giving my reasons for the step I have taken, though I can assure you they were sound and logical. Perhaps had I been blessed with a mother, or a sister, or a female friend of another sort tenderly devoted to me, I might have thought it worthwhile to continue my present existence. I have long dreamt of such an unattainable creature, as you know, and she, this undiscoverable, elusive one, inspired my last volume; the imaginary woman alone, for, in spite of what has been said in some quarters, there is no real woman behind the title. She has continued to the last unrevealed, unmet, unwon. I think it desirable to mention this in order that no blame may attach to any real woman as having been the cause of my decease by cruel or cavalier treatment of me. Tell my landlady that I am sorry to have caused her this

unpleasantness; but my occupancy of the rooms will soon be forgotten. There are ample funds in my name at the bank to pay all expenses.

R. Trewe.'

Ella sat for a while as if stunned, then rushed into the adjoining chamber and flung herself upon her face on the bed.

Her grief and distraction shook her to pieces; and she lay in this frenzy of sorrow for more than an hour. Broken words came every now and then from her quivering lips: 'O, if he had only known of me—known of me—me! ...O, if I had only once met him—only once; and put my hand upon his hot forehead—kissed him—let him know how I loved him—that I would have suffered shame and scorn, would have lived and died, for him! Perhaps it would have saved his dear life! ...But no—it was not allowed! God is a jealous God; and that happiness was not for him and me!'

All possibilities were over; the meeting was stultified. Yet it was almost visible to her in her fantasy even now, though it could never be substantiated—

'The hour which might have been, yet might not be,
Which man's and woman's heart conceived and bore,
Yet whereof life was barren.'

She wrote to the landlady at Solentsea in the third person, in as subdued a style as she could command, enclosing a postal order for a sovereign, and informing Mrs Hooper that Mrs Marchmill had seen in the papers the sad account of the poet's death, and having been, as Mrs Hooper was aware, much interested in Mr Trewe during her stay at Coburg House, she would be obliged if Mrs Hooper could obtain a small portion of his hair before his coffin was closed down, and send it her as a memorial of him, as also the photograph that was in the frame.

By the return-post a letter arrived containing what had been requested. Ella wept over the portrait and secured it in her private drawer; the lock of hair she tied with white ribbon and put in her bosom, whence she drew it and kissed it every now and then in some unobserved nook.

'What's the matter?' said her husband, looking up from his newspaper on one of these occasions. 'Crying over something? A lock of hair? Whose is it?'

'He's dead!' she murmured.

'Who?'

'I don't want to tell you, Will, just now, unless you insist!' she said, a sob hanging heavy in her voice.

'O, all right.'

'Do you mind my refusing? I will tell you some day.'

'It doesn't matter in the least, of course.'

He walked away whistling a few bars of no tune in particular; and when he had got down to his factory in the city the subject came into Marchmill's head again.

He, too, was aware that a suicide had taken place recently at the house they had occupied at Solentsea. Having seen the volume of poems in his wife's hand of late, and heard fragments of the landlady's conversation about Trewe when they were her tenants, he all at once said to himself; 'Why of course it's he! How the devil did she get to know him? What sly animals women are!'

Then he placidly dismissed the matter, and went on with his daily affairs. By this time Ella at home had come to a determination. Mrs Hooper, in sending the hair and photograph, had informed her of the day of the funeral; and as the morning and noon wore on an overpowering wish to know where they were laying him took possession of the sympathetic woman. Caring very little now what her husband or anyone else might think of her eccentricities; she wrote Marchmill a brief note, stating that she was called away for the afternoon and evening, but would return on the following morning. This she left on his desk, and having given the same information to the servants, went out of the house on foot.

When Mr Marchmill reached home early in the afternoon the servants looked anxious. The nurse took him privately aside, and hinted that her mistress's sadness during the past few days had been such that she feared she had gone out to drown herself. Marchmill reflected. Upon the whole he thought that she had not done that. Without saying whither he was bound he also started off, telling them not to sit up for him. He drove to the railway-station, and took a ticket for Solentsea.

It was dark when he reached the place, though he had come by a fast train, and he knew that if his wife had preceded him thither it could only have been by a slower train, arriving not a great while before his own. The season at Solentsea was now past: the parade was gloomy, and the flys were few and cheap. He asked the way to the Cemetery, and soon reached it. The gate was locked, but the keeper let him in, declaring, however, that there was nobody within the precincts. Although it was not late, the autumnal darkness had now become intense; and he found some difficulty in keeping to the serpentine path which led to the quarter where, as the man had told him, the one or two interments for the day had taken place. He stepped upon the grass, and, stumbling over some pegs, stooped now and then to discern if possible a figure against the sky.

He could see none; but lighting on a spot where the soil was trodden, beheld a crouching object beside a newly made grave. She heard him, and sprang up.

'Ell, how silly this is!' he said indignantly. 'Running away from home—I never heard such a thing! Of course I am not jealous of this unfortunate man; but it is too ridiculous that you, a married woman with three children and a fourth coming, should go losing your head like this over a dead lover! ...Do you know you were locked in? You might not have been able to get out all night.'

She did not answer.

'I hope it didn't go far between you and him, for your own sake.'

'Don't insult me, Will.'

'Mind, I won't have any more of this sort of thing; do you hear?'

'Very well,' she said.

He drew her arm within his own, and conducted her out of the Cemetery. It was impossible to get back that night; and not wishing to be recognised in their present sorry condition, he took her to a miserable little coffee-house close to the station, whence they departed early in the morning, travelling almost without speaking, under the sense that it was one of those dreary situations occurring in married life which words could not mend, and reaching their own door at noon.

The months passed, and neither of the twain ever ventured to start a conversation upon this episode. Ella seemed to be only too frequently in a sad and listless mood, which might almost have been

146

called pining. The time was approaching when she would have to undergo the stress of childbirth for a fourth time, and that apparently did not tend to raise her spirits.

'I don't think I shall get over it this time!' she said one day.

'Pooh! what childish foreboding! Why shouldn't it be as well now as ever?'

She shook her head. 'I feel almost sure I am going to die; and I should be glad, if it were not for Nelly, and Frank, and Tiny.'

'And me!'

'You'll soon find somebody to fill my place,' she murmured, with a sad smile. 'And you'll have a perfect right to; I assure you of that.'

'Ell, you are not thinking still about that—poetical friend of yours?'

She neither admitted nor denied the charge. 'I am not going to get over my illness this time,' she reiterated. 'Something tells me I shan't.'

This view of things was rather a bad beginning, as it usually is; and, in fact, six weeks later, in the month of May, she was lying in her room, pulseless and bloodless, with hardly strength enough left to follow up one feeble breath with another, the infant for whose unnecessary life she was slowly parting with her own being fat and well. Just before her death she spoke to Marchmill softly:—

'Will, I want to confess to you the entire circumstances of that—about you know what—that time we visited Solentsea. I can't tell what possessed me—how I could forget you so, my husband! But I had got into a morbid state: I thought you had been unkind; that you had neglected me; that you weren't up to my intellectual level, while he was, and far above it. I wanted a fuller appreciator, perhaps, rather than another lover–'

She could get no further then for very exhaustion; and she went off in sudden collapse a few hours later, without having said anything more to her husband on the subject of her love for the poet. William Marchmill, in truth, like most husbands of several years' standing, was little disturbed by retrospective jealousies, and had not shown the least anxiety to press her for confessions concerning a man dead and gone beyond any power of inconveniencing him more.

147

But when she had been buried a couple of years it chanced one day that, in turning over some forgotten papers that he wished to destroy before his second wife entered the house, he lighted on a lock of hair in an envelope, with the photograph of the deceased poet, a date being written on the back in his late wife's hand. It was that of the time they spent at Solentsea.

Marchmill looked long and musingly at the hair and portrait, for something struck him. Fetching the little boy who had been the death of his mother, now a noisy toddler, he took him on his knee, held the lock of hair against the child's head, and set up the photograph on the table behind, so that he could closely compare the features each countenance presented. There were undoubtedly strong traces of resemblance; the dreamy and peculiar expression of the poet's face sat, as the transmitted idea, upon the child's, and the hair was of the same hue.

'I'm damned if I didn't think so!' murmured Marchmill. 'Then she did play me false with that fellow at the lodgings! Let me see: the dates—the second week in August... the third week in May... Yes... yes... Get away, you poor little brat! You are nothing to me!'

Thomas Hardy (1840–1928) was born in Stinsford, Dorset, and became one of the great literary figures of the Victorian period, writing such acclaimed novels as Tess of the d'Urbervilles *(1891) and* Jude the Obscure *(1895) as well as numerous short stories, many of which were set in the partly fictionalised region of Wessex in southwest England. 'An Imaginative Woman', written in 1894 and added to the 1896 edition of* Wessex Tales, *was among his later short stories. Hardy's own experience of married life, to Emma Lavinia Gifford, was not happy: they married in 1874 but later became estranged. Emma's death in 1912 had a profound effect upon Hardy and prompted him to express his remorse in poetry rather than prose. He did, however, marry again, to his secretary Florence Emily Dugdale, in 1914 and they remained together until his death.*

Two of Them

J.M. Barrie

She is a very pretty girl, though that counts for nothing with either of us, and her frock is yellow and brown, with pins here and there. Some of these pins are nearly a foot long, and when they are not in use she keeps them in her hat, through which she stabs them far down into her brain. This makes me shudder; but, so is she constructed that it does not seem to hurt, and in that human pin-cushion the daggers remain until it is time for her to put on her jacket again. Her size is six-and-a-quarter, and she can also get into sixes.

She comes here occasionally (always looking as if she had been born afresh that morning) to sit in the big chair and discuss what sort of girl she is, with other matters of moment. When she suddenly flings herself forward—clasping her hands on her knee—and says 'Oh!' I know that she has remembered something which must out at once or endanger her health; and whether it be 'I don't believe in anybody or anything—there!' or 'Why do we die so soon?' or 'I buy chocolate drops by the half pound', I am expected to regard it, for the time being, as one of the biggest things of the day. I allow her, but no other, to mend my fire; and some of her most profound thoughts have come to her with a jerk while holding the poker. However, she is not always serious, for, though her face is often so wistful that to be within a yard of it is too close for safety, she sometimes jests gleefully, clapping her hands; but I never laugh, rather continue smoking hard; and this she (very properly) puts down to my lack of humour. The reason we get on so well is because I treat her exactly as if she were a man, as per agreement. Ours is a platonic friendship, or, at least, was, for she went off half-an-hour ago with her head in the air.

THE BARGAIN

After only one glance in the mirror, she had spread herself out in the big chair, which seems to me to put its arms round her. Then this jumped out:

'And I had thought you so trustworthy!' (She always begins in the middle.)

'What have I done?' I asked, though I knew.

'Yesterday,' she said; 'when you put me into that cab. Oh, you didn't do it, but you tried to.'

'Do what?'

She screwed her mouth, whereupon I smoked hard, lest I should attempt to do it again. But she would have an answer.

'Men are all alike,' she said, indignantly.

'And you actually think,' I broke out, bitterly, 'that if I did meditate such an act (for one brief moment), I was yielding to the wretched impulses to which other men give way! Miss Gunnings, do you know me no better than that?'

'I don't see what you mean,' she replied. (Her directness is sometimes a little annoying.)

I wagged my head mournfully, and there ensued a pause, for I did not quite know what I meant myself.

'What do you mean!' she asked, more gently, my face showing her that I was deeply hurt—not angry, but hurt.

I laid my pipe on the mantelpiece, and speaking very sadly, proved to her that I had nothing in common with other young men, though I forget now how I proved it. If I seemed to act as they did my motives were quite different, and therefore I should be judged from another standpoint. Also I looked upon her as a child, while I felt very old. (There are six years between us.)

'And now,' said I, with emotion, 'as you still think that I tried to—to do it from the wretched, ordinary motive (namely, because I wanted to) I suppose you and I must part. I have explained the affair to you because it is painful to me to be misunderstood. Good-by, I shall always think of you with sincere regard.'

Despite an apparent effort to control it, my voice broke. Then she gave way. She put her hand into mine, and with tears in her eyes, asked me to forgive her, which I did.

This little incident it was that showed her how different I am from other men, and led to the drawing up of our platonic agreement, which we signed, so to speak, that afternoon over the poker. I promised to be to her such a friend as I am to Mr Thomson; I even undertook, if necessary, to scold her though she cried (as she hinted she should probably do), and she was to see that it was for her good, just as Thomson sees it when I scold him.

A NECESSARY CONSEQUENCE

'I shall have to call you "Mary".'

'I don't see that.'

'Yes, it is customary among real friends. They expect it of each other.'

I was not looking her in the face, so cannot tell how she took this at first. However, after she had eaten a chocolate drop in silence, she said 'But you don't call Mr Thomson by his Christian name?'

'Certainly I do.'

'And he would feel slighted if you did not?'

'He would be extremely pained.'

'What is his Christian name?'

'Thomson's Christian name? Oh, his Christian name. Thomson's Christian name is—ah—Harry.'

'But I thought his initials were J. T.? Those are the initials on that umbrella you never returned to him.'

'Is that so! Then my suspicions were correct, the umbrella is not his own. How like him!'

'I had an idea that you merely called him Thomson?'

'Before other people only. Men friends address each other in one way in company, but in quite another way when they are alone.'

'Oh, well, if it is customary.'

'If it were not I would not propose such a thing.'

Another chocolate drop, and then, 'Mary, dear–'

'*Dear!*'

'That is what I said.'

'I don't think it worthy of you. It is taking two chocolate drops

151

when I only said you could have one.'

'Well, when I get my hand into the bag I admit—I—I mean Thomson would have not been so niggardly.'

'I am certain you don't call him "Harry, dear"'

'Not, perhaps, as a rule, but at times men friends are more demonstrative than you think them. For instance, if Thom—I mean Harry—was ill–'

'But I am quite well.'

'Still, with all this influenza about–'

HER BACK

She had put her jacket on the table, her chocolate drops on the mantelpiece, her gloves on the couch. Indeed, the room was full of her, and I was holding her scarf, just as I hold Thomson's.

'I walked down Regent Street behind you yesterday,' I said, sternly, 'and your back told me that you were vain.'

'I am not vain of my personal appearance, at any rate.'

'How could you be?'

She looked at me sharply, but my face was without expression, and she sighed. She remembered that I had no humour.

'Whatever my faults are, and they are many, vanity is not one of them.'

'When I said you had a bad temper you made the same remark about it. Also when–'

'That was last week, stupid! But, of course, if you think me *ugly*–'

'I did not say that.'

'Yes, you did.'

'But if you think nothing of your personal appearance, why blame me if I agree with you!'

She rose haughtily.

'Sit down.'

'I won't. Give me my scarf.' Her eyes were flashing. She has all sorts of eyes.

'If you really want to know what I think of your personal

appearance–'

'I don't.'

I resumed my pipe.

'Well?' she said.

'Well?'

'Oh, I thought you were going to say something.'

'Only that your back pleased me in certain other respects.'

She let the chair take her back into its embrace.

'Mary, dear!'

It is a fact that she was crying. After I had made a remark or two:

'I am so glad you think me pretty,' she said, frankly, 'for though I don't think so myself, I like other people to think it, and somehow I thought you considered me *plain*. My nose is all wrong, isn't it?'

'Let me see.'

'So you admit you were entirely mistaken in calling me vain?'

'You have proved that I was.'

However, after she had drawn the daggers out of her head and put them into the scarf (or whatever part of a lady's dress it is that is worked with daggers), and when the door had closed on her, she opened it and hurriedly fired these shots at me:

'Yes, I am horridly vain—I do my hair every night before I go to bed—I was sure you admired me the very first time we met—I *know* I have a pretty nose—good-afternoon.'

HER SELFISHNESS

She was making spills for me, because those Thomson made for me had run down.

'Mary.'

'Well?'

'Mary, dear!'

'I am listening.'

'That is all.'

'You have such a curious, *wasteful* habit of saying one's name as if it was a remark by itself.'

'Yes, Thomson has noticed that also. However, I think I meant to

153

add that it is very good of you to make those spills. I wonder if you would do something else for me?'

'As a friend?'

'Yes. I want you to fill my pipe, and ram down the tobacco with your little finger.'

'You and Mr Thomson do that for each other?'

'Often.'

'Very well; give it me. This way?'

'It smokes beautifully. You are a dear, good girl.'

She let the poker fall.

'Oh, I'm not,' she wailed. 'I am not *really* kindhearted; it is all selfishness.'

This came out with a rush, but I am used to her, and kept my pipe in.

'Even my charities are only a hideous kind of selfishness,' she continued, with clasped hands. 'There is that poor man who sells matchboxes at the corner of this street, for instance. I sometimes give him twopence.' (She carries an enormous purse, but there is never more than twopence in it.)

'That is surely not selfish,' I said.

'It is,' said she, seizing the poker as if intending to do for herself that instant. 'I never give him anything simply because I see he needs it, but only occasionally when I feel happier than usual. I am only thinking of my own happiness when I give it him. That is the personification of selfishness.'

'Mary!'

'Well, if that isn't, this is. I only give him something when I am passing him, at any rate. I never dream of crossing the street on purpose to do it. Oh, I should need to be terrifically happy before I would bother crossing to give him anything. There! what do you think of me now?'

'You gave him something on Monday when I was with you?'

'Yes.'

'Then you were happy at that time?'

'What has that got to do with it?'

'A great deal.'

I rose.

'Mary, dear—'

'No! Go and sit over there.'

STAGGERERS

The subjects we have discussed over the poker! For instance:

The rapidity with which we grow old.

What on earth Mr Meredith means by saying that woman will be the last thing civilised by man?

Thomson.

What will it all matter a hundred years hence?

How strangely unlike other people we two are!

The nicest name for a woman. (Mary.)

The mystery of Being and not Being.

Why does Mary exist?

Does Mary exist?

She had come in, looking very doleful, and the reason was, that the more she thought it over, the less could she see why she existed. This came of reading a work entitled 'Why Do We Exist?'—a kind of book that ought not to be published, for it only makes people unhappy. Mary stared at the problem with wide, fixed eyes until I compelled her to wink by putting another in front of it, namely, 'Do You Exist?' In her ignorance she thought there was no doubt of this, but I lent her a 'Bishop Berkeley', and since then she has taken to pinching herself on the sly, just to make sure that she is still there.

HER SCARF

So far I had not (as will have been noticed) by a word or look or sign broken the agreement which rendered our platonic friendship possible. I had not even called her darling, and this because, having reflected a good deal on the subject, I could not persuade myself that this was one of my ways of addressing Thomson. And I would have continued the same treatment had it not been for her scarf, which has proved beyond all bearing. That scarf is entirely responsible for what happened to-day.

It is a stripe of faded terra-cotta, and she ties it round her mouth

155

before going out into the fog. Her face is then sufficiently irritating, but I could endure it by looking another way, did she not recklessly make farewell remarks through the scarf, which is very thin. Then her mouth— in short, I can't put up with this. I had warned her repeatedly. But she was like a mad girl, or, perhaps, she did not understand my meaning.

'Don't come near me with that thing round your mouth,' I have told her a dozen times. I have refused firmly to tie it for her. I have put the table between me and it, and she asked why (through the scarf). She was quite mad.

And to-day, when I was feeling rather strange at any rate! It all occurred in a moment.

'Don't attempt to speak with that scarf round you,' I had said, and said it with my back to her.

'You think I can't, because it is too tight?' she asked.

'Go away,' I said.

She turned me round.

'Why,' she said, wonderingly, 'it is quite loose. I believe I could whistle through it.'

She did whistle through it. That finished our platonic friendship.

FIVE MINUTES AFTERWARD

I spoke wildly, fiercely, exultingly; and she, all the time, was trying to put on her jacket, and could not find the sleeve.

'It was your own fault; but I am glad. I warned you. Cry away. I like to see you crying.'

'I hate you!'

'No, you don't.'

'A friend–'

'Friend! Pooh! Bah! Pshaw!'

'Mr Thomson–'

'Thomson! Tehut! Thomson! His Christian name isn't Harry. I don't know what it is. I don't care!'

'You said–'

'It was a lie. Don't screw your mouth in that way.'

'I will, if I like.'

'I warn you!'

'I don't care. Oh! Oh!'

'I warned you.'

'Now I know you in your true colours.'

'You do, and I glory in it. Platonic friendship—fudge! I quarrelled with you that time to be able to hold your hands when we made it up. When you thought I was reading your character I- Don't—screw—your—mouth!'

'Give me my scarf.'

'I lent you Berkeley so that I could take hold of you by the shoulders on the pretence that I was finding out whether you existed.'

'Good-by *forever*!'

'All the time we were discussing the mystery of Being I was thinking how much I should like to put my hands beneath your chin and flick it.'

'If you ever dare to speak to me again–'

'Don't—screw—your—mouth. And I would rather put my fingers through your hair than write the greatest poem in–'

She was gone, leaving the scarf behind her.

My heart sank. I flung open my window (six hansoms came immediately), and I could have jumped after her. But I did not. What I saw had a remarkable effect on my spirits. *I saw her cross the street on purpose* to give twopence to the old man who sells the matches.

All's well with the world. As soon as I can lay down the scarf I am going west to the house where Mary, dear, lives.

James Matthew Barrie (1860–1937) was born in Kirriemuir, Angus, in Scotland, and is remembered chiefly today for the classic children's story Peter Pan, *although he also wrote a number of other successful plays, novels and short stories. Barrie's personal life has long been a subject of speculation, focusing in particular upon his obsessive relationship with the children of Arthur Llewellyn Davies. Barrie himself claimed, after the death of the children's widowed mother, that he and Mrs Llewellyn Davies had been engaged to be married. His own marriage to the actress Mary Ansell ended in divorce after he discovered that she had had an affair.*

Amy Foster
Joseph Conrad

Kennedy is a country doctor, and lives in Colebrook, on the shores of Eastbay. The high ground rising abruptly behind the red roofs of the little town crowds the quaint High Street against the wall which defends it from the sea. Beyond the sea-wall there curves for miles in a vast and regular sweep the barren beach of shingle, with the village of Brenzett standing out darkly across the water, a spire in a clump of trees; and still further out the perpendicular column of a lighthouse, looking in the distance no bigger than a lead pencil, marks the vanishing-point of the land. The country at the back of Brenzett is low and flat, but the bay is fairly well sheltered from the seas, and occasionally a big ship, windbound or through stress of weather, makes use of the anchoring ground a mile and a half due north from you as you stand at the back door of the 'Ship Inn' in Brenzett. A dilapidated windmill near by lifting its shattered arms from a mound no loftier than a rubbish heap, and a Martello tower squatting at the water's edge half a mile to the south of the Coastguard cottages, are familiar to the skippers of small craft. These are the official seamarks for the patch of trustworthy bottom represented on the Admiralty charts by an irregular oval of dots enclosing several figures six, with a tiny anchor engraved among them, and the legend 'mud and shells' over all.

The brow of the upland overtops the square tower of the Colebrook Church. The slope is green and looped by a white road. Ascending along this road, you open a valley broad and shallow, a wide green trough of pastures and hedges merging inland into a vista of purple tints and flowing lines closing the view.

In this valley down to Brenzett and Colebrook and up to Darnford, the market town fourteen miles away, lies the practice of my friend Kennedy. He had begun life as surgeon in the Navy, and afterwards had been the companion of a famous traveller, in the days when there were continents with unexplored interiors. His papers on the fauna and flora made him known to scientific societies. And now he had come to a country practice—from choice. The penetrating power of his mind, acting like a corrosive fluid, had destroyed his ambition, I fancy. His intelligence is of a scientific order, of an investigating habit, and of that unappeasable curiosity which believes that there is a particle of a general truth in every mystery.

A good many years ago now, on my return from abroad, he invited me to stay with him. I came readily enough, and as he could not neglect his patients to keep me company, he took me on his rounds— thirty miles or so of an afternoon, sometimes. I waited for him on the roads; the horse reached after the leafy twigs, and, sitting in the dogcart, I could hear Kennedy's laugh through the half-open door left open of some cottage. He had a big, hearty laugh that would have fitted a man twice his size, a brisk manner, a bronzed face, and a pair of grey, profoundly attentive eyes. He had the talent of making people talk to him freely, and an inexhaustible patience in listening to their tales.

One day, as we trotted out of a large village into a shady bit of road, I saw on our left hand a low, black cottage, with diamond panes in the windows, a creeper on the end wall, a roof of shingle, and some roses climbing on the rickety trellis-work of the tiny porch. Kennedy pulled up to a walk. A woman, in full sunlight, was throwing a dripping blanket over a line stretched between two old apple-trees. And as the bobtailed, long-necked chestnut, trying to get his head, jerked the left hand, covered by a thick dog-skin glove, the doctor raised his voice over the hedge: 'How's your child, Amy?'

I had the time to see her dull face, red, not with a mantling blush, but as if her flat cheeks had been vigorously slapped, and to take in the squat figure, the scanty, dusty brown hair drawn into a tight knot at the back of the head. She looked quite young. With a distinct catch in her breath, her voice sounded low and timid.

'He's well, thank you.'

We trotted again. 'A young patient of yours,' I said; and the doctor, flicking the chestnut absently, muttered, 'Her husband used to be.'

'She seems a dull creature,' I remarked listlessly.

'Precisely,' said Kennedy. 'She is very passive. It's enough to look at the red hands hanging at the end of those short arms, at those slow, prominent brown eyes, to know the inertness of her mind—an inertness that one would think made it everlastingly safe from all the surprises of imagination. And yet which of us is safe? At any rate, such as you see her, she had enough imagination to fall in love. She's the daughter of one Isaac Foster, who from a small farmer has sunk into a shepherd; the beginning of his misfortunes dating from his runaway marriage with the cook of his widowed father—a well-to-do, apoplectic grazier, who passionately struck his name off his will, and had been heard to utter threats against his life. But this old affair, scandalous enough to serve as a motive for a Greek tragedy, arose from the similarity of their characters. There are other tragedies, less scandalous and of a subtler poignancy, arising from irreconcilable differences and from that fear of the Incomprehensible that hangs over all our heads— over all our heads...'

The tired chestnut dropped into a walk; and the rim of the sun, all red in a speckless sky, touched familiarly the smooth top of a ploughed rise near the road as I had seen it times innumerable touch the distant horizon of the sea. The uniform brownness of the harrowed field glowed with a rosy tinge, as though the powdered clods had sweated out in minute pearls of blood the toil of uncounted ploughmen. From the edge of a copse a waggon with two horses was rolling gently along the ridge. Raised above our heads upon the sky-line, it loomed up against the red sun, triumphantly big, enormous, like a chariot of giants drawn by two slow-stepping steeds of legendary proportions. And the clumsy figure of the man plodding at the head of the leading horse projected itself on the background of the Infinite with a heroic uncouthness. The end of his carter's whip quivered high up in the blue. Kennedy discoursed.

'She's the eldest of a large family. At the age of fifteen they put her out to service at the New Barns Farm. I attended Mrs Smith, the tenant's wife, and saw that girl there for the first time. Mrs Smith, a genteel person with a sharp nose, made her put on a black dress every afternoon. I don't know what induced me to notice her at all. There are faces that call your attention by a curious want of definiteness in their whole aspect, as, walking in a mist, you peer attentively at a vague shape which, after all, may be nothing more curious or strange than a signpost. The only peculiarity I perceived in her was a slight hesitation in her utterance, a sort of preliminary stammer which passes away with the first word. When sharply spoken to, she was apt to lose her head at once; but her heart was of the kindest. She had never been heard to express a dislike for a single human being, and she was tender to every living creature. She was devoted to Mrs Smith, to Mr Smith, to their dogs, cats, canaries; and as to Mrs Smith's grey parrot, its peculiarities exercised upon her a positive fascination. Nevertheless, when that outlandish bird, attacked by the cat, shrieked for help in human accents, she ran out into the yard stopping her ears, and did not prevent the crime. For Mrs Smith this was another evidence of her stupidity; on the other hand, her want of charm, in view of Smith's well-known frivolousness, was a great recommendation. Her short-sighted eyes would swim with pity for a poor mouse in a trap, and she had been seen once by some boys on her knees in the wet grass helping a toad in difficulties. If it's true, as some German fellow has said, that without phosphorus there is no thought, it is still more true that there is no kindness of heart without a certain amount of imagination. She had some. She had even more than is necessary to understand suffering and to be moved by pity. She fell in love under circumstances that leave no room for doubt in the matter; for you need imagination to form a notion of beauty at all, and still more to discover your ideal in an unfamiliar shape.

'How this aptitude came to her, what it did feed upon, is an inscrutable mystery. She was born in the village, and had never been further away from it than Colebrook or perhaps Darnford. She lived for four years with the Smiths. New Barns is an isolated farmhouse a mile away from the road, and she was content to look day after day at the same fields, hollows, rises; at the trees and the hedgerows; at the faces of the four men about the farm, always the same—day after day, month after month, year after year. She never showed a desire for conversation, and, as it seemed to me, she did not know how to smile. Sometimes of a fine Sunday afternoon she would put on her best dress, a pair of stout boots, a large grey hat trimmed with a black feather (I've seen her in that finery), seize an absurdly slender parasol, climb over two stiles, tramp over three fields and along two hundred yards of road—never further. There stood Foster's cottage. She would help her mother to give their tea to the younger children, wash up the crockery, kiss the little ones, and go back to the farm. That was all. All the rest, all the change, all the relaxation. She never seemed to wish for anything more. And then she fell in love. She fell in love silently, obstinately—perhaps helplessly. It came slowly, but when it came it worked like a powerful spell; it was love as the Ancients understood it: an irresistible and fateful impulse—a possession! Yes, it was in her to become haunted and possessed by a face, by a presence, fatally, as though she had been a pagan worshipper of form under a joyous sky—and to be awakened at last from that mysterious forgetfulness of self, from that enchantment, from that transport, by a fear resembling the unaccountable terror of a brute...'

With the sun hanging low on its western limit, the expanse of the grass-lands framed in the counter-scarps of the rising ground took on a gorgeous and sombre aspect. A sense of penetrating sadness, like that inspired by a grave strain of music, disengaged itself from the silence of the fields. The men we met walked past slow, unsmiling, with downcast eyes, as if the melancholy of an over-burdened earth had weighted their feet, bowed their shoulders, borne down their glances.

'Yes,' said the doctor to my remark, 'one would think the earth is under a curse, since of all her children these that cling to her the closest are uncouth in body and as leaden of gait as if their very hearts were loaded with chains. But here on this same road you might have seen amongst these heavy men a being lithe, supple, and long-limbed, straight like a pine with something striving upwards in his appearance as though the heart within him had been buoyant. Perhaps it was only the force of the contrast, but when he was passing one of these villagers here, the soles of his feet did not seem to me to touch the dust of the road. He vaulted over the stiles, paced these slopes with a long elastic stride that made him noticeable at a great distance, and had lustrous black eyes. He was so different from the mankind around that, with his freedom of movement, his soft—a little startled, glance, his olive complexion and graceful bearing, his humanity suggested to me the nature of a woodland creature. He came from there.'

The doctor pointed with his whip, and from the summit of the descent seen over the rolling tops of the trees in a park by the side of the road, appeared the level sea far below us, like the floor of an immense edifice inlaid with bands of dark ripple, with still trails of glitter, ending in a belt of glassy water at the foot of the sky. The light blur of smoke, from an invisible steamer, faded on the great clearness of the horizon like the mist of a breath on a mirror; and, inshore, the white sails of a coaster,

162

with the appearance of disentangling themselves slowly from under the branches, floated clear of the foliage of the trees.

'Shipwrecked in the bay?' I said.

'Yes; he was a castaway. A poor emigrant from Central Europe bound to America and washed ashore here in a storm. And for him, who knew nothing of the earth, England was an undiscovered country. It was some time before he learned its name; and for all I know he might have expected to find wild beasts or wild men here, when, crawling in the dark over the sea-wall, he rolled down the other side into a dyke, where it was another miracle he didn't get drowned. But he struggled instinctively like an animal under a net, and this blind struggle threw him out into a field. He must have been, indeed, of a tougher fibre than he looked to withstand without expiring such buffetings, the violence of his exertions, and so much fear. Later on, in his broken English that resembled curiously the speech of a young child, he told me himself that he put his trust in God, believing he was no longer in this world. And truly—he would add—how was he to know? He fought his way against the rain and the gale on all fours, and crawled at last among some sheep huddled close under the lee of a hedge. They ran off in all directions, bleating in the darkness, and he welcomed the first familiar sound he heard on these shores. It must have been two in the morning then. And this is all we know of the manner of his landing, though he did not arrive unattended by any means. Only his grisly company did not begin to come ashore till much later in the day...'

The doctor gathered the reins, clicked his tongue; we trotted down the hill. Then turning, almost directly, a sharp corner into the High Street, we rattled over the stones and were home.

Late in the evening Kennedy, breaking a spell of moodiness that had come over him, returned to the story. Smoking his pipe, he paced the long room from end to end. A reading-lamp concentrated all its light upon the papers on his desk; and, sitting by the open window, I saw, after the windless, scorching day, the frigid splendour of a hazy sea lying motionless under the moon. Not a whisper, not a splash, not a stir of the shingle, not a footstep, not a sigh came up from the earth below—never a sign of life but the scent of climbing jasmine; and Kennedy's voice, speaking behind me, passed through the wide casement, to vanish outside in a chill and sumptuous stillness.

'...The relations of shipwrecks in the olden time tell us of much suffering. Often the castaways were only saved from drowning to die miserably from starvation on a barren coast; others suffered violent death or else slavery, passing through years of precarious existence with people to whom their strangeness was an object of suspicion, dislike or fear. We read about these things, and they are very pitiful. It is indeed hard upon a man to find himself a lost stranger, helpless, incomprehensible, and of a mysterious origin, in some obscure corner of the earth. Yet amongst all the adventurers shipwrecked in all the wild parts of the world there is not one, it seems to me, that ever had to suffer a fate so simply tragic as the man I am speaking of, the most innocent of adventurers cast out by the sea in the bight of this bay, almost within sight from this very window.

'He did not know the name of his ship. Indeed, in the course of time we discovered he did not even know that ships had names—'like Christian people'; and when, one day, from the top of the Talfourd Hill, he beheld the sea lying open to his view, his eyes roamed afar, lost in an air of wild surprise, as though he had never seen such a sight before. And probably he had not. As far as I could make out, he had been hustled together with many others on board an emigrant-ship lying at the mouth of the Elbe, too bewildered to take note of his surroundings, too weary to see anything, too anxious to care. They were driven below into the 'tweendeck and battened down from the very start. It was a low timber dwelling—he would say—with wooden beams overhead, like the houses in his country, but you went into it down a ladder. It was very large, very cold, damp and sombre, with places in the manner of wooden boxes where people had to sleep, one above another, and it kept on rocking all ways at once all the time. He crept into one of these boxes and laid down there in the clothes in which he had left his home many days before, keeping his bundle and his stick by his side. People groaned, children cried, water dripped, the lights went out, the walls of the place creaked, and everything was being shaken so that in one's little box one dared not lift one's head. He had lost touch with his only companion (a young man from the same valley, he said), and all the time a great noise of wind went on outside and heavy blows fell—boom! boom! An awful sickness overcame him, even to the point of making him neglect his prayers. Besides, one could not tell whether it was morning or evening. It seemed always to be night in that place.

'Before that he had been travelling a long, long time on the iron track. He looked out of the window, which had a wonderfully clear glass in it, and the trees, the houses, the fields, and the long roads seemed to fly round and round about him till his head swam. He gave me to understand that he had on his passage beheld uncounted multitudes of people—whole nations—all dressed in such clothes as the rich wear. Once he was made to get out of the carriage, and slept through a night on a bench in a house of bricks with his bundle under his head; and once for many hours he had to sit on a floor of flat stones dozing, with his knees up and with his bundle between his feet. There was a roof over him, which seemed made of glass, and was so high that the tallest mountain-pine he had ever seen would have had room to grow under it. Steam-machines rolled in at one end and out at the other. People swarmed more than you can see on a feast-day round the miraculous Holy Image in the yard of the Carmelite Convent down in the plains where, before he left his home, he drove his mother in a wooden cart—a pious old woman who wanted to offer prayers and make a vow for his safety. He could not give me an idea of how large and lofty and full of noise and smoke and gloom, and clang of iron, the place was, but someone had told him it was called Berlin. Then they rang a bell, and another steam-machine came in, and again he was taken on and on through a land that wearied his eyes by its flatness without a single bit of a hill to be seen anywhere. One more night he spent shut up in a building like a good stable with a litter of straw on the floor, guarding his bundle amongst a lot of men, of whom not one could understand a single word he said. In the morning they were all led down to the stony shores of an extremely broad muddy river, flowing not between hills but between houses that seemed immense. There was a steam-machine that went on the water, and they all stood upon it packed tight, only now there were with them many women and children who made much noise. A cold rain fell, the wind blew in his face; he was wet through, and his teeth chattered. He and the young man from the same valley took each other by the hand.

'They thought they were being taken to America straight away, but suddenly the steam-machine bumped against the side of a thing like a house on the water. The walls were smooth and black, and there uprose, growing from the roof as it were, bare trees in the shape of crosses, extremely high. That's how it appeared to him then, for he had never seen a ship before. This was the ship that was going to swim all the way to America. Voices shouted, everything swayed; there was a ladder dipping up and down. He went up on his hands and knees in mortal fear of falling into the water below, which made a great splashing. He got separated from his companion, and when he descended into the bottom of that ship his heart seemed to melt suddenly within him.

'It was then also, as he told me, that he lost contact for good and all with one of those three men who the summer before had been going about through all the little towns in the foothills of his country. They would arrive on market days driving in a peasant's cart, and would set up an office in an inn or some other Jew's house. There were three of them, of whom one with a long beard looked venerable; and they had red cloth collars round their necks and gold lace on their sleeves like Government officials. They sat proudly behind a long table; and in the next room, so that the common people shouldn't hear, they kept a cunning telegraph machine, through which they could talk to the Emperor of America. The fathers hung about the door, but the young men of the mountains would crowd up to the table asking many questions, for there was work to be got all the year round at three dollars a day in America, and no military service to do.

'But the American Kaiser would not take everybody. Oh, no! He himself had a great difficulty in getting accepted, and the venerable man in uniform had to go out of the room several times to work the telegraph on his behalf. The American Kaiser engaged him at last at three dollars, he being young and strong. However, many able young men backed out, afraid of the great distance; besides, those only who had some money could be taken. There were some who sold their huts and their land because it cost a lot of money to get to America; but then, once there, you had three dollars a day, and if you were clever you could find places where true gold could be picked up on the ground. His father's house was getting over full. Two of his brothers were married and had children. He promised to send money home from America by post twice a year. His father sold an old cow, a pair of piebald mountain ponies of his own raising, and a cleared plot of fair pasture land on the sunny slope of a pine-clad pass to a Jew inn-keeper in order to pay the people of the ship that took men to America to get rich in a short time.

'He must have been a real adventurer at heart, for how many of the greatest enterprises in the conquest of the earth had for their beginning just such a bargaining away of the paternal cow for the mirage or true gold far away! I have been telling you more or less in my own words what I learned fragmentarily in the course of two or three years, during which I seldom missed an opportunity of a friendly chat with him. He told me this story of his adventure with many flashes of white teeth and lively glances of black eyes, at first in a sort of anxious baby-talk, then, as he acquired the language, with great fluency, but always with that singing, soft, and at the same time vibrating intonation that instilled a strangely penetrating power into the sound of the most familiar English words, as if they had been the words of an unearthly language. And he always would come to an end, with many emphatic shakes of his head, upon that awful sensation of his heart melting within him directly he set foot on board that ship. Afterwards there seemed to come for him a period of blank ignorance, at any rate as to facts. No doubt he must have been abominably sea-sick and abominably unhappy—this soft and passionate adventurer, taken thus out of his knowledge, and feeling bitterly as he lay in his emigrant bunk his utter loneliness; for his was a highly sensitive nature. The next thing we know of him for certain is that he had been hiding in Hammond's pig-pound by the side of the road to Norton six miles, as the crow flies, from the sea. Of these experiences he was unwilling to speak: they seemed to have seared into his soul a sombre sort of wonder and indignation. Through the rumours of the country-side, which lasted for a good many days after his arrival, we know that the fishermen of West Colebrook had been disturbed and startled by heavy knocks against the walls of weatherboard cottages, and by a voice crying piercingly strange words in the night. Several of them turned out even, but, no doubt, he had fled in sudden alarm at their rough angry tones hailing each other in the darkness. A sort of frenzy must have helped him up the steep Norton hill. It was he, no doubt, who early the following morning had been seen lying (in a swoon, I should say) on the roadside grass by the Brenzett carrier, who actually got down to have a nearer look, but drew back, intimidated by the perfect immobility, and by something queer in the aspect of that tramp, sleeping so still under the showers. As the day advanced, some children came dashing into school at Norton in such a fright that the schoolmistress went out and spoke indignantly to a "horrid-looking man" on the road. He edged away, hanging his head, for a few steps, and then suddenly ran off with extraordinary fleetness. The driver of Mr Bradley's milk-cart made no secret of it that he had lashed with his whip at a hairy sort of gipsy fellow who, jumping up at a turn of the road by the Vents, made a snatch at the pony's bridle. And he caught him a good one too, right over the face, he said, that made him drop down in the mud a jolly sight quicker than he had jumped up; but it was a good half-a-mile before he could stop the pony. Maybe that in his desperate endeavours to get help, and in his need to get in touch with someone, the poor devil had tried to stop the cart. Also three boys confessed afterwards to throwing stones at a funny tramp, knocking about all wet and muddy, and, it seemed, very drunk, in the narrow deep lane by the limekilns. All this was the talk of three villages for days; but we have Mrs Finn's (the wife of Smith's waggoner) unimpeachable testimony that she saw him get over the low wall of Hammond's pig-pound and lurch straight at her, babbling aloud in a voice that was enough to make one die of fright. Having the baby with her in a perambulator, Mrs Finn called out to him to go away, and as he persisted in coming nearer, she hit him courageously with her umbrella over the head and, without once looking back, ran like the wind with the perambulator as far as the first house in the village. She stopped then, out of breath, and spoke to old Lewis, hammering there at a heap of stones; and the old chap, taking off his immense black wire goggles, got up on his shaky legs to look where she pointed. Together they followed with their eyes the figure of the man running over a field; they saw him fall down, pick himself up, and run on again, staggering and waving his long arms above his head, in the direction of the New Barns Farm. From that moment he is plainly in the toils of his obscure and touching destiny. There is no doubt after this of what happened to him. All is certain now: Mrs Smith's intense terror; Amy Foster's stolid conviction held against the other's nervous attack, that the man 'meant no harm'; Smith's exasperation (on his return from Darnford Market) at finding the dog barking himself into a fit, the back-door locked, his wife in hysterics; and all for an unfortunate dirty tramp, supposed to be even then lurking in his stackyard. Was he? He would teach him to frighten women.

'Smith is notoriously hot-tempered, but the sight of some nondescript and miry creature sitting cross-legged amongst a lot of loose straw, and swinging itself to and fro like a bear in a cage, made him pause. Then this tramp stood up silently before him, one mass of mud and filth from head to foot. Smith, alone amongst his stacks with this apparition, in the stormy twilight ringing with the infuriated barking of the dog, felt the dread of an inexplicable strangeness. But when that being, parting with his black hands the long matted locks that hung before his face, as you part the two halves of a curtain, looked out at him with glistening, wild, black-and-white eyes, the weirdness of this silent encounter fairly staggered him. He had admitted since (for the story has been a legitimate subject of conversation about here for years) that he made more than one step backwards. Then a sudden burst of rapid, senseless speech persuaded him at once that he had to do with an escaped lunatic. In fact, that impression never wore off completely. Smith has not in his heart given up his secret conviction of the man's essential insanity to this very day.

'As the creature approached him, jabbering in a most discomposing manner, Smith (unaware that he was being addressed as 'gracious lord', and adjured in God's name to afford food and shelter) kept on speaking firmly but gently to it, and retreating all the time into the other yard. At last, watching his chance, by a sudden charge he bundled him headlong into the wood-lodge, and instantly shot the bolt. Thereupon he wiped his brow, though the day was cold. He had done his duty to the community by shutting up a wandering and probably dangerous maniac. Smith isn't a hard man at all, but he had room in his brain only for that one idea of lunacy. He was not imaginative enough to ask himself whether the man might not be perishing with cold and hunger. Meantime, at first, the maniac made a great deal of noise in the lodge. Mrs Smith was screaming upstairs, where she had locked herself in her bedroom; but Amy Foster sobbed piteously at the kitchen door, wringing her hands and muttering, 'Don't! don't!' I daresay Smith had a rough time of it that evening with one noise and another, and this insane, disturbing voice crying obstinately through the door only added to his irritation. He couldn't possibly have connected this troublesome lunatic with the sinking of a ship in Eastbay, of which there had been a rumour in the Darnford marketplace. And I daresay the man inside had been very near to insanity on that night. Before his excitement collapsed and he became unconscious he was throwing himself violently about in the dark, rolling on some dirty sacks, and biting his fists with rage, cold, hunger, amazement, and despair.

'He was a mountaineer of the eastern range of the Carpathians, and the vessel sunk the night before in Eastbay was the Hamburg emigrant-ship *Herzogin Sophia-Dorothea*, of appalling memory.

'A few months later we could read in the papers the accounts of the bogus "Emigration Agencies" among the Sclavonian peasantry in the more remote provinces of Austria. The object of these scoundrels was to get hold of the poor ignorant people's homesteads, and they were in league with the local usurers. They exported their victims through Hamburg mostly. As to the ship, I had watched her out of this very window, reaching close-hauled under short canvas into the bay on a dark, threatening afternoon. She came to an anchor, correctly by the chart, off the Brenzett Coastguard station. I remember before the night fell looking out again at the outlines of her spars and rigging that stood out dark and pointed on a background of ragged, slaty clouds like another and a slighter spire to the left of the Brenzett church-tower. In the evening the wind rose. At midnight I could hear in my bed the terrific gusts and the sounds of a driving deluge.

'About that time the Coastguardmen thought they saw the lights of a steamer over the anchoring-ground. In a moment they vanished; but it is clear that another vessel of some sort had tried for shelter in the bay on that awful, blind night, had rammed the German ship amidships (a breach—as one of the divers told me afterwards—'that you could sail a Thames barge through'), and then had gone out either scathless or damaged, who shall say; but had gone out, unknown, unseen, and fatal, to perish mysteriously at sea. Of her nothing ever came to light, and yet the hue and cry that was raised all over the world would have found her out if she had been in existence anywhere on the face of the waters.

'A completeness without a clue, and a stealthy silence as of a neatly executed crime, characterise this murderous disaster, which, as you may remember, had its gruesome celebrity. The wind would have prevented the loudest outcries from reaching the shore; there had been evidently no time for signals of distress. It was death without any sort of fuss. The Hamburg ship, filling all at once, capsized as she sank, and at daylight there was not even the end of a spar to be seen above water. She was missed, of course, and at first the Coastguardmen surmised that she had either dragged her anchor or parted her cable some time during the night, and had been blown out to sea. Then, after the tide turned, the wreck must have shifted a little and released some of the bodies, because a child—a little fair-haired child in a red frock—came ashore abreast of the Martello tower. By the afternoon you could see along three miles of beach dark figures with bare legs dashing in and out of the tumbling foam, and rough-looking men, women with hard faces, children, mostly fair-haired, were being carried, stiff and dripping, on stretchers, on wattles, on ladders, in a long procession past the door of the 'Ship Inn', to be laid out in a row under the north wall of the Brenzett Church.

'Officially, the body of the little girl in the red frock is the first thing that came ashore from that ship. But I have patients amongst the seafaring population of West Colebrook, and, unofficially, I am informed that very early that morning two brothers, who went down to look after their cobble hauled up on the beach, found, a good way from Brenzett, an ordinary ship's hencoop lying high and dry on the shore, with eleven drowned ducks inside. Their families ate the birds, and the hencoop was split into firewood with a hatchet. It is possible that a man (supposing he happened to be on deck at the time of the accident) might have floated ashore on that hencoop. He might. I admit it is improbable, but there was the man—and for days, nay, for weeks—it didn't enter our heads that we had amongst us the only living soul that had escaped from that disaster. The man himself, even when he learned to speak intelligibly, could tell us very little. He remembered he had felt better (after the ship had anchored, I suppose), and that the darkness, the wind, and the rain took his breath away. This looks as if he had been on deck some time during that night. But we mustn't forget he had been taken out of his knowledge, that he had been sea-sick and battened down below for four days, that he had no general notion of a ship or of the sea, and therefore could have no definite idea of what was happening to him. The rain, the wind, the darkness he knew; he understood the bleating of the sheep, and he remembered the pain of his wretchedness and misery, his heartbroken astonishment that it was neither seen nor understood, his dismay at finding all the men angry and all the women fierce. He had approached them as a beggar, it is true, he said; but in his country, even if they gave nothing, they spoke gently to beggars. The children in his country were not taught to throw stones at those who asked for compassion. Smith's strategy overcame him completely. The wood-lodge presented the horrible aspect of a dungeon. What would be done to him next?... No wonder that Amy Foster appeared to his eyes with the aureole of an angel of light. The girl had not been able to sleep for thinking of the poor man, and in the morning, before the Smiths were up, she slipped out across the back yard. Holding the door of the wood-lodge ajar, she looked in and extended to him half a loaf of white bread—'such bread as the rich eat in my country,' he used to say.

'At this he got up slowly from amongst all sorts of rubbish, stiff, hungry, trembling, miserable, and doubtful. "Can you eat this?" she asked in her soft and timid voice. He must have taken her for a "gracious lady". He devoured ferociously, and tears were falling on the crust. Suddenly he dropped the bread, seized her wrist, and imprinted a kiss on her hand. She was not frightened. Through his forlorn condition she had observed that he was good-looking. She shut the door and walked back slowly to the kitchen. Much later on, she told Mrs Smith, who shuddered at the bare idea of being touched by that creature.

'Through this act of impulsive pity he was brought back again within the pale of human relations with his new surroundings. He never forgot it—never.

'That very same morning old Mr Swaffer (Smith's nearest neighbour) came over to give his advice, and ended by carrying him off. He stood, unsteady on his legs, meek, and caked over in half-dried mud, while the two men talked around him in an incomprehensible tongue. Mrs Smith had refused to come downstairs till the madman was off the premises; Amy Foster, far from within the dark kitchen, watched through the open back door; and he obeyed the signs that were made to him to the best of his ability. But Smith was full of mistrust. 'Mind, sir! It may be all his cunning,' he cried repeatedly in a tone of warning. When Mr Swaffer started the mare, the deplorable being sitting humbly by his side, through weakness, nearly fell out over the back of the high two-wheeled cart. Swaffer took him straight home. And it is then that I come upon the scene.

'I was called in by the simple process of the old man beckoning to me with his forefinger over the gate of his house as I happened to be driving past. I got down, of course.

'"I've got something here," he mumbled, leading the way to an outhouse at a little distance from his other farm-buildings.

172

'It was there that I saw him first, in a long low room taken upon the space of that sort of coach-house. It was bare and whitewashed, with a small square aperture glazed with one cracked, dusty pane at its further end. He was lying on his back upon a straw pallet; they had given him a couple of horse-blankets, and he seemed to have spent the remainder of his strength in the exertion of cleaning himself. He was almost speechless; his quick breathing under the blankets pulled up to his chin, his glittering, restless black eyes reminded me of a wild bird caught in a snare. While I was examining him, old Swaffer stood silently by the door, passing the tips of his fingers along his shaven upper lip. I gave some directions, promised to send a bottle of medicine, and naturally made some inquiries.

'"Smith caught him in the stackyard at New Barns," said the old chap in his deliberate, unmoved manner, and as if the other had been indeed a sort of wild animal. "That's how I came by him. Quite a curiosity, isn't he? Now tell me, doctor—you've been all over the world—don't you think that's a bit of a Hindoo we've got hold of here."

'I was greatly surprised. His long black hair scattered over the straw bolster contrasted with the olive pallor of his face. It occurred to me he might be a Basque. It didn't necessarily follow that he should understand Spanish; but I tried him with the few words I know, and also with some French. The whispered sounds I caught by bending my ear to his lips puzzled me utterly. That afternoon the young ladies from the Rectory (one of them read Goethe with a dictionary, and the other had struggled with Dante for years), coming to see Miss Swaffer, tried their German and Italian on him from the doorway. They retreated, just the least bit scared by the flood of passionate speech which, turning on his pallet, he let out at them. They admitted that the sound was pleasant, soft, musical—but, in conjunction with his looks perhaps, it was startling—so excitable, so utterly unlike anything one had ever heard. The village boys climbed up the bank to have a peep through the little square aperture. Everybody was wondering what Mr Swaffer would do with him.

'He simply kept him.

'Swaffer would be called eccentric were he not so much respected. They will tell you that Mr Swaffer sits up as late as ten o'clock at night to read books, and they will tell you also that he can write a cheque for two hundred pounds without thinking twice about it.

He himself would tell you that the Swaffers had owned land between this and Darnford for these three hundred years. He must be eighty-five to-day, but he does not look a bit older than when I first came here. He is a great breeder of sheep, and deals extensively in cattle. He attends market days for miles around in every sort of weather, and drives sitting bowed low over the reins, his lank grey hair curling over the collar of his warm coat, and with a green plaid rug round his legs. The calmness of advanced age gives a solemnity to his manner. He is clean-shaved; his lips are thin and sensitive; something rigid and monarchal in the set of his features lends a certain elevation to the character of his face. He has been known to drive miles in the rain to see a new kind of rose in somebody's garden, or a monstrous cabbage grown by a cottager. He loves to hear tell of or to be shown something that he calls 'outlandish'. Perhaps it was just that outlandishness of the man which influenced old Swaffer. Perhaps it was only an inexplicable caprice. All I know is that at the end of three weeks I caught sight of Smith's lunatic digging in Swaffer's kitchen garden. They had found out he could use a spade. He dug barefooted.

'His black hair flowed over his shoulders. I suppose it was Swaffer who had given him the striped old cotton shirt; but he wore still the national brown cloth trousers (in which he had been washed ashore) fitting to the leg almost like tights; was belted with a broad leathern belt studded with little brass discs; and had never yet ventured into the village. The land he looked upon seemed to him kept neatly, like the grounds round a landowner's house; the size of the cart-horses struck him with astonishment; the roads resembled garden walks, and the aspect of the people, especially on Sundays, spoke of opulence. He wondered what made them so hardhearted and their children so bold. He got his food at the back door, carried it in both hands carefully to his outhouse, and, sitting alone on his pallet, would make the sign of the cross before he began. Beside the same pallet, kneeling in the early darkness of the short days, he recited aloud the Lord's Prayer before he slept. Whenever he saw old Swaffer he would bow with veneration from the waist, and stand erect while the old man, with his fingers over his upper lip, surveyed him silently. He bowed also to Miss Swaffer, who kept house frugally for her father—a broad-shouldered, big-boned woman of forty-five, with the pocket of her dress full of keys, and a grey, steady eye. She was Church—as people said (while her father was one of the trustees of the Baptist Chapel)—and wore a little steel cross at her waist. She dressed severely in black, in memory of one of the innumerable Bradleys of the neighbourhood, to whom she had been engaged some twenty-five years ago—a young farmer who broke his neck out hunting on the eve of the wedding day. She had the unmoved countenance of the deaf, spoke very seldom, and her lips, thin like her father's, astonished one sometimes by a mysteriously ironic curl.

'These were the people to whom he owed allegiance, and an overwhelming loneliness seemed to fall from the leaden sky of that winter without sunshine. All the faces were sad. He could talk to no one, and had no hope of ever understanding anybody. It was as if these had been the faces of people from the other world—dead people—he used to tell me years afterwards. Upon my word, I wonder he did not go mad. He didn't know where he was. Somewhere very far from his mountains—somewhere over the water. Was this America, he wondered?

'If it hadn't been for the steel cross at Miss Swaffer's belt he would not, he confessed, have known whether he was in a Christian country at all. He used to cast stealthy glances at it, and feel comforted. There was nothing here the same as in his country! The earth and the water were different; there were no images of the Redeemer by the roadside. The very grass was different, and the trees. All the trees but the three old Norway pines on the bit of lawn before Swaffer's house, and these reminded him of his country. He had been detected once, after dusk, with his forehead against the trunk of one of them, sobbing, and talking to himself. They had been like brothers to him at that time, he affirmed. Everything else was strange. Conceive you the kind of an existence overshadowed, oppressed, by the everyday material appearances, as if by the visions of a nightmare. At night, when he could not sleep, he kept on thinking of the girl who gave him the first piece of bread he had eaten in this foreign land. She had been neither fierce nor angry, nor frightened. Her face he remembered as the only comprehensible face amongst all these faces that were as closed, as mysterious, and as mute as the faces of the dead who are possessed of a knowledge beyond the comprehension of the living. I wonder whether the memory of her compassion prevented him from cutting his throat. But there! I suppose I am an old sentimentalist, and forget the instinctive love of life which it takes all the strength of an uncommon despair to overcome.

'He did the work which was given him with an intelligence which surprised old Swaffer. By-and-by it was discovered that he could help at the ploughing, could milk the cows, feed the bullocks in the cattle-yard, and was of some use with the sheep. He began to pick up words, too, very fast; and suddenly, one fine morning in spring, he rescued from an untimely death a grand-child of old Swaffer.

'Swaffer's younger daughter is married to Willcox, a solicitor and the Town Clerk of Colebrook. Regularly twice a year they come to stay with the old man for a few days. Their only child, a little girl not three years old at the time, ran out of the house alone in her little white pinafore, and, toddling across the grass of a terraced garden, pitched herself over a low wall head first into the horse-pond in the yard below.

'Our man was out with the waggoner and the plough in the field nearest to the house, and as he was leading the team round to begin a fresh furrow, he saw, through the gap of the gate, what for anybody else would have been a mere flutter of something white. But he had straight-glancing, quick, far-reaching eyes, that only seemed to flinch and lose their amazing power before the immensity of the sea. He was barefooted, and looking as outlandish as the heart of Swaffer could desire. Leaving the horses on the turn, to the inexpressible disgust of the waggoner he bounded off, going over the ploughed ground in long leaps, and suddenly appeared before the mother, thrust the child into her arms, and strode away.

'The pond was not very deep; but still, if he had not had such good eyes, the child would have perished—miserably suffocated in the foot or so of sticky mud at the bottom. Old Swaffer walked out slowly into the field, waited till the plough came over to his side, had a good look at him, and without saying a word went back to the house. But from that time they laid out his meals on the kitchen table; and at first, Miss Swaffer, all in black and with an inscrutable face, would come and stand in the doorway of the living-room to see him make a big sign of the cross before he fell to. I believe that from that day, too, Swaffer began to pay him regular wages.

'I can't follow step by step his development. He cut his hair short, was seen in the village and along the road going to and fro to his work like any other man. Children ceased to shout after him. He became aware of social differences, but remained for a long time surprised at the bare poverty of the churches among so much wealth. He couldn't understand either why they were kept shut up on week days. There was nothing to steal in them. Was it to keep people from praying too often? The rectory took much notice of him about that time, and I believe the young ladies attempted to prepare the ground for his conversion. They could not, however, break him of his habit of crossing himself, but he went so far as to take off the string with a couple of brass medals the size of a sixpence, a tiny metal cross, and a square sort of scapulary which he wore round his neck. He hung them on the wall by the side of his bed, and he was still to be heard every evening reciting the Lord's Prayer, in incomprehensible words and in a slow, fervent tone, as he had heard his old father do at the head of all the kneeling family, big and little, on every evening of his life. And though he wore corduroys at work, and a slop-made pepper-and-salt suit on Sundays, strangers would turn round to look after him on the road. His foreignness had a peculiar and indelible stamp. At last people became used to see him. But they never became used to him. His rapid, skimming walk; his swarthy complexion; his hat cocked on the left ear; his habit, on warm evenings, of wearing his coat over one shoulder, like a hussar's dolman; his manner of leaping over the stiles, not as a feat of agility, but in the ordinary course of progression—all these peculiarities were, as one may say, so many causes of scorn and offence to the inhabitants of the village. *They* wouldn't in their dinner hour lie flat on their backs on the grass to stare at the sky. Neither did they go about the fields screaming dismal tunes. Many times have I heard his high-pitched voice from behind the ridge of some sloping sheep-walk, a voice light and soaring, like a lark's, but with a melancholy human note, over our fields that hear only the song of birds. And I should be startled myself. Ah! He was different: innocent of heart, and full of good will, which nobody wanted, this castaway, that, like a man transplanted into another planet, was separated by an immense space from his past and by an immense ignorance from his future. His quick, fervent utterance positively shocked everybody. 'An excitable devil,' they called him. One evening, in the tap-room of the Coach and Horses (having drunk some whisky), he upset them all by singing a love song of his country. They hooted him down, and he was pained; but

Preble, the lame wheelwright, and Vincent, the fat blacksmith, and the other notables too, wanted to drink their evening beer in peace. On another occasion he tried to show them how to dance. The dust rose in clouds from the sanded floor; he leaped straight up amongst the deal tables, struck his heels together, squatted on one heel in front of old Preble, shooting out the other leg, uttered wild and exulting cries, jumped up to whirl on one foot, snapping his fingers above his head—and a strange carter who was having a drink in there began to swear, and cleared out with his half-pint in his hand into the bar. But when suddenly he sprang upon a table and continued to dance among the glasses, the landlord interfered. He didn't want any 'acrobat tricks in the taproom'. They laid their hands on him. Having had a glass or two, Mr Swaffer's foreigner tried to expostulate: was ejected forcibly: got a black eye.

'I believe he felt the hostility of his human surroundings. But he was tough—tough in spirit, too, as well as in body. Only the memory of the sea frightened him, with that vague terror that is left by a bad dream. His home was far away; and he did not want now to go to America. I had often explained to him that there is no place on earth where true gold can be found lying ready and to be got for the trouble of the picking up. How then, he asked, could he ever return home with empty hands when there had been sold a cow, two ponies, and a bit of land to pay for his going? His eyes would fill with tears, and, averting them from the immense shimmer of the sea, he would throw himself face down on the grass. But sometimes, cocking his hat with a little conquering air, he would defy my wisdom. He had found his bit of true gold. That was Amy Foster's heart; which was 'a golden heart, and soft to people's misery', he would say in the accents of overwhelming conviction.

'He was called Yanko. He had explained that this meant little John; but as he would also repeat very often that he was a mountaineer (some word sounding in the dialect of his country like Goorall) he got it for his surname. And this is the only trace of him that the succeeding ages may find in the marriage register of the parish. There it stands—Yanko Goorall—in the rector's handwriting. The crooked cross made by the castaway, a cross whose tracing no doubt seemed to him the most solemn part of the whole ceremony, is all that remains now to perpetuate the memory of his name.

'His courtship had lasted some time—ever since he got his

precarious footing in the community. It began by his buying for Amy Foster a green satin ribbon in Darnford. This was what you did in his country. You bought a ribbon at a Jew's stall on a fair-day. I don't suppose the girl knew what to do with it, but he seemed to think that his honourable intentions could not be mistaken.

'It was only when he declared his purpose to get married that I fully understood how, for a hundred futile and inappreciable reasons, how—shall I say odious?—he was to all the countryside. Every old woman in the village was up in arms. Smith, coming upon him near the farm, promised to break his head for him if he found him about again. But he twisted his little black moustache with such a bellicose air and rolled such big, black fierce eyes at Smith that this promise came to nothing. Smith, however, told the girl that she must be mad to take up with a man who was surely wrong in his head. All the same, when she heard him in the gloaming whistle from beyond the orchard a couple of bars of a weird and mournful tune, she would drop whatever she had in her hand—she would leave Mrs Smith in the middle of a sentence—and she would run out to his call. Mrs Smith called her a shameless hussy. She answered nothing. She said nothing at all to anybody, and went on her way as if she had been deaf. She and I alone all in the land, I fancy, could see his very real beauty. He was very good-looking, and most graceful in his bearing, with that something wild as of a woodland creature in his aspect. Her mother moaned over her dismally whenever the girl came to see her on her day out. The father was surly, but pretended not to know; and Mrs Finn once told her plainly that 'this man, my dear, will do you some harm some day yet.' And so it went on. They could be seen on the roads, she tramping stolidly in her finery—grey dress, black feather, stout boots, prominent white cotton gloves that caught your eye a hundred yards away; and he, his coat slung picturesquely over one shoulder, pacing by her side, gallant of bearing and casting tender glances upon the girl with the golden heart. I wonder whether he saw how plain she was. Perhaps among types so different from what he had ever seen, he had not the power to judge; or perhaps he was seduced by the divine quality of her pity.

'Yanko was in great trouble meantime. In his country you get an old man for an ambassador in marriage affairs. He did not know how to proceed. However, one day in the midst of sheep in a field (he was now

179

Swaffer's under-shepherd with Foster) he took off his hat to the father and declared himself humbly. 'I daresay she's fool enough to marry you,' was all Foster said. 'And then,' he used to relate, 'he puts his hat on his head, looks black at me as if he wanted to cut my throat, whistles the dog, and off he goes, leaving me to do the work.' The Fosters, of course, didn't like to lose the wages the girl earned: Amy used to give all her money to her mother. But there was in Foster a very genuine aversion to that match. He contended that the fellow was very good with sheep, but was not fit for any girl to marry. For one thing, he used to go along the hedges muttering to himself like a dam' fool; and then, these foreigners behave very queerly to women sometimes. And perhaps he would want to carry her off somewhere—or run off himself. It was not safe. He preached it to his daughter that the fellow might ill-use her in some way. She made no answer. It was, they said in the village, as if the man had done something to her. People discussed the matter. It was quite an excitement, and the two went on "walking out" together in the face of opposition. Then something unexpected happened.

'I don't know whether old Swaffer ever understood how much he was regarded in the light of a father by his foreign retainer. Anyway the relation was curiously feudal. So when Yanko asked formally for an interview—'and the Miss too' (he called the severe, deaf Miss Swaffer simply *Miss*)—it was to obtain their permission to marry. Swaffer heard him unmoved, dismissed him by a nod, and then shouted the intelligence into Miss Swaffer's best ear. She showed no surprise, and only remarked grimly, in a veiled blank voice, 'He certainly won't get any other girl to marry him.'

'It is Miss Swaffer who has all the credit of the munificence: but in a very few days it came out that Mr Swaffer had presented Yanko with a cottage (the cottage you've seen this morning) and something like an acre of ground—had made it over to him in absolute property. Willcox expedited the deed, and I remember him telling me he had a great pleasure in making it ready. It recited: "In consideration of saving the life of my beloved grandchild, Bertha Willcox."

'Of course, after that no power on earth could prevent them from getting married.

'Her infatuation endured. People saw her going out to meet him in the evening. She stared with unblinking, fascinated eyes up the road where he was expected to appear, walking freely, with a swing from the hip, and humming one of the love-tunes of his country. When the boy was born, he got elevated at the "Coach and Horses", essayed again a song and a dance, and was again ejected. People expressed their commiseration for a woman married to that Jack-in-the-box. He didn't care. There was a man now (he told me boastfully) to whom he could sing and talk in the language of his country, and show how to dance by-and-by.

'But I don't know. To me he appeared to have grown less springy of step, heavier in body, less keen of eye. Imagination, no doubt; but it seems to me now as if the net of fate had been drawn closer round him already.

'One day I met him on the footpath over the Talfourd Hill. He told me that "women were funny". I had heard already of domestic differences. People were saying that Amy Foster was beginning to find out what sort of man she had married. He looked upon the sea with indifferent, unseeing eyes. His wife had snatched the child out of his arms one day as he sat on the doorstep crooning to it a song such as the mothers sing to babies in his mountains. She seemed to think he was doing it some harm. Women are funny. And she had objected to him praying aloud in the evening. Why? He expected the boy to repeat the prayer aloud after him by-and-by, as he used to do after his old father when he was a child—in his own country. And I discovered he longed for their boy to grow up so that he could have a man to talk with in that language that to our ears sounded so disturbing, so passionate, and so bizarre. Why his wife should dislike the idea he couldn't tell. But that would pass, he said. And tilting his head knowingly, he tapped his breastbone to indicate that she had a good heart: not hard, not fierce, open to compassion, charitable to the poor!

'I walked away thoughtfully; I wondered whether his difference, his strangeness, were not penetrating with repulsion that dull nature they had begun by irresistibly attracting. I wondered...'

The Doctor came to the window and looked out at the frigid splendour of the sea, immense in the haze, as if enclosing all the earth with all the hearts lost among the passions of love and fear.

'Physiologically, now,' he said, turning away abruptly, 'it was possible. It was possible.'

He remained silent. Then went on—'At all events, the next time I saw him he was ill—lung trouble. He was tough, but I daresay he was not acclimatised as well as I had supposed. It was a bad winter; and, of course, these mountaineers do get fits of home sickness; and a state of depression would make him vulnerable. He was lying half dressed on a couch downstairs.

'A table covered with a dark oilcloth took up all the middle of the little room. There was a wicker cradle on the floor, a kettle spouting steam on the hob, and some child's linen lay drying on the fender. The room was warm, but the door opens right into the garden, as you noticed perhaps.

'He was very feverish, and kept on muttering to himself. She sat on a chair and looked at him fixedly across the table with her brown, blurred eyes. "Why don't you have him upstairs?" I asked. With a start and a confused stammer she said, "Oh! ah! I couldn't sit with him upstairs, Sir."

'I gave her certain directions; and going outside, I said again that he ought to be in bed upstairs. She wrung her hands. "I couldn't. I couldn't. He keeps on saying something—I don't know what." With the memory of all the talk against the man that had been dinned into her ears, I looked at her narrowly. I looked into her shortsighted eyes, at her dumb eyes that once in her life had seen an enticing shape, but seemed, staring at me, to see nothing at all now. But I saw she was uneasy.

'"What's the matter with him?" she asked in a sort of vacant trepidation. "He doesn't look very ill. I never did see anybody look like this before..."

'"Do you think," I asked indignantly, "he is shamming?"

'"I can't help it, sir," she said stolidly. And suddenly she clapped her hands and looked right and left. "And there's the baby. I am so frightened. He wanted me just now to give him the baby. I can't understand what he says to it."

'"Can't you ask a neighbour to come in tonight?" I asked.

'"Please, sir, nobody seems to care to come," she muttered, dully resigned all at once.

'I impressed upon her the necessity of the greatest care, and then had to go. There was a good deal of sickness that winter. "Oh, I hope he won't talk!" she exclaimed softly just as I was going away.

'I don't know how it is I did not see—but I didn't. And yet, turning in my trap, I saw her lingering before the door, very still, and as if meditating a flight up the miry road.

'Towards the night his fever increased.

'He tossed, moaned, and now and then muttered a complaint. And she sat with the table between her and the couch, watching every movement and every sound, with the terror, the unreasonable terror, of that man she could not understand creeping over her. She had drawn the wicker cradle close to her feet. There was nothing in her now but the maternal instinct and that unaccountable fear.

'Suddenly coming to himself, parched, he demanded a drink of water. She did not move. She had not understood, though he may have thought he was speaking in English. He waited, looking at her, burning with fever, amazed at her silence and immobility, and then he shouted impatiently, "Water! Give me water!"

'She jumped to her feet, snatched up the child, and stood still. He spoke to her, and his passionate remonstrances only increased her fear of that strange man. I believe he spoke to her for a long time, entreating, wondering, pleading, ordering, I suppose. She says she bore it as long as she could. And then a gust of rage came over him.

'He sat up and called out terribly one word—some word. Then he got up as though he hadn't been ill at all, she says. And as in fevered dismay, indignation, and wonder he tried to get to her round the table, she simply opened the door and ran out with the child in her arms. She heard him call twice after her down the road in a terrible voice—and fled... Ah! but you should have seen stirring behind the dull, blurred glance of these eyes the spectre of the fear which had hunted her on that night three miles and a half to the door of Foster's cottage! I did the next day.

'And it was I who found him lying face down and his body in a puddle, just outside the little wicket-gate.

'I had been called out that night to an urgent case in the village, and on my way home at daybreak passed by the cottage. The door stood open. My man helped me to carry him in. We laid him on the couch. The lamp smoked, the fire was out, the chill of the stormy night oozed from the cheerless yellow paper on the wall. "Amy!" I called aloud, and my voice seemed to lose itself in the emptiness of this tiny house as if I had cried in a desert. He opened his eyes. "Gone!" he said distinctly. "I had only asked for water—only for a little water..."

'He was muddy. I covered him up and stood waiting in silence, catching a painfully gasped word now and then. They were no longer in his own language. The fever had left him, taking with it the heat of life. And with his panting breast and lustrous eyes he reminded me again of a wild creature under the net; of a bird caught in a snare. She had left him. She had left him—sick—helpless—thirsty. The spear of the hunter had entered his very soul. "Why?" he cried in the penetrating and indignant voice of a man calling to a responsible Maker. A gust of wind and a swish of rain answered.

'And as I turned away to shut the door he pronounced the word "Merciful!" and expired.

'Eventually I certified heart-failure as the immediate cause of death. His heart must have indeed failed him, or else he might have stood this night of storm and exposure, too. I closed his eyes and drove away. Not very far from the cottage I met Foster walking sturdily between the dripping hedges with his collie at his heels.

'"Do you know where your daughter is?" I asked.

'"Don't I!" he cried. "I am going to talk to him a bit. Frightening a poor woman like this."

'"He won't frighten her any more," I said. "He is dead."

'He struck with his stick at the mud.

'"And there's the child."

'Then, after thinking deeply for a while—"I don't know that it isn't for the best."

'That's what he said. And she says nothing at all now. Not a word of him. Never. Is his image as utterly gone from her mind as his lithe and striding figure, his carolling voice are gone from our fields? He is no longer before her eyes to excite her imagination into a passion of love or fear; and his memory seems to have vanished from her dull brain as a shadow passes away upon a white screen. She lives in the cottage and works for Miss Swaffer. She is Amy Foster for everybody, and the child is "Amy Foster's boy". She calls him Johnny—which means Little John.

'It is impossible to say whether this name recalls anything to her. Does she ever think of the past? I have seen her hanging over the boy's cot in a very passion of maternal tenderness. The little fellow was lying on his back, a little frightened at me, but very still, with his big black eyes, with his fluttered air of a bird in a snare. And looking at him I seemed to see again the other one—the father, cast out mysteriously by the sea to perish in the supreme disaster of loneliness and despair.'

Joseph Conrad (1857–1924) was born Józef Teodor Konrad Korzeniowski in the Ukrainian town of Berdychiv of Polish descent, though he was granted British nationality in 1886 and wrote in English. Such novels as Heart of Darkness *(1899),* Lord Jim *(1900) and* Nostromo *(1904) rank high among the annals of world literature, but he was also admired for his shorter works, many of which reflect his long experience of life at sea as a young man. A complex, somewhat depressive personality himself, Conrad surprised his more aristocratic friends in 1896 by marrying Jessie George, a working-class girl sixteen years his junior. The couple defied unkind remarks made at the time and had an enduring relationship that produced two sons; the stability of their marriage is thought to have contributed greatly to the author's continued success.*

The Storm

Kate Chopin

I

The leaves were so still that even Bibi thought it was going to rain. Bobinôt, who was accustomed to converse on terms of perfect equality with his little son, called the child's attention to certain sombre clouds that were rolling with sinister intention from the west, accompanied by a sullen, threatening roar. They were at Friedheimer's store and decided to remain there till the storm had passed. They sat within the door on two empty kegs. Bibi was four years old and looked very wise.

'Mama'll be 'fraid, yes, he suggested with blinking eyes.

'She'll shut the house. Maybe she got Sylvie helpin' her this evenin',' Bobinôt responded reassuringly.

'No; she ent got Sylvie. Sylvie was helpin' her yistiday,' piped Bibi.

Bobinôt arose and going across to the counter purchased a can of shrimps, of which Calixta was very fond. Then he returned to his perch on the keg and sat stolidly holding the can of shrimps while the storm burst. It shook the wooden store and seemed to be ripping great furrows in the distant field. Bibi laid his little hand on his father's knee and was not afraid.

II

Calixta, at home, felt no uneasiness for their safety. She sat at a side window sewing furiously on a sewing machine. She was greatly occupied and did not notice the approaching storm. But she felt very warm and often stopped to mop her face on which the perspiration gathered in beads. She unfastened her white sacque at the throat. It began to grow dark, and suddenly realising the situation she got up hurriedly and went about closing windows and doors.

Out on the small front gallery she had hung Bobinôt's Sunday clothes to dry and she hastened out to gather them before the rain fell. As she stepped outside, Alcée Laballière rode in at the gate. She had not seen him very often since her marriage, and never alone. She stood there with Bobinôt's coat in her hands, and the big rain drops began to fall. Alcée rode his horse under the shelter of a side projection where the chickens had huddled and there were ploughs and a harrow piled up in the corner.

'May I come and wait on your gallery till the storm is over, Calixta?' he asked.

Come 'long in, M'sieur Alcée.'

His voice and her own startled her as if from a trance, and she seized Bobinôt's vest. Alcée, mounting to the porch, grabbed the trousers and snatched Bibi's braided jacket that was about to be carried away by a sudden gust of wind. He expressed an intention to remain outside, but it was soon apparent that he might as well have been out in the open: the water beat in upon the boards in driving sheets, and he went inside, closing the door after him. It was even necessary to put something beneath the door to keep the water out.

'My! what a rain! It's good two years sence it rain' like that,' exclaimed Calixta as she rolled up a piece of bagging and Alcée helped her to thrust it beneath the crack.

She was a little fuller of figure than five years before when she married; but she had lost nothing of her vivacity. Her blue eyes still retained their melting quality; and her yellow hair, dishevelled by the wind and rain, kinked more stubbornly than ever about her ears and temples.

The rain beat upon the low, shingled roof with a force and clatter that threatened to break an entrance and deluge them there. They were in the dining room—the sitting room—the general utility room. Adjoining was her bedroom, with Bibi's couch alongside her own. The door stood open, and the room with its white, monumental bed, its closed shutters, looked dim and mysterious.

Alcée flung himself into a rocker and Calixta nervously began to gather up from the floor the lengths of a cotton sheet which she had been sewing.

'If this keeps up, Dieu sait if the levees goin' to stan' it!' she exclaimed.

'What have you got to do with the levees?'

'I got enough to do! An' there's Bobinôt with Bibi out in that storm—if he only didn' left Friedheimer's!'

'Let us hope, Calixta, that Bobinôt's got sense enough to come in out of a cyclone.'

She went and stood at the window with a greatly disturbed look on her face. She wiped the frame that was clouded with moisture. It was stiflingly hot. Alcée got up and joined her at the window, looking over her shoulder. The rain was coming down in sheets obscuring the view of far-off cabins and enveloping the distant wood in a grey mist. The playing of the lightning was incessant. A bolt struck a tall chinaberry tree at the edge of the field. It filled all visible space with a blinding glare and the crash seemed to invade the very boards they stood upon.

Calixta put her hands to her eyes, and with a cry, staggered backward. Alcée's arm encircled her, and for an instant he drew her close and spasmodically to him.

'Bonté!' she cried, releasing herself from his encircling arm and retreating from the window, the house'll go next! If I only knew w'ere Bibi was!' She would not compose herself; she would not be seated. Alcée clasped her shoulders and looked into her face. The contact of her warm, palpitating body when he had unthinkingly drawn her into his arms, had aroused all the old-time infatuation and desire for her flesh.

'Calixta,' he said, 'don't be frightened. Nothing can happen. The house is too low to be struck, with so many tall trees standing about. There! aren't you going to be quiet? say, aren't you?' He pushed her hair back from her face that was warm and steaming. Her lips were as red and moist as pomegranate seed. Her white neck and a glimpse of her full, firm bosom disturbed him powerfully. As she glanced up at him the fear in her liquid blue eyes had given place to a drowsy gleam that unconsciously betrayed a sensuous desire. He looked down into her eyes and there was nothing for him to do but to gather her lips in a kiss. It reminded him of Assumption.

'Do you remember—in Assumption, Calixta?' he asked in a low voice broken by passion. Oh! she remembered; for in Assumption he had kissed her and kissed and kissed her; until his senses would well nigh fail, and to save her he would resort to a desperate flight. If she was not an immaculate dove in those days, she was still inviolate; a passionate creature whose very defencelessness had made her defence, against which his honour forbade him to prevail. Now—well, now—her lips seemed in a manner free to be tasted, as well as her round, white throat and her whiter breasts.

They did not heed the crashing torrents, and the roar of the elements made her laugh as she lay in his arms. She was a revelation in that dim, mysterious chamber; as white as the couch she lay upon. Her firm, elastic flesh that was knowing for the first time its birthright, was like a creamy lily that the sun invites to contribute its breath and perfume to the undying life of the world.

The generous abundance of her passion, without guile or trickery, was like a white flame which penetrated and found response in depths of his own sensuous nature that had never yet been reached.

When he touched her breasts they gave themselves up in quivering ecstasy, inviting his lips. Her mouth was a fountain of delight. And when he possessed her, they seemed to swoon together at the very borderland of life's mystery.

He stayed cushioned upon her, breathless, dazed, enervated, with his heart beating like a hammer upon her. With one hand she clasped his head, her lips lightly touching his forehead. The other hand stroked with a soothing rhythm his muscular shoulders.

The growl of the thunder was distant and passing away. The rain beat softly upon the shingles, inviting them to drowsiness and sleep. But they dared not yield.

III

The rain was over; and the sun was turning the glistening green world into a palace of gems. Calixta, on the gallery, watched Alcée ride away. He turned and smiled at her with a beaming face; and she lifted her pretty chin in the air and laughed aloud.

Bobinôt and Bibi, trudging home, stopped without at the cistern to make themselves presentable.

'My! Bibi, w'at will yo' mama say! You ought to be ashame'. You oughta' put on those good pants. Look at 'em! An' that mud on yo' collar! How you got that mud on yo' collar, Bibi? I never saw such a boy!' Bibi was the picture of pathetic resignation. Bobinôt was the embodiment of serious solicitude as he strove to remove from his own person and his son's the signs of their tramp over heavy roads and through wet fields. He scraped the mud off Bibi's bare legs and feet with a stick and carefully removed all traces from his heavy brogans. Then, prepared for the worst—the meeting with an over-scrupulous housewife, they entered cautiously at the back door.

Calixta was preparing supper. She had set the table and was dripping coffee at the hearth. She sprang up as they came in.

'Oh, Bobinôt! You back! My! but I was uneasy. W'ere you been during the rain? An' Bibi? he ain't wet? he ain't hurt?' She had clasped Bibi and was kissing him effusively. Bobinôt's explanations and apologies which he had been composing all along the way, died on his lips as Calixta felt him to see if he were dry, and seemed to express nothing but satisfaction at their safe return.

'I brought you some shrimps, Calixta,' offered Bobinôt, hauling the can from his ample side pocket and laying it on the table.

'Shrimps! Oh, Bobinôt! you too good fo' anything!' and she gave him a smacking kiss on the cheek that resounded, 'J'vous réponds, we'll have a feas' to-night! umph-umph!'

Bobinôt and Bibi began to relax and enjoy themselves, and when the three seated themselves at table they laughed much and so loud that anyone might have heard them as far away as Laballière's.

IV

Alcée Laballière wrote to his wife, Clarisse, that night. It was a loving letter, full of tender solicitude. He told her not to hurry back, but if she and the babies liked it at Biloxi, to stay a month longer. He was getting on nicely; and though he missed them, he was willing to bear the separation a while longer—realising that their health and pleasure were the first things to be considered.

V

As for Clarisse, she was charmed upon receiving her husband's letter. She and the babies were doing well. The society was agreeable; many of her old friends and acquaintances were at the bay. And the first free breath since her marriage seemed to restore the pleasant liberty of her maiden days. Devoted as she was to her husband, their intimate conjugal life was something which she was more than willing to forego for a while.

So the storm passed and everyone was happy.

Kate Chopin was the pen name of Katherine O'Flaherty (1850–1904), who was born and died in St Louis, Missouri, and is now recognised as one of America's leading women writers. Most of her short stories are set among the Cajun inhabitants of Louisiana, and Chopin is particularly admired for her capturing of local dialects. 'The Storm', written in 1898, is a sequel to 'At the Cadian Ball' (1892), which depicts how Calixta is attracted by the handsome Alcée but ends up with Bobinôt after the former goes off with Clarisse.

The Cold Embrace
Mary E. Braddon

He was an artist—such things as happened to him happen sometimes to artists.

He was a German—such things as happened to him happen sometimes to Germans.

He was young, handsome, studious, enthusiastic, metaphysical, reckless, unbelieving, heartless.

And being young, handsome and eloquent, he was beloved.

He was an orphan, under the guardianship of his dead father's brother, his uncle Wilhelm, in whose house he had been brought up from a little child; and she who loved him was his cousin—his cousin Gertrude, whom he swore he loved in return.

Did he love her? Yes, when he first swore it. It soon wore out, this passionate love; how threadbare and wretched a sentiment it became at last in the selfish heart of the student! But in its golden dawn, when he was only nineteen, and had just returned from his apprenticeship to a great painter at Antwerp, and they wandered together in the most romantic outskirts of the city at rosy sunset, by holy moonlight, or bright and joyous morning, how beautiful a dream!

They keep it a secret from Wilhelm, as he has the father's ambition of a wealthy suitor for his only child—a cold and dreary vision beside the lover's dream.

So they are betrothed; and standing side by side when the dying sun and the pale rising moon divide the heavens, he puts the betrothal ring upon her finger, the white and taper finger whose slender shape he knows so well. This ring is a peculiar one, a massive golden serpent, its tail in its mouth, the symbol of eternity; it had been his mother's, and he would know it amongst a thousand. If he were to become blind tomorrow, he could select it from amongst a thousand by the touch alone.

He places it on her finger, and they swear to be true to each other for ever and ever—through trouble and danger—sorrow and change—in wealth or poverty. Her father must needs be won to consent to their

192

union by and by, for they were now betrothed, and death alone could part them.

But the young student, the scoffer at revelation, yet the enthusiastic adorer of the mystical, asks:

'Can death part us? I would return to you from the grave, Gertrude. My soul would come back to be near my love. And you—you, if you died before me—the cold earth would not hold you from me; if you loved me, you would return, and again these fair arms would be clasped round my neck as they are now.'

But she told him, with a holier light in her deep-blue eyes than had ever shone in his—she told him that the dead who die at peace with God are happy in heaven, and cannot return to the troubled earth; and that it is only the suicide—the lost wretch on whom sorrowful angels shut the door of Paradise—whose unholy spirit haunts the footsteps of the living.

The first year of their betrothal is passed, and she is alone, for he has gone to Italy, on a commission for some rich man, to copy Raphaels, Titians, Guidos, in a gallery at Florence. He has gone to win fame, perhaps; but it is not the less bitter—he is gone!

Of course her father misses his young nephew, who has been as a son to him; and he thinks his daughter's sadness no more than a cousin should feel for a cousin's absence.

In the meantime, the weeks and months pass. The lover writes— often at first, then seldom—at last, not at all.

How many excuses she invents for him! How many times she goes to the distant little post-office, to which he is to address his letters! How many times she hopes, only to be disappointed! How many times she despairs, only to hope again!

But real despair comes at last, and will not be put off any more. The rich suitor appears on the scene, and her father is determined. She is to marry at once. The wedding-day is fixed—the fifteenth of June.

The date seems to burn into her brain.

The date, written in fire, dances for ever before her eyes.

The date, shrieked by the Furies, sounds continually in her ears.

But there is time yet—it is the middle of May—there is time for a letter to reach him at Florence; there is time for him to come to

Brunswick, to take her away and marry her, in spite of her father—in spite of the whole world.

But the days and the weeks fly by, and he does not write—he does not come. This is indeed despair which usurps her heart, and will not be put away.

It is the fourteenth of June. For the last time she goes to the little post-office; for the last time she asks the old question, and they give her for the last time the dreary answer, 'No; no letter.'

For the last time—for tomorrow is the day appointed for the bridal. Her father will hear no entreaties; her rich suitor will not listen to her prayers. They will not be put off a day—an hour; to-night alone is hers—this night, which she may employ as she will.

She takes another path than that which leads home; she hurries through some by-streets of the city, out on to a lonely bridge, where he and she had stood so often in the sunset, watching the rose-coloured light glow, fade, and die upon the river.

He returns from Florence. He had received her letter. That letter, blotted with tears, entreating, despairing—he had received it, but he loved her no longer. A young Florentine, who has sat to him for a model, had bewitched his fancy—that fancy which with him stood in place of a heart—and Gertrude had been half-forgotten. If she had a rich suitor, good; let her marry him; better for her, better far for himself. He had no wish to fetter himself with a wife. Had he not his art always?—his eternal bride, his unchanging mistress.

Thus he thought it wiser to delay his journey to Brunswick, so that he should arrive when the wedding was over—arrive in time to salute the bride.

And the vows—the mystical fancies—the belief in his return, even after death, to the embrace of his beloved? O, gone out of his life; melted away for ever, those foolish dreams of his boyhood.

So on the fifteenth of June he enters Brunswick, by that very bridge on which she stood, the stars looking down on her, the night before. He strolls across the bridge and down by the water's edge, a great rough dog at his heels, and the smoke from his short meerschaum-pipe curling in blue wreaths fantastically in the pure morning air. He has his sketch-book under his arm, and attracted now and then by some object that catches his artist's eye, stops to draw: a few weeds and pebbles on the river's brink—a crag on the opposite shore—a group of pollard willows in the distance. When he has done, he admires his drawing, shuts his sketch-book, empties the ashes from his pipe, refills from his tobacco-pouch, sings the refrain of a gay drinking-song, calls to his dog, smokes again, and walks on. Suddenly he opens his sketch-book again; this time that which attracts him is a group of figures: but what is it?

It is not a funeral, for there are no mourners.

It is not a funeral, but a corpse lying on a rude bier, covered with an old sail, carried between two bearers.

It is not a funeral, for the bearers are fishermen—fishermen in their everyday garb.

About a hundred yards from him they rest their burden on a bank—one stands at the head of the bier, the other throws himself down at the foot of it.

And thus they form the perfect group; he walks back two or three paces, selects his point of sight, and begins to sketch a hurried outline. He has finished it before they move; he hears their voices, though he cannot hear their words, and wonders what they can be talking of. Presently he walks on and joins them.

'You have a corpse there, my friends?' he says.

'Yes; a corpse washed ashore an hour ago.'

'Drowned?'

'Yes, drowned. A young girl, very handsome.'

'Suicides are always handsome,' says the painter; and then he stands for a little while idly smoking and meditating, looking at the sharp outline of the corpse and the stiff folds of the rough canvas covering.

Life is such a golden holiday for him—young, ambitious, clever—that it seems as though sorrow and death could have no part in his destiny.

At last he says that, as this poor suicide is so handsome, he should like to make a sketch of her.

He gives the fishermen some money, and they offer to remove the sailcloth that covers her features.

No; he will do it himself. He lifts the rough, coarse, wet canvas from her face. What face?

The face that shone on the dreams of his foolish boyhood; the face which once was the light of his uncle's home. His cousin Gertrude—his betrothed!

He sees, as in one glance, while he draws one breath, the rigid features—the marble arms—the hands crossed on the cold bosom; and, on the third finger of the left hand, the ring which had been his mother's—the golden serpent; the ring which, if he were to become blind, he could select from a thousand others by the touch alone.

But he is a genius and a metaphysician—grief, true grief, is not for such as he. His first thought is flight—flight anywhere out of that accursed city—anywhere far from the brink of that hideous river—anywhere away from remorse—anywhere to forget.

He is miles on the road that leads away from Brunswick before he knows that he has walked a step.

It is only when his dog lies down panting at his feet that he feels how exhausted he is himself, and sits down upon a bank to rest. How the landscape spins round and round before his dazzled eyes, while his morning's sketch of the two fishermen and the canvas-covered bier glares redly at him out of the twilight.

At last, after sitting a long time by the roadside, idly playing with his dog, idly smoking, idly lounging, looking as any idle, light-hearted travelling student might look, yet all the while acting over that morning's scene in his burning brain a hundred times a minute; at last he grows a little more composed, and tries presently to think of himself as he is, apart from his cousin's suicide. Apart from that, he was no worse off than he was yesterday. His genius was not gone; the money he had earned at Florence still lined his pocket-book; he was his own master, free to go whither he would.

And while he sits on the roadside, trying to separate himself from the scene of that morning—trying to put away the image of the corpse covered with the damp canvas sail—trying to think of what he should do next, where he should go, to be farthest away from Brunswick and remorse, the old diligence comes rumbling and jingling along. He remembers it; it goes from Brunswick to Aix-la-Chapelle.

He whistles to the dog, shouts to the postillion to stop, and springs into the *coupé*.

During the whole evening, through the long night, though he

does not once close his eyes, he never speaks a word; but when morning dawns, and the other passengers awake and begin to talk to each other, he joins in the conversation. He tells them that he is an artist, that he is going to Cologne and to Antwerp to copy Rubenses, and the great picture by Quentin Matsys, in the museum. He remembered afterwards that he talked and laughed boisterously, and that when he was talking and laughing loudest, a passenger, older and graver than the rest, opened the window near him, and told him to put his head out. He remembered the fresh air blowing in his face, the singing of the birds in his ears, and the flat fields and roadside reeling before his eyes. He remembered this, and then falling in a lifeless heap on the floor of the diligence.

It is a fever that keeps him for six long weeks on a bed at a hotel in Aix-la-Chapelle.

He gets well, and, accompanied by his dog, starts on foot for Cologne. By this time he is his former self once more. Again the blue smoke from his short meerschaum curls upwards in the morning air— again he sings some old university drinking song—again stops here and there, meditating and sketching.

He is happy, and has forgotten his cousin—and so on to Cologne.

It is by the great cathedral he is standing, with his dog at his side. It is night, the bells have just chimed the hour, and the clocks are striking eleven; the moonlight shines full upon the magnificent pile, over which the artist's eye wanders, absorbed in the beauty of form.

He is not thinking of his drowned cousin, for he has forgotten her and is happy.

Suddenly someone, something from behind him, puts two cold arms round his neck, and clasps its hands on his breast.

And yet there is no one behind him, for on the flags bathed in the broad moonlight there are only two shadows, his own and his dog's. He turns quickly round—there is no one—nothing to be seen in the broad square but himself and his dog; and though he feels, he cannot see the cold arms clasped round his neck.

It is not ghostly, this embrace, for it is palpable to the touch—it cannot be real, for it is invisible.

He tries to throw off the cold caress. He clasps the hands in his own to tear them asunder, and to cast them off his neck. He can feel the long delicate fingers cold and wet beneath his touch, and on the third finger of the left hand he can feel the ring which was his mother's—the golden serpent—the ring which he has always said he would know among a thousand by the touch alone. He knows it now!

His dead cousin's cold arms are round his neck—his dead cousin's wet hands are clasped upon his breast. He asks himself if he is mad. 'Up, Leo!' he shouts. 'Up, up, boy!' and the Newfoundland leaps to his shoulders—the dog's paws are on the dead hands, and the animal utters a terrific howl, and springs away from his master.

The student stands in the moonlight, the dead arms around his neck, and the dog at a little distance moaning piteously.

Presently a watchman, alarmed by the howling of the dog, comes into the square to see what is wrong.

In a breath the cold arms are gone.

He takes the watchman home to the hotel with him and gives him money; in his gratitude he could have given the man half his little fortune.

Will it ever come to him again, this embrace of the dead?

He tries never to be alone; he makes a hundred acquaintances, and shares the chamber of another student. He starts up if he is left by himself in the public room of the inn where he is staying, and runs into the street. People notice his strange actions, and begin to think that he is mad.

But, in spite of all, he is alone once more; for one night the public room being empty for a moment, when on some idle pretence he strolls into the street, the street is empty too, and for the second time he feels the cold arms round his neck, and for the second time, when he calls his dog, the animal shrinks away from him with a piteous howl.

After this he leaves Cologne, still travelling on foot—of necessity now, for his money is getting low. He joins travelling hawkers, he walks side by side with labourers, he talks to every foot-passenger he falls in with, and tries from morning till night to get company on the road.

At night he sleeps by the fire in the kitchen of the inn at which he stops; but do what he will, he is often alone, and it is now a common thing for him to feel the cold arms around his neck.

Many months have passed since his cousin's death—autumn,

winter, early spring. His money is nearly gone, his health is utterly broken, he is the shadow of his former self, and he is getting near to Paris. He will reach that city at the time of the Carnival. To this he looks forward. In Paris, in Carnival time, he need never, surely, be alone, never feel that deadly caress; he may even recover his lost gaiety, his lost health, once more resume his profession, once more earn fame and money by his art.

How hard he tries to get over the distance that divides him from Paris, while day by day he grows weaker, and his step slower and more heavy!

But there is an end at last; the long dreary roads are passed. This is Paris, which he enters for the first time—Paris, of which he has dreamed so much—Paris, whose million voices are to exorcise his phantom.

To him to-night Paris seems one vast chaos of lights, music, and confusion—lights which dance before his eyes and will not be still—music that rings in his ears and deafens him—confusion which makes his head whirl round and round.

But, in spite of all, he finds the opera-house, where there is a masked ball. He has enough money left to buy a ticket of admission, and to hire a domino to throw over his shabby dress. It seems only a moment after his entering the gates of Paris that he is in the very midst of all the wild gaiety of the opera-house ball.

No more darkness, no more loneliness, but a mad crowd, shouting and dancing, and a lovely Débardeuse hanging on his arm.

The boisterous gaiety he feels surely is his old light-heartedness come back. He hears the people round him talking of the outrageous conduct of some drunken student, and it is to him they point when they say this—to him, who has not moistened his lips since yesterday at noon, for even now he will not drink; though his lips are parched, and his throat burning, he cannot drink. His voice is thick and hoarse, and his utterance indistinct; but still this must be his old light-heartedness come back that makes him so wildly gay.

The little Débardeuse is wearied out—her arm rests on his shoulder heavier than lead—the other dancers one by one drop off.

The lights in the chandeliers one by one die out.

The decorations look pale and shadowy in that dim light which is neither night nor day.

A faint glimmer from the dying lamps, a pale streak of cold grey light from the new-born day, creeping in through half-opened shutters.

And by this light the bright-eyed Débardeuse fades sadly. He looks her in the face. How the brightness of her eyes dies out! Again he looks her in the face. How white that face has grown! Again—and now it is the shadow of a face alone that looks in his.

Again—and they are gone—the bright eyes, the face, the shadow of the face. He is alone; alone in that vast saloon.

Alone, and, in the terrible silence, he hears the echoes of his own footsteps in that dismal dance which has no music.

No music but the beating of his heart against his breast. For the cold arms are round his neck—they whirl him round, they will not be flung off, or cast away; he can no more escape from their icy grasp than he can escape from death. He looks behind him—there is nothing but himself in the great empty *salle*; but he can feel—cold, deathlike, but O, how palpable!—the long slender fingers, and the ring which was his mother's.

He tries to shout, but he has no power in his burning throat. The silence of the place is only broken by the echoes of his own footsteps in the dance from which he cannot extricate himself. Who says he has no partner? The cold hands are clasped on his breast, and now he does not shun their caress. No! One more polka, if he drops down dead.

The lights are all out, and, half an hour after, the *gendarmes* come in with a lantern to see that the house is empty; they are followed by a great dog that they have found seated howling on the steps of the theatre. Near the principal entrance they stumble over–

The body of a student, who has died from want of food, exhaustion, and the breaking of a blood-vessel.

Mary Elizabeth Braddon (1835–1915) was born in London and worked as an actress before establishing a reputation as a popular novelist, enjoying her greatest success with the melodrama Lady Audley's Secret *(1862). Her own private life was somewhat complicated by the fact that she was unable to marry her lover, the publisher John Maxwell, until his wife, confined to an asylum, finally died in 1874. Several streets in Richmond, where she lived in her later years, are named after characters in her stories.*

The Little Mermaid
Hans Christian Andersen

Far out in the ocean, where the water is as blue as the prettiest cornflower, and as clear as crystal, it is very, very deep; so deep, indeed, that no cable could fathom it: many church steeples, piled one upon another, would not reach from the ground beneath to the surface of the water above. There dwell the Sea King and his subjects. We must not imagine that there is nothing at the bottom of the sea but bare yellow sand. No, indeed; the most singular flowers and plants grow there; the leaves and stems of which are so pliant, that the slightest agitation of the water causes them to stir as if they had life. Fishes, both large and small, glide between the branches, as birds fly among the trees here upon land. In the deepest spot of all, stands the castle of the Sea King. Its walls are built of coral, and the long, gothic windows are of the clearest amber. The roof is formed of shells, that open and close as the water flows over them. Their appearance is very beautiful, for in each lies a glittering pearl, which would be fit for the diadem of a queen.

The Sea King had been a widower for many years, and his aged mother kept house for him. She was a very wise woman, and exceedingly proud of her high birth; on that account she wore twelve oysters on her tail; while others, also of high rank, were only allowed to wear six. She was, however, deserving of very great praise, especially for her care of the little sea-princesses, her grand-daughters. They were six beautiful children; but the youngest was the prettiest of them all; her skin was as clear and delicate as a rose-leaf, and her eyes as blue as the deepest sea; but, like all the others, she had no feet, and her body ended in a fish's tail. All day long they played in the great halls of the castle, or among the living flowers that grew out of the walls. The large amber windows were open, and the fish swam in, just as the swallows fly into our houses when we open the windows, excepting that the fishes swam up to the princesses, ate out of their hands, and allowed themselves to be stroked. Outside the castle there was a beautiful garden, in which grew bright red and dark blue flowers, and blossoms like flames of fire; the fruit glittered like gold, and the leaves and stems waved to and fro continually. The earth itself was the finest sand, but blue as the flame of burning sulphur. Over everything lay a peculiar blue radiance, as if it were surrounded by the air from above, through which the blue sky shone, instead of the dark depths of the sea. In calm weather the sun could be seen, looking like a purple flower, with the light streaming from the calyx. Each of the young princesses had a little plot of ground in the garden, where she might dig and plant as she pleased. One arranged her flower-bed into the form of a whale; another thought it better to make hers like the figure of a little mermaid; but that of the youngest was round like the sun, and contained flowers as red as his rays at sunset. She was a strange child, quiet and thoughtful; and while her sisters would be delighted with the wonderful things which they obtained from the wrecks of vessels, she cared for nothing but her pretty red flowers, like the sun, excepting a beautiful marble statue. It was the representation of a handsome boy, carved out of pure white stone, which had fallen to the bottom of the sea from a wreck. She planted by the statue a rose-coloured weeping willow. It grew splendidly, and very soon hung its fresh branches over the statue, almost down to the blue sands. The shadow had a violet tint, and waved to and fro like the branches; it seemed as if the crown of the tree and the root were at play, and trying to kiss each other. Nothing gave her so much pleasure as to hear about the world above the sea. She made her old grandmother tell her all she knew of the ships and of the towns, the people and the animals. To her it seemed most wonderful and beautiful to hear that the flowers of the land should have fragrance, and not those below the sea; that the trees of the forest should be green; and that the fishes among the trees could sing so sweetly, that it was quite a pleasure to hear them. Her grandmother called the little birds fishes, or she would not have understood her; for she had never seen birds.

'When you have reached your fifteenth year,' said the grandmother, 'you will have permission to rise up out of the sea, to sit on the rocks in the moonlight, while the great ships are sailing by; and then you will see both forests and towns.'

In the following year, one of the sisters would be fifteen: but as each was a year younger than the other, the youngest would have to wait five years before her turn came to rise up from the bottom of the ocean, and see the earth as we do. However, each promised to tell the others what she saw on her first visit, and what she thought the most beautiful; for their grandmother could not tell them enough; there were so many things on which they wanted information. None of them longed so much for her turn to come as the youngest, she who had the longest time to wait, and who was so quiet and thoughtful. Many nights she stood by the open window, looking up through the dark blue water, and watching the fish as they splashed about with their fins and tails. She could see the moon and stars shining faintly; but through the water they looked larger than they do to our eyes. When something like a black cloud passed between her and them, she knew that it was either a whale swimming over her head, or a ship full of human beings, who never imagined that a pretty little mermaid was standing beneath them, holding out her white hands towards the keel of their ship.

As soon as the eldest was fifteen, she was allowed to rise to the surface of the ocean. When she came back, she had hundreds of things to talk about; but the most beautiful, she said, was to lie in the moonlight, on a sandbank, in the quiet sea, near the coast, and to gaze on a large town nearby, where the lights were twinkling like hundreds of stars; to listen to the sounds of the music, the noise of carriages, and the voices of human beings, and then to hear the merry bells peal out from the church steeples; and because she could not go near to all those wonderful things, she longed for them more than ever. Oh, did not the youngest sister listen eagerly to all these descriptions? and afterwards, when she stood at the open window looking up through the dark blue water, she thought of the great city, with all its bustle and noise, and even fancied she could hear the sound of the church bells, down in the depths of the sea.

In another year the second sister received permission to rise to the surface of the water, and to swim about where she pleased. She rose just as the sun was setting, and this, she said, was the most beautiful sight of all. The whole sky looked like gold, while violet and rose-coloured clouds, which she could not describe, floated over her; and, still more rapidly than the clouds, flew a large flock of wild swans towards the setting sun, looking like a long white veil across the sea. She also swam towards the sun; but it sunk into the waves, and the rosy tints faded from the clouds and from the sea.

The third sister's turn followed; she was the boldest of them all, and she swam up a broad river that emptied itself into the sea. On the banks she saw green hills covered with beautiful vines; palaces and castles peeped out from amid the proud trees of the forest; she heard the birds singing, and the rays of the sun were so powerful that she was obliged often to dive down under the water to cool her burning face. In a narrow creek she found a whole troop of little human children, quite naked, and sporting about in the water; she wanted to play with them, but they fled in a great fright; and then a little black animal came to the water; it was a dog, but she did not know that, for she had never before seen one. This animal barked at her so terribly that she became frightened, and rushed back to the open sea. But she said she should never forget the beautiful forest, the green hills, and the pretty little children who could swim in the water, although they had not fish's tails.

The fourth sister was more timid; she remained in the midst of the sea, but she said it was quite as beautiful there as nearer the land. She could see for so many miles around her, and the sky above looked like a bell of glass. She had seen the ships, but at such a great distance that they looked like sea-gulls. The dolphins sported in the waves, and the great whales spouted water from their nostrils till it seemed as if a hundred fountains were playing in every direction.

The fifth sister's birthday occurred in the winter; so when her turn came, she saw what the others had not seen the first time they went up. The sea looked quite green, and large icebergs were floating about, each like a pearl, she said, but larger and loftier than the churches built by men. They were of the most singular shapes, and glittered like diamonds. She had seated herself upon one of the largest, and let the wind play with her long hair, and she remarked that all the ships sailed by rapidly, and steered as far away as they could from the iceberg, as if they were afraid of it. Towards evening, as the sun went down, dark clouds covered the sky, the thunder rolled and the lightning flashed, and the red light glowed on the icebergs as they rocked and tossed on the heaving sea. On all the ships the sails were reefed with fear and trembling, while she sat calmly on the floating iceberg, watching the blue lightning, as it darted its forked flashes into the sea.

When first the sisters had permission to rise to the surface, they were each delighted with the new and beautiful sights they saw; but now, as grown-up girls, they could go when they pleased, and they had become indifferent about it. They wished themselves back again in the water, and after a month had passed they said it was much more beautiful down below, and pleasanter to be at home. Yet often, in the evening hours, the five sisters would twine their arms round each other, and rise to the surface, in a row. They had more beautiful voices than any human being could have; and before the approach of a storm, and when they expected a ship would be lost, they swam before the vessel, and sang sweetly of the delights to be found in the depths of the sea, and begging the sailors not to fear if they sank to the bottom. But the sailors could not understand the song, they took it for the howling of the storm. And these things were never to be beautiful for them; for if the ship sank, the men were drowned, and their dead bodies alone reached the palace of the Sea King.

When the sisters rose, arm-in-arm, through the water in this way, their youngest sister would stand quite alone, looking after them, ready to cry, only that the mermaids have no tears, and therefore they suffer more. 'Oh, were I but fifteen years old,' said she: 'I know that I shall love the world up there, and all the people who live in it.'

At last she reached her fifteenth year. 'Well, now, you are grown up,' said the old dowager, her grandmother; 'so you must let me adorn you like your other sisters;' and she placed a wreath of white lilies in her hair, and every flower leaf was half a pearl. Then the old lady ordered eight great oysters to attach themselves to the tail of the princess to show her high rank.

'But they hurt me so,' said the little mermaid.

'Pride must suffer pain,' replied the old lady. Oh, how gladly she would have shaken off all this grandeur, and laid aside the heavy wreath! The red flowers in her own garden would have suited her much better, but she could not help herself: so she said, 'Farewell', and rose as lightly as a bubble to the surface of the water. The sun had just set as she raised her head above the waves; but the clouds were tinted with crimson and gold, and through the glimmering twilight beamed the evening star in all its beauty. The sea was calm, and the air mild and fresh. A large ship, with three masts, lay becalmed on the water, with only one sail set; for not a breeze stiffed, and the sailors sat idle on deck or amongst the rigging. There was music and song on board; and, as darkness came on, a hundred coloured lanterns were lighted, as if the flags of all nations waved in the air. The little mermaid swam close to the cabin windows;

and now and then, as the waves lifted her up, she could look in through clear glass window-panes, and see a number of well-dressed people within. Among them was a young prince, the most beautiful of all, with large black eyes; he was sixteen years of age, and his birthday was being kept with much rejoicing. The sailors were dancing on deck, but when the prince came out of the cabin, more than a hundred rockets rose in the air, making it as bright as day. The little mermaid was so startled that she dived under water; and when she again stretched out her head, it appeared as if all the stars of heaven were falling around her, she had never seen such fireworks before. Great suns spurted fire about, splendid fireflies flew into the blue air, and everything was reflected in the clear, calm sea beneath. The ship itself was so brightly illuminated that all the people, and even the smallest rope, could be distinctly and plainly seen. And how handsome the young prince looked, as he pressed the hands of all present and smiled at them, while the music resounded through the clear night air.

It was very late; yet the little mermaid could not take her eyes from the ship, or from the beautiful prince. The coloured lanterns had been extinguished, no more rockets rose in the air, and the cannon had ceased firing; but the sea became restless, and a moaning, grumbling sound could be heard beneath the waves: still the little mermaid remained by the cabin window, rocking up and down on the water, which enabled her to look in. After a while, the sails were quickly unfurled, and the noble ship continued her passage; but soon the waves rose higher, heavy clouds darkened the sky, and lightning appeared in the distance. A dreadful storm was approaching; once more the sails were reefed, and the great ship pursued her flying course over the raging sea. The waves rose mountains high, as if they would have overtopped the mast; but the ship dived like a swan between them, and then rose again on their lofty, foaming crests. To the little mermaid this appeared pleasant sport; not so to the sailors. At length the ship groaned and creaked; the thick planks gave way under the lashing of the sea as it broke over the deck; the mainmast snapped asunder like a reed; the ship lay over on her side; and the water rushed in. The little mermaid now perceived that the crew were in danger; even she herself was obliged to be careful to avoid the beams and planks of the wreck which lay scattered on the water. At one moment it was so pitch dark that she could not see a single object, but a flash of lightning revealed the whole scene; she could see everyone who had been on board excepting the prince; when the ship parted, she had seen him sink into the deep waves, and she was glad, for she thought he would now be with her; and then she remembered that human beings could not live in the water, so that when he got down to her father's palace he would be quite dead. But he must not die. So she swam about among the beams and planks which strewed the surface of the sea, forgetting that they could crush her to pieces. Then she dived deeply under the dark waters, rising and falling with the waves, till at length she managed to reach the young prince, who was fast losing the power of swimming in that stormy sea. His limbs were failing him, his beautiful eyes were closed, and he would have died had not the little mermaid come to his assistance. She held his head above the water, and let the waves drift them where they would.

In the morning the storm had ceased; but of the ship not a single fragment could be seen. The sun rose up red and glowing from the water, and its beams brought back the hue of health to the prince's cheeks; but his eyes remained closed. The mermaid kissed his high, smooth forehead, and stroked back his wet hair; he seemed to her like the marble statue in her little garden, and she kissed him again, and wished that he might live. Presently they came in sight of land; she saw lofty blue mountains, on which the white snow rested as if a flock of swans were lying upon them. Near the coast were beautiful green forests, and close by stood a large building, whether a church or a convent she could not tell. Orange and citron trees grew in the garden, and before the door stood lofty palms. The sea here formed a little bay, in which the water was quite still, but very deep; so she swam with the handsome prince to the beach, which was covered with fine, white sand, and there she laid him in the warm sunshine, taking care to raise his head higher than his body. Then bells sounded in the large white building, and a number of young girls came into the garden. The little mermaid swam out farther from the shore and placed herself between some high rocks that rose out of the water; then she covered her head and neck with the foam of the sea so that her little face might not be seen, and watched to see what would become of the poor prince. She did not wait long before she saw a young girl approach the spot where he lay. She seemed frightened at first, but only for a moment; then she fetched a number of people, and the mermaid saw that the prince came to life again, and smiled upon those who stood round him. But to her he sent no smile; he knew not that she had saved him. This made her very unhappy, and when he was led away into the great building, she dived down sorrowfully into the water, and returned to her father's castle. She had always been silent and thoughtful, and now she was more so than ever. Her sisters asked her what she had seen during her first visit to the surface of the water; but she would tell them nothing. Many an evening and morning did she rise to the place where she had left the prince. She saw the fruits in the garden ripen till they were gathered, the snow on the tops of the mountains melt away; but she never saw the prince, and therefore she returned home, always more sorrowful than before. It was her only comfort to sit in her own little garden, and fling her arm round the beautiful marble statue which was like the prince; but she gave up tending her flowers, and they grew in wild confusion over the paths, twining their long leaves and stems round the branches of the trees, so that the whole place became dark and gloomy. At length she could bear it no longer, and told one of her sisters all about it. Then the others heard the secret, and very soon it became known to two mermaids whose intimate friend happened to know who the prince was. She had also seen the festival on board ship, and she told them where the prince came from, and where his palace stood.

'Come, little sister,' said the other princesses; then they entwined their arms and rose up in a long row to the surface of the water, close by the spot where they knew the prince's palace stood. It was built of bright yellow shining stone, with long flights of marble steps, one of which reached quite down to the sea. Splendid gilded cupolas rose over the roof, and between the pillars that surrounded the whole building stood life-like statues of marble. Through the clear crystal of the lofty windows could be seen noble rooms, with costly silk curtains and hangings of tapestry; while the walls were covered with beautiful paintings which were a pleasure to look at. In the centre of the largest saloon a fountain threw its sparkling jets high up into the glass cupola of the ceiling, through which the sun shone down upon the water and upon the beautiful plants growing round the basin of the fountain. Now that she knew where he lived, she spent many an evening and many a night on the water near the palace. She would swim much nearer the shore than any of the others ventured to do; indeed once she went quite up the narrow channel under the marble balcony, which threw a broad shadow on the water. Here she would sit and watch the young prince, who thought himself quite alone in the bright moonlight. She saw him many times of an evening sailing in a pleasant boat, with music playing and flags waving. She peeped out from among the green rushes, and if the wind caught her long silvery-white veil, those who saw it believed it to be a swan, spreading out its wings. On many a night, too, when the fishermen, with their torches, were out at sea, she heard them relate so many good things about the doings of the young prince, that she was glad she had saved his life when he had been tossed about half-dead on the waves. And she remembered that his head had rested on her bosom, and how heartily she had kissed him; but he knew nothing of all this, and could not even dream of her. She grew more and more fond of human beings, and wished more and more to be able to wander about with those whose world seemed to be so much larger than her own. They could fly over the sea in ships, and mount the high hills which were far above the clouds; and the lands they possessed, their woods and their fields, stretched far away beyond the reach of her sight. There was so much that she wished to know, and her sisters were unable to answer all her questions. Then she applied to her old grandmother, who knew all about the upper world, which she very rightly called the lands above the sea.

'If human beings are not drowned,' asked the little mermaid, 'can they live forever? do they never die as we do here in the sea?'

'Yes,' replied the old lady, 'they must also die, and their term of life is even shorter than ours. We sometimes live to three hundred years, but when we cease to exist here we only become the foam on the surface of the water, and we have not even a grave down here of those we love. We have not immortal souls, we shall never live again; but, like the green sea-weed, when once it has been cut off, we can never flourish more. Human beings, on the contrary, have a soul which lives forever, lives after the body has been turned to dust. It rises up through the clear, pure air beyond the glittering stars. As we rise out of the water, and behold all the land of the earth, so do they rise to unknown and glorious regions which we shall never see.'

'Why have not we an immortal soul?' asked the little mermaid mournfully; 'I would give gladly all the hundreds of years that I have to live, to be a human being only for one day, and to have the hope of knowing the happiness of that glorious world above the stars.'

'You must not think of that,' said the old woman; 'we feel ourselves to be much happier and much better off than human beings.'

'So I shall die,' said the little mermaid, 'and as the foam of the sea I shall be driven about never again to hear the music of the waves, or to see the pretty flowers nor the red sun. Is there anything I can do to win an immortal soul?'

'No,' said the old woman, 'unless a man were to love you so much that you were more to him than his father or mother; and if all his thoughts and all his love were fixed upon you, and the priest placed his right hand in yours, and he promised to be true to you here and hereafter, then his soul would glide into your body and you would obtain a share in the future happiness of mankind. He would give a soul to you and retain his own as well; but this can never happen. Your fish's tail, which amongst us is considered so beautiful, is thought on earth to be quite ugly; they do not know any better, and they think it necessary to have two stout props, which they call legs, in order to be handsome.'

Then the little mermaid sighed, and looked sorrowfully at her fish's tail. 'Let us be happy,' said the old lady, 'and dart and spring about during the three hundred years that we have to live, which is really quite long enough; after that we can rest ourselves all the better. This evening we are going to have a court ball.'

It is one of those splendid sights which we can never see on earth. The walls and the ceiling of the large ball-room were of thick, but transparent crystal. May hundreds of colossal shells, some of a deep red, others of a grass green, stood on each side in rows, with blue fire in them, which lighted up the whole saloon, and shone through the walls, so that the sea was also illuminated. Innumerable fishes, great and small, swam past the crystal walls; on some of them the scales glowed with a purple brilliancy, and on others they shone like silver and gold. Through the halls flowed a broad stream, and in it danced the mermen and the mermaids to the music of their own sweet singing. No one on earth has such a lovely voice as theirs. The little mermaid sang more sweetly than them all. The whole court applauded her with hands and tails; and for a moment her heart felt quite gay, for she knew she had the loveliest voice of any on earth or in the sea. But she soon thought again of the world above her, for she could not forget the charming prince, nor her sorrow that she had not an immortal soul like his; therefore she crept away silently out of her father's palace, and while everything within was gladness and song, she sat in her own little garden sorrowful and alone. Then she heard the bugle sounding through the water, and thought—'He is certainly sailing above, he on whom my wishes depend, and in whose hands I should like to place the happiness of my life. I will venture all for him, and to win an immortal soul, while my sisters are dancing in my father's palace, I will go to the sea witch, of whom I have always been so much afraid, but she can give me counsel and help.'

And then the little mermaid went out from her garden, and took the road to the foaming whirlpools, behind which the sorceress lived. She had never been that way before: neither flowers nor grass grew there; nothing but bare, grey, sandy ground stretched out to the whirlpool, where the water, like foaming mill-wheels, whirled round everything that it seized, and cast it into the fathomless deep. Through the midst of these crushing whirlpools the little mermaid was obliged to pass, to reach the dominions of the sea witch; and also for a long distance the only road lay right across a quantity of warm, bubbling mire, called by the witch her turfmoor. Beyond this stood her house, in the centre of a strange forest, in which all the trees and flowers were polypi, half animals and half plants; they looked like serpents with a hundred heads growing out of the ground. The branches were long slimy arms, with fingers like flexible worms, moving limb after limb from the root to the top. All that could be reached in the sea they seized upon, and held fast, so that it never escaped from their clutches. The little mermaid was so alarmed at what she saw, that she stood still, and her heart beat with fear, and she was very nearly turning back; but she thought of the prince, and of the human soul for which she longed, and her courage returned. She fastened her long flowing hair round her head, so that the polypi might not seize hold of it. She laid her hands together across her bosom, and then she darted forward as a fish shoots through the water, between the supple arms and fingers of the ugly polypi, which were stretched out on each side of her. She saw that each held in its grasp something it had seized with its numerous little arms, as if they were iron bands. The white skeletons of human beings who had perished at sea, and had sunk down into the deep waters, skeletons of land animals, oars, rudders, and chests of ships were lying tightly grasped by their clinging arms; even a little mermaid, whom they had caught and strangled; and this seemed the most shocking of all to the little princess.

She now came to a space of marshy ground in the wood, where large, fat water-snakes were rolling in the mire, and showing their ugly, drab-coloured bodies. In the midst of this spot stood a house, built with the bones of shipwrecked human beings. There sat the sea witch, allowing a toad to eat from her mouth, just as people sometimes feed a canary with a piece of sugar. She called the ugly water-snakes her little chickens, and allowed them to crawl all over her bosom.

'I know what you want,' said the sea witch; 'it is very stupid of you, but you shall have your way, and it will bring you to sorrow, my pretty princess. You want to get rid of your fish's tail, and to have two supports instead of it, like human beings on earth, so that the young prince may fall in love with you, and that you may have an immortal soul.' And then the witch laughed so loud and disgustingly, that the toad and the snakes fell to the ground, and lay there wriggling about. 'You are but just in time,' said the witch; 'for after sunrise to-morrow I should not be able to help you till the end of another year. I will prepare a draught for you, with which you must swim to land tomorrow before sunrise, and sit down on the shore and drink it. Your tail will then disappear, and shrink up into what mankind calls legs, and you will feel great pain, as if a sword were passing through you. But all who see you will say that you are the prettiest little human being they ever saw. You will still have the same floating gracefulness of movement, and no dancer will ever tread so lightly; but at every step you take it will feel as if you were treading upon sharp knives, and that the blood must flow. If you will bear all this, I will help you.'

'Yes, I will,' said the little princess in a trembling voice, as she thought of the prince and the immortal soul.

'But think again,' said the witch; 'for when once your shape has become like a human being, you can no more be a mermaid. You will never return through the water to your sisters, or to your father's palace again; and if you do not win the love of the prince, so that he is willing to forget his father and mother for your sake, and to love you with his whole soul, and allow the priest to join your hands that you may be man and wife, then you will never have an immortal soul. The first morning after he marries another your heart will break, and you will become foam on the crest of the waves.'

'I will do it,' said the little mermaid, and she became pale as death.

'But I must be paid also,' said the witch, 'and it is not a trifle that I ask. You have the sweetest voice of any who dwell here in the depths of the sea, and you believe that you will be able to charm the prince with it also, but this voice you must give to me; the best thing you possess will I have for the price of my draught. My own blood must be mixed with it, that it may be as sharp as a two-edged sword.'

'But if you take away my voice,' said the little mermaid, 'what is left for me?'

'Your beautiful form, your graceful walk, and your expressive eyes; surely with these you can enchain a man's heart. Well, have you lost your courage? Put out your little tongue that I may cut it off as my payment; then you shall have the powerful draught.'

'It shall be,' said the little mermaid.

Then the witch placed her cauldron on the fire, to prepare the magic draught.

'Cleanliness is a good thing,' said she, scouring the vessel with snakes, which she had tied together in a large knot; then she pricked herself in the breast, and let the black blood drop into it. The steam that rose formed itself into such horrible shapes that no one could look at them without fear. Every moment the witch threw something else into the vessel, and when it began to boil, the sound was like the weeping of a crocodile. When at last the magic draught was ready, it looked like the clearest water. 'There it is for you,' said the witch. Then she cut off the mermaid's tongue, so that she became dumb, and would never again speak or sing. 'If the polypi should seize hold of you as you return through the wood,' said the witch, 'throw over them a few drops of the potion, and their fingers will be torn into a thousand pieces.' But the little mermaid had no occasion to do this, for the polypi sprang back in terror when they caught sight of the glittering draught, which shone in her hand like a twinkling star.

So she passed quickly through the wood and the marsh, and between the rushing whirlpools. She saw that in her father's palace the torches in the ballroom were extinguished, and all within asleep; but she did not venture to go in to them, for now she was dumb and going to leave them forever, she felt as if her heart would break. She stole into the garden, took a flower from the flower-beds of each of her sisters, kissed her hand a thousand times towards the palace, and then rose up through the dark blue waters. The sun had not risen when she came in sight of the prince's palace, and approached the beautiful marble steps, but the moon shone clear and bright. Then the little mermaid drank the magic draught, and it seemed as if a two-edged sword went through her delicate body: she fell into a swoon, and lay like one dead. When the sun arose and shone over the sea, she recovered, and felt a sharp pain; but just before her stood the handsome young prince. He fixed his coal-black eyes upon her so earnestly that she cast down her own, and then became aware that her fish's tail was gone, and that she had as pretty a pair of white legs and tiny feet as any little maiden could have; but she had no clothes, so she wrapped herself in her long, thick hair. The prince asked her who she was, and where she came from, and she looked at him mildly and sorrowfully with her deep blue eyes; but she could not speak. Every step she took was as the witch had said it would be, she felt as if treading upon the points of needles or sharp knives; but she bore it willingly, and stepped as lightly by the prince's side as a soap-bubble, so that he and all who saw her wondered at her graceful-swaying movements. She was very soon arrayed in costly robes of silk and muslin, and was the most beautiful creature in the palace; but she was dumb, and could neither speak nor sing.

Beautiful female slaves, dressed in silk and gold, stepped forward and sang before the prince and his royal parents: one sang better than all the others, and the prince clapped his hands and smiled at her. This was great sorrow to the little mermaid; she knew how much more sweetly she herself could sing once, and she thought, 'Oh if he could only know that! I have given away my voice forever, to be with him.'

The slaves next performed some pretty fairy-like dances, to the sound of beautiful music. Then the little mermaid raised her lovely white arms, stood on the tips of her toes, and glided over the floor, and danced as no one yet had been able to dance. At each moment her beauty became more revealed, and her expressive eyes appealed more directly to the heart than the songs of the slaves. Everyone was enchanted, especially the prince, who called her his little foundling; and she danced again quite readily, to please him, though each time her foot touched the floor it seemed as if she trod on sharp knives.

The prince said she should remain with him always, and she received permission to sleep at his door, on a velvet cushion. He had a page's dress made for her, that she might accompany him on horseback. They rode together through the sweet-scented woods, where the green boughs touched their shoulders, and the little birds sang among the fresh leaves. She climbed with the prince to the tops of high mountains; and although her tender feet bled so that even her steps were marked, she only laughed, and followed him till they could see the clouds beneath them looking like a flock of birds travelling to distant lands. While at the prince's palace, and when all the household were asleep, she would go and sit on the broad marble steps; for it eased her burning feet to bathe them in the cold sea-water; and then she thought of all those below in the deep.

Once during the night her sisters came up arm-in-arm, singing sorrowfully, as they floated on the water. She beckoned to them, and then they recognised her, and told her how she had grieved them. After that, they came to the same place every night; and once she saw in the distance her old grandmother, who had not been to the surface of the sea for many years, and the old Sea King, her father, with his crown on his head. They stretched out their hands towards her, but they did not venture so near the land as her sisters did.

As the days passed, she loved the prince more fondly, and he loved her as he would love a little child, but it never came into his head to make her his wife; yet, unless he married her, she could not receive an immortal soul; and, on the morning after his marriage with another, she would dissolve into the foam of the sea.

'Do you not love me the best of them all?' the eyes of the little mermaid seemed to say, when he took her in his arms, and kissed her fair forehead.

'Yes, you are dear to me,' said the prince; 'for you have the best heart, and you are the most devoted to me; you are like a young maiden whom I once saw, but whom I shall never meet again. I was in a ship that was wrecked, and the waves cast me ashore near a holy temple, where several young maidens performed the service. The youngest of them found me on the shore, and saved my life. I saw her but twice, and she is the only one in the world whom I could love; but you are like her, and you have almost driven her image out of my mind. She belongs to the holy temple, and my good fortune has sent you to me instead of her; and we will never part.'

'Ah, he knows not that it was I who saved his life,' thought the little mermaid. 'I carried him over the sea to the wood where the temple stands: I sat beneath the foam, and watched till the human beings came to help him. I saw the pretty maiden that he loves better than he loves me;' and the mermaid sighed deeply, but she could not shed tears. 'He says the maiden belongs to the holy temple, therefore she will never return to the world. They will meet no more: while I am by his side, and see him every day. I will take care of him, and love him, and give up my life for his sake.'

Very soon it was said that the prince must marry, and that the beautiful daughter of a neighbouring king would be his wife, for a fine ship was being fitted out. Although the prince gave out that he merely intended to pay a visit to the king, it was generally supposed that he really went to see his daughter. A great company were to go with him. The little mermaid smiled, and shook her head. She knew the prince's thoughts better than any of the others.

'I must travel,' he had said to her; 'I must see this beautiful princess; my parents desire it; but they will not oblige me to bring her home as my bride. I cannot love her; she is not like the beautiful maiden in the temple, whom you resemble. If I were forced to choose a bride, I would rather choose you, my dumb foundling, with those expressive eyes.' And then he kissed her rosy mouth, played with her long waving hair, and laid his head on her heart, while she dreamed of human happiness and an immortal soul. 'You are not afraid of the sea, my dumb child,' said he, as they stood on the deck of the noble ship which was to carry them to the country of the neighbouring king. And then he told her of storm and of calm, of strange fishes in the deep beneath them, and of what the divers had seen there; and she smiled at his descriptions, for she knew better than anyone what wonders were at the bottom of the sea.

In the moonlight, when all on board were asleep, excepting the man at the helm, who was steering, she sat on the deck, gazing down through the clear water. She thought she could distinguish her father's castle, and upon it her aged grandmother, with the silver crown on her head, looking through the rushing tide at the keel of the vessel. Then her sisters came up on the waves, and gazed at her mournfully, wringing their white hands. She beckoned to them, and smiled, and wanted to tell them how happy and well off she was; but the cabin-boy approached, and when her sisters dived down he thought it was only the foam of the sea which he saw.

The next morning the ship sailed into the harbour of a beautiful town belonging to the king whom the prince was going to visit. The church bells were ringing, and from the high towers sounded a flourish of trumpets; and soldiers, with flying colours and glittering bayonets, lined the rocks through which they passed. Every day was a festival; balls and entertainments followed one another.

But the princess had not yet appeared. People said that she was being brought up and educated in a religious house, where she was learning every royal virtue. At last she came. Then the little mermaid, who was very anxious to see whether she was really beautiful, was obliged to acknowledge that she had never seen a more perfect vision of beauty. Her skin was delicately fair, and beneath her long dark eye-lashes her laughing blue eyes shone with truth and purity.

'It was you,' said the prince, 'who saved my life when I lay dead on the beach,' and he folded his blushing bride in his arms. 'Oh, I am too happy,' said he to the little mermaid; 'my fondest hopes are all fulfilled. You will rejoice at my happiness; for your devotion to me is great and sincere.'

The little mermaid kissed his hand, and felt as if her heart were already broken. His wedding morning would bring death to her, and she would change into the foam of the sea. All the church bells rung, and the heralds rode about the town proclaiming the betrothal. Perfumed oil was burning in costly silver lamps on every altar. The priests waved the censers, while the bride and bridegroom joined their hands and received the blessing of the bishop. The little mermaid, dressed in silk and gold, held up the bride's train; but her ears heard nothing of the festive music, and her eyes saw not the holy ceremony; she thought of the night of death which was coming to her, and of all she had lost in the world. On the same evening the bride and bridegroom went on board ship; cannons were roaring, flags waving, and in the centre of the ship a costly tent of purple and gold had been erected. It contained elegant couches, for the reception of the bridal pair during the night. The ship, with swelling sails and a favourable wind, glided away smoothly and lightly over the calm sea. When it grew dark a number of coloured lamps were lit, and the sailors danced merrily on the deck. The little mermaid could not help thinking of her first rising out of the sea, when she had seen similar festivities and joys; and she joined in the dance, poised herself in the air as a swallow when he pursues his prey, and all present cheered her with wonder. She had never danced so elegantly before. Her tender feet felt as if cut with sharp knives, but she cared not for it; a sharper pang had pierced through her heart. She knew this was the last evening she should ever see the prince, for whom she had forsaken her kindred and her home; she had given up her beautiful voice, and suffered unheard-of pain daily for him, while he knew nothing of it. This was the last evening that she would breathe the same air with him, or gaze on the starry sky and the deep sea; an eternal night, without a thought or a dream, awaited her: she had no soul and now she could never win one. All was joy and gaiety on board ship till long after midnight; she laughed and danced with the rest, while the thoughts of death were in her heart. The prince kissed his beautiful bride, while she played with his raven hair, till they went arm-in-arm to rest in the splendid tent. Then all became still on board the ship; the helmsman, alone awake, stood at the helm. The little mermaid leaned her white arms on the edge of the vessel, and looked towards the east for the first blush of morning, for that first ray of dawn that would bring her death. She saw her sisters rising out of the flood: they were as pale as herself; but their long beautiful hair waved no more in the wind, and had been cut off.

'We have given our hair to the witch,' said they, 'to obtain help for you, that you may not die to-night. She has given us a knife: here it is, see it is very sharp. Before the sun rises you must plunge it into the heart of the prince; when the warm blood falls upon your feet they will grow together again, and form into a fish's tail, and you will be once more a mermaid, and return to us to live out your three hundred years before you die and change into the salt sea foam. Haste, then; he or you must die before sunrise. Our old grandmother moans so for you, that her white hair is falling off from sorrow, as ours fell under the witch's scissors. Kill the prince and come back; hasten: do you not see the first red streaks in the sky? In a few minutes the sun will rise, and you must die.' And then they sighed deeply and mournfully, and sank down beneath the waves.

The little mermaid drew back the crimson curtain of the tent, and beheld the fair bride with her head resting on the prince's breast. She bent down and kissed his fair brow, then looked at the sky on which the rosy dawn grew brighter and brighter; then she glanced at the sharp knife, and again fixed her eyes on the prince, who whispered the name of his bride in his dreams. She was in his thoughts, and the knife trembled in the hand of the little mermaid: then she flung it far away from her into the waves; the water turned red where it fell, and the drops that spurted up looked like blood. She cast one more lingering, half-fainting glance at the prince, and then threw herself from the ship into the sea, and thought her body was dissolving into foam. The sun rose above the waves, and his warm rays fell on the cold foam of the little mermaid, who did not feel as if she were dying. She saw the bright sun, and all around her floated hundreds of transparent beautiful beings; she could see through them the white sails of the ship, and the red clouds in the sky; their speech was melodious, but too ethereal to be heard by mortal ears, as they were also unseen by mortal eyes. The little mermaid perceived that she had a body like theirs, and that she continued to rise higher and higher out of the foam. 'Where am I?' asked she, and her voice sounded ethereal, as the voice of those who were with her; no earthly music could imitate it.

'Among the daughters of the air,' answered one of them. 'A mermaid has not an immortal soul, nor can she obtain one unless she wins the love of a human being. On the power of another hangs her eternal destiny. But the daughters of the air, although they do not possess an immortal soul, can, by their good deeds, procure one for themselves. We fly to warm countries, and cool the sultry air that destroys mankind with the pestilence. We carry the perfume of the flowers to spread health and restoration. After we have striven for three hundred years to all the good in our power, we receive an immortal soul and take part in the happiness of mankind. You, poor little mermaid, have tried with your whole heart to do as we are doing; you have suffered and endured and raised yourself to the spirit-world by your good deeds; and now, by striving for three hundred years in the same way, you may obtain an immortal soul.'

The little mermaid lifted her glorified eyes towards the sun, and felt them, for the first time, filling with tears. On the ship, in which she had left the prince, there were life and noise; she saw him and his beautiful bride searching for her; sorrowfully they gazed at the pearly foam, as if they knew she had thrown herself into the waves. Unseen she kissed the forehead of her bride, and fanned the prince, and then mounted with the other children of the air to a rosy cloud that floated through the aether.

'After three hundred years, thus shall we float into the kingdom of heaven,' said she. 'And we may even get there sooner,' whispered one of her companions. 'Unseen we can enter the houses of men, where there are children, and for every day on which we find a good child, who is the joy of his parents and deserves their love, our time of probation is shortened. The child does not know, when we fly through the room, that we smile with joy at his good conduct, for we can count one year less of our three hundred years. But when we see a naughty or a wicked child, we shed tears of sorrow, and for every tear a day is added to our time of trial!'

Hans Christian Andersen (1805–75) was born in Odense, Denmark, and is celebrated today throughout the world as the author of numerous much-loved fairy tales. 'The Little Mermaid', one of his most famous stories, was first published in 1837 and is thought to have been offered as a message of love to the unattainable Edvard Collin after the latter announced his engagement. Although shy with females, Andersen himself fell in love with a series of women and girls who sadly did not reciprocate his feelings.

The Lady, or the Tiger?

Frank R. Stockton

In the very olden time there lived a semi-barbaric king, whose ideas, though somewhat polished and sharpened by the progressiveness of distant Latin neighbours, were still large, florid, and untrammelled, as became the half of him which was barbaric. He was a man of exuberant fancy, and, withal, of an authority so irresistible that, at his will, he turned his varied fancies into facts. He was greatly given to self-communing, and, when he and himself agreed upon anything, the thing was done. When every member of his domestic and political systems moved smoothly in its appointed course, his nature was bland and genial; but, whenever there was a little hitch, and some of his orbs got out of their orbits, he was blander and more genial still, for nothing pleased him so much as to make the crooked straight and crush down uneven places.

Among the borrowed notions by which his barbarism had become semified was that of the public arena, in which, by exhibitions of manly and beastly valour, the minds of his subjects were refined and cultured.

But even here the exuberant and barbaric fancy asserted itself. The arena of the king was built, not to give the people an opportunity of hearing the rhapsodies of dying gladiators, nor to enable them to view the inevitable conclusion of a conflict between religious opinions and hungry jaws, but for purposes far better adapted to widen and develop the mental energies of the people. This vast amphitheatre, with its encircling galleries, its mysterious vaults, and its unseen passages, was an agent of poetic justice, in which crime was punished, or virtue rewarded, by the decrees of an impartial and incorruptible chance.

When a subject was accused of a crime of sufficient importance to interest the king, public notice was given that on an appointed day the fate of the accused person would be decided in the king's arena, a structure which well deserved its name, for, although its form and plan were borrowed from afar, its purpose emanated solely from the brain of this man, who, every barleycorn a king, knew no tradition to which he owed more allegiance than pleased his fancy, and who ingrafted on every adopted form of human thought and action the rich growth of his barbaric idealism.

When all the people had assembled in the galleries, and the king, surrounded by his court, sat high up on his throne of royal state on one side of the arena, he gave a signal, a door beneath him opened, and the accused subject stepped out into the amphitheatre. Directly opposite him, on the other side of the inclosed space, were two doors, exactly alike and side by side. It was the duty and the privilege of the person on trial to walk directly to these doors and open one of them. He could open either door he pleased; he was subject to no guidance or influence but that of the aforementioned impartial and incorruptible chance. If he opened the one, there came out of it a hungry tiger, the fiercest and most cruel that could be procured, which immediately sprang upon him and tore him to pieces as a punishment for his guilt. The moment that the case of the criminal was thus decided, doleful iron bells were clanged, great wails went up from the hired mourners posted on the outer rim of the arena, and the vast audience, with bowed heads and downcast hearts, wended slowly their homeward way, mourning greatly that one so young and fair, or so old and respected, should have merited so dire a fate.

But, if the accused person opened the other door, there came forth from it a lady, the most suitable to his years and station that his majesty could select among his fair subjects, and to this lady he was immediately married, as a reward of his innocence. It mattered not that he might already possess a wife and family, or that his affections might be engaged upon an object of his own selection; the king allowed no such subordinate arrangements to interfere with his great scheme of retribution and reward. The exercises, as in the other instance, took place immediately, and in the arena. Another door opened beneath the king, and a priest, followed by a band of choristers, and dancing maidens blowing joyous airs on golden horns and treading an epithalamic measure, advanced to where the pair stood, side by side, and the wedding was promptly and cheerily solemnised. Then the gay brass bells rang forth their merry peals, the people shouted glad hurrahs, and the innocent man, preceded by children strewing flowers on his path, led his bride to his home.

This was the king's semi-barbaric method of administering

justice. Its perfect fairness is obvious. The criminal could not know out of which door would come the lady; he opened either he pleased, without having the slightest idea whether, in the next instant, he was to be devoured or married. On some occasions the tiger came out of one door, and on some out of the other. The decisions of this tribunal were not only fair, they were positively determinate: the accused person was instantly punished if he found himself guilty, and, if innocent, he was rewarded on the spot, whether he liked it or not. There was no escape from the judgements of the king's arena.

The institution was a very popular one. When the people gathered together on one of the great trial days, they never knew whether they were to witness a bloody slaughter or a hilarious wedding. This element of uncertainty lent an interest to the occasion which it could not otherwise have attained. Thus, the masses were entertained and pleased, and the thinking part of the community could bring no charge of unfairness against this plan, for did not the accused person have the whole matter in his own hands?

This semi-barbaric king had a daughter as blooming as his most florid fancies, and with a soul as fervent and imperious as his own. As is usual in such cases, she was the apple of his eye, and was loved by him above all humanity. Among his courtiers was a young man of that fineness of blood and lowness of station common to the conventional heroes of romance who love royal maidens. This royal maiden was well satisfied with her lover, for he was handsome and brave to a degree unsurpassed in all this kingdom, and she loved him with an ardour that had enough of barbarism in it to make it exceedingly warm and strong.

This love affair moved on happily for many months, until one day the king happened to discover its existence. He did not hesitate nor waver in regard to his duty in the premises. The youth was immediately cast into prison, and a day was appointed for his trial in the king's arena. This, of course, was an especially important occasion, and his majesty, as well as all the people, was greatly interested in the workings and development of this trial. Never before had such a case occurred; never before had a subject dared to love the daughter of the king. In after years such things became commonplace enough, but then they were in no slight degree novel and startling.

The tiger-cages of the kingdom were searched for the most

savage and relentless beasts, from which the fiercest monster might be selected for the arena; and the ranks of maiden youth and beauty throughout the land were carefully surveyed by competent judges in order that the young man might have a fitting bride in case fate did not determine for him a different destiny. Of course, everybody knew that the deed with which the accused was charged had been done. He had loved the princess, and neither he, she, nor anyone else, thought of denying the fact; but the king would not think of allowing any fact of this kind to interfere with the workings of the tribunal, in which he took such great delight and satisfaction. No matter how the affair turned out, the youth would be disposed of, and the king would take an aesthetic pleasure in watching the course of events, which would determine whether or not the young man had done wrong in allowing himself to love the princess.

The appointed day arrived. From far and near the people gathered, and thronged the great galleries of the arena, and crowds, unable to gain admittance, massed themselves against its outside walls. The king and his court were in their places, opposite the twin doors, those fateful portals, so terrible in their similarity.

All was ready. The signal was given. A door beneath the royal party opened, and the lover of the princess walked into the arena. Tall, beautiful, fair, his appearance was greeted with a low hum of admiration and anxiety. Half the audience had not known so grand a youth had lived among them. No wonder the princess loved him! What a terrible thing for him to be there!

As the youth advanced into the arena he turned, as the custom was, to bow to the king, but he did not think at all of that royal personage. His eyes were fixed upon the princess, who sat to the right of her father. Had it not been for the moiety of barbarism in her nature it is probable that lady would not have been there, but her intense and fervid soul would not allow her to be absent on an occasion in which she was so terribly interested. From the moment that the decree had gone forth that her lover should decide his fate in the king's arena, she had thought of nothing, night or day, but this great event and the various subjects connected with it. Possessed of more power, influence, and force of character than anyone who had ever before been interested in such a case, she had done what no other person had done,—she had possessed herself of the secret of the doors. She knew in which of the two rooms, that lay behind those doors, stood the cage of the tiger, with its open front, and in which waited the lady. Through these thick doors, heavily curtained with skins on the inside, it was impossible that any noise or suggestion should come from within to the person who should approach to raise the latch of one of them. But gold, and the power of a woman's will, had brought the secret to the princess.

And not only did she know in which room stood the lady ready to emerge, all blushing and radiant, should her door be opened, but she knew who the lady was. It was one of the fairest and loveliest of the damsels of the court who had been selected as the reward of the accused youth, should he be proved innocent of the crime of aspiring to one so far above him; and the princess hated her. Often had she seen, or imagined that she had seen, this fair creature throwing glances of admiration upon the person of her lover, and sometimes she thought these glances were perceived, and even returned. Now and then she had seen them talking together; it was but for a moment or two, but much can be said in a brief space; it may have been on most unimportant topics, but how could she know that? The girl was lovely, but she had dared to raise her eyes to the loved one of the princess; and, with all the intensity of the savage blood transmitted to her through long lines of wholly barbaric ancestors, she hated the woman who blushed and trembled behind that silent door.

When her lover turned and looked at her, and his eye met hers as she sat there, paler and whiter than anyone in the vast ocean of anxious faces about her, he saw, by that power of quick perception which is given to those whose souls are one, that she knew behind which door crouched the tiger, and behind which stood the lady. He had expected her to know it. He understood her nature, and his soul was assured that she would never rest until she had made plain to herself this thing, hidden to all other lookers-on, even to the king. The only hope for the youth in which there was any element of certainty was based upon the success of the princess in discovering this mystery; and the moment he looked upon her, he saw she had succeeded, as in his soul he knew she would succeed.

Then it was that his quick and anxious glance asked the question: 'Which?' It was as plain to her as if he shouted it from where he stood. There was not an instant to be lost. The question was asked in a flash; it must be answered in another.

Her right arm lay on the cushioned parapet before her. She raised her hand, and made a slight, quick movement toward the right. No one but her lover saw her. Every eye but his was fixed on the man in the arena.

He turned, and with a firm and rapid step he walked across the empty space. Every heart stopped beating, every breath was held, every eye was fixed immovably upon that man. Without the slightest hesitation, he went to the door on the right, and opened it.

Now, the point of the story is this: Did the tiger come out of that door, or did the lady?

The more we reflect upon this question, the harder it is to answer. It involves a study of the human heart which leads us through devious mazes of passion, out of which it is difficult to find our way. Think of it, fair reader, not as if the decision of the question depended upon yourself, but upon that hot-blooded, semi-barbaric princess, her soul at a white heat beneath the combined fires of despair and jealousy. She had lost him, but who should have him?

How often, in her waking hours and in her dreams, had she started in wild horror, and covered her face with her hands as she thought of her lover opening the door on the other side of which waited the cruel fangs of the tiger!

But how much oftener had she seen him at the other door! How in her grievous reveries had she gnashed her teeth, and torn her hair, when she saw his start of rapturous delight as he opened the door of the lady! How her soul had burned in agony when she had seen him rush to meet that woman, with her flushing cheek and sparkling eye of triumph; when she had seen him lead her forth, his whole frame kindled with the joy of recovered life; when she had heard the glad shouts from the multitude, and the wild ringing of the happy bells; when she had seen the priest, with his joyous followers, advance to the couple, and make them man and wife before her very eyes; and when she had seen them walk away together upon their path of flowers, followed by the tremendous shouts of the hilarious multitude, in which her one despairing shriek was lost and drowned!

Would it not be better for him to die at once, and go to wait for her in the blessed regions of semi-barbaric futurity?

And yet, that awful tiger, those shrieks, that blood!

Her decision had been indicated in an instant, but it had been made after days and nights of anguished deliberation. She had known she would be asked, she had decided what she would answer, and, without the slightest hesitation, she had moved her hand to the right.

The question of her decision is one not to be lightly considered, and it is not for me to presume to set myself up as the one person able to answer it. And so I leave it with all of you: Which came out of the opened door,—the lady, or the tiger?

Frank Richard Stockton (1834–1902) was born in Philadelphia and established a reputation as one of America's most popular writers and humorists, remembered especially for his fables and children's fairytales. 'The Lady, or the Tiger?', published in 1882, is perhaps his best-known story. Stockton himself never hinted at what he thought the outcome of the story would be.

Rappaccini's Daughter
Nathaniel Hawthorne

(From the Writings of Aubepine)

We do not remember to have seen any translated specimens of the productions of M. de l'Aubepine—a fact the less to be wondered at, as his very name is unknown to many of his own countrymen as well as to the student of foreign literature. As a writer, he seems to occupy an unfortunate position between the Transcendentalists (who, under one name or another, have their share in all the current literature of the world) and the great body of pen-and-ink men who address the intellect and sympathies of the multitude. If not too refined, at all events too remote, too shadowy, and unsubstantial in his modes of development to suit the taste of the latter class, and yet too popular to satisfy the spiritual or metaphysical requisitions of the former, he must necessarily find himself without an audience, except here and there an individual or possibly an isolated clique. His writings, to do them justice, are not altogether destitute of fancy and originality; they might have won him greater reputation but for an inveterate love of allegory, which is apt to invest his plots and characters with the aspect of scenery and people in the clouds, and to steal away the human warmth out of his conceptions. His fictions are sometimes historical, sometimes of the present day, and sometimes, so far as can be discovered, have little or no reference either to time or space. In any case, he generally contents himself with a very slight embroidery of outward manners,—the faintest possible counterfeit of real life,—and endeavours to create an interest by some less obvious peculiarity of the subject. Occasionally a breath of Nature, a raindrop of pathos and tenderness, or a gleam of humour, will find its way into the midst of his fantastic imagery, and make us feel as if, after all, we were yet within the limits of our native earth. We will only add to this very cursory notice that M. de l'Aubepine's productions, if the reader chance to take them in precisely the proper point of view, may amuse a leisure hour as well as those of a brighter man; if otherwise, they can hardly fail to look excessively like nonsense.

Our author is voluminous; he continues to write and publish with as much praiseworthy and indefatigable prolixity as if his efforts were crowned with the brilliant success that so justly attends those of Eugene Sue. His first appearance was by a collection of stories in a long series of volumes entitled 'Contes deux fois racontees'. The titles of some of his more recent works (we quote from memory) are as follows: 'Le Voyage Celeste a Chemin de Fer', 3 tom., 1838; 'Le nouveau Pere Adam et la nouvelle Mere Eve', 2 tom., 1839; 'Roderic; ou le Serpent a l'estomac', 2 tom., 1840; 'Le Culte du Feu', a folio volume of ponderous research into the religion and ritual of the old Persian Ghebers, published in 1841; 'La Soiree du Chateau en Espagne', 1 tom., 8vo, 1842; and 'L'Artiste du Beau; ou le Papillon Mecanique', 5 tom., 4to, 1843. Our somewhat wearisome perusal of this startling catalogue of volumes has left behind it a certain personal affection and sympathy, though by no means admiration, for M. de l'Aubepine; and we would fain do the little in our power towards introducing him favourably to the American public. The ensuing tale is a translation of his 'Beatrice; ou la Belle Empoisonneuse', recently published in 'La Revue Anti-Aristocratique'. This journal, edited by the Comte de Bearhaven, has for some years past led the defence of liberal principles and popular rights with a faithfulness and ability worthy of all praise.

A young man, named Giovanni Guasconti, came, very long ago, from the more southern region of Italy, to pursue his studies at the University of Padua. Giovanni, who had but a scanty supply of gold ducats in his pocket, took lodgings in a high and gloomy chamber of an old edifice which looked not unworthy to have been the palace of a Paduan noble, and which, in fact, exhibited over its entrance the armorial bearings of a family long since extinct. The young stranger, who was not unstudied in the great poem of his country, recollected that one of the ancestors of this family, and perhaps an occupant of this very mansion, had been pictured by Dante as a partaker of the immortal agonies of his Inferno. These reminiscences and associations, together with the tendency to heartbreak natural to a young man for the first time out of his native sphere, caused Giovanni to sigh heavily as he looked around the desolate and ill-furnished apartment.

'Holy Virgin, signor!' cried old Dame Lisabetta, who, won by the youth's remarkable beauty of person, was kindly endeavouring to give the chamber a habitable air, 'what a sigh was that to come out of a young man's heart! Do you find this old mansion gloomy? For the love of Heaven, then, put your head out of the window, and you will see as bright sunshine as you have left in Naples.'

Guasconti mechanically did as the old woman advised, but could not quite agree with her that the Paduan sunshine was as cheerful as that of southern Italy. Such as it was, however, it fell upon a garden beneath the window and expended its fostering influences on a variety of plants, which seemed to have been cultivated with exceeding care.

'Does this garden belong to the house?' asked Giovanni.

'Heaven forbid, signor, unless it were fruitful of better pot herbs than any that grow there now,' answered old Lisabetta. 'No; that garden is cultivated by the own hands of Signor Giacomo Rappaccini, the famous doctor, who, I warrant him, has been heard of as far as Naples. It is said that he distils these plants into medicines that are as potent as a charm. Oftentimes you may see the signor doctor at work, and perchance the signora, his daughter, too, gathering the strange flowers that grow in the garden.'

The old woman had now done what she could for the aspect of the chamber; and, commending the young man to the protection of the saints, took her departure.

Giovanni still found no better occupation than to look down into the garden beneath his window. From its appearance, he judged it to be one of those botanic gardens which were of earlier date in Padua than elsewhere in Italy or in the world. Or, not improbably, it might once have been the pleasure-place of an opulent family; for there was the ruin of a marble fountain in the centre, sculptured with rare art, but so woefully shattered that it was impossible to trace the original design from the chaos of remaining fragments. The water, however, continued to gush and sparkle into the sunbeams as cheerfully as ever. A little gurgling sound ascended to the young man's window, and made him feel as if the fountain were an immortal spirit that sung its song unceasingly and without heeding the vicissitudes around it, while one century imbodied it in marble and another scattered the perishable garniture on the soil. All about the pool into which the water subsided grew various plants, that seemed to require a plentiful supply of moisture for the nourishment of gigantic leaves, and in some instances, flowers gorgeously magnificent. There was one shrub in particular, set in a marble vase in the midst of the pool, that bore a profusion of purple blossoms, each of which had the lustre and richness of a gem; and the whole together made a show so resplendent that it seemed enough to illuminate the garden, even had there been no sunshine. Every portion of the soil was peopled with plants and herbs, which, if less beautiful, still bore tokens of assiduous care, as if all had their individual virtues, known to the scientific mind that fostered them. Some were placed in urns, rich with old carving, and others in common garden pots; some crept serpent-like along the ground or climbed on high, using whatever means of ascent was offered them. One plant had wreathed itself round a statue of Vertumnus, which was thus quite veiled and shrouded in a drapery of hanging foliage, so happily arranged that it might have served a sculptor for a study.

While Giovanni stood at the window he heard a rustling behind a screen of leaves, and became aware that a person was at work in the garden. His figure soon emerged into view, and showed itself to be that of no common labourer, but a tall, emaciated, sallow, and sickly-looking man, dressed in a scholar's garb of black. He was beyond the middle term of life, with grey hair, a thin, grey beard, and a face singularly marked with intellect and cultivation, but which could never, even in his more youthful days, have expressed much warmth of heart.

Nothing could exceed the intentness with which this scientific gardener examined every shrub which grew in his path: it seemed as if he was looking into their inmost nature, making observations in regard to their creative essence, and discovering why one leaf grew in this shape and another in that, and wherefore such and such flowers differed among themselves in hue and perfume. Nevertheless, in spite of this deep intelligence on his part, there was no approach to intimacy between himself and these vegetable existences. On the contrary, he avoided their actual touch or the direct inhaling of their odours with a caution that impressed Giovanni most disagreeably; for the man's demeanour was that of one walking among malignant influences, such as savage beasts, or deadly snakes, or evil spirits, which, should he allow them one moment of licence, would wreak upon him some terrible fatality. It was strangely frightful to the young man's imagination to see this air of insecurity in a person cultivating a garden, that most simple and innocent of human toils, and which had been alike the joy and labour of the unfallen parents of the race. Was this garden, then, the Eden of the present world? And this man, with such a perception of harm in what his own hands caused to grow,—was he the Adam?

The distrustful gardener, while plucking away the dead leaves or pruning the too luxuriant growth of the shrubs, defended his hands with a pair of thick gloves. Nor were these his only armour. When, in his walk through the garden, he came to the magnificent plant that hung its purple gems beside the marble fountain, he placed a kind of mask over his mouth and nostrils, as if all this beauty did but conceal a deadlier malice; but, finding his task still too dangerous, he drew back, removed the mask, and called loudly, but in the infirm voice of a person affected with inward disease, 'Beatrice! Beatrice!'

'Here am I, my father. What would you?' cried a rich and youthful voice from the window of the opposite house—a voice as rich as a tropical sunset, and which made Giovanni, though he knew not why, think of deep hues of purple or crimson and of perfumes heavily delectable. 'Are you in the garden?'

'Yes, Beatrice,' answered the gardener, 'and I need your help.'

Soon there emerged from under a sculptured portal the figure of a young girl, arrayed with as much richness of taste as the most splendid of the flowers, beautiful as the day, and with a bloom so deep and vivid that one shade more would have been too much. She looked redundant with life, health, and energy; all of which attributes were bound down and compressed, as it were and girdled tensely, in their luxuriance, by her virgin zone. Yet Giovanni's fancy must have grown morbid while he looked down into the garden; for the impression which the fair stranger made upon him was as if here were another flower, the human sister of those vegetable ones, as beautiful as they, more beautiful than the richest of them, but still to be touched only with a glove, nor to be approached without a mask. As Beatrice came down the garden path, it was observable that she handled and inhaled the odour of several of the plants which her father had most sedulously avoided.

'Here, Beatrice,' said the latter, 'see how many needful offices require to be done to our chief treasure. Yet, shattered as I am, my life might pay the penalty of approaching it so closely as circumstances demand. Henceforth, I fear, this plant must be consigned to your sole charge.'

'And gladly will I undertake it,' cried again the rich tones of the young lady, as she bent towards the magnificent plant and opened her arms as if to embrace it. 'Yes, my sister, my splendour, it shall be Beatrice's task to nurse and serve thee; and thou shalt reward her with thy kisses and perfumed breath, which to her is as the breath of life.'

Then, with all the tenderness in her manner that was so strikingly expressed in her words, she busied herself with such attentions as the plant seemed to require; and Giovanni, at his lofty window, rubbed his eyes and almost doubted whether it were a girl tending her favourite flower, or one sister performing the duties of affection to another. The scene soon terminated. Whether Dr Rappaccini had finished his labours in the garden, or that his watchful eye had caught the stranger's face, he now took his daughter's arm and retired. Night was already closing in; oppressive exhalations seemed to proceed from the plants and steal upward past the open window; and Giovanni, closing the lattice, went to his couch and dreamed of a rich flower and beautiful girl. Flower and maiden were different, and yet the same, and fraught with some strange peril in either shape.

But there is an influence in the light of morning that tends to rectify whatever errors of fancy, or even of judgement, we may have incurred during the sun's decline, or among the shadows of the night, or in the less wholesome glow of moonshine. Giovanni's first movement, on starting from sleep, was to throw open the window and gaze down into the garden which his dreams had made so fertile of mysteries. He was surprised and a little ashamed to find how real and matter-of-fact an affair it proved to be, in the first rays of the sun which gilded the dew-drops that hung upon leaf and blossom, and, while giving a brighter beauty to each rare flower, brought everything within the limits of ordinary experience. The young man rejoiced that, in the heart of the barren city, he had the privilege of overlooking this spot of lovely and luxuriant vegetation. It would serve, he said to himself, as a symbolic language to keep him in communion with Nature. Neither the sickly and thoughtworn Dr Giacomo Rappaccini, it is true, nor his brilliant daughter, were now visible; so that Giovanni could not determine how much of the singularity which he attributed to both was due to their own qualities and how much to his wonder-working fancy; but he was inclined to take a most rational view of the whole matter.

In the course of the day he paid his respects to Signor Pietro Baglioni, professor of medicine in the university, a physician of eminent repute to whom Giovanni had brought a letter of introduction. The professor was an elderly personage, apparently of genial nature, and habits that might almost be called jovial. He kept the young man to dinner, and made himself very agreeable by the freedom and liveliness of his conversation, especially when warmed by a flask or two of Tuscan wine. Giovanni, conceiving that men of science, inhabitants of the same city, must needs be on familiar terms with one another, took an opportunity to mention the name of Dr Rappaccini. But the professor did not respond with so much cordiality as he had anticipated.

'Ill would it become a teacher of the divine art of medicine,' said Professor Pietro Baglioni, in answer to a question of Giovanni, 'to withhold due and well-considered praise of a physician so eminently skilled as Rappaccini; but, on the other hand, I should answer it but scantily to my conscience were I to permit a worthy youth like yourself, Signor Giovanni, the son of an ancient friend, to imbibe erroneous ideas respecting a man who might hereafter chance to hold your life and death in his hands. The truth is, our worshipful Dr Rappaccini has as much science as any member of the faculty—with perhaps one single exception—in Padua, or all Italy; but there are certain grave objections to his professional character.'

'And what are they?' asked the young man.

'Has my friend Giovanni any disease of body or heart, that he is so inquisitive about physicians?' said the professor, with a smile. 'But as for Rappaccini, it is said of him—and I, who know the man well, can answer for its truth—that he cares infinitely more for science than for mankind. His patients are interesting to him only as subjects for some new experiment. He would sacrifice human life, his own among the rest, or whatever else was dearest to him, for the sake of adding so much as a grain of mustard seed to the great heap of his accumulated knowledge.'

'Methinks he is an awful man indeed,' remarked Guasconti, mentally recalling the cold and purely intellectual aspect of Rappaccini. 'And yet, worshipful professor, is it not a noble spirit? Are there many men capable of so spiritual a love of science?'

'God forbid,' answered the professor, somewhat testily; 'at least, unless they take sounder views of the healing art than those adopted by Rappaccini. It is his theory that all medicinal virtues are comprised within those substances which we term vegetable poisons. These he cultivates with his own hands, and is said even to have produced new varieties of poison, more horribly deleterious than Nature, without the assistance of this learned person, would ever have plagued the world withal. That the signor doctor does less mischief than might be expected with such dangerous substances is undeniable. Now and then, it must be owned, he has effected, or seemed to effect, a marvellous cure; but, to tell you my private mind, Signor Giovanni, he should receive little credit for such instances of success,—they being probably the work of chance,—but should be held strictly accountable for his failures, which may justly be considered his own work.'

The youth might have taken Baglioni's opinions with many grains of allowance had he known that there was a professional warfare of long continuance between him and Dr Rappaccini, in which the latter was generally thought to have gained the advantage. If the reader be inclined to judge for himself, we refer him to certain black-letter tracts on both sides, preserved in the medical department of the University of Padua.

'I know not, most learned professor,' returned Giovanni, after musing on what had been said of Rappaccini's exclusive zeal for science,—'I know not how dearly this physician may love his art; but surely there is one object more dear to him. He has a daughter.'

'Aha!' cried the professor, with a laugh. 'So now our friend Giovanni's secret is out. You have heard of this daughter, whom all the young men in Padua are wild about, though not half a dozen have ever had the good hap to see her face. I know little of the Signora Beatrice save that Rappaccini is said to have instructed her deeply in his science, and that, young and beautiful as fame reports her, she is already qualified to fill a professor's chair. Perchance her father destines her for mine! Other absurd rumours there be, not worth talking about or listening to. So now, Signor Giovanni, drink off your glass of lachryma.'

Guasconti returned to his lodgings somewhat heated with the wine he had quaffed, and which caused his brain to swim with strange fantasies in reference to Dr Rappaccini and the beautiful Beatrice. On his way, happening to pass by a florist's, he bought a fresh bouquet of flowers.

Ascending to his chamber, he seated himself near the window, but within the shadow thrown by the depth of the wall, so that he could look down into the garden with little risk of being discovered. All beneath his eye was a solitude. The strange plants were basking in the sunshine, and now and then nodding gently to one another, as if in acknowledgement of sympathy and kindred. In the midst, by the shattered fountain, grew the magnificent shrub, with its purple gems clustering all over it; they glowed in the air, and gleamed back again out of the depths of the pool, which thus seemed to overflow with coloured radiance from the rich reflection that was steeped in it. At first, as we have said, the garden was a solitude. Soon, however,—as Giovanni had half hoped, half feared, would be the case,—a figure appeared beneath the antique sculptured portal, and came down between the rows of plants, inhaling their various perfumes as if she were one of those beings of old classic fable that lived upon sweet odours. On again beholding Beatrice, the young man was even startled to perceive how much her beauty exceeded his recollection of it; so brilliant, so vivid, was its character, that she glowed amid the sunlight, and, as Giovanni whispered to himself, positively illuminated the more shadowy intervals of the garden path. Her face being now more revealed than on the former occasion, he was struck by its expression of simplicity and sweetness,—qualities that had not entered into his idea of her character, and which made him ask anew what manner of mortal she might be. Nor did he fail again to observe, or imagine, an analogy between the beautiful girl and the gorgeous shrub that hung its gemlike flowers over the fountain,—a resemblance which Beatrice seemed to have indulged a fantastic humour in heightening, both by the arrangement of her dress and the selection of its hues.

Approaching the shrub, she threw open her arms, as with a passionate ardour, and drew its branches into an intimate embrace—so intimate that her features were hidden in its leafy bosom and her glistening ringlets all intermingled with the flowers.

'Give me thy breath, my sister,' exclaimed Beatrice; 'for I am faint with common air. And give me this flower of thine, which I separate with gentlest fingers from the stem and place it close beside my heart.'

With these words the beautiful daughter of Rappaccini plucked one of the richest blossoms of the shrub, and was about to fasten it in her bosom. But now, unless Giovanni's draughts of wine had bewildered his senses, a singular incident occurred. A small orange-coloured reptile, of the lizard or chameleon species, chanced to be creeping along the path, just at the feet of Beatrice. It appeared to Giovanni,—but, at the distance from which he gazed, he could scarcely have seen anything so minute,— it appeared to him, however, that a drop or two of moisture from the broken stem of the flower descended upon the lizard's head. For an instant the reptile contorted itself violently, and then lay motionless in the sunshine. Beatrice observed this remarkable phenomenon and crossed herself, sadly, but without surprise; nor did she therefore hesitate to arrange the fatal flower in her bosom. There it blushed, and almost glimmered with the dazzling effect of a precious stone, adding to her dress and aspect the one appropriate charm which nothing else in the world could have supplied. But Giovanni, out of the shadow of his window, bent forward and shrank back, and murmured and trembled.

'Am I awake? Have I my senses?' said he to himself. 'What is this being? Beautiful shall I call her, or inexpressibly terrible?'

Beatrice now strayed carelessly through the garden, approaching closer beneath Giovanni's window, so that he was compelled to thrust his head quite out of its concealment in order to gratify the intense and painful curiosity which she excited. At this moment there came a beautiful insect over the garden wall; it had, perhaps, wandered through the city, and found no flowers or verdure among those antique haunts of men until the heavy perfumes of Dr Rappaccini's shrubs had lured it from afar. Without alighting on the flowers, this winged brightness seemed to be attracted by Beatrice, and lingered in the air and fluttered about her head. Now, here it could not be but that Giovanni Guasconti's eyes deceived him. Be that as it might, he fancied that, while Beatrice was gazing at the insect with childish delight, it grew faint and fell at her feet; its bright wings shivered; it was dead—from no cause that he could discern, unless it were the atmosphere of her breath. Again Beatrice crossed herself and sighed heavily as she bent over the dead insect.

An impulsive movement of Giovanni drew her eyes to the window. There she beheld the beautiful head of the young man—rather a

Grecian than an Italian head, with fair, regular features, and a glistening of gold among his ringlets—gazing down upon her like a being that hovered in mid air. Scarcely knowing what he did, Giovanni threw down the bouquet which he had hitherto held in his hand.

'Signora,' said he, 'there are pure and healthful flowers. Wear them for the sake of Giovanni Guasconti.'

'Thanks, signor,' replied Beatrice, with her rich voice, that came forth as it were like a gush of music, and with a mirthful expression half childish and half woman-like. 'I accept your gift, and would fain recompense it with this precious purple flower; but if I toss it into the air it will not reach you. So Signor Guasconti must even content himself with my thanks.'

She lifted the bouquet from the ground, and then, as if inwardly ashamed at having stepped aside from her maidenly reserve to respond to a stranger's greeting, passed swiftly homeward through the garden. But few as the moments were, it seemed to Giovanni, when she was on the point of vanishing beneath the sculptured portal, that his beautiful bouquet was already beginning to wither in her grasp. It was an idle thought; there could be no possibility of distinguishing a faded flower from a fresh one at so great a distance.

For many days after this incident the young man avoided the window that looked into Dr Rappaccini's garden, as if something ugly and monstrous would have blasted his eyesight had he been betrayed into a glance. He felt conscious of having put himself, to a certain extent, within the influence of an unintelligible power by the communication which he had opened with Beatrice. The wisest course would have been, if his heart were in any real danger, to quit his lodgings and Padua itself at once; the next wiser, to have accustomed himself, as far as possible, to the familiar and daylight view of Beatrice—thus bringing her rigidly and systematically within the limits of ordinary experience. Least of all, while avoiding her sight, ought Giovanni to have remained so near this extraordinary being that the proximity and possibility even of intercourse should give a kind of substance and reality to the wild vagaries which his imagination ran riot continually in producing. Guasconti had not a deep heart—or, at all events, its depths were not sounded now; but he had a quick fancy, and an ardent southern temperament, which rose every instant to a higher fever pitch. Whether or no Beatrice possessed those terrible attributes, that fatal breath, the affinity with those so beautiful and deadly flowers which were indicated by what Giovanni had witnessed, she had at least instilled a fierce and subtle poison into his system. It was not love, although her rich beauty was a madness to him; nor horror, even while he fancied her spirit to be imbued with the same baneful essence that seemed to pervade her physical frame; but a wild offspring of both love and horror that had each parent in it, and burned like one and shivered like the other. Giovanni knew not what to dread; still less did he know what to hope; yet hope and dread kept a continual warfare in his breast, alternately vanquishing one another and starting up afresh to renew the contest. Blessed are all simple emotions, be they dark or bright! It is the lurid intermixture of the two that produces the illuminating blaze of the infernal regions.

Sometimes he endeavoured to assuage the fever of his spirit by a rapid walk through the streets of Padua or beyond its gates: his footsteps kept time with the throbbings of his brain, so that the walk was apt to accelerate itself to a race. One day he found himself arrested; his arm was seized by a portly personage, who had turned back on recognising the young man and expended much breath in overtaking him.

'Signor Giovanni! Stay, my young friend!' cried he. 'Have you forgotten me? That might well be the case if I were as much altered as yourself.'

It was Baglioni, whom Giovanni had avoided ever since their first meeting, from a doubt that the professor's sagacity would look too deeply into his secrets. Endeavouring to recover himself, he stared forth wildly from his inner world into the outer one and spoke like a man in a dream.

'Yes; I am Giovanni Guasconti. You are Professor Pietro Baglioni. Now let me pass!'

'Not yet, not yet, Signor Giovanni Guasconti,' said the professor, smiling, but at the same time scrutinising the youth with an earnest glance. 'What! did I grow up side by side with your father? and shall his son pass me like a stranger in these old streets of Padua? Stand still, Signor Giovanni; for we must have a word or two before we part.'

'Speedily, then, most worshipful professor, speedily,' said Giovanni, with feverish impatience. 'Does not your worship see that I am in haste?'

Now, while he was speaking there came a man in black along the street, stooping and moving feebly like a person in inferior health. His face was all overspread with a most sickly and sallow hue, but yet so pervaded with an expression of piercing and active intellect that an observer might easily have overlooked the merely physical attributes and have seen only this wonderful energy. As he passed, this person exchanged a cold and distant salutation with Baglioni, but fixed his eyes upon Giovanni with an intentness that seemed to bring out whatever was within him worthy of notice. Nevertheless, there was a peculiar quietness in the look, as if taking merely a speculative, not a human interest, in the young man.

'It is Dr Rappaccini!' whispered the professor when the stranger had passed. 'Has he ever seen your face before?'

'Not that I know,' answered Giovanni, starting at the name.

'He *has* seen you! he must have seen you!' said Baglioni, hastily. 'For some purpose or other, this man of science is making a study of you. I know that look of his! It is the same that coldly illuminates his face as he bends over a bird, a mouse, or a butterfly, which, in pursuance of some experiment, he has killed by the perfume of a flower; a look as deep as Nature itself, but without Nature's warmth of love. Signor Giovanni, I will stake my life upon it, you are the subject of one of Rappaccini's experiments!'

'Will you make a fool of me?' cried Giovanni, passionately. '*that*, signor professor, were an untoward experiment.'

'Patience! patience!' replied the imperturbable professor. 'I tell thee, my poor Giovanni, that Rappaccini has a scientific interest in thee. Thou hast fallen into fearful hands! And the Signora Beatrice,—what part does she act in this mystery?'

But Guasconti, finding Baglioni's pertinacity intolerable, here broke away, and was gone before the professor could again seize his arm. He looked after the young man intently and shook his head.

'This must not be,' said Baglioni to himself. 'The youth is the son of my old friend, and shall not come to any harm from which the arcana of medical science can preserve him. Besides, it is too insufferable an impertinence in Rappaccini, thus to snatch the lad out of my own hands, as I may say, and make use of him for his infernal experiments. This daughter of his! It shall be looked to. Perchance, most learned Rappaccini, I may foil you where you little dream of it!'

Meanwhile Giovanni had pursued a circuitous route, and at length found himself at the door of his lodgings. As he crossed the threshold he was met by old Lisabetta, who smirked and smiled, and was evidently desirous to attract his attention; vainly, however, as the ebullition of his feelings had momentarily subsided into a cold and dull vacuity. He turned his eyes full upon the withered face that was puckering itself into a smile, but seemed to behold it not. The old dame, therefore, laid her grasp upon his cloak.

'Signor! signor!' whispered she, still with a smile over the whole breadth of her visage, so that it looked not unlike a grotesque carving in wood, darkened by centuries. 'Listen, signor! There is a private entrance into the garden!'

'What do you say?' exclaimed Giovanni, turning quickly about, as if an inanimate thing should start into feverish life. 'A private entrance into Dr Rappaccini's garden?'

'Hush! hush! not so loud!' whispered Lisabetta, putting her hand over his mouth. 'Yes; into the worshipful doctor's garden, where you may see all his fine shrubbery. Many a young man in Padua would give gold to be admitted among those flowers.'

Giovanni put a piece of gold into her hand.

'Show me the way,' said he.

A surmise, probably excited by his conversation with Baglioni, crossed his mind, that this interposition of old Lisabetta might perchance be connected with the intrigue, whatever were its nature, in which the professor seemed to suppose that Dr Rappaccini was involving him. But such a suspicion, though it disturbed Giovanni, was inadequate to restrain him. The instant that he was aware of the possibility of approaching Beatrice, it seemed an absolute necessity of his existence to do so. It mattered not whether she were angel or demon; he was irrevocably within her sphere, and must obey the law that whirled him onward, in ever-lessening circles, towards a result which he did not attempt to foreshadow; and yet, strange to say, there came across him a sudden doubt whether this intense interest on his part were not delusory; whether it were really of so deep and positive a nature as to justify him in now thrusting himself into an incalculable position; whether it were not merely the fantasy of a young man's brain, only slightly or not at all connected with his heart.

He paused, hesitated, turned half about, but again went on. His withered guide led him along several obscure passages, and finally undid a door, through which, as it was opened, there came the sight and sound of rustling leaves, with the broken sunshine glimmering among them. Giovanni stepped forth, and, forcing himself through the entanglement of a shrub that wreathed its tendrils over the hidden entrance, stood beneath his own window in the open area of Dr Rappaccini's garden.

How often is it the case that, when impossibilities have come to pass and dreams have condensed their misty substance into tangible realities, we find ourselves calm, and even coldly self-possessed, amid circumstances which it would have been a delirium of joy or agony to anticipate! Fate delights to thwart us thus. Passion will choose his own time to rush upon the scene, and lingers sluggishly behind when an appropriate adjustment of events would seem to summon his appearance. So was it now with Giovanni. Day after day his pulses had throbbed with feverish blood at the improbable idea of an interview with Beatrice, and of standing with her, face to face, in this very garden, basking in the Oriental sunshine of her beauty, and snatching from her full gaze the mystery which he deemed the riddle of his own existence. But now there was a singular and untimely equanimity within his breast. He threw a glance around the garden to discover if Beatrice or her father were present, and, perceiving that he was alone, began a critical observation of the plants.

The aspect of one and all of them dissatisfied him; their gorgeousness seemed fierce, passionate, and even unnatural. There was hardly an individual shrub which a wanderer, straying by himself through a forest, would not have been startled to find growing wild, as if an unearthly face had glared at him out of the thicket. Several also would have shocked a delicate instinct by an appearance of artificialness indicating that there had been such commixture, and, as it were, adultery, of various vegetable species, that the production was no longer of God's making, but the monstrous offspring of man's depraved fancy, glowing with only an evil mockery of beauty. They were probably the result of experiment, which in one or two cases had succeeded in mingling plants individually lovely into a compound possessing the questionable and ominous character that distinguished the whole growth of the garden. In fine, Giovanni recognised but two or three plants in the collection, and those of a kind that he well knew to be poisonous. While busy with these contemplations he heard the rustling of a silken garment, and, turning, beheld Beatrice emerging from beneath the sculptured portal.

Giovanni had not considered with himself what should be his deportment; whether he should apologise for his intrusion into the garden, or assume that he was there with the privity at least, if not by the desire, of Dr Rappaccini or his daughter; but Beatrice's manner placed him at his ease, though leaving him still in doubt by what agency he had gained admittance. She came lightly along the path and met him near the broken fountain. There was surprise in her face, but brightened by a simple and kind expression of pleasure.

'You are a connoisseur in flowers, signor,' said Beatrice, with a smile, alluding to the bouquet which he had flung her from the window. 'It is no marvel, therefore, if the sight of my father's rare collection has tempted you to take a nearer view. If he were here, he could tell you many strange and interesting facts as to the nature and habits of these shrubs; for he has spent a lifetime in such studies, and this garden is his world.'

'And yourself, lady,' observed Giovanni, 'if fame says true,— you likewise are deeply skilled in the virtues indicated by these rich blossoms and these spicy perfumes. Would you deign to be my instructress, I should prove an apter scholar than if taught by Signor Rappaccini himself.'

'Are there such idle rumours?' asked Beatrice, with the music of a pleasant laugh. 'Do people say that I am skilled in my father's science of plants? What a jest is there! No; though I have grown up among these flowers, I know no more of them than their hues and perfume; and sometimes methinks I would fain rid myself of even that small knowledge. There are many flowers here, and those not the least brilliant, that shock and offend me when they meet my eye. But pray, signor, do not believe these stories about my science. Believe nothing of me save what you see with your own eyes.'

'And must I believe all that I have seen with my own eyes?' asked Giovanni, pointedly, while the recollection of former scenes made him shrink. 'No, signora; you demand too little of me. Bid me believe nothing save what comes from your own lips.'

It would appear that Beatrice understood him. There came a deep flush to her cheek; but she looked full into Giovanni's eyes, and responded to his gaze of uneasy suspicion with a queenlike haughtiness.

'I do so bid you, signor,' she replied. 'Forget whatever you may have fancied in regard to me. If true to the outward senses, still it may be false in its essence; but the words of Beatrice Rappaccini's lips are true from the depths of the heart outward. Those you may believe.'

A fervour glowed in her whole aspect and beamed upon Giovanni's consciousness like the light of truth itself; but while she spoke there was a fragrance in the atmosphere around her, rich and delightful, though evanescent, yet which the young man, from an indefinable reluctance, scarcely dared to draw into his lungs. It might be the odour of the flowers. Could it be Beatrice's breath which thus embalmed her words with a strange richness, as if by steeping them in her heart? A faintness passed like a shadow over Giovanni and flitted away; he seemed to gaze through the beautiful girl's eyes into her transparent soul, and felt no more doubt or fear.

The tinge of passion that had coloured Beatrice's manner vanished; she became gay, and appeared to derive a pure delight from her communion with the youth not unlike what the maiden of a lonely island might have felt conversing with a voyager from the civilised world. Evidently her experience of life had been confined within the limits of that garden. She talked now about matters as simple as the daylight or summer clouds, and now asked questions in reference to the city, or Giovanni's distant home, his friends, his mother, and his sisters—questions indicating such seclusion, and such lack of familiarity with modes and forms, that Giovanni responded as if to an infant. Her spirit gushed out before him like a fresh rill that was just catching its first glimpse of the sunlight and wondering at the reflections of earth and sky which were flung into its bosom. There came thoughts, too, from a deep source, and fantasies of a gemlike brilliancy, as if diamonds and rubies sparkled upward among the bubbles of the fountain. Ever and anon there gleamed across the young man's mind a sense of wonder that he should be walking side by side with the being who had so wrought upon his imagination, whom he had idealised in such hues of terror, in whom he had positively witnessed such manifestations of dreadful attributes,—that he should be conversing with Beatrice like a brother, and should find her so human and so maidenlike. But such reflections were only momentary; the effect of her character was too real not to make itself familiar at once.

In this free intercourse they had strayed through the garden, and now, after many turns among its avenues, were come to the shattered fountain, beside which grew the magnificent shrub, with its treasury of glowing blossoms. A fragrance was diffused from it which Giovanni recognised as identical with that which he had attributed to Beatrice's breath, but incomparably more powerful. As her eyes fell upon it, Giovanni beheld her press her hand to her bosom as if her heart were throbbing suddenly and painfully.

'For the first time in my life,' murmured she, addressing the shrub, 'I had forgotten thee.'

'I remember, signora,' said Giovanni, 'that you once promised to reward me with one of these living gems for the bouquet which I had the happy boldness to fling to your feet. Permit me now to pluck it as a memorial of this interview.'

He made a step towards the shrub with extended hand; but Beatrice darted forward, uttering a shriek that went through his heart like a dagger. She caught his hand and drew it back with the whole force of her slender figure. Giovanni felt her touch thrilling through his fibres.

'Touch it not!' exclaimed she, in a voice of agony. 'Not for thy life! It is fatal!'

Then, hiding her face, she fled from him and vanished beneath the sculptured portal. As Giovanni followed her with his eyes, he beheld the emaciated figure and pale intelligence of Dr Rappaccini, who had been watching the scene, he knew not how long, within the shadow of the entrance.

No sooner was Guasconti alone in his chamber than the image of Beatrice came back to his passionate musings, invested with all the witchery that had been gathering around it ever since his first glimpse of her, and now likewise imbued with a tender warmth of girlish womanhood. She was human; her nature was endowed with all gentle and feminine qualities; she was worthiest to be worshipped; she was capable, surely, on her part, of the height and heroism of love. Those tokens which he had hitherto considered as proofs of a frightful peculiarity in her physical and moral system were now either forgotten, or, by the subtle sophistry of passion transmitted into a golden crown of enchantment, rendering Beatrice the more admirable by so much as she was the more unique. Whatever had looked ugly was now beautiful; or, if incapable of such a change, it stole away and hid itself among those shapeless half ideas which throng the dim region beyond the daylight of our perfect consciousness. Thus did he spend the night, nor fell asleep until the dawn had begun to awake the slumbering flowers in Dr Rappaccini's garden, whither Giovanni's dreams doubtless led him. Up rose the sun in his due season, and, flinging his beams upon the young man's eyelids, awoke him to a sense of pain. When thoroughly aroused, he became sensible of a burning and tingling agony in his hand—in his right hand—the very hand which Beatrice had grasped in her own when he was on the point of plucking one of the gemlike flowers. On the back of that hand there was now a purple print like that of four small fingers, and the likeness of a slender thumb upon his wrist.

Oh, how stubbornly does love,—or even that cunning semblance of love which flourishes in the imagination, but strikes no depth of root into the heart,—how stubbornly does it hold its faith until the moment comes when it is doomed to vanish into thin mist! Giovanni wrapped a handkerchief about his hand and wondered what evil thing had stung him, and soon forgot his pain in a reverie of Beatrice.

After the first interview, a second was in the inevitable course of what we call fate. A third; a fourth; and a meeting with Beatrice in the garden was no longer an incident in Giovanni's daily life, but the whole space in which he might be said to live; for the anticipation and memory of that ecstatic hour made up the remainder. Nor was it otherwise with the daughter of Rappaccini. She watched for the youth's appearance, and flew to his side with confidence as unreserved as if they had been playmates from early infancy—as if they were such playmates still. If, by any unwonted chance, he failed to come at the appointed moment, she stood beneath the window and sent up the rich sweetness of her tones to float around him in his chamber and echo and reverberate throughout his heart: 'Giovanni! Giovanni! Why tarriest thou? Come down!' And down he hastened into that Eden of poisonous flowers.

But, with all this intimate familiarity, there was still a reserve in Beatrice's demeanour, so rigidly and invariably sustained that the idea of infringing it scarcely occurred to his imagination. By all appreciable signs, they loved; they had looked love with eyes that conveyed the holy secret from the depths of one soul into the depths of the other, as if it were too sacred to be whispered by the way; they had even spoken love in those gushes of passion when their spirits darted forth in articulated breath like tongues of long-hidden flame; and yet there had been no seal of lips, no clasp of hands, nor any slightest caress such as love claims and hallows. He had never touched one of the gleaming ringlets of her hair; her garment—so marked was the physical barrier between them—had never been waved against him by a breeze. On the few occasions when Giovanni had seemed tempted to overstep the limit, Beatrice grew so sad, so stern, and withal wore such a look of desolate separation, shuddering at itself, that not a spoken word was requisite to repel him. At such times he was startled at the horrible suspicions that rose, monster-like, out of the caverns of his heart and stared him in the face; his love grew thin and faint as the morning mist, his doubts alone had substance. But, when Beatrice's face brightened again after the momentary shadow, she was transformed at once from the mysterious, questionable being whom he had watched with so much awe and horror; she was now the beautiful and unsophisticated girl whom he felt that his spirit knew with a certainty beyond all other knowledge.

A considerable time had now passed since Giovanni's last meeting with Baglioni. One morning, however, he was disagreeably surprised by a visit from the professor, whom he had scarcely thought of for whole weeks, and would willingly have forgotten still longer. Given up as he had long been to a pervading excitement, he could tolerate no companions except upon condition of their perfect sympathy with his present state of feeling. Such sympathy was not to be expected from Professor Baglioni.

The visitor chatted carelessly for a few moments about the gossip of the city and the university, and then took up another topic.

'I have been reading an old classic author lately,' said he, 'and met with a story that strangely interested me. Possibly you may remember it. It is of an Indian prince, who sent a beautiful woman as a present to Alexander the Great. She was as lovely as the dawn and gorgeous as the sunset; but what especially distinguished her was a certain rich perfume in her breath—richer than a garden of Persian roses. Alexander, as was natural to a youthful conqueror, fell in love at first sight with this magnificent stranger; but a certain sage physician, happening to be present, discovered a terrible secret in regard to her.'

'And what was that?' asked Giovanni, turning his eyes downward to avoid those of the professor.

'That this lovely woman,' continued Baglioni, with emphasis, 'had been nourished with poisons from her birth upward, until her whole nature was so imbued with them that she herself had become the deadliest poison in existence. Poison was her element of life. With that rich perfume of her breath she blasted the very air. Her love would have been poison—her embrace death. Is not this a marvellous tale?'

'A childish fable,' answered Giovanni, nervously starting from his chair. 'I marvel how your worship finds time to read such nonsense among your graver studies.'

'By the by,' said the professor, looking uneasily about him, 'what singular fragrance is this in your apartment? Is it the perfume of your gloves? It is faint, but delicious; and yet, after all, by no means agreeable. Were I to breathe it long, methinks it would make me ill. It is like the breath of a flower; but I see no flowers in the chamber.'

'Nor are there any,' replied Giovanni, who had turned pale as the professor spoke; 'nor, I think, is there any fragrance except in your worship's imagination. Odours, being a sort of element combined of the sensual and the spiritual, are apt to deceive us in this manner. The recollection of a perfume, the bare idea of it, may easily be mistaken for a present reality.'

'Ay; but my sober imagination does not often play such tricks,' said Baglioni; 'and, were I to fancy any kind of odour, it would be that of some vile apothecary drug, wherewith my fingers are likely enough to be imbued. Our worshipful friend Rappaccini, as I have heard, tinctures his medicaments with odours richer than those of Araby. Doubtless, likewise, the fair and learned Signora Beatrice would minister to her patients with draughts as sweet as a maiden's breath; but woe to him that sips them!'

Giovanni's face evinced many contending emotions. The tone in which the professor alluded to the pure and lovely daughter of Rappaccini was a torture to his soul; and yet the intimation of a view of her character opposite to his own, gave instantaneous distinctness to a thousand dim suspicions, which now grinned at him like so many demons. But he strove hard to quell them and to respond to Baglioni with

249

a true lover's perfect faith.

'Signor professor,' said he, 'you were my father's friend; perchance, too, it is your purpose to act a friendly part towards his son. I would fain feel nothing towards you save respect and deference; but I pray you to observe, signor, that there is one subject on which we must not speak. You know not the Signora Beatrice. You cannot, therefore, estimate the wrong—the blasphemy, I may even say—that is offered to her character by a light or injurious word.'

'Giovanni! my poor Giovanni!' answered the professor, with a calm expression of pity, 'I know this wretched girl far better than yourself. You shall hear the truth in respect to the poisoner Rappaccini and his poisonous daughter; yes, poisonous as she is beautiful. Listen; for, even should you do violence to my grey hairs, it shall not silence me. That old fable of the Indian woman has become a truth by the deep and deadly science of Rappaccini and in the person of the lovely Beatrice.'

Giovanni groaned and hid his face

'Her father,' continued Baglioni, 'was not restrained by natural affection from offering up his child in this horrible manner as the victim of his insane zeal for science; for, let us do him justice, he is as true a man of science as ever distilled his own heart in an alembic. What, then, will be your fate? Beyond a doubt you are selected as the material of some new experiment. Perhaps the result is to be death; perhaps a fate more awful still. Rappaccini, with what he calls the interest of science before his eyes, will hesitate at nothing.'

'It is a dream,' muttered Giovanni to himself; 'surely it is a dream.'

'But,' resumed the professor, 'be of good cheer, son of my friend. It is not yet too late for the rescue. Possibly we may even succeed in bringing back this miserable child within the limits of ordinary nature, from which her father's madness has estranged her. Behold this little silver vase! It was wrought by the hands of the renowned Benvenuto Cellini, and is well worthy to be a love gift to the fairest dame in Italy. But its contents are invaluable. One little sip of this antidote would have rendered the most virulent poisons of the Borgias innocuous. Doubt not that it will be as efficacious against those of Rappaccini. Bestow the vase, and the precious liquid within it, on your Beatrice, and hopefully await the result.'

Baglioni laid a small, exquisitely wrought silver vial on the table and withdrew, leaving what he had said to produce its effect upon the young man's mind.

'We will thwart Rappaccini yet,' thought he, chuckling to himself, as he descended the stairs; 'but, let us confess the truth of him, he is a wonderful man—a wonderful man indeed; a vile empiric, however, in his practice, and therefore not to be tolerated by those who respect the good old rules of the medical profession.'

Throughout Giovanni's whole acquaintance with Beatrice, he had occasionally, as we have said, been haunted by dark surmises as to her character; yet so thoroughly had she made herself felt by him as a simple, natural, most affectionate, and guileless creature, that the image now held up by Professor Baglioni looked as strange and incredible as if it were not in accordance with his own original conception. True, there were ugly recollections connected with his first glimpses of the beautiful girl; he could not quite forget the bouquet that withered in her grasp, and the insect that perished amid the sunny air, by no ostensible agency save the fragrance of her breath. These incidents, however, dissolving in the pure light of her character, had no longer the efficacy of facts, but were acknowledged as mistaken fantasies, by whatever testimony of the senses they might appear to be substantiated. There is something truer and more real than what we can see with the eyes and touch with the finger. On such better evidence had Giovanni founded his confidence in Beatrice, though rather by the necessary force of her high attributes than by any deep and generous faith on his part. But now his spirit was incapable of sustaining itself at the height to which the early enthusiasm of passion had exalted it; he fell down, grovelling among earthly doubts, and defiled therewith the pure whiteness of Beatrice's image. Not that he gave her up; he did but distrust. He resolved to institute some decisive test that should satisfy him, once for all, whether there were those dreadful peculiarities in her physical nature which could not be supposed to exist without some corresponding monstrosity of soul. His eyes, gazing down afar, might have deceived him as to the lizard, the insect, and the flowers; but if he could witness, at the distance of a few paces, the sudden blight of one fresh and healthful flower in Beatrice's hand, there would be room for no further question. With this idea he hastened to the florist's and purchased a bouquet that was still gemmed with the morning dew-drops.

It was now the customary hour of his daily interview with Beatrice. Before descending into the garden, Giovanni failed not to look at his figure in the mirror,—a vanity to be expected in a beautiful young man, yet, as displaying itself at that troubled and feverish moment, the token of a certain shallowness of feeling and insincerity of character. He did gaze, however, and said to himself that his features had never before possessed so rich a grace, nor his eyes such vivacity, nor his cheeks so warm a hue of superabundant life.

'At least,' thought he, 'her poison has not yet insinuated itself into my system. I am no flower to perish in her grasp.'

With that thought he turned his eyes on the bouquet, which he had never once laid aside from his hand. A thrill of indefinable horror shot through his frame on perceiving that those dewy flowers were already beginning to droop; they wore the aspect of things that had been fresh and lovely yesterday. Giovanni grew white as marble, and stood motionless before the mirror, staring at his own reflection there as at the likeness of something frightful. He remembered Baglioni's remark about the fragrance that seemed to pervade the chamber. It must have been the poison in his breath! Then he shuddered—shuddered at himself. Recovering from his stupor, he began to watch with curious eye a spider that was busily at work hanging its web from the antique cornice of the apartment, crossing and recrossing the artful system of interwoven lines—as vigorous and active a spider as ever dangled from an old ceiling. Giovanni bent towards the insect, and emitted a deep, long breath. The spider suddenly ceased its toil; the web vibrated with a tremor originating in the body of the small artisan. Again Giovanni sent forth a breath, deeper, longer, and imbued with a venomous feeling out of his heart: he knew not whether he were wicked, or only desperate. The spider made a convulsive gripe with his limbs and hung dead across the window.

'Accursed! accursed!' muttered Giovanni, addressing himself. 'Hast thou grown so poisonous that this deadly insect perishes by thy breath?'

At that moment a rich, sweet voice came floating up from the garden.

'Giovanni! Giovanni! It is past the hour! Why tarriest thou?

Come down!'

'Yes,' muttered Giovanni again. 'She is the only being whom my breath may not slay! Would that it might!'

He rushed down, and in an instant was standing before the bright and loving eyes of Beatrice. A moment ago his wrath and despair had been so fierce that he could have desired nothing so much as to wither her by a glance; but with her actual presence there came influences which had too real an existence to be at once shaken off: recollections of the delicate and benign power of her feminine nature, which had so often enveloped him in a religious calm; recollections of many a holy and passionate outgush of her heart, when the pure fountain had been unsealed from its depths and made visible in its transparency to his mental eye; recollections which, had Giovanni known how to estimate them, would have assured him that all this ugly mystery was but an earthly illusion, and that, whatever mist of evil might seem to have gathered over her, the real Beatrice was a heavenly angel. Incapable as he was of such high faith, still her presence had not utterly lost its magic. Giovanni's rage was quelled into an aspect of sullen insensibility. Beatrice, with a quick spiritual sense, immediately felt that there was a gulf of blackness between them which neither he nor she could pass. They walked on together, sad and silent, and came thus to the marble fountain and to its pool of water on the ground, in the midst of which grew the shrub that bore gem-like blossoms. Giovanni was affrighted at the eager enjoyment—the appetite, as it were—with which he found himself inhaling the fragrance of the flowers.

'Beatrice,' asked he, abruptly, 'whence came this shrub?'

'My father created it,' answered she, with simplicity.

'Created it! created it!' repeated Giovanni. 'What mean you, Beatrice?'

'He is a man fearfully acquainted with the secrets of Nature,' replied Beatrice; 'and, at the hour when I first drew breath, this plant sprang from the soil, the offspring of his science, of his intellect, while I was but his earthly child. Approach it not!' continued she, observing with terror that Giovanni was drawing nearer to the shrub. 'It has qualities that you little dream of. But I, dearest Giovanni,—I grew up and blossomed with the plant and was nourished with its breath. It was my sister, and I loved it with a human affection; for, alas!—hast thou not suspected it?—there was an awful doom.'

Here Giovanni frowned so darkly upon her that Beatrice paused and trembled. But her faith in his tenderness reassured her, and made her blush that she had doubted for an instant.

'There was an awful doom,' she continued, 'the effect of my father's fatal love of science, which estranged me from all society of my kind. Until Heaven sent thee, dearest Giovanni, oh, how lonely was thy poor Beatrice!'

'Was it a hard doom?' asked Giovanni, fixing his eyes upon her.

'Only of late have I known how hard it was,' answered she, tenderly. 'Oh, yes; but my heart was torpid, and therefore quiet.'

Giovanni's rage broke forth from his sullen gloom like a lightning flash out of a dark cloud.

'Accursed one!' cried he, with venomous scorn and anger. 'And, finding thy solitude wearisome, thou hast severed me likewise from all the warmth of life and enticed me into thy region of unspeakable horror!'

'Giovanni!' exclaimed Beatrice, turning her large bright eyes upon his face. The force of his words had not found its way into her mind; she was merely thunderstruck.

'Yes, poisonous thing!' repeated Giovanni, beside himself with passion. 'Thou hast done it! Thou hast blasted me! Thou hast filled my veins with poison! Thou hast made me as hateful, as ugly, as loathsome and deadly a creature as thyself—a world's wonder of hideous monstrosity! Now, if our breath be happily as fatal to ourselves as to all others, let us join our lips in one kiss of unutterable hatred, and so die!'

'What has befallen me?' murmured Beatrice, with a low moan out of her heart. 'Holy Virgin, pity me, a poor heart-broken child!'

'Thou,—dost thou pray?' cried Giovanni, still with the same fiendish scorn. 'Thy very prayers, as they come from thy lips, taint the atmosphere with death. Yes, yes; let us pray! Let us to church and dip our fingers in the holy water at the portal! They that come after us will perish as by a pestilence! Let us sign crosses in the air! It will be scattering curses abroad in the likeness of holy symbols!'

'Giovanni,' said Beatrice, calmly, for her grief was beyond passion, 'why dost thou join thyself with me thus in those terrible words? I, it is true, am the horrible thing thou namest me. But thou,—what hast thou to do, save with one other shudder at my hideous misery to go forth out of the garden and mingle with thy race, and forget there ever crawled on earth such a monster as poor Beatrice?'

'Dost thou pretend ignorance?' asked Giovanni, scowling upon her. 'Behold! this power have I gained from the pure daughter of Rappaccini.'

There was a swarm of summer insects flitting through the air in search of the food promised by the flower odours of the fatal garden. They circled round Giovanni's head, and were evidently attracted towards him by the same influence which had drawn them for an instant within the sphere of several of the shrubs. He sent forth a breath among them, and smiled bitterly at Beatrice as at least a score of the insects fell dead upon the ground.

'I see it! I see it!' shrieked Beatrice. 'It is my father's fatal science! No, no, Giovanni; it was not I! Never! never! I dreamed only to love thee and be with thee a little time, and so to let thee pass away, leaving but thine image in mine heart; for, Giovanni, believe it, though my body be nourished with poison, my spirit is God's creature, and craves love as its daily food. But my father,—he has united us in this fearful sympathy. Yes; spurn me, tread upon me, kill me! Oh, what is death after such words as thine? But it was not I. Not for a world of bliss would I have done it.'

Giovanni's passion had exhausted itself in its outburst from his lips. There now came across him a sense, mournful, and not without tenderness, of the intimate and peculiar relationship between Beatrice and himself. They stood, as it were, in an utter solitude, which would be made none the less solitary by the densest throng of human life. Ought not, then, the desert of humanity around them to press this insulated pair closer together? If they should be cruel to one another, who was there to be kind to them? Besides, thought Giovanni, might there not still be a hope of his returning within the limits of ordinary nature, and leading Beatrice, the redeemed Beatrice, by the hand? O, weak, and selfish, and unworthy spirit, that could dream of an earthly union and earthly happiness as possible, after such deep love had been so bitterly wronged as was Beatrice's love by Giovanni's blighting words! No, no; there could be no such hope. She must pass heavily, with that broken heart, across the borders of Time—she must bathe her hurts in some fount of paradise, and forget her grief in the light of immortality, and *there* be well.

But Giovanni did not know it.

'Dear Beatrice,' said he, approaching her, while she shrank away as always at his approach, but now with a different impulse, 'dearest Beatrice, our fate is not yet so desperate. Behold! there is a medicine, potent, as a wise physician has assured me, and almost divine in its efficacy. It is composed of ingredients the most opposite to those by which thy awful father has brought this calamity upon thee and me. It is distilled of blessed herbs. Shall we not quaff it together, and thus be purified from evil?'

'Give it me!' said Beatrice, extending her hand to receive the little silver vial which Giovanni took from his bosom. She added, with a peculiar emphasis, 'I will drink; but do thou await the result.'

She put Baglioni's antidote to her lips; and, at the same moment, the figure of Rappaccini emerged from the portal and came slowly towards the marble fountain. As he drew near, the pale man of science seemed to gaze with a triumphant expression at the beautiful youth and maiden, as might an artist who should spend his life in achieving a picture or a group of statuary and finally be satisfied with his success. He paused; his bent form grew erect with conscious power; he spread out his hands over them in the attitude of a father imploring a blessing upon his children; but those were the same hands that had thrown poison into the stream of their lives. Giovanni trembled. Beatrice shuddered nervously, and pressed her hand upon her heart.

'My daughter,' said Rappaccini, 'thou art no longer lonely in the world. Pluck one of those precious gems from thy sister shrub and bid thy bridegroom wear it in his bosom. It will not harm him now. My science and the sympathy between thee and him have so wrought within his system that he now stands apart from common men, as thou dost, daughter of my pride and triumph, from ordinary women. Pass on, then, through the world, most dear to one another and dreadful to all besides!'

'My father,' said Beatrice, feebly,—and still as she spoke she kept her hand upon her heart,—'wherefore didst thou inflict this miserable doom upon thy child?'

'Miserable!' exclaimed Rappaccini. 'What mean you, foolish girl? Dost thou deem it misery to be endowed with marvellous gifts against which no power nor strength could avail an enemy—misery, to be able to quell the mightiest with a breath—misery, to be as terrible as thou art beautiful? Wouldst thou, then, have preferred the condition of a weak woman, exposed to all evil and capable of none?'

'I would fain have been loved, not feared,' murmured Beatrice, sinking down upon the ground. 'But now it matters not. I am going, father, where the evil which thou hast striven to mingle with my being will pass away like a dream—like the fragrance of these poisonous flowers, which will no longer taint my breath among the flowers of Eden. Farewell, Giovanni! Thy words of hatred are like lead within my heart; but they, too, will fall away as I ascend. Oh, was there not, from the first, more poison in thy nature than in mine?'

To Beatrice,—so radically had her earthly part been wrought upon by Rappaccini's skill,—as poison had been life, so the powerful antidote was death; and thus the poor victim of man's ingenuity and of thwarted nature, and of the fatality that attends all such efforts of perverted wisdom, perished there, at the feet of her father and Giovanni. Just at that moment Professor Pietro Baglioni looked forth from the window, and called loudly, in a tone of triumph mixed with horror, to the thunderstricken man of science, 'Rappaccini! Rappaccini! and is *this* the upshot of your experiment!'

Nathaniel Hawthorne (1804–1864) was born in Salem, Massachusetts, and is celebrated today as one of the great American authors, whose most famous works include the novels The Scarlet Letter *(1850) and* The House of the Seven Gables *(1851). 'Rappaccini's Daughter' was among the stories collected as* Mosses from an Old Manse *(1846), the Old Manse being the name of the house in which Hawthorne and his wife spent the first three years of their married life. The central notion of a poisonous but beautiful maiden has been traced back to Indian myths, although there is no evidence that Hawthorne knew of these earlier stories.*

Araby

James Joyce

North Richmond Street, being blind, was a quiet street except at the hour when the Christian Brothers' School set the boys free. An uninhabited house of two storeys stood at the blind end, detached from its neighbours in a square ground. The other houses of the street, conscious of decent lives within them, gazed at one another with brown imperturbable faces.

The former tenant of our house, a priest, had died in the back drawing-room. Air, musty from having been long enclosed, hung in all the rooms, and the waste room behind the kitchen was littered with old useless papers. Among these I found a few paper-covered books, the pages of which were curled and damp: *The Abbot*, by Walter Scott, *The Devout Communicant* and *The Memoirs of Vidocq*. I liked the last best because its leaves were yellow. The wild garden behind the house contained a central apple-tree and a few straggling bushes under one of which I found the late tenant's rusty bicycle-pump. He had been a very charitable priest; in his will he had left all his money to institutions and the furniture of his house to his sister.

When the short days of winter came dusk fell before we had well eaten our dinners. When we met in the street the houses had grown sombre. The space of sky above us was the colour of ever-changing violet and towards it the lamps of the street lifted their feeble lanterns. The cold air stung us and we played till our bodies glowed. Our shouts echoed in the silent street. The career of our play brought us through the dark muddy lanes behind the houses where we ran the gauntlet of the rough tribes from the cottages, to the back doors of the dark dripping gardens where odours arose from the ashpits, to the dark odorous stables where a coachman smoothed and combed the horse or shook music from the buckled harness. When we returned to the street light from the kitchen windows had filled the areas. If my uncle was seen turning the corner we hid in the shadow until we had seen him safely housed. Or if Mangan's sister came out on the doorstep to call her brother in to his tea we watched her from our shadow peer up and down the street. We waited to see whether she would remain or go in and, if she remained, we left our shadow and walked up to Mangan's steps resignedly. She was waiting for us, her figure defined by the light from the half-opened door. Her brother always teased her before he obeyed and I stood by the railings looking at her. Her dress swung as she moved her body and the soft rope of her hair tossed from side to side.

Every morning I lay on the floor in the front parlour watching her door. The blind was pulled down to within an inch of the sash so that I could not be seen. When she came out on the doorstep my heart leaped. I ran to the hall, seized my books and followed her. I kept her brown figure always in my eye and, when we came near the point at which our ways diverged, I quickened my pace and passed her. This happened morning after morning. I had never spoken to her, except for a few casual words, and yet her name was like a summons to all my foolish blood.

Her image accompanied me even in places the most hostile to romance. On Saturday evenings when my aunt went marketing I had to go to carry some of the parcels. We walked through the flaring streets, jostled by drunken men and bargaining women, amid the curses of labourers, the shrill litanies of shop-boys who stood on guard by the barrels of pigs' cheeks, the nasal chanting of street-singers, who sang a come-all-you about O'Donovan Rossa, or a ballad about the troubles in our native land. These noises converged in a single sensation of life for me: I imagined that I bore my chalice safely through a throng of foes. Her name sprang to my lips at moments in strange prayers and praises which I myself did not understand. My eyes were often full of tears (I could not tell why) and at times a flood from my heart seemed to pour itself out into my bosom. I thought little of the future. I did not know whether I would ever speak to her or not or, if I spoke to her, how I could tell her of my confused adoration. But my body was like a harp and her words and gestures were like fingers running upon the wires.

One evening I went into the back drawing-room in which the priest had died. It was a dark rainy evening and there was no sound in the house. Through one of the broken panes I heard the rain impinge upon the earth, the fine incessant needles of water playing in the sodden beds. Some distant lamp or lighted window gleamed below me. I was thankful that I could see so little. All my senses seemed to desire to veil themselves and, feeling that I was about to slip from them, I pressed the palms of my hands together until they trembled, murmuring: 'O love! O love!' many times.

At last she spoke to me. When she addressed the first words to me I was so confused that I did not know what to answer. She asked me was I going to Araby. I forgot whether I answered yes or no. It would be a splendid bazaar, she said; she would love to go.

'And why can't you?' I asked.

While she spoke she turned a silver bracelet round and round her wrist. She could not go, she said, because there would be a retreat that week in her convent. Her brother and two other boys were fighting for their caps and I was alone at the railings. She held one of the spikes, bowing her head towards me. The light from the lamp opposite our door caught the white curve of her neck, lit up her hair that rested there and, falling, lit up the hand upon the railing. It fell over one side of her dress and caught the white border of a petticoat, just visible as she stood at ease.

'It's well for you,' she said.

'If I go,' I said, 'I will bring you something.'

What innumerable follies laid waste my waking and sleeping thoughts after that evening! I wished to annihilate the tedious intervening days. I chafed against the work of school. At night in my bedroom and by day in the classroom her image came between me and the page I strove to read. The syllables of the word Araby were called to me through the silence in which my soul luxuriated and cast an Eastern enchantment over me. I asked for leave to go to the bazaar on Saturday night. My aunt was surprised and hoped it was not some Freemason affair. I answered few questions in class. I watched my master's face pass from amiability to sternness; he hoped I was not beginning to idle. I could not call my wandering thoughts together. I had hardly any patience with the serious work of life which, now that it stood between me and my desire, seemed to me child's play, ugly monotonous child's play.

On Saturday morning I reminded my uncle that I wished to go to the bazaar in the evening. He was fussing at the hallstand, looking for the hat-brush, and answered me curtly:

'Yes, boy, I know.'

As he was in the hall I could not go into the front parlour and lie at the window. I left the house in bad humour and walked slowly towards the school. The air was pitilessly raw and already my heart misgave me.

When I came home to dinner my uncle had not yet been home. Still it was early. I sat staring at the clock for some time and, when its ticking began to irritate me, I left the room. I mounted the staircase and gained the upper part of the house. The high cold empty gloomy rooms liberated me and I went from room to room singing. From the front window I saw my companions playing below in the street. Their cries reached me weakened and indistinct and, leaning my forehead against the cool glass, I looked over at the dark house where she lived. I may have stood there for an hour, seeing nothing but the brown-clad figure cast by my imagination, touched discreetly by the lamplight at the curved neck, at the hand upon the railings and at the border below the dress.

When I came downstairs again I found Mrs Mercer sitting at the fire. She was an old garrulous woman, a pawnbroker's widow, who collected used stamps for some pious purpose. I had to endure the gossip of the tea-table. The meal was prolonged beyond an hour and still my uncle did not come. Mrs Mercer stood up to go: she was sorry she couldn't wait any longer, but it was after eight o'clock and she did not like to be out late as the night air was bad for her. When she had gone I began to walk up and down the room, clenching my fists. My aunt said:

'I'm afraid you may put off your bazaar for this night of Our Lord.'

At nine o'clock I heard my uncle's latchkey in the halldoor. I heard him talking to himself and heard the hallstand rocking when it had received the weight of his overcoat. I could interpret these signs. When he was midway through his dinner I asked him to give me the money to go to the bazaar. He had forgotten.

'The people are in bed and after their first sleep now,' he said.

I did not smile. My aunt said to him energetically:

'Can't you give him the money and let him go? You've kept him late enough as it is.'

My uncle said he was very sorry he had forgotten. He said he believed in the old saying: 'All work and no play makes Jack a dull boy.' He asked me where I was going and, when I had told him a second time he asked me did I know 'The Arab's Farewell to his Steed'. When I left the kitchen he was about to recite the opening lines of the piece to my

261

aunt.

I held a florin tightly in my hand as I strode down Buckingham Street towards the station. The sight of the streets thronged with buyers and glaring with gas recalled to me the purpose of my journey. I took my seat in a third-class carriage of a deserted train. After an intolerable delay the train moved out of the station slowly. It crept onward among ruinous houses and over the twinkling river. At Westland Row Station a crowd of people pressed to the carriage doors; but the porters moved them back, saying that it was a special train for the bazaar. I remained alone in the bare carriage. In a few minutes the train drew up beside an improvised wooden platform. I passed out on to the road and saw by the lighted dial of a clock that it was ten minutes to ten. In front of me was a large building which displayed the magical name.

I could not find any sixpenny entrance and, fearing that the bazaar would be closed, I passed in quickly through a turnstile, handing a shilling to a weary-looking man. I found myself in a big hall girdled at half its height by a gallery. Nearly all the stalls were closed and the greater part of the hall was in darkness. I recognised a silence like that which pervades a church after a service. I walked into the centre of the bazaar timidly. A few people were gathered about the stalls which were still open. Before a curtain, over which the words Cafe Chantant were written in coloured lamps, two men were counting money on a salver. I listened to the fall of the coins.

Remembering with difficulty why I had come I went over to one of the stalls and examined porcelain vases and flowered tea-sets. At the door of the stall a young lady was talking and laughing with two young gentlemen. I remarked their English accents and listened vaguely to their conversation.

'O, I never said such a thing!'

'O, but you did!'

'O, but I didn't!'

'Didn't she say that?'

'Yes. I heard her.'

'O, there's a... fib!'

Observing me the young lady came over and asked me did I wish to buy anything. The tone of her voice was not encouraging; she seemed to have spoken to me out of a sense of duty. I looked humbly at the great jars that stood like eastern guards at either side of the dark entrance to the stall and murmured:

'No, thank you.'

The young lady changed the position of one of the vases and went back to the two young men. They began to talk of the same subject. Once or twice the young lady glanced at me over her shoulder.

I lingered before her stall, though I knew my stay was useless, to make my interest in her wares seem the more real. Then I turned away slowly and walked down the middle of the bazaar. I allowed the two pennies to fall against the sixpence in my pocket. I heard a voice call from one end of the gallery that the light was out. The upper part of the hall was now completely dark.

Gazing up into the darkness I saw myself as a creature driven and derided by vanity; and my eyes burned with anguish and anger.

James Augustine Aloysius Joyce (1882–1941) was born in Dublin and is revered today as one of the greatest, if controversial, names in Irish literature. The author of such innovative and uniquely Irish novels as A Portrait of the Artist as a Young Man *(1916),* Ulysses *(1922), and* Finnegans Wake *(1939), he was also acclaimed for his short stories. 'Araby' was one of the stories published in the collection* Dubliners *(1914); constituting a vivid evocation of first love, it drew on Joyce's childhood in Dublin, in particular his memories of his father, upon whom the uncle in the story was probably modelled.*

The White Stocking

D.H. Lawrence

I

'I'm getting up, Teddilinks,' said Mrs Whiston, and she sprang out of bed briskly.

'What the Hanover's got you?' asked Whiston.

'Nothing. Can't I get up?' she replied animatedly.

It was about seven o'clock, scarcely light yet in the cold bedroom. Whiston lay still and looked at his wife. She was a pretty little thing, with her fleecy, short black hair all tousled... He watched her as she dressed quickly, flicking her small, delightful limbs, throwing her clothes about her. Her slovenliness and untidiness did not trouble him. When she picked up the edge of her petticoat, ripped off a torn string of white lace, and flung it on the dressing-table, her careless abandon made his spirit glow. She stood before the mirror and roughly scrambled together her profuse little mane of hair. He watched the quickness and softness of her young shoulders, calmly, like a husband, and appreciatively.

'Rise up,' she cried, turning to him with a quick wave of her arm—'and shine forth.'

They had been married two years. But still, when she had gone out of the room, he felt as if all his light and warmth were taken away, he became aware of the raw, cold morning. So he rose himself, wondering casually what had roused her so early. Usually she lay in bed as late as she could.

Whiston fastened a belt round his loins and went downstairs in shirt and trousers. He heard her singing in her snatchy fashion. The stairs creaked under his weight. He passed down the narrow little passage, which she called a hall, of the seven and sixpenny house which was his first home.

He was a shapely young fellow of about twenty-eight, sleepy now and easy with well-being. He heard the water drumming into the kettle, and she began to whistle. He loved the quick way she dodged the supper cups under the tap to wash them for breakfast. She looked an untidy minx, but she was quick and handy enough.

'Teddilinks,' she cried.

'What?'

'Light a fire, quick.'

She wore an old, sack-like dressing-jacket of black silk pinned across her breast. But one of the sleeves, coming unfastened, showed some delightful pink upper-arm.

'Why don't you sew your sleeve up?' he said, suffering from the sight of the exposed soft flesh.

'Where?' she cried, peering round. 'Nuisance,' she said, seeing the gap, then with light fingers went on drying the cups.

The kitchen was of fair size, but gloomy. Whiston poked out the dead ashes.

Suddenly a thud was heard at the door down the passage.

'I'll go,' cried Mrs Whiston, and she was gone down the hall.

The postman was a ruddy-faced man who had been a soldier. He smiled broadly, handing her some packages.

'They've not forgot you,' he said impudently.

'No—lucky for them,' she said, with a toss of the head. But she was interested only in her envelopes this morning. The postman waited inquisitively, smiling in an ingratiating fashion. She slowly, abstractedly, as if she did not know anyone was there, closed the door in his face, continuing to look at the addresses on her letters.

She tore open the thin envelope. There was a long, hideous, cartoon valentine. She smiled briefly and dropped it on the floor. Struggling with the string of a packet, she opened a white cardboard box, and there lay a white silk handkerchief packed neatly under the paper lace of the box, and her initial, worked in heliotrope, fully displayed. She smiled pleasantly, and gently put the box aside. The third envelope contained another white packet—apparently a cotton handkerchief neatly folded. She shook it out. It was a long white stocking, but there was a little weight in the toe. Quickly, she thrust down her arm, wriggling her fingers into the toe of the stocking, and brought out a small box. She peeped inside the box, then hastily opened a door on her left hand, and went into the little, cold sitting-room. She had her lower lip caught earnestly between her teeth.

With a little flash of triumph, she lifted a pair of pearl ear-rings from the small box, and she went to the mirror. There, earnestly, she began to hook them through her ears, looking at herself sideways in the glass. Curiously concentrated and intent she seemed as she fingered the lobes of her ears, her head bent on one side.

Then the pearl ear-rings dangled under her rosy, small ears. She shook her head sharply, to see the swing of the drops. They went chill against her neck, in little, sharp touches. Then she stood still to look at herself, bridling her head in the dignified fashion. Then she simpered at herself. Catching her own eye, she could not help winking at herself and laughing.

She turned to look at the box. There was a scrap of paper with this posy:

'Pearls may be fair, but thou art fairer.
Wear these for me, and I'll love the wearer.'

She made a grimace and a grin. But she was drawn to the mirror again, to look at her ear-rings.

Whiston had made the fire burn, so he came to look for her. When she heard him, she started round quickly, guiltily. She was watching him with intent blue eyes when he appeared.

He did not see much, in his morning-drowsy warmth. He gave her, as ever, a feeling of warmth and slowness. His eyes were very blue, very kind, his manner simple.

'What ha' you got?' he asked.

'Valentines,' she said briskly, ostentatiously turning to show him the silk handkerchief. She thrust it under his nose. 'Smell how good,' she said.

'Who's that from?' he replied, without smelling.

'It's a valentine,' she cried. 'How da I know who it's from?'

'I'll bet you know,' he said.

'Ted!—I don't!' she cried, beginning to shake her head, then stopping because of the ear-rings.

He stood still a moment, displeased.

'They've no right to send you valentines, now,' he said.

'Ted!—Why not? You're not jealous, are you? I haven't the least idea who it's from. Look—there's my initial'—she pointed with an emphatic finger at the heliotrope embroidery—

'E for Elsie,
Nice little gelsie,'

she sang.

'Get out,' he said. 'You know who it's from.'

'Truth, I don't,' she cried.

He looked round, and saw the white stocking lying on a chair.

'Is this another?' he said.

'No, that's a sample,' she said. 'There's only a comic.' And she fetched in the long cartoon.

He stretched it out and looked at it solemnly.

'Fools!' he said, and went out of the room.

She flew upstairs and took off the ear-rings. When she returned, he was crouched before the fire blowing the coals. The skin of his face was flushed, and slightly pitted, as if he had had small-pox. But his neck was white and smooth and goodly. She hung her arms round his neck as he crouched there, and clung to him. He balanced on his toes.

'This fire's a slow-coach,' he said.

'And who else is a slow-coach?' she said.

'One of us two, I know,' he said, and he rose carefully. She remained clinging round his neck, so that she was lifted off her feet.

'Ha!—-swing me,' she cried.

He lowered his head, and she hung in the air, swinging from his neck, laughing. Then she slipped off.

'The kettle is singing,' she sang, flying for the teapot. He bent down again to blow the fire. The veins in his neck stood out, his shirt collar seemed too tight.

'Doctor Wyer,
Blow the fire,
Puff! puff! puff!'

she sang, laughing.

He smiled at her.

She was so glad because of her pearl ear-rings.

Over the breakfast she grew serious. He did not notice. She became portentous in her gravity. Almost it penetrated through his steady good-humour to irritate him.

'Teddy!' she said at last.

'What?' he asked.

'I told you a lie,' she said, humbly tragic.

His soul stirred uneasily.

'Oh aye?' he said casually.

She was not satisfied. He ought to be more moved.

'Yes,' she said.

He cut a piece of bread.

'Was it a good one?' he asked.

She was piqued. Then she considered—*was* it a good one? Then she laughed.

'No,' she said, 'it wasn't up to much.'

'Ah!' he said easily, but with a steady strength of fondness for her in his tone. 'Get it out then.'

It became a little more difficult.

'You know that white stocking,' she said earnestly. 'I told you a lie. It wasn't a sample. It was a valentine.'

A little frown came on his brow.

'Then what did you invent it as a sample for?' he said. But he knew this weakness of hers. The touch of anger in his voice frightened her.

'I was afraid you'd be cross,' she said pathetically.

'I'll bet you were vastly afraid,' he said.

'I *was*, Teddy.'

There was a pause. He was resolving one or two things in his mind.

'And who sent it?' he asked.

'I can guess,' she said, 'though there wasn't a word with it—except–'

She ran to the sitting-room and returned with a slip of paper.

'Pearls may be fair, but thou art fairer.
Wear these for me, and I'll love the wearer.'

He read it twice, then a dull red flush came on his face.

'And *who* do you guess it is?' he asked, with a ringing of anger in his voice.

'I suspect it's Sam Adams,' she said, with a little virtuous indignation.

Whiston was silent for a moment.

'Fool!' he said. 'An' what's it got to do with pearls?—and how can he say 'wear these for me' when there's only one? He hasn't got the brain to invent a proper verse.'

He screwed the sup of paper into a ball and flung it into the fire.

'I suppose he thinks it'll make a pair with the one last year,' she said.

'Why, did he send one then?'

'Yes. I thought you'd be wild if you knew.'

His jaw set rather sullenly.

Presently he rose, and went to wash himself, rolling back his sleeves and pulling open his shirt at the breast. It was as if his fine, clear-cut temples and steady eyes were degraded by the lower, rather brutal part of his face. But she loved it. As she whisked about, clearing the table, she loved the way in which he stood washing himself. He was such a man. She liked to see his neck glistening with water as he swilled it. It amused her and pleased her and thrilled her. He was so sure, so permanent, he had her so utterly in his power. It gave her a delightful, mischievous sense of liberty. Within his grasp, she could dart about excitingly.

He turned round to her, his face red from the cold water, his eyes fresh and very blue.

'You haven't been seeing anything of him, have you?' he asked roughly.

'Yes,' she answered, after a moment, as if caught guilty. 'He got into the tram with me, and he asked me to drink a coffee and a Benedictine in the Royal.'

'You've got it off fine and glib,' he said sullenly. 'And did you?'

'Yes,' she replied, with the air of a traitor before the rack.

The blood came up into his neck and face, he stood motionless, dangerous.

'It was cold, and it was such fun to go into the Royal,' she said.

'You'd go off with a nigger for a packet of chocolate,' he said, in anger and contempt, and some bitterness. Queer how he drew away from her, cut her off from him.

'Ted—how beastly!' she cried. 'You know quite well—' She caught her lip, flushed, and the tears came to her eyes.

He turned away, to put on his necktie. She went about her work, making a queer pathetic little mouth, down which occasionally dripped a tear.

He was ready to go. With his hat jammed down on his head, and his overcoat buttoned up to his chin, he came to kiss her. He would be miserable all the day if he went without. She allowed herself to be kissed. Her cheek was wet under his lips, and his heart burned. She hurt him so deeply. And she felt aggrieved, and did not quite forgive him.

In a moment she went upstairs to her ear-rings. Sweet they looked nestling in the little drawer—sweet! She examined them with voluptuous pleasure, she threaded them in her ears, she looked at herself, she posed and postured and smiled, and looked sad and tragic and winning and appealing, all in turn before the mirror. And she was happy, and very pretty.

She wore her ear-rings all morning, in the house. She was self-conscious, and quite brilliantly winsome, when the baker came, wondering if he would notice. All the tradesmen left her door with a glow in them, feeling elated, and unconsciously favouring the delightful little creature, though there had been nothing to notice in her behaviour.

She was stimulated all the day. She did not think about her husband. He was the permanent basis from which she took these giddy little flights into nowhere. At night, like chickens and curses, she would come home to him, to roost.

Meanwhile Whiston, a traveller and confidential support of a small firm, hastened about his work, his heart all the while anxious for her, yearning for surety, and kept tense by not getting it.

II

She had been a warehouse girl in Adams's lace factory before she was married. Sam Adams was her employer. He was a bachelor of forty, growing stout, a man well dressed and florid, with a large brown moustache and thin hair. From the rest of his well-groomed, showy appearance, it was evident his baldness was a chagrin to him. He had a good presence, and some Irish blood in his veins.

His fondness for the girls, or the fondness of the girls for him, was notorious. And Elsie, quick, pretty, almost witty little thing—she *seemed* witty, although, when her sayings were repeated, they were entirely trivial—she had a great attraction for him. He would come into the warehouse dressed in a rather sporting reefer coat, of fawn colour, and trousers of fine black-and-white check, a cap with a big peak and a scarlet carnation in his button-hole, to impress her. She was only half impressed. He was too loud for her good taste. Instinctively perceiving this, he sobered down to navy blue. Then a well-built man, florid, with large brown whiskers, smart navy blue suit, fashionable boots, and manly hat, he was the irreproachable. Elsie was impressed.

But meanwhile Whiston was courting her, and she made splendid little gestures, before her bedroom mirror, of the constant-and-true sort.

'True, true till death–'

That was her song. Whiston was made that way, so there was no need to take thought for him.

Every Christmas Sam Adams gave a party at his house, to which he invited his superior work-people—not factory hands and labourers, but those above. He was a generous man in his way, with a real warm feeling for giving pleasure.

Two years ago Elsie had attended this Christmas-party for the last time. Whiston had accompanied her. At that time he worked for Sam Adams.

She had been very proud of herself, in her close-fitting, full-skirted dress of blue silk. Whiston called for her. Then she tripped beside him, holding her large cashmere shawl across her breast. He strode with long strides, his trousers handsomely strapped under his boots, and her silk shoes bulging the pockets of his full-skirted overcoat.

They passed through the park gates, and her spirits rose. Above them the Castle Rock looked grandly in the night, the naked trees stood still and dark in the frost, along the boulevard.

They were rather late. Agitated with anticipation, in the cloakroom she gave up her shawl, donned her silk shoes, and looked at herself in the mirror. The loose bunches of curls on either side her face danced prettily, her mouth smiled.

She hung a moment in the door of the brilliantly lighted room. Many people were moving within the blaze of lamps, under the crystal chandeliers, the full skirts of the women balancing and floating, the side-whiskers and white cravats of the men bowing above. Then she entered the light.

In an instant Sam Adams was coming forward, lifting both his arms in boisterous welcome. There was a constant red laugh on his face.

'Come late, would you,' he shouted, 'like royalty.'

He seized her hands and led her forward. He opened his mouth wide when he spoke, and the effect of the warm, dark opening behind the brown whiskers was disturbing. But she was floating into the throng on his arm. He was very gallant.

'Now then,' he said, taking her card to write down the dances, 'I've got carte blanche, haven't I?'

'Mr Whiston doesn't dance,' she said.

'I am a lucky man!' he said, scribbling his initials. 'I was born with an *amourette* in my mouth.'

He wrote on, quietly. She blushed and laughed, not knowing what it meant.

'Why, what is that?' she said.

'It's you, even littler than you are, dressed in little wings,' he said.

'I should have to be pretty small to get in your mouth,' she said.

'You think you're too big, do you!' he said easily.

He handed her her card, with a bow.

'Now I'm set up, my darling, for this evening,' he said.

Then, quick, always at his ease, he looked over the room. She waited in front of him. He was ready. Catching the eye of the band, he

272

nodded. In a moment, the music began. He seemed to relax, giving himself up.

'Now then, Elsie,' he said, with a curious caress in his voice that seemed to lap the outside of her body in a warm glow, delicious. She gave herself to it. She liked it.

He was an excellent dancer. He seemed to draw her close in to him by some male warmth of attraction, so that she became all soft and pliant to him, flowing to his form, whilst he united her with him and they lapsed along in one movement. She was just carried in a kind of strong, warm flood, her feet moved of themselves, and only the music threw her away from him, threw her back to him, to his clasp, in his strong form moving against her, rhythmically, deliriously.

When it was over, he was pleased and his eyes had a curious gleam which thrilled her and yet had nothing to do with her. Yet it held her. He did not speak to her. He only looked straight into her eyes with a curious, gleaming look that disturbed her fearfully and deliriously. But also there was in his look some of the automatic irony of the *roué*. It left her partly cold. She was not carried away.

She went, driven by an opposite, heavier impulse, to Whiston. He stood looking gloomy, trying to admit that she had a perfect right to enjoy herself apart from him. He received her with rather grudging kindliness.

'Aren't you going to play whist?' she asked.

'Aye,' he said. 'Directly.'

'I do wish you could dance.'

'Well, I can't,' he said. 'So you enjoy yourself.'

'But I should enjoy it better if I could dance with you.'

'Nay, you're all right,' he said. 'I'm not made that way.'

'Then you ought to be!' she cried.

'Well, it's my fault, not yours. You enjoy yourself,' he bade her. Which she proceeded to do, a little bit irked.

She went with anticipation to the arms of Sam Adams, when the time came to dance with him. It *was* so gratifying, irrespective of the man. And she felt a little grudge against Whiston, soon forgotten when her host was holding her near to him, in a delicious embrace. And she watched his eyes, to meet the gleam in them, which gratified her.

She was getting warmed right through, the glow was penetrating

273

into her, driving away everything else. Only in her heart was a little tightness, like conscience.

When she got a chance, she escaped from the dancing-room to the card-room. There, in a cloud of smoke, she found Whiston playing cribbage. Radiant, roused, animated, she came up to him and greeted him. She was too strong, too vibrant a note in the quiet room. He lifted his head, and a frown knitted his gloomy forehead.

'Are you playing cribbage? Is it exciting? How are you getting on?' she chattered.

He looked at her. None of these questions needed answering, and he did not feel in touch with her. She turned to the cribbage-board.

'Are you white or red?' she asked.

'He's red,' replied the partner.

'Then you're losing,' she said, still to Whiston. And she lifted the red peg from the board. 'One—two—three—four—five—six—seven—eight—Right up there you ought to jump–'

'Now put it back in its right place,' said Whiston.

'Where was it?' she asked gaily, knowing her transgression. He took the little red peg away from her and stuck it in its hole.

The cards were shuffled.

'What a shame you're losing!' said Elsie.

'You'd better cut for him,' said the partner.

She did so, hastily. The cards were dealt. She put her hand on his shoulder, looking at his cards.

'It's good,' she cried, 'isn't it?'

He did not answer, but threw down two cards. It moved him more strongly than was comfortable, to have her hand on his shoulder, her curls dangling and touching his ears, whilst she was roused to another man. It made the blood flame over him.

At that moment Sam Adams appeared, florid and boisterous, intoxicated more with himself, with the dancing, than with wine. In his eyes the curious, impersonal light gleamed.

'I thought I should find you here, Elsie,' he cried boisterously, a disturbing, high note in his voice.

'What made you think so?' she replied, the mischief rousing in her.

The florid, well-built man narrowed his eyes to a smile.

'I should never look for you among the ladies,' he said, with a kind of intimate, animal call to her. He laughed, bowed, and offered her his arm.

'Madam, the music waits.'

She went almost helplessly, carried along with him, unwilling, yet delighted.

That dance was an intoxication to her. After the first few steps, she felt herself slipping away from herself. She almost knew she was going, she did not even want to go. Yet she must have chosen to go. She lay in the arm of the steady, close man with whom she was dancing, and she seemed to swim away out of contact with the room, into him. She had passed into another, denser element of him, an essential privacy. The room was all vague around her, like an atmosphere, like under sea, with a flow of ghostly, dumb movements. But she herself was held real against her partner, and it seemed she was connected with him, as if the movements of his body and limbs were her own movements, yet not her own movements—and oh, delicious! He also was given up, oblivious, concentrated, into the dance. His eye was unseeing. Only his large, voluptuous body gave off a subtle activity. His fingers seemed to search into her flesh. Every moment, and every moment, she felt she would give way utterly, and sink molten: the fusion point was coming when she would fuse down into perfect unconsciousness at his feet and knees. But he bore her round the room in the dance, and he seemed to sustain all her body with his limbs, his body, and his warmth seemed to come closer into her, nearer, till it would fuse right through her, and she would be as liquid to him, as an intoxication only.

It was exquisite. When it was over, she was dazed, and was scarcely breathing. She stood with him in the middle of the room as if she were alone in a remote place. He bent over her. She expected his lips on her bare shoulder, and waited. Yet they were not alone, they were not alone. It was cruel.

''Twas good, wasn't it, my darling?' he said to her, low and delighted. There was a strange impersonality about his low, exultant call that appealed to her irresistibly. Yet why was she aware of some part shut off in her? She pressed his arm, and he led her towards the door.

She was not aware of what she was doing, only a little grain of resistant trouble was in her. The man, possessed, yet with a superficial presence of mind, made way to the dining-room, as if to give her refreshment, cunningly working to his own escape with her. He was molten hot, filmed over with presence of mind, and bottomed with cold disbelief.

In the dining-room was Whiston, carrying coffee to the plain, neglected ladies. Elsie saw him, but felt as if he could not see her. She was beyond his reach and ken. A sort of fusion existed between her and the large man at her side. She ate her custard, but an incomplete fusion all the while sustained and contained her within the being of her employer.

But she was growing cooler. Whiston came up. She looked at him, and saw him with different eyes. She saw his slim, young man's figure real and enduring before her. That was he. But she was in the spell with the other man, fused with him, and she could not be taken away.

'Have you finished your cribbage?' she asked, with hasty evasion of him.

'Yes,' he replied. 'Aren't you getting tired of dancing?'

'Not a bit,' she said.

'Not she,' said Adams heartily. 'No girl with any spirit gets tired of dancing.—Have something else, Elsie. Come—sherry. Have a glass of sherry with us, Whiston.'

Whilst they sipped the wine, Adams watched Whiston almost cunningly, to find his advantage.

'We'd better be getting back—there's the music,' he said. 'See the women get something to eat, Whiston, will you, there's a good chap.'

And he began to draw away. Elsie was drifting helplessly with him. But Whiston put himself beside them, and went along with them. In silence they passed through to the dancing-room. There Adams hesitated, and looked round the room. It was as if he could not see.

A man came hurrying forward, claiming Elsie, and Adams went to his other partner. Whiston stood watching during the dance. She was conscious of him standing there observant of her, like a ghost, or a judgement, or a guardian angel. She was also conscious, much more intimately and impersonally, of the body of the other man moving somewhere in the room. She still belonged to him, but a feeling of distraction possessed her, and helplessness. Adams danced on, adhering to Elsie, waiting his time, with the persistence of cynicism.

276

The dance was over. Adams was detained. Elsie found herself beside Whiston. There was something shapely about him as he sat, about his knees and his distinct figure, that she clung to. It was as if he had enduring form. She put her hand on his knee.

'Are you enjoying yourself?' he asked.

'*Ever* so,' she replied, with a fervent, yet detached tone.

'It's going on for one o'clock,' he said.

'Is it?' she answered. It meant nothing to her.

'Should we be going?' he said.

She was silent. For the first time for an hour or more an inkling of her normal consciousness returned. She resented it.

'What for?' she said.

'I thought you might have had enough,' he said.

A slight soberness came over her, an irritation at being frustrated of her illusion.

'Why?' she said.

'We've been here since nine,' he said.

That was no answer, no reason. It conveyed nothing to her. She sat detached from him. Across the room Sam Adams glanced at her. She sat there exposed for him.

'You don't want to be too free with Sam Adams,' said Whiston cautiously, suffering. 'You know what he is.'

'How, free?' she asked.

'Why—you don't want to have too much to do with him.'

She sat silent. He was forcing her into consciousness of her position. But he could not get hold of her feelings, to change them. She had a curious, perverse desire that he should not.

'I like him,' she said.

'What do you find to like in him?' he said, with a hot heart.

'I don't know—but I like him,' she said.

She was immutable. He sat feeling heavy and dulled with rage. He was not clear as to what he felt. He sat there unliving whilst she danced. And she, distracted, lost to herself between the opposing forces of the two men, drifted. Between the dances, Whiston kept near to her. She was scarcely conscious. She glanced repeatedly at her card, to see when she would dance again with Adams, half in desire, half in dread. Sometimes she met his steady, glaucous eye as she passed him in the dance. Sometimes she saw the steadiness of his flank as he danced. And it was always as if she rested on his arm, were borne along, upborne by him, away from herself. And always there was present the other's antagonism. She was divided.

The time came for her to dance with Adams. Oh, the delicious closing of contact with him, of his limbs touching her limbs, his arm supporting her. She seemed to resolve. Whiston had not made himself real to her. He was only a heavy place in her consciousness.

But she breathed heavily, beginning to suffer from the closeness of strain. She was nervous. Adams also was constrained. A tightness, a tension was coming over them all. And he was exasperated, feeling something counteracting physical magnetism, feeling a will stronger with her than his own, intervening in what was becoming a vital necessity to him.

Elsie was almost lost to her own control. As she went forward with him to take her place at the dance, she stooped for her pocket-handkerchief. The music sounded for quadrilles. Everybody was ready. Adams stood with his body near her, exerting his attraction over her. He was tense and fighting. She stooped for her pocket-handkerchief, and shook it as she rose. It shook out and fell from her hand. With agony, she saw she had taken a white stocking instead of a handkerchief. For a second it lay on the floor, a twist of white stocking. Then, in an instant, Adams picked it up, with a little, surprised laugh of triumph.

'That'll do for me,' he whispered—seeming to take possession of her. And he stuffed the stocking in his trousers pocket, and quickly offered her his handkerchief.

The dance began. She felt weak and faint, as if her will were turned to water. A heavy sense of loss came over her. She could not help herself any more. But it was peace.

When the dance was over, Adams yielded her up. Whiston came to her.

'What was it as you dropped?' Whiston asked.

'I thought it was my handkerchief—I'd taken a stocking by mistake,' she said, detached and muted.

'And he's got it?'

'Yes.'

'What does he mean by that?'

She lifted her shoulders.

'Are you going to let him keep it?' he asked.

'I don't let him.'

There was a long pause.

'Am I to go and have it out with him?' he asked, his face flushed, his blue eyes going hard with opposition.

'No,' she said, pale.

'Why?'

'No—I don't want to say anything about it.'

He sat exasperated and nonplussed.

'You'll let him keep it, then?' he asked.

She sat silent and made no form of answer.

'What do you mean by it?' he said, dark with fury. And he started up.

'No!' she cried. 'Ted!' And she caught hold of him, sharply detaining him.

It made him black with rage.

'Why?' he said.

Then something about her mouth was pitiful to him. He did not understand, but he felt she must have her reasons.

'Then I'm not stopping here,' he said. 'Are you coming with me?'

She rose mutely, and they went out of the room. Adams had not noticed.

In a few moments they were in the street.

'What the hell do you mean?' he said, in a black fury.

She went at his side, in silence, neutral.

'That great hog, an' all,' he added.

Then they went a long time in silence through the frozen, deserted darkness of the town. She felt she could not go indoors. They were drawing near her house.

'I don't want to go home,' she suddenly cried in distress and anguish. 'I don't want to go home.'

He looked at her.

'Why don't you?' he said.

'I don't want to go home,' was all she could sob.

He heard somebody coming.

'Well, we can walk a bit further,' he said.

She was silent again. They passed out of the town into the fields. He held her by the arm—they could not speak.

'What's a-matter?' he asked at length, puzzled.

She began to cry again.

At last he took her in his arms, to soothe her. She sobbed by herself, almost unaware of him.

'Tell me what's a-matter, Elsie,' he said. 'Tell me what's a-matter—my dear—tell me, then–'

He kissed her wet face, and caressed her. She made no response. He was puzzled and tender and miserable.

At length she became quiet. Then he kissed her, and she put her arms round him, and clung to him very tight, as if for fear and anguish. He held her in his arms, wondering.

'Ted!' she whispered, frantic. 'Ted!'

'What, my love?' he answered, becoming also afraid.

'Be good to me,' she cried. 'Don't be cruel to me.'

'No, my pet,' he said, amazed and grieved. 'Why?'

'Oh, be good to me,' she sobbed.

And he held her very safe, and his heart was white-hot with love for her. His mind was amazed. He could only hold her against his chest that was white-hot with love and belief in her. So she was restored at last.

III

She refused to go to her work at Adams's any more. Her father had to submit and she sent in her notice—she was not well. Sam Adams was ironical. But he had a curious patience. He did not fight.

In a few weeks, she and Whiston were married. She loved him with passion and worship, a fierce little abandon of love that moved him to the depths of his being, and gave him a permanent surety and sense of realness in himself. He did not trouble about himself any more: he felt he was fulfilled and now he had only the many things in the world to busy himself about. Whatever troubled him, at the bottom was surety. He had found himself in this love.

They spoke once or twice of the white stocking.

'Ah!' Whiston exclaimed. 'What does it matter?'

He was impatient and angry, and could not bear to consider the matter. So it was left unresolved.

She was quite happy at first, carried away by her adoration of her husband. Then gradually she got used to him. He always was the ground of her happiness, but she got used to him, as to the air she breathed. He never got used to her in the same way.

Inside of marriage she found her liberty. She was rid of the responsibility of herself. Her husband must look after that. She was free to get what she could out of her time.

So that, when, after some months, she met Sam Adams, she was not quite as unkind to him as she might have been. With a young wife's new and exciting knowledge of men, she perceived he was in love with her, she knew he had always kept an unsatisfied desire for her. And, sportive, she could not help playing a little with this, though she cared not one jot for the man himself.

When Valentine's day came, which was near the first anniversary of her wedding day, there arrived a white stocking with a little amethyst brooch. Luckily Whiston did not see it, so she said nothing of it to him. She had not the faintest intention of having anything to do with Sam Adams, but once a little brooch was in her possession, it was hers, and she did not trouble her head for a moment how she had come by it. She kept it.

Now she had the pearl ear-rings. They were a more valuable and a more conspicuous present. She would have to ask her mother to give them to her, to explain their presence. She made a little plan in her head. And she was extraordinarily pleased. As for Sam Adams, even if he saw her wearing them, he would not give her away. What fun, if he saw her wearing his ear-rings! She would pretend she had inherited them from her grandmother, her mother's mother. She laughed to herself as she went down town in the afternoon, the pretty drops dangling in front of her curls. But she saw no one of importance.

Whiston came home tired and depressed. All day the male in him had been uneasy, and this had fatigued him. She was curiously against him, inclined, as she sometimes was nowadays, to make mock of him and jeer at him and cut him off. He did not understand this, and it angered him deeply. She was uneasy before him.

She knew he was in a state of suppressed irritation. The veins stood out on the backs of his hands, his brow was drawn stiffly. Yet she could not help goading him.

'What did you do wi' that white stocking?' he asked, out of a gloomy silence, his voice strong and brutal.

'I put it in a drawer—why?' she replied flippantly.

'Why didn't you put it on the fire back?' he said harshly. 'What are you hoarding it up for?'

'I'm not hoarding it up,' she said. 'I've got a pair.'

He relapsed into gloomy silence. She, unable to move him, ran away upstairs, leaving him smoking by the fire. Again she tried on the ear-rings. Then another little inspiration came to her. She drew on the white stockings, both of them.

Presently she came down in them. Her husband still sat immovable and glowering by the fire.

'Look!' she said. 'They'll do beautifully.'

And she picked up her skirts to her knees, and twisted round, looking at her pretty legs in the neat stockings.

He filled with unreasonable rage, and took the pipe from his mouth.

'Don't they look nice?' she said. 'One from last year and one from this, they just do. Save you buying a pair.'

And she looked over her shoulders at her pretty calves, and the dangling frills of her knickers.

'Put your skirts down and don't make a fool of yourself,' he said.

'Why a fool of myself?' she asked.

And she began to dance slowly round the room, kicking up her feet half reckless, half jeering, in a ballet-dancer's fashion. Almost fearfully, yet in defiance, she kicked up her legs at him, singing as she did so. She resented him.

'You little fool, ha' done with it,' he said. 'And you'll backfire them stockings, I'm telling you.' He was angry. His face flushed dark, he kept his head bent. She ceased to dance.

'I shan't,' she said. 'They'll come in very useful.'

He lifted his head and watched her, with lighted, dangerous eyes.

'You'll put 'em on the fire back, I tell you,' he said.

It was a war now. She bent forward, in a ballet-dancer's fashion, and put her tongue between her teeth.

'I shan't backfire them stockings,' she sang, repeating his words, 'I shan't, I shan't, I shan't.'

And she danced round the room doing a high kick to the tune of her words. There was a real biting indifference in her behaviour.

'We'll see whether you will or not,' he said, 'trollops! You'd like Sam Adams to know you was wearing 'em, wouldn't you? That's what would please you.'

'Yes, I'd like him to see how nicely they fit me, he might give me some more then.'

And she looked down at her pretty legs.

He knew somehow that she *would* like Sam Adams to see how pretty her legs looked in the white stockings. It made his anger go deep, almost to hatred.

'Yer nasty trolley,' he cried. 'Put yer petticoats down, and stop being so foul-minded.'

'I'm not foul-minded,' she said. 'My legs are my own. And why shouldn't Sam Adams think they're nice?'

There was a pause. He watched her with eyes glittering to a point.

'Have you been havin' owt to do with him?' he asked.

'I've just spoken to him when I've seen him,' she said. 'He's not as bad as you would make out.'

'Isn't he?' he cried, a certain wakefulness in his voice. 'Them who has anything to do wi' him is too bad for me, I tell you.'

'Why, what are you frightened of him for?' she mocked.

She was rousing all his uncontrollable anger. He sat glowering. Every one of her sentences stirred him up like a red-hot iron. Soon it would be too much. And she was afraid herself; but she was neither conquered nor convinced.

A curious little grin of hate came on his face. He had a long score against her.

'What am I frightened of him for?' he repeated automatically. 'What am I frightened of him for? Why, for you, you stray-running little bitch.'

She flushed. The insult went deep into her, right home.

'Well, if you're so dull–' she said, lowering her eyelids, and speaking coldly, haughtily.

'If I'm so dull I'll break your neck the first word you speak to him,' he said, tense.

'Pf!' she sneered. 'Do you think I'm frightened of you?' She spoke coldly, detached.

She was frightened, for all that, white round the mouth.

His heart was getting hotter.

'You *will* be frightened of me, the next time you have anything to do with him,' he said.

'Do you think *you'd* ever be told—ha!'

Her jeering scorn made him go white-hot, molten. He knew he was incoherent, scarcely responsible for what he might do. Slowly, unseeing, he rose and went out of doors, stifled, moved to kill her.

He stood leaning against the garden fence, unable either to see or hear. Below him, far off, fumed the lights of the town. He stood still, unconscious with a black storm of rage, his face lifted to the night.

Presently, still unconscious of what he was doing, he went indoors again. She stood, a small stubborn figure with tight-pressed lips and big, sullen, childish eyes, watching him, white with fear. He went heavily across the floor and dropped into his chair.

There was a silence.

'*You're* not going to tell me everything I shall do, and everything I shan't,' she broke out at last.

He lifted his head.

'I tell you *this*,' he said, low and intense. 'Have anything to do with Sam Adams, and I'll break your neck.'

She laughed, shrill and false.

'How I hate your word "break your neck",' she said, with a grimace of the mouth. 'It sounds so common and beastly. Can't you say something else–'

There was a dead silence.

'And besides,' she said, with a queer chirrup of mocking laughter, 'what do you know about anything? He sent me an amethyst brooch and a pair of pearl ear-rings.'

'He what?' said Whiston, in a suddenly normal voice. His eyes were fixed on her.

'Sent me a pair of pearl ear-rings, and an amethyst brooch,' she repeated, mechanically, pale to the lips.

And her big, black, childish eyes watched him, fascinated, held in her spell.

He seemed to thrust his face and his eyes forward at her, as he rose slowly and came to her. She watched transfixed in terror. Her throat made a small sound, as she tried to scream.

Then, quick as lightning, the back of his hand struck her with a crash across the mouth, and she was flung back blinded against the wall. The shock shook a queer sound out of her. And then she saw him still coming on, his eyes holding her, his fist drawn back, advancing slowly. At any instant the blow might crash into her.

Mad with terror, she raised her hands with a queer clawing movement to cover her eyes and her temples, opening her mouth in a dumb shriek. There was no sound. But the sight of her slowly arrested him. He hung before her, looking at her fixedly, as she stood crouched against the wall with open, bleeding mouth, and wide-staring eyes, and two hands clawing over her temples. And his lust to see her bleed, to break her and destroy her, rose from an old source against her. It carried him. He wanted satisfaction.

But he had seen her standing there, a piteous, horrified thing, and he turned his face aside in shame and nausea. He went and sat heavily in his chair, and a curious ease, almost like sleep, came over his brain.

She walked away from the wall towards the fire, dizzy, white to the lips, mechanically wiping her small, bleeding mouth. He sat motionless. Then, gradually, her breath began to hiss, she shook, and was sobbing silently, in grief for herself. Without looking, he saw. It made his mad desire to destroy her come back.

At length he lifted his head. His eyes were glowing again, fixed on her.

'And what did he give them you for?' he asked, in a steady, unyielding voice.

Her crying dried up in a second. She also was tense.

'They came as valentines,' she replied, still not subjugated, even if beaten.

'When, to-day?'

'The pearl ear-rings to-day—the amethyst brooch last year.'

'You've had it a year?'

'Yes.'

She felt that now nothing would prevent him if he rose to kill her. She could not prevent him any more. She was yielded up to him. They both trembled in the balance, unconscious.

'What have you had to do with him?' he asked, in a barren voice.

'I've not had anything to do with him,' she quavered.

'You just kept 'em because they were jewellery?' he said.

A weariness came over him. What was the worth of speaking any more of it? He did not care any more. He was dreary and sick.

She began to cry again, but he took no notice. She kept wiping her mouth on her handkerchief. He could see it, the blood-mark. It made him only more sick and tired of the responsibility of it, the violence, the shame.

When she began to move about again, he raised his head once more from his dead, motionless position.

'Where are the things?' he said.

'They are upstairs,' she quavered. She knew the passion had gone down in him.

'Bring them down,' he said.

'I won't,' she wept, with rage. 'You're not going to bully me and hit me like that on the mouth.'

And she sobbed again. He looked at her in contempt and compassion and in rising anger.

'Where are they?' he said.

'They're in the little drawer under the looking-glass,' she sobbed.

He went slowly upstairs, struck a match, and found the trinkets. He brought them downstairs in his hand.

'These?' he said, looking at them as they lay in his palm.

She looked at them without answering. She was not interested in them any more.

He looked at the little jewels. They were pretty.

'It's none of their fault,' he said to himself.

And he searched round slowly, persistently, for a box. He tied the things up and addressed them to Sam Adams. Then he went out in his slippers to post the little package.

When he came back she was still sitting crying.

'You'd better go to bed,' he said.

She paid no attention. He sat by the fire. She still cried.

'I'm sleeping down here,' he said. 'Go you to bed.'

In a few moments she lifted her tear-stained, swollen face and looked at him with eyes all forlorn and pathetic. A great flash of anguish went over his body. He went over, slowly, and very gently took her in his hands. She let herself be taken. Then as she lay against his shoulder, she sobbed aloud:

'I never meant–'

'My love—my little love–' he cried, in anguish of spirit, holding her in his arms.

David Herbert Lawrence (1885–1930) was born in Eastwood, Nottinghamshire, but after a time as a teacher escaped the working-class coal-mining community he grew up in and went on to establish a reputation as one of the most brilliant and controversial writers of his generation. As well as such classic novels as Sons and Lovers, Women in Love *and* Lady Chatterley's Lover, *he wrote many acclaimed short stories. 'The White Stocking' was one of the stories included in his early short story collection* The Prussian Officer and Other Stories *(1914). The story was written not long after the author eloped with the already-married Frieda Weekley (née von Richtofen); they were to remain together until his death.*

Eve's Diary

Mark Twain

SATURDAY.—I am almost a whole day old, now. I arrived yesterday. That is as it seems to me. And it must be so, for if there was a day-before-yesterday I was not there when it happened, or I should remember it. It could be, of course, that it did happen, and that I was not noticing. Very well; I will be very watchful now, and if any day-before-yesterdays happen I will make a note of it. It will be best to start right and not let the record get confused, for some instinct tells me that these details are going to be important to the historian some day. For I feel like an experiment, I feel exactly like an experiment; it would be impossible for a person to feel more like an experiment than I do, and so I am coming to feel convinced that that is what I AM—an experiment; just an experiment, and nothing more.

Then if I am an experiment, am I the whole of it? No, I think not; I think the rest of it is part of it. I am the main part of it, but I think the rest of it has its share in the matter. Is my position assured, or do I have to watch it and take care of it? The latter, perhaps. Some instinct tells me that eternal vigilance is the price of supremacy. (That is a good phrase, I think, for one so young.)

Everything looks better today than it did yesterday. In the rush of finishing up yesterday, the mountains were left in a ragged condition, and some of the plains were so cluttered with rubbish and remnants that the aspects were quite distressing. Noble and beautiful works of art should not be subjected to haste; and this majestic new world is indeed a most noble and beautiful work. And certainly marvellously near to being perfect, notwithstanding the shortness of the time. There are too many stars in some places and not enough in others, but that can be remedied presently, no doubt. The moon got loose last night, and slid down and fell out of the scheme—a very great loss; it breaks my heart to think of it. There isn't another thing among the ornaments and decorations that is comparable to it for beauty and finish. It should have been fastened better. If we can only get it back again–

But of course there is no telling where it went to. And besides, whoever gets it will hide it; I know it because I would do it myself. I believe I can be honest in all other matters, but I already begin to realise that the core and centre of my nature is love of the beautiful, a passion for the beautiful, and that it would not be safe to trust me with a moon that belonged to another person and that person didn't know I had it. I could give up a moon that I found in the daytime, because I should be afraid someone was looking; but if I found it in the dark, I am sure I should find some kind of an excuse for not saying anything about it. For I do love moons, they are so pretty and so romantic. I wish we had five or six; I would never go to bed; I should never get tired lying on the moss-bank and looking up at them.

Stars are good, too. I wish I could get some to put in my hair. But I suppose I never can. You would be surprised to find how far off they are, for they do not look it. When they first showed, last night, I tried to knock some down with a pole, but it didn't reach, which astonished me; then I tried clods till I was all tired out, but I never got one. It was because I am left-handed and cannot throw good. Even when I aimed at the one I wasn't after I couldn't hit the other one, though I did make some close shots, for I saw the black blot of the clod sail right into the midst of the golden clusters forty or fifty times, just barely missing them, and if I could have held out a little longer maybe I could have got one.

So I cried a little, which was natural, I suppose, for one of my age, and after I was rested I got a basket and started for a place on the extreme rim of the circle, where the stars were close to the ground and I could get them with my hands, which would be better, anyway, because I could gather them tenderly then, and not break them. But it was farther than I thought, and at last I had to give it up; I was so tired I couldn't drag my feet another step; and besides, they were sore and hurt me very much.

I couldn't get back home; it was too far and turning cold; but I found some tigers and nestled in among them and was most adorably comfortable, and their breath was sweet and pleasant, because they live on strawberries. I had never seen a tiger before, but I knew them in a minute by the stripes. If I could have one of those skins, it would make a lovely gown.

Today I am getting better ideas about distances. I was so eager to get hold of every pretty thing that I giddily grabbed for it, sometimes when it was too far off, and sometimes when it was but six inches away but seemed a foot—alas, with thorns between! I learned a lesson; also I made an axiom, all out of my own head—my very first one; THE SCRATCHED EXPERIMENT SHUNS THE THORN. I think it is a very good one for one so young.

I followed the other Experiment around, yesterday afternoon, at a distance, to see what it might be for, if I could. But I was not able to make (it) out. I think it is a man. I had never seen a man, but it looked like one, and I feel sure that that is what it is. I realise that I feel more curiosity about it than about any of the other reptiles. If it is a reptile, and I suppose it is; for it has frowzy hair and blue eyes, and looks like a reptile. It has no hips; it tapers like a carrot; when it stands, it spreads itself apart like a derrick; so I think it is a reptile, though it may be architecture.

I was afraid of it at first, and started to run every time it turned around, for I thought it was going to chase me; but by and by I found it was only trying to get away, so after that I was not timid any more, but tracked it along, several hours, about twenty yards behind, which made it nervous and unhappy. At last it was a good deal worried, and climbed a tree. I waited a good while, then gave it up and went home.

Today the same thing over. I've got it up the tree again.

SUNDAY.—It is up there yet. Resting, apparently. But that is a subterfuge: Sunday isn't the day of rest; Saturday is appointed for that. It looks to me like a creature that is more interested in resting than in anything else. It would tire me to rest so much. It tires me just to sit around and watch the tree. I do wonder what it is for; I never see it do anything.

They returned the moon last night, and I was SO happy! I think it is very honest of them. It slid down and fell off again, but I was not distressed; there is no need to worry when one has that kind of neighbours; they will fetch it back. I wish I could do something to show my appreciation. I would like to send them some stars, for we have more than we can use. I mean I, not we, for I can see that the reptile cares nothing for such things.

It has low tastes, and is not kind. When I went there yesterday evening in the gloaming it had crept down and was trying to catch the little speckled fishes that play in the pool, and I had to clod it to make it go up the tree again and let them alone. I wonder if THAT is what it is for? Hasn't it any heart? Hasn't it any compassion for those little creatures? Can it be that it was designed and manufactured for such ungentle work? It has the look of it. One of the clods took it back of the ear, and it used language. It gave me a thrill, for it was the first time I had ever heard speech, except my own. I did not understand the words, but they seemed expressive.

When I found it could talk I felt a new interest in it, for I love to talk; I talk, all day, and in my sleep, too, and I am very interesting, but if I had another to talk to I could be twice as interesting, and would never stop, if desired.

If this reptile is a man, it isn't an IT, is it? That wouldn't be grammatical, would it? I think it would be HE. I think so. In that case one would parse it thus: nominative, HE; dative, HIM; possessive, HIS'N. Well, I will consider it a man and call it he until it turns out to be something else. This will be handier than having so many uncertainties.

NEXT WEEK SUNDAY.—All the week I tagged around after him and tried to get acquainted. I had to do the talking, because he was shy, but I didn't mind it. He seemed pleased to have me around, and I used the sociable 'we' a good deal, because it seemed to flatter him to be included.

WEDNESDAY.—We are getting along very well indeed, now, and getting better and better acquainted. He does not try to avoid me any more, which is a good sign, and shows that he likes to have me with him. That pleases me, and I study to be useful to him in every way I can, so as to increase his regard.

During the last day or two I have taken all the work of naming things off his hands, and this has been a great relief to him, for he has no gift in that line, and is evidently very grateful. He can't think of a rational name to save him, but I do not let him see that I am aware of his defect. Whenever a new creature comes along I name it before he has time to expose himself by an awkward silence. In this way I have saved him many embarrassments. I have no defect like this. The minute I set eyes on an animal I know what it is. I don't have to reflect a moment; the right name comes out instantly, just as if it were an inspiration, as no doubt it is, for I am sure it wasn't in me half a minute before. I seem to know just by the shape of the creature and the way it acts what animal it is.

When the dodo came along he thought it was a wildcat—I saw it in his eye. But I saved him. And I was careful not to do it in a way that could hurt his pride. I just spoke up in a quite natural way of pleasing surprise, and not as if I was dreaming of conveying information, and said, 'Well, I do declare, if there isn't the dodo!' I explained—without seeming to be explaining—how I know it for a dodo, and although I thought maybe he was a little piqued that I knew the creature when he didn't, it was quite evident that he admired me. That was very agreeable, and I thought of it more than once with gratification before I slept. How little a thing can make us happy when we feel that we have earned it!

THURSDAY.—my first sorrow. Yesterday he avoided me and seemed to wish I would not talk to him. I could not believe it, and thought there was some mistake, for I loved to be with him, and loved to hear him talk, and so how could it be that he could feel unkind toward me when I had not done anything? But at last it seemed true, so I went away and sat lonely in the place where I first saw him the morning that we were made and I did not know what he was and was indifferent about him; but now it was a mournful place, and every little thing spoke of him, and my heart was very sore. I did not know why very clearly, for it was a new feeling; I had not experienced it before, and it was all a mystery, and I could not make it out.

But when night came I could not bear the lonesomeness, and went to the new shelter which he has built, to ask him what I had done that was wrong and how I could mend it and get back his kindness again; but he put me out in the rain, and it was my first sorrow.

SUNDAY.—It is pleasant again, now, and I am happy; but those were heavy days; I do not think of them when I can help it.

I tried to get him some of those apples, but I cannot learn to throw straight. I failed, but I think the good intention pleased him. They are forbidden, and he says I shall come to harm; but so I come to harm through pleasing him, why shall I care for that harm?

MONDAY.—This morning I told him my name, hoping it would interest him. But he did not care for it. It is strange. If he should tell me his name, I would care. I think it would be pleasanter in my ears than any other sound.

He talks very little. Perhaps it is because he is not bright, and is sensitive about it and wishes to conceal it. It is such a pity that he should feel so, for brightness is nothing; it is in the heart that the values lie. I wish I could make him understand that a loving good heart is riches, and riches enough, and that without it intellect is poverty.

Although he talks so little, he has quite a considerable vocabulary. This morning he used a surprisingly good word. He evidently recognised, himself, that it was a good one, for he worked it in twice afterward, casually. It was good casual art, still it showed that he possesses a certain quality of perception. Without a doubt that seed can be made to grow, if cultivated.

Where did he get that word? I do not think I have ever used it.

No, he took no interest in my name. I tried to hide my disappointment, but I suppose I did not succeed. I went away and sat on the moss-bank with my feet in the water. It is where I go when I hunger for companionship, someone to look at, someone to talk to. It is not enough—that lovely white body painted there in the pool—but it is something, and something is better than utter loneliness. It talks when I talk; it is sad when I am sad; it comforts me with its sympathy; it says, 'Do not be downhearted, you poor friendless girl; I will be your friend.' It IS a good friend to me, and my only one; it is my sister.

That first time that she forsook me! ah, I shall never forget that—never, never. My heart was lead in my body! I said, 'She was all I had, and now she is gone!' In my despair I said, 'Break, my heart; I cannot bear my life any more!' and hid my face in my hands, and there was no solace for me. And when I took them away, after a little, there she was again, white and shining and beautiful, and I sprang into her arms!

That was perfect happiness; I had known happiness before, but it was not like this, which was ecstasy. I never doubted her afterward. Sometimes she stayed away—maybe an hour, maybe almost the whole day, but I waited and did not doubt; I said, 'She is busy, or she is gone on a journey, but she will come.' And it was so: she always did. At night she would not come if it was dark, for she was a timid little thing; but if there was a moon she would come. I am not afraid of the dark, but she is younger than I am; she was born after I was. Many and many are the visits I have paid her; she is my comfort and my refuge when my life is hard—and it is mainly that.

TUESDAY.—All the morning I was at work improving the estate; and I purposely kept away from him in the hope that he would get lonely and come. But he did not.

At noon I stopped for the day and took my recreation by flitting all about with the bees and the butterflies and revelling in the flowers, those beautiful creatures that catch the smile of God out of the sky and preserve it! I gathered them, and made them into wreaths and garlands and clothed myself in them while I ate my luncheon—apples, of course; then I sat in the shade and wished and waited. But he did not come.

But no matter. Nothing would have come of it, for he does not care for flowers. He called them rubbish, and cannot tell one from another, and thinks it is superior to feel like that. He does not care for me, he does not care for flowers, he does not care for the painted sky at eventide—is there anything he does care for, except building shacks to coop himself up in from the good clean rain, and thumping the melons, and sampling the grapes, and fingering the fruit on the trees, to see how those properties are coming along?

I laid a dry stick on the ground and tried to bore a hole in it with another one, in order to carry out a scheme that I had, and soon I got an awful fright. A thin, transparent bluish film rose out of the hole, and I dropped everything and ran! I thought it was a spirit, and I WAS so frightened! But I looked back, and it was not coming; so I leaned against a rock and rested and panted, and let my limbs go on trembling until they got steady again; then I crept warily back, alert, watching, and ready to fly if there was occasion; and when I was come near, I parted the branches of a rose-bush and peeped through—wishing the man was about, I was looking so cunning and pretty—but the sprite was gone. I went there, and there was a pinch of delicate pink dust in the hole. I put my finger in, to feel it, and said OUCH! and took it out again. It was a cruel pain. I put my finger in my mouth; and by standing first on one foot and then the other, and grunting, I presently eased my misery; then I was full of interest, and began to examine.

I was curious to know what the pink dust was. Suddenly the name of it occurred to me, though I had never heard of it before. It was FIRE! I was as certain of it as a person could be of anything in the world. So without hesitation I named it that—fire.

I had created something that didn't exist before; I had added a new thing to the world's uncountable properties; I realised this, and was proud of my achievement, and was going to run and find him and tell him about it, thinking to raise myself in his esteem—but I reflected, and did not do it. No—he would not care for it. He would ask what it was good for, and what could I answer? for if it was not GOOD for something, but only beautiful, merely beautiful–

So I sighed, and did not go. For it wasn't good for anything; it could not build a shack, it could not improve melons, it could not hurry a fruit crop; it was useless, it was a foolishness and a vanity; he would despise it and say cutting words. But to me it was not despicable; I said, 'Oh, you fire, I love you, you dainty pink creature, for you are BEAUTIFUL—and that is enough!' and was going to gather it to my breast. But refrained. Then I made another maxim out of my head, though it was so nearly like the first one that I was afraid it was only a plagiarism: 'THE BURNT EXPERIMENT SHUNS THE FIRE.'

I wrought again; and when I had made a good deal of fire-dust I emptied it into a handful of dry brown grass, intending to carry it home and keep it always and play with it; but the wind struck it and it sprayed up and spat out at me fiercely, and I dropped it and ran. When I looked back the blue spirit was towering up and stretching and rolling away like a cloud, and instantly I thought of the name of it—SMOKE!—though, upon my word, I had never heard of smoke before.

Soon brilliant yellow and red flares shot up through the smoke, and I named them in an instant—FLAMES—and I was right, too, though these were the very first flames that had ever been in the world. They climbed the trees, then flashed splendidly in and out of the vast and increasing volume of tumbling smoke, and I had to clap my hands and laugh and dance in my rapture, it was so new and strange and so wonderful and so beautiful!

He came running, and stopped and gazed, and said not a word for many minutes. Then he asked what it was. Ah, it was too bad that he should ask such a direct question. I had to answer it, of course, and I did. I said it was fire. If it annoyed him that I should know and he must ask; that was not my fault; I had no desire to annoy him. After a pause he asked:

'How did it come?'

Another direct question, and it also had to have a direct answer.

'I made it.'

The fire was travelling farther and farther off. He went to the edge of the burned place and stood looking down, and said:

'What are these?'

'Fire-coals.'

He picked up one to examine it, but changed his mind and put it down again. Then he went away. NOTHING interests him.

But I was interested. There were ashes, grey and soft and delicate and pretty—I knew what they were at once. And the embers; I knew the embers, too. I found my apples, and raked them out, and was glad; for I am very young and my appetite is active. But I was disappointed; they were all burst open and spoiled. Spoiled apparently; but it was not so; they were better than raw ones. Fire is beautiful; some day it will be useful, I think.

FRIDAY.—I saw him again, for a moment, last Monday at nightfall, but only for a moment. I was hoping he would praise me for trying to improve the estate, for I had meant well and had worked hard. But he was not pleased, and turned away and left me. He was also displeased on another account: I tried once more to persuade him to stop going over the Falls. That was because the fire had revealed to me a new passion—quite new, and distinctly different from love, grief, and those others which I had already discovered—FEAR. And it is horrible!—I wish I had never discovered it; it gives me dark moments, it spoils my happiness, it makes me shiver and tremble and shudder. But I could not persuade him, for he has not discovered fear yet, and so he could not understand me.

Extract from Adam's Diary

Perhaps I ought to remember that she is very young, a mere girl and make allowances. She is all interest, eagerness, vivacity, the world is to her a charm, a wonder, a mystery, a joy; she can't speak for delight when she finds a new flower, she must pet it and caress it and smell it and talk to it, and pour out endearing names upon it. And she is colour-mad: brown rocks, yellow sand, grey moss, green foliage, blue sky; the pearl of the dawn, the purple shadows on the mountains, the golden islands floating in crimson seas at sunset, the pallid moon sailing through the shredded cloud-rack, the star-jewels glittering in the wastes of space—none of them is of any practical value, so far as I can see, but because they have colour and majesty, that is enough for her, and she loses her mind over them. If she could quiet down and keep still a couple minutes at a time, it would be a reposeful spectacle. In that case I think I could enjoy looking at her; indeed I am sure I could, for I am coming to realise that she is a quite remarkably comely creature—lithe, slender, trim, rounded, shapely, nimble, graceful; and once when she was standing marble-white and sun-drenched on a boulder, with her young head tilted back and her hand shading her eyes, watching the flight of a bird in the sky, I recognised that she was beautiful.

MONDAY NOON.—If there is anything on the planet that she is not interested in it is not in my list. There are animals that I am indifferent to, but it is not so with her. She has no discrimination, she takes to all of them, she thinks they are all treasures, every new one is welcome.

When the mighty brontosaurus came striding into camp, she regarded it as an acquisition, I considered it a calamity; that is a good sample of the lack of harmony that prevails in our views of things. She wanted to domesticate it, I wanted to make it a present of the homestead and move out. She believed it could be tamed by kind treatment and would be a good pet; I said a pet twenty-one feet high and eighty-four feet long would be no proper thing to have about the place, because, even with the best intentions and without meaning any harm, it could sit down on the house and mash it, for anyone could see by the look of its eye that it was absent-minded.

Still, her heart was set upon having that monster, and she couldn't give it up. She thought we could start a dairy with it, and wanted me to help milk it; but I wouldn't; it was too risky. The sex wasn't right, and we hadn't any ladder anyway. Then she wanted to ride it, and look at the scenery. Thirty or forty feet of its tail was lying on the ground, like a fallen tree, and she thought she could climb it, but she was mistaken; when she got to the steep place it was too slick and down she came, and would have hurt herself but for me.

Was she satisfied now? No. Nothing ever satisfies her but demonstration; untested theories are not in her line, and she won't have them. It is the right spirit, I concede it; it attracts me; I feel the influence of it; if I were with her more I think I should take it up myself. Well, she had one theory remaining about this colossus: she thought that if we could tame it and make him friendly we could stand in the river and use him for a bridge. It turned out that he was already plenty tame enough— at least as far as she was concerned—so she tried her theory, but it failed: every time she got him properly placed in the river and went ashore to cross over him, he came out and followed her around like a pet mountain. Like the other animals. They all do that.

Tuesday—Wednesday—Thursday—and today: all without seeing him. It is a long time to be alone; still, it is better to be alone than unwelcome.

FRIDAY—I HAD to have company—I was made for it, I think—so I made friends with the animals. They are just charming, and they have the kindest disposition and the politest ways; they never look sour, they never let you feel that you are intruding, they smile at you and wag their tail, if they've got one, and they are always ready for a romp or an excursion or anything you want to propose. I think they are perfect gentlemen. All these days we have had such good times, and it hasn't been lonesome for me, ever.

Lonesome! No, I should say not. Why, there's always a swarm of them around—sometimes as much as four or five acres—you can't count them; and when you stand on a rock in the midst and look out over the furry expanse it is so mottled and splashed and gay with colour and frisking sheen and sun-flash, and so rippled with stripes, that you might think it was a lake, only you know it isn't; and there's storms of sociable birds, and hurricanes of whirring wings; and when the sun strikes all that feathery commotion, you have a blazing up of all the colours you can think of, enough to put your eyes out.

We have made long excursions, and I have seen a great deal of the world; almost all of it, I think; and so I am the first traveller, and the only one. When we are on the march, it is an imposing sight—there's nothing like it anywhere. For comfort I ride a tiger or a leopard, because it is soft and has a round back that fits me, and because they are such pretty animals; but for long distance or for scenery I ride the elephant. He hoists me up with his trunk, but I can get off myself; when we are ready to camp, he sits and I slide down the back way.

The birds and animals are all friendly to each other, and there are no disputes about anything. They all talk, and they all talk to me, but it must be a foreign language, for I cannot make out a word they say; yet they often understand me when I talk back, particularly the dog and the elephant. It makes me ashamed. It shows that they are brighter than I am, for I want to be the principal Experiment myself—and I intend to be, too.

I have learned a number of things, and am educated, now, but I wasn't at first. I was ignorant at first. At first it used to vex me because, with all my watching, I was never smart enough to be around when the water was running uphill; but now I do not mind it. I have experimented and experimented until now I know it never does run uphill, except in the dark. I know it does in the dark, because the pool never goes dry, which it would, of course, if the water didn't come back in the night. It is best to prove things by actual experiment; then you KNOW; whereas if you depend on guessing and supposing and conjecturing, you never get educated.

Some things you CAN'T find out; but you will never know you can't by guessing and supposing: no, you have to be patient and go on experimenting until you find out that you can't find out. And it is delightful to have it that way, it makes the world so interesting. If there wasn't anything to find out, it would be dull. Even trying to find out and not finding out is just as interesting as trying to find out and finding out, and I don't know but more so. The secret of the water was a treasure until I GOT it; then the excitement all went away, and I recognised a sense of loss.

By experiment I know that wood swims, and dry leaves, and feathers, and plenty of other things; therefore by all that cumulative evidence you know that a rock will swim; but you have to put up with simply knowing it, for there isn't any way to prove it—up to now. But I shall find a way—then THAT excitement will go. Such things make me sad; because by and by when I have found out everything there won't be any more excitements, and I do love excitements so! The other night I couldn't sleep for thinking about it.

At first I couldn't make out what I was made for, but now I think it was to search out the secrets of this wonderful world and be happy and thank the Giver of it all for devising it. I think there are many things to learn yet—I hope so; and by economising and not hurrying too fast I think they will last weeks and weeks. I hope so. When you cast up a feather it sails away on the air and goes out of sight; then you throw up a clod and it doesn't. It comes down, every time. I have tried it and tried it, and it is always so. I wonder why it is? Of course it DOESN'T come down, but why should it SEEM to? I suppose it is an optical illusion. I mean, one of them is. I don't know which one. It may be the feather, it may be the clod; I can't prove which it is, I can only demonstrate that one or the other is a fake, and let a person take his choice.

By watching, I know that the stars are not going to last. I have seen some of the best ones melt and run down the sky. Since one can melt, they can all melt; since they can all melt, they can all melt the same night. That sorrow will come—I know it. I mean to sit up every night and look at them as long as I can keep awake; and I will impress those sparkling fields on my memory, so that by and by when they are taken away I can by my fancy restore those lovely myriads to the black sky and make them sparkle again, and double them by the blur of my tears.

After the Fall

When I look back, the Garden is a dream to me. It was beautiful, surpassingly beautiful, enchantingly beautiful; and now it is lost, and I shall not see it any more.

The Garden is lost, but I have found HIM, and am content. He loves me as well as he can; I love him with all the strength of my passionate nature, and this, I think, is proper to my youth and sex. If I ask myself why I love him, I find I do not know, and do not really much care to know; so I suppose that this kind of love is not a product of reasoning and statistics, like one's love for other reptiles and animals. I think that this must be so. I love certain birds because of their song; but I do not love Adam on account of his singing—no, it is not that; the more he sings the more I do not get reconciled to it. Yet I ask him to sing, because I wish to learn to like everything he is interested in. I am sure I can learn, because at first I could not stand it, but now I can. It sours the milk, but it doesn't matter; I can get used to that kind of milk.

It is not on account of his brightness that I love him—no, it is not that. He is not to blame for his brightness, such as it is, for he did not make it himself; he is as God make him, and that is sufficient. There was a wise purpose in it, THAT I know. In time it will develop, though I think it will not be sudden; and besides, there is no hurry; he is well enough just as he is.

It is not on account of his gracious and considerate ways and his delicacy that I love him. No, he has lacks in this regard, but he is well enough just so, and is improving.

It is not on account of his industry that I love him—no, it is not that. I think he has it in him, and I do not know why he conceals it from me. It is my only pain. Otherwise he is frank and open with me, now. I am sure he keeps nothing from me but this. It grieves me that he should have a secret from me, and sometimes it spoils my sleep, thinking of it, but I will put it out of my mind; it shall not trouble my happiness, which is otherwise full to overflowing.

It is not on account of his education that I love him—no, it is not that. He is self-educated, and does really know a multitude of things, but they are not so.

It is not on account of his chivalry that I love him—no, it is not that. He told on me, but I do not blame him; it is a peculiarity of sex, I think, and he did not make his sex. Of course I would not have told on him, I would have perished first; but that is a peculiarity of sex, too, and I do not take credit for it, for I did not make my sex.

Then why is it that I love him? MERELY BECAUSE HE IS MASCULINE, I think.

At bottom he is good, and I love him for that, but I could love him without it. If he should beat me and abuse me, I should go on loving him. I know it. It is a matter of sex, I think.

He is strong and handsome, and I love him for that, and I admire him and am proud of him, but I could love him without those qualities. If he were plain, I should love him; if he were a wreck, I should love him; and I would work for him, and slave over him, and pray for him, and watch by his bedside until I died.

Yes, I think I love him merely because he is MINE and is MASCULINE. There is no other reason, I suppose. And so I think it is as I first said: that this kind of love is not a product of reasonings and statistics. It just COMES—none knows whence—and cannot explain itself. And doesn't need to.

It is what I think. But I am only a girl, the first that has examined this matter, and it may turn out that in my ignorance and inexperience I have not got it right.

Forty Years Later

It is my prayer, it is my longing, that we may pass from this life together—a longing which shall never perish from the earth, but shall have place in the heart of every wife that loves, until the end of time; and it shall be called by my name.

But if one of us must go first, it is my prayer that it shall be I; for he is strong, I am weak, I am not so necessary to him as he is to me—life without him would not be life; how could I endure it? This prayer is also immortal, and will not cease from being offered up while my race continues. I am the first wife; and in the last wife I shall be repeated.

At Eve's Grave

ADAM: Wheresoever she was, THERE was Eden.

Mark Twain (1835–1910) was born Samuel Langhorne Clemens in Florida, Missouri, and worked as a printer and as a Mississippi riverboat pilot before achieving fame as an author and humorist. His most popular works include the novels The Adventures of Tom Sawyer *(1876) and* Adventures of Huckleberry Finn *(1885) as well as numerous short stories and articles. 'Eve's Diary', which was first published in 1905 in the magazine* Harper's Bazaar, *caused a considerable stir on account of the accompanying illustrations depicting the naked Eve. It has been speculated that the author wrote the piece as a love-letter to his wife Olivia, who died in June 1904.*

Also available by the same author

Classic Short Stories
Classic Ghost Stories
Classic Ghost Stories 2
Classic Horror Stories
Classic Horror Stories 2
Dictionary of Witchcraft
Dictionary of Superstitions
And Stones Shall Dance (novel)
Things Lost and Other Short Stories